For Brenda Pandos

BOOKS BY KRISTIE COOK

SOUL SAVERS

Recommended Reading Order:

A Demon's Promise

An Angel's Purpose

Genesis: A Soul Savers Novella

Dangerous Devotion

Dark Power

Sacred Wrath

Unholy Torment

Fractured Faith

Age of Angels Part I: Awakened

Age of Angels Part II: Lost

Age of Angels Part III: Marked

Prophecy of the Wolves: (A Soul Savers Tie-In Novella)

Wonder: A Soul Savers Collection of Holiday Short Stories &
Recipes

HAVENWOOD FALLS

Recommended Reading Order:

Forget You Not

Lose You Not

Break Me Not

The Collector: Awakening

Savage Salvation (Sin & Silk)

Sun & Moon Academy Book One: Fall Semester

Sun & Moon Academy Book Two: Fall Semester

The Winged & the Wicked (with T.V. Hahn)

Havenwood Falls Short Story Anthology 2018

Havenwood Falls Short Story Anthology 2019

Havenwood Falls Short Story Anthology 2020

BOOK OF PHOENIX

The Space Between

The Space Beyond

The Space Within

SOUL SAVERS BOOK 4

DARK POWER

KRISTIE COOK

CHAPTER 1

Just breathe.

Something I shouldn't have to remind myself to do, but at the moment, the task was easier said than done. Pushing the air out of my tight lungs proved simple enough, but in through the nose was a different story, as each inhale brought with it an eye-watering fetor of body odor, liquor, cigarette smoke, and vomit pooled somewhere in the dark corners. I could handle the stench, as well as the flashing lights, the pulsating music, and a sea of Norman bodies dry-humping to the beat, but making it all exponentially worse were the drunken mind signatures, swirling and gyrating and pinging all over the place.

A nightclub in the middle of a seaside tourist village was probably the last place a new telepath should be hanging out. Yet here I was.

I hadn't been off Amadis Island for eight months, since the trial last September, and didn't particularly want to be here either. I preferred to be in one of my usual spots, next to either Rina or Lilith, both still comatose from the dark magic inflicted by Kali the sorceress. But my Amadis power seemed to be doing neither of them much good, and Vanessa had recently been seen in this small town, which meant something was going on.

The Daemoni simply didn't hang out here—not anywhere on this little key in the Aegean Sea that was the Amadis Island's closest neighbor. Too many Amadis passed through here on their way to and from our island, and many came for a day or weekend of mainstreaming without wandering too far away from the safety of our haven. So Vanessa being here was perplexing—as well as bold and stupid on her part. Except the vampire wasn't stupid, which meant she wouldn't be here alone for long. The Daemoni seemed to be planning an ambush, and our current strategy was for me to hear her thoughts and learn their plan. She'd also stolen something precious from me, and I needed it back.

Unfortunately, I hadn't been able to find her mind signature tonight, so here I was, hoping to pick up a thought of someone who'd seen her today or knew where she stayed. The sensory overload made my head pound and set my teeth on edge. The packs of women not so discreetly waiting their turns to hit on my husband certainly didn't help my mood.

Tristan's long and hard body leaned against the bar on the other side of the room from me, blue and green lights from the dance floor flashing over his perfect features. An American girl in a sundress and stilettos twirled her red hair around her fingers as she and a similarly dressed brunette talked to him. More small groups of women stood nearby at the bar and tables, stealing glances his way to see if he'd dismissed these two yet. After all, he'd been dismissing foolish women practically falling at his feet all night, but for some reason, each newcomer thought she'd be the exception.

His eyes slid over to me, and he smirked. I fought the ridiculously immature but overwhelming urge to stick my tongue out. Instead, I turned away from him and gave my full attention to the intoxicated Greek god offering to buy me a drink. Well, I tried my best to give it to him, but I could barely provide more than a forced smile while my mind scanned the thoughts of the women talking to Tristan. If they knew anything about the vampire-bitch, they weren't thinking about her. In fact, their minds were pretty focused on how they'd be willing to give Tristan a threesome if that's what it took to get him into bed. No wonder he was smirking.

Just breathe, I reminded myself again. *It was your idea to separate. This is your own doing.* Right. I needed to focus. Even if I didn't find Vanessa, scanning mind signatures and thoughts in this kind of environment provided good practice, which I needed.

I'd acquired the telepathy during my *Ang'dora* last year and fought it and its intricacies for a while. Well, I still had some issues, but I experienced a big breakthrough last September when I protected Tristan from being banished for betrayal and saved the Amadis by exposing the real traitor. I'd been trying ever since to embrace the gift, but the only people I could practice on were the people in the Amadis village, and they were nothing compared to this. Especially since the Amadis knew I could hear their thoughts, so they kept them subdued. Here, thoughts exploded from inebriated minds like fireworks, some bright and cheery and others simply loud and obnoxious.

I could hardly fathom how all these people could be here partying it up with everything else going on in the world. Of course, they didn't know what I did—the increased homicide rates, animal attacks, and missing persons reports weren't solely a result of depressed economies and political unrest as the media told them, but rather, the workings of the Daemoni. Norms only joked about the world going to Hell, not realizing how right they were. They hadn't attended funeral after funeral as I had in the last few months.

Or, perhaps, they had. Perhaps they sought to forget it all in the alcohol, drugs, dancing, and sex. Perhaps if I delved deeper into their thoughts, beneath the blanket of intoxication, I'd find they were on vacation here to escape their own terrible realities. Escapism was a part of human nature, after all, and the people here had apparently found what they needed.

I didn't delve, though. Invading people's private thoughts was one of the issues I still had with this ability. Luckily, those thoughts didn't automatically blast in my mind, or I'd never be able to live with myself. As an introvert, I needed my head to be my own and couldn't imagine a constant party going on inside it. That would have been so much worse than the situation I was in now, which was bad enough.

Skimming along the surfaces of tourists' minds to listen for the smallest hint of Vanessa's whereabouts, I concluded no one else was suffering a near anxiety attack like I was. Everyone else seemed to be enjoying the loud music, the strobe lights, and the press of the crowd around them.

I accepted the drink from the beautiful man with the dark but glassed-over eyes, and threw it back, grimacing at the ouzo's burn as it slid down my throat, wishing this would be the shot that would dull the senses. But, of course, it wouldn't. I couldn't get drunk. Unlike the norms, I couldn't find my own escape.

"You okay?" Tristan silently asked me.

I clenched my jaw, not wanting to lie, but not wanting to give in, either. *Don't worry about me.*

"As if I could stop. I always worry about you."

I stared directly at him and all the girls surrounding him, particularly the one he smiled at even as he thought his concern toward me.

Well, don't, I thought to him as I drew in a steadying breath. *I can take care of myself.*

"Are you sure?" he asked precisely when the guy in front of me asked me to dance. I nodded, although I truly just wanted to get out of here. *"Alexis, don't think—"*

I never heard the rest of his sentence—what he didn't want

me to think. The handsome stranger thought I'd nodded to him and had me by the hand, stumbling over his own feet as he dragged me to the dance area. As soon as we stepped onto the sunken floor, his hands were on my hips, pulling me close to him. For a brief moment, I forgot about all the mind signatures, the twirling lights, and the pounding music, and could only think about how strange it was to be that close to a man other than Tristan.

But only for a brief moment. Before I could even do anything, a growl ripped through the music—or maybe just through my head—and Tristan suddenly stood between the guy and me, his back to me and his arms out protectively. The drunk guy swung without even looking, and Tristan caught his wrist in mid-air. With the pain of the grip, the guy finally looked up into Tristan's face. His eyes grew wide, and his Adam's apple bobbed as he gulped. Without so much as an apology to me, he carefully stepped away from the dance floor.

Tristan turned to me and wrapped his hands around my waist, pulling me to him as he swayed to the music. I looked up at him with a raised eyebrow.

"You can talk to girls all night, but I can't dance once?"

His nostrils flared. "There's a difference. His hands were all over you."

"I had things under control."

He leaned closer to me and growled in my ear. "I didn't like it."

I stepped back. I should have been warmed by his concern, but his eyes were alit with real anger and his tone acidic.

"I told you. I can take care of myself." I added silently, *He's only a norm, after all.*

Tristan cocked his head and considered me for a long moment, then jerked his hands off my hips.

"Of course you can," he snapped before walking off.

I stared after him, clenching my jaw to keep it from falling open. Warrior Boy seemed to have lost his cool. Which wasn't, well, cool, considering the circumstances.

Tristan!

I stomped off the dance floor and toward the front door of the club, expecting him to follow me, but he sauntered back to his place at the bar amidst all the girls who now looked at me like wild cats about to pounce. I almost gave in to the urge to lift my lip and snarl at them as Tristan had done to my Greek god, but I didn't. Only because something else caught my attention as I reached the door. The mind signature I'd been searching for all night.

Tristan, come on. Game's over. Found her. I looked over my shoulder to see him still leaning against the bar. *Are you coming?*

He shrugged without looking away from the blonde who'd moved in on him. "*You can take care of yourself.*"

I turned to glare at him, but he still ignored me. What was *wrong* with him? It had been my idea to go in separately, to appear as though we were single so the norms would be more likely to talk to us, but Tristan was taking it too far. I wanted to clock him, knock some sense into him. Vanessa's mind signature was on the move, though, and I didn't want to lose her. So I rushed outside, knowing Tristan would come to his senses and follow, while mentally reaching out for the other nearby Amadis. They were all on the other side of the island, keeping their distance, as was part of the plan.

Vanessa must not have sensed me yet, because she didn't move toward the club, as expected. Too many people stood outside to see me flash, so I jogged down the street toward her mind signature as it continued to slowly move away from me, as if she were taking an evening stroll at two in the morning. Probably looking for her midnight snack.

I tried following her signature to her thoughts, but although she remained in my range, my mind struggled to grasp them. My head physically hurt from the effort, probably because of the bombardment it had already suffered in the nightclub, but I pushed harder, desperate to discover her plan.

But I didn't latch on fast enough. Several new mind signatures popped into existence about a half-mile away. All of them Daemoni.

Vanessa's mind prickled, but she didn't move. She remained frozen in place. I didn't wait to find out what she was thinking. If the Daemoni attacked the nightclub—the only place on the island with so many norms in one spot at this time of night—they'd have to go through Tristan and me first.

Tristan, they're here! I yelled at him as I ran toward the club.

I stopped at the door, waiting for him to come out, and wondering if I should somehow get the outside loiterers indoors to safety. My heart pounded, but rather than feeling scared as I always had in the past, I actually felt excitement as the adrenaline pumped through my veins. I hadn't been in a fight in ages—in fact, I wore my leathers and carried my dagger for the first time tonight since last September. I palmed the hilt of my cloaked dagger, and a burst of power surged through me, as if the weapon knew it was finally released from its spot in the boring closet and returned to where it belonged: in my hand. For the first time ever, I felt like the warrior I was supposed to be, every bit as powerful as Tristan.

But that didn't mean I didn't want him with me. So why did I sense him still inside, as if nothing was going on out here?

Tristan! Get your ass out here.

I felt out for the Daemoni as I waited. They hadn't moved yet from where they'd flashed onto the island, close to the shore on the far side of the nightclub. And a new signature popped right into the middle of them. A familiar one, although we hadn't heard from its owner since he disappeared after the trial. The sounds of a fight broke out immediately. Vanessa's mind signature finally moved at an inhuman speed.

Owen's here! He's fighting them by himself. Let's go!

Confident that would get Tristan's attention, I bounced on the balls of my feet with impatience, but he didn't come flying through the door. Where was he? Was he really that distracted? I couldn't stand here doing nothing anymore. I ran toward the fight, Vanessa close behind me. *Ah, shit.* She was *herding* me right toward the cluster of Daemoni.

I stopped, ready to take her on by herself. But she blurred right past me. Surely she had to have smelled me, but she didn't even hesitate. She headed straight for the others.

I stood in the middle of the dark street, flabbergasted for a moment. But I knew what I had to do—I couldn't let Owen fight unassisted. My heart raced harder, and my hand shook a little as my thumb slid over the stone in the dagger's hilt to expose the weapon. It would be stupid to do this alone, but if Tristan didn't get his act together, I'd lose the opportunity to recover my pendant *and* my protector.

"*You are not alone.*"

I nearly jumped out of my skin at the sound of the soft woman's voice in my head, vaguely familiar but not mine. However, it wasn't attached to any mind signature around. And although the internal voice didn't belong to me, I somehow knew it came from inside me.

"*You have what you need within you, Alexis. I am here.*"

The voice did anything but comfort me. Memories of Psycho and Evil Alexis came to mind instead, and I wondered if I was losing my sanity. I'd slowly but surely become used to voices in my head since the *Ang'dora*, but this was different. I hadn't sought it out. I released my hold on the dagger's hilt and massaged my temples.

Get a grip. You're just panicking.

I drew in a deep breath and blew it out slowly. The voice didn't return. Hopefully, it had been some strange fluke, my subconscious finding a different way to try to calm me. My mind remained quiet, even as I reached out again to track the nearby mind signatures.

The fight between Owen and the Daemoni had escalated, and Vanessa was about to land in the middle of it all. A yelp of pain in the voice of my protector shot through the quiet night, and my body immediately responded.

Tristan, I'm going in without you. I called out as my legs carried me down the street. I reached out to the other Amadis soldiers, as well, ordering them to join us. Tristan finally appeared by my side. *Owen, we're coming!*

"*Leave me alone, Alexis,*" Owen barked in my mind just as we rounded the corner to the fight. Just as the Amadis appeared, too. And just as the Daemoni flashed out of sight, Owen on their trails, and Vanessa on his. But we were physically too far away to catch hers.

"Owen," I shouted as I reached out for their mind signatures. They were gone. Not on the island at all. They could be anywhere in a hundred-mile radius. I spun on Tristan and pounded him with my fists. "Where were you?" I yelled at him. "What is wrong with you? If you'd been here—"

He grabbed my wrists and pulled me to him, and the rest of the Amadis slipped away into the shadows, not wanting to be a part of *this*. "I know, *ma lykita*. I'm sorry."

I jerked backwards out of his grasp. "You're *sorry*? Don't you think you took that 'let's pretend we're not together' thing a little too far? And now Owen *and* Vanessa *and* my pendant are gone. Again! It'll probably be another eight months before we get another chance, Tristan. Eight. Months!" I threw my hands in the air with my violent frustration. "Actually, we'll be lucky to ever see Owen again considering what he just flung himself into. What the *hell*, Tristan?"

He looked at me with guilt-filled hazel eyes, the gold flecks dim. He scrubbed his hands over his face and exhaled slowly.

"I don't know." He rolled his neck and his shoulders, then

stared at something off to the side, avoiding eye contact with me. His jaw muscle twitched. "An off night for me, I guess."

"An off night?" I echoed, my words dripping with venom. "*You* don't have off nights. *You* are the warrior who's supposed to be ready for anything and everything. Remember that? Besides, you sure didn't look off to me. In fact, you looked to be pretty *on* with all those women."

His gaze returned to me. "I admit I lost focus, but not because of them. Because of you. I didn't like the damn act, especially when that guy put his hands on you. Then I was pissed and . . . I don't know. Not right."

"We're supposed to be a team, Tristan. I *need* you."

He pressed his lips together and nodded. Whatever had happened in that nightclub, he knew he'd been wrong. But he obviously had nothing else to say, so I broke my eyes from his, and my gaze traveled around the street where we stood. Stucco houses glowed white in the moonlight, and many flights of stairs twisted and wound around the homes, leading to those at the top of the hill. Not a single person sat outside on the various verandas and rooftops; no one climbed the steps. I opened my mind but Daemoni and Amadis alike were gone.

"Let's just go," I said with a groan.

I didn't know what to think about Tristan's behavior. We were on a mission. How could Tristan—*Tristan*, the experienced warrior—become so distracted? We'd fought side-by-side before. He couldn't blame me, especially when he pretty much ignored me when I needed him most. But what else could have been going on?

We flashed to right outside the Amadis Island's shield, then swam the rest of the way in. The physical exertion quieted my anger and frustration with Tristan, and then I completely forgot about it when a new idea occurred to me.

"Were they there for Owen?" I asked once we stood on the beach of the Amadis Island, dripping wet. I'd thought Vanessa was corralling me into the arms of the enemy, but she'd shown no interest in me. Had Owen been the one they wanted? But why? "What if …?"

I couldn't finish the thought of what may have happened to him.

"I've told you before. Scarecrow can handle himself," Tristan said, taking my hand. "Remember, he's pretty damn powerful, even for a warlock."

How could I forget? His extraordinary power was exactly why he was gone. He'd disappeared the day he learned the source of all his power: Kali, the evil sorceress whose spirit had taken over the body of Owen's father, Martin.

I shook my head. "I still don't get it. Why would he throw himself into the middle of so many of them? I don't care how great he is, that was plain stupid."

"You know why. He still needs time."

I let out a harrumph. Everyone, including Mom, kept saying Owen was a grown man and needed to work things out the way he felt was right. Although the Amadis had rules, each member had free will. Well, everyone but us daughters, since the council tried to control us at every chance they could, but we're a different story. As for Owen, if he wanted to abandon us to deal with his own issues, he could choose to do so. And apparently, that's what he chose, still. But he'd been so close to home. There had to have been a reason he showed up on that island tonight. He had to have been thinking of coming back. But if that were true, why would he follow the Daemoni when they'd left the island?

I kicked a stray rock on the path from the beach to the mansion, thinking about how much I missed my protector, my friend. Tristan missed him, too, I knew, and Dorian constantly asked about his uncle. But the way Owen had snapped at me earlier—he didn't sound worried about my safety. Rather, he made sure I knew the door to his life remained closed. Why did he shut us all out when he needed us most? *Because he's a man.* That's all I could figure.

As we walked into the mansion, I expected to find it quiet and dark with Mom sitting in Rina's quarters and Bree staying with Lilith. Dorian slept in his room—I sensed his dreaming mind signature. But Mom wasn't in Rina's suite. She came rushing from the sitting room, tears streaming down her face.

"Alexis, Tristan," she croaked, her wet eyes flitting between us. Her hand covered her mouth as she shook her head. Mom rarely cried. Something was terribly wrong, and considering both Rina and Lilith had been on the brink of death for so many months, it wasn't hard to guess what. And Mom had been down here, waiting for us, while Bree was noticeably absent.

"Oh, my God," I whispered. Tristan's arm around me was the only thing keeping me upright as my knees gave out from under me. Whatever had happened between him and me tonight became a distant memory—we would need each other in the days to come.

CHAPTER 2

The late spring breeze whipped at the hem of my skirt, promising to bring a thunderstorm within the next few hours. Salty sea air filled my nose and coated the back of my throat as we stood on the edge of the cliff, saying our farewells. My hair lashed at my face, but the tears that stung my eyes rose from the deeper pain in my heart. Grief and the boulder of guilt that had replaced my insides made it difficult to breathe.

Tristan stood tightly against me, his hand intertwined in mine, returning the squeezes I gave every few minutes. Reassuring me that he didn't hate me. "It's not your fault," he'd told me numerous times over the last two days, and I'd tried to make the statement my mantra. Still, I couldn't help but feel that it was all my fault.

Mom stood at the head of our group, leading us in the prayer that we'd said and heard much too often these last few months. Bree stood on the other side of Tristan and Solomon to my right. No one else had come to this private funeral, but only one major absence bothered me.

Owen had missed them all, of course, but since this one hit closer to the heart, I'd hoped he'd make an appearance. But no. Still no word from him since the other night. Perhaps he was unable to make it. Perhaps we'd be holding his funeral next. *Don't think that way. No news is good news.* That's what everyone kept telling me. After all, if the Daemoni killed or even held Owen captive, they'd certainly be bragging about it.

Trying to push Owen out of my mind, I refocused on Mom and the pyre she stood next to. The body lain out on top, with her hands folded over her stomach, looked so tiny, so helpless, so vulnerable. So still. The tears brimmed the rims of my eyes and slid down my cheeks. I'd tried so hard to help her. I gave her as much Amadis power as I possibly could over the months, trying to fill her with goodness and eradicate the darkness within her. Trying to draw her out of her coma. But giving her all I could still hadn't been enough. I hadn't saved her.

Even if Tristan didn't hate me, I didn't understand how Bree could not. She'd given up her own world, the Otherworld, and her faerie life to serve the Angels and give them Tristan, only to lose him to the Daemoni when he was six years old. Lilith had been her everything for the past three hundred years. And now her daughter, Tristan's sister, was gone. Because I'd failed. I shouldn't have been at that stupid nightclub the other night. Maybe if I'd been here right before she died, I could have done something at the last minute.

Mom finished the eulogy, and Solomon moved forward with a match as long as a chopstick. Tristan let go of me, stepped up, and placed a hand on Solomon's arm.

"Please. Let me," Tristan said, his voice low and gruff.

Solomon returned to my side as Tristan moved to the pyre. He lifted his hand to Lilith, caressed her forehead and smoothed her blond hair away from her face, so peaceful now, so much like Dorian's when he slept. Tristan's other hand faced the pile of logs and twitched. A flame shot out of his palm and ignited the wood. I dropped my head and closed my eyes, too much of a coward to watch. When Tristan returned to my side, though, I forced myself to give Lilith all that I had left to give her.

Mom, Bree, Tristan, and I lifted our hands and the burning pyre rose from the ground. We sent it over the edge of the cliff and let it hover there for what felt like hours, waiting, but nothing happened. In the other funerals, the pyre—body and all—had disappeared before incineration.

We'd given Lilith an Amadis send-off, but she apparently wasn't Amadis enough for the Angels to take her in the same way they had the others.

Because I had failed.

Plumes of black smoke with a tinge of purple began to darken the sky in front of us as the flames grew bigger and licked at the frail little body. A sob caught in my throat, choking me. *I can't watch this.* I forced myself to keep my eyes open.

"Lower her to the sea," Bree whispered. "Please. She would like that."

With our powers, we carefully lowered the flame-engulfed pyre to the sea below and silently watched.

"*Ms. Alexis! Ms. Alexis!*" Ophelia's voice cried out.

I automatically turned toward the woods that separated this part of the island from the mansion, although the sound came in my head. Panic immediately swept over me at her urgent tone. Ophelia served as the head of staff at the Amadis mansion and often babysat my son.

Dorian? I asked her in response.

"*He is fine. He is fine. It is Ms. Katerina! Please, send Ms. Sophia. Now!*"

My heart stuttered at her desperation, and if the grief of Lilith's death hadn't already swallowed my ability to breathe, news about Rina did. I mentally passed the message to everyone else. Mom's head snapped toward me, her eyes wide. Then she disappeared.

I looked up at Tristan. He gave my hand a squeeze, leaned over, and pressed his lips to my temple.

"Go," he said. "Solomon, too. Bree and I'd like to be alone, anyway."

A popping sound behind me meant Solomon didn't wait to be told twice. But I couldn't bring myself to leave Tristan's side. Not with that look darkening his beautiful hazel eyes. He'd kept telling me he'd never known Lilith as a sister, that he didn't feel the same kind of grief, but I knew he'd hoped to develop a relationship with her, and that hope was now incinerating in the flames below.

I lifted my hand to his cheek, and he leaned into my palm. "I don't want to leave you, though."

"My love," he whispered, "Rina might need you. You must go."

And although he didn't say the words, I thought them: *Don't fail Rina, too.*

I swallowed the lump in my throat and nodded. With another look at the blaze floating on the sea below, I said a silent goodbye to Lilith before flashing to the mansion on the other side of the island.

Bedroom suites had a special shield that only allowed their owners to flash inside them, so I appeared in the hallway of Rina's wing. Her suite door stood wide open, and I rushed through the ornately decorated front room, into her bedroom of browns and beiges, dimly lit by a few candles and lanterns set upon the antique furniture.

Ophelia, the ancient witch, stood at the end of the bed, wringing her wrinkly hands, her severely creased face pulled tight with worry. Julia, the dark-haired vampire who rarely left Rina's suite, paced along the near side of my grandmother's bed. Solomon's cornrows hung around his face as he watched Rina from his stance on the far side. Mom sat on the bed in front of him, holding Rina's hand and whispering to her.

And Rina's eyes shifted to me.

Rina's eyes shifted to me!

They were open! For the first time in eight months, almost to the day, Rina's beautiful, mahogany eyes, so much like mine and Mom's, were open on her own volition.

"Rina!" I gasped, a new sob filling my throat. Tears of joy replaced those of grief as I hurried to her bedside, nearly knocking Julia out of my way.

As I knelt beside her bed, stretched my arm across the dark-chocolate brown duvet and took Rina's hand into mine, Mom looked over at me with pursed lips. Surprised by her dim expression, I glanced at everyone else. Julia still paced. Ophelia continued to wring her hands. Solomon's eyes were tight, the corners of his mouth pulled down. Why weren't they overjoyed?

I studied Rina's face, which normally looked maybe eight or nine years older than mine but now appeared as though she'd aged decades. She stared at me, her face expressionless and her eyes vacant. Her dry lips parted but formed no words. She blinked, then her brows pushed close together, as though she concentrated hard on trying to speak.

"Lil . . . ith . . . good," she grunted. Then her eyes fluttered closed again. We all froze and watched my grandmother's body with bated breath, waiting for her to open her eyes again, but she didn't.

"She's just sleeping," Mom said after a few minutes of monitoring Rina's vital signs. "She didn't slip back under."

A collective sigh of relief whooshed around the room.

Julia sunk down onto the end of the bed and stared at the clasped fingers in her lap, and Ophelia dropped her hands to her side, only to anxiously twist them into the hem of her apron.

"Is she . . . okay?" I asked.

Mom shook her head, and her chestnut hair, pulled into the ponytail swung across the nape of her neck. "I don't know.

She didn't respond normally. She couldn't even speak. Julia, what happened?"

The vampire slowly lifted her head and looked at Rina. "I was sitting right here. As always. Praying for her to wake up, as always. And then . . . her eyes slowly opened and she eventually focused on me. That's when I called for Ophelia to retrieve you. She looked around the room, as if lost. Confused. Even when she saw you."

Mom nodded. "Yes, I noticed that, too."

"She . . . she does not recognize us?" Ophelia asked, her voice tight with worry.

"She has been unconscious for eight months," Mom said. "Although Tristan and I have thought her brain waves appeared fairly normal, she may have trouble returning to us completely. At least at first. We don't know the extent of the dark magic's effects on her."

Before we'd defeated Kali at Tristan's trial, she had blasted Rina with a powerful spell. At least, we thought we had defeated Kali. We truly had no idea what happened to her soul after leaving Martin's body. Or what happened to Martin's body, for that matter. It had disappeared before anyone had noticed its absence.

Lilith and I had been hit by a similar spell in the Florida Everglades, but somehow I had recovered. Lilith never had. Hopefully, Rina will, although she'd been hit at a much closer range than either Lilith or me.

"Now that she's come out of it, maybe I can reach her mind," I suggested as I gazed at Rina's once again still face. My telepathy had been useless with both her and Lilith before. Their brains were too far under to reach.

Mom nodded, and I gave it a go. Rina's mind signature definitely felt different than it had the last several months, as if it had more substance, but still not the same as it had been before. And when I followed it to her thoughts, they were thin, gauzy, like a mist trying to take shape but unable to solidify. I concentrated harder, as if I could focus her mind for her, but, of course, I couldn't.

"At least she *has* thoughts now," I said. "I just can't tell what they are."

"Well, that's better than the complete blank you were getting before," Mom said.

"I hope they clear." I squeezed Rina's hand, giving her as much Amadis power as I could. Between sharing it with her and Lilith for so long, however, pushing all that I had into them to heal their bodies and souls, I was drained.

"Alexis, you need a break," Mom said. "I'll stay with her today and tonight."

"I'm fine." I laid my head on Rina's bed. "I just need to rest a little."

"You need to *sleep*," she corrected. "You need to recharge and regenerate."

"Rina needs me," I said sleepily.

"She needs your full power. Go. Get some real sleep. Spend some time with your family. You need it."

I opened my mouth to protest. I didn't care what I needed. Not when I'd failed Lilith because I hadn't given her enough of what she needed. Not when I could still fail Rina.

"Your *family* needs it," Mom said, cutting me off. "Rina needs you to do it."

She knew how to get to me. I sighed with resignation, but couldn't bring myself to move from Rina's bed. It wouldn't have been the first time I'd slept in her bed, but as long as I did while keeping my hand tightly around hers and feeding her my Amadis power, I'd never truly regenerate. Mom was right. I was depleted. Exhausted. Too tired to even move.

The next thing I knew, I woke up in my own bed.

A large, hard body pressed against the back of mine, and a heavy arm draped over me and held me tightly. I wrapped my hand over Tristan's and entwined my fingers with his. A thick, strong river of his love washed into me, filling every cell as though I'd immersed myself under a waterfall of emotion. Besides sleep, this was exactly what I needed. I drew on his love with a hunger I hadn't realized I'd had, as if my soul had been starving for this connection. *How blessed I am to be his*, I thought as my power began to rebuild within me.

Then Tristan stirred, and his mind signature brightened with consciousness as he awoke. And the strength of the love flowing from him diminished into a narrow stream.

That thought pricked at my heart. *Why would his love lessen?* That couldn't be right. *No, not an actual lessening. Just normal restraint. We all do it.* Of course that was it—consciousness kept his emotions in check. Tristan was so good at controlling his emotions, but I'd never before realized how much he kept his love hidden, even from me.

"Good morning, *ma lykita*," he whispered against my ear.

I peered around the darkness of our suite.

"It's still night."

"Hmm . . . I'd say about three a.m. Technically morning." He rolled away from me, onto his back. I turned over, saw his eyes still closed, and laid my head in the soft crook between his shoulder and chest.

"Still night," I said, closing my eyes. His mind signature relaxed again, and his current of love strengthened. I drank it in as I drifted to sleep.

"I don't want to go!" Dorian crossed his arms over his chest, flipped his light blond hair out of his hazel eyes, and scowled at me as I leaned against the wardrobe in his room at the mansion, having delivered the news that he and Tristan would be going home tomorrow. "I don't want to leave you. Why aren't you coming with us?"

He gave a football on the floor a kick across the room. Good thing the wall was made of stone; plaster would have been ruined with the force. I pressed my lips together and breathed deeply through my nose, practicing my own emotional restraint.

As much as I hated being separated from my two men, I needed to stay to help Mom with Rina and with everything else. Mom couldn't do it all—manage the entire Amadis as acting matriarch and also nurse Rina back to health—on her own.

"I'll be coming home as soon as I can," I promised. "As soon as Rina's all better. And look on the bright side—you'll have Dad all to yourself."

He didn't respond to this, but I could see in his eyes that he liked this perk.

I hated it. Well, for me. It would be good for Tristan and Dorian to have some extended one-on-one time together, but I hated that they had to leave. However, it was unavoidable and not unexpected. Dorian had celebrated his eighth birthday a couple of months ago, and the older he became, the more likely he'd keep memories into adulthood—memories of Amadis secrets he'd take with him when he went to the Daemoni. *If he goes to the Daemoni. IF, dammit.* I refused to accept its inevitability.

We'd been able to keep him on the island this long because Tristan and I both had reason to be here. With Lilith gone and Bree leaving, though, we were out of excuses for Tristan's presence, which meant he could take Dorian home. Especially now that Rina was awake and we all knew it wouldn't be long before I could leave, too.

"I'll miss you," Dorian said. He looked away from me and stared out the window. "I'll miss this place."

I felt his pain. Since Dorian had discovered the village on the other end of the island and the people within it, we began taking him there on occasion. After all, if we couldn't somehow break the curse that would allow the Daemoni to claim him, it wasn't as though the fact of a village or magical people living here would be such a great secret for him to share. The Daemoni already knew about that.

He hadn't exactly made friends here—the adults didn't appreciate the idea of Dorian, their future enemy, getting too close to their kids, as if the curse, if there even was one, might rub off on them. But at least the kids here didn't make fun of him as they had at the Norman schools, and they understood him better than any Norman kids ever would. Even if he hadn't forged a tight bond with any of them, he obviously felt a sense of community here.

I opened my arms to him. He ignored me for a moment, his fists on his hips and the corners of his mouth still pulled down. But then he rushed across the room to me and threw his arms around my neck.

"I'm sorry, little man," I said, hugging him tightly. "You still have Dad and me and Sasha, though."

"But not . . . not Uncle Owen." And the dam that had been containing his tears burst. He sobbed against my shoulder. "Why did he leave us? Is he ever coming back? What if you don't come home, either?"

I blinked away my own tears at the realization of his true fear. He didn't want to leave here, but his feelings had less to do about *where* he was, and more about whom he was with. Since Tristan had been gone most of his life, he feared that we'd each disappear on him. He didn't want to lose his loved ones. *This is good. He needs to know love as deeply as possible.* I counted on love—ours for him and his for us—to help fight the curse or whatever it was that compelled our sons to convert to the Daemoni.

"Uncle Owen will be back," I said for the hundredth time, praying it was true. "And I'll definitely be coming home. I can't stay away from my two men for long."

Dorian pulled away just enough to look at my face. "Maybe Rina will be better tomorrow, and you can come with us."

I chuckled. "That would be wonderful. But really, little man, don't worry. I'll be home with you and Dad before you know it."

After some more coaxing and soothing, he finally gave in, and we spent the remainder of the day together as a family. I needed their love to rejuvenate me and took advantage of the last chance I had to absorb it and boost my Amadis power. I already missed them. I'd been spending so much time bouncing between Rina and Lilith, I hadn't been able to spend nearly enough time with my own little family. And now they'd be leaving.

After putting Dorian to bed that night, Tristan and I snuck off to our private place on the island, a little clearing in the woods, far from the mansion and even farther from the village. Having to stay here for so long and my little problem with my gift during sex had led us to finding a place far enough away that I could let my shield down. We were right on the edge of the island, not far from where we held the funerals.

We lay on the plush blanket afterward, the full length of our naked bodies pressed together, and stared at the diamond-studded sky.

"I wish there was another way," Tristan murmured, turning to press his lips to my temple. His warm breath tickled my ear. "I already miss you."

"I know." I burrowed my face against his wide, muscular chest, and inhaled deeply, tasting his tangy-sweet scent of mangos, papayas, lime, and sage on my lips, on my tongue. "Me, too."

He trailed his hand down the length of my side, sending a current over my skin. "I already miss this."

"Me, too," I breathed against him. "Not long, though, right?"

"Rina looked good when I saw her today. As good as can

be expected anyway. She'll be back to herself soon, I'm sure, especially with your power."

My hand slid up his rippled abs and hard pecs, along his neck, and up to his velvety soft face where I held him. My thumb stroked his cheek. "I love you, my sweet Tristan."

"I love you, too, *ma lykita*." He showed me again with his body exactly how much.

And, although he made me feel as incredible as always, something seemed to be . . . missing.

CHAPTER 3

*R*ina's eyes glassed over as she looked away from
Mom and stared out the open French doors to the
balcony, though she didn't appear to be gazing at the view of
the cypress trees with the Aegean Sea sparkling behind them.
She sat in her oversized bed, propped by a mountain of
pillows, but her mind had traveled to another place . . . to
another time. Perhaps to when she'd first met the people
whose names Mom had just mentioned, or maybe to when
she'd ordained them to her council.

"Adolf and Shihab," she murmured, dabbing a finger at the
corners of her eyes. "And you said others?"

"Yes, but we don't need to discuss this right now," Mom
said, studying Rina's haggard face as she adjusted the covers.
My grandmother's brown eyes looked even larger than usual in
her thin face, accented by dark purple half-moons under her
lower lids.

Tristan had been both right and wrong about Rina's quick
recovery—she regained a good portion of her mental capacity
the day after he and Dorian had left and had continued
showing improvement in the ten days since, but physically she
struggled. With as many hours of the day that she slept, her

body should have restored itself twenty times over by now, but her cells weren't regenerating as they should have been.

"Yes, we *do* need to discuss it right now," Rina said, shooing Mom's fussing hands away with a flick of her own.

Mom pulled back and instead made herself busy by pouring Rina a cup of tea. "Mother, it can wait—"

Rina's eyes snapped to Mom's face. "My people are *dying*, Sophia. It can *not* wait!" Her chest rose and fell in a calming breath before she took the teacup and saucer from Mom. "Who else?"

Mom pinched the bridge of her nose and squinted her eyes. She looked as tired as I felt. Now that Rina was awake and coherent, Mom and I had been spending more time in here with her, gradually bringing her up to date on the state of the Amadis. As her mind began to clear, one of Rina's first questions had been about whether Tristan and I had recovered the pendant yet.

I hadn't been surprised she'd focused on the pendant, especially since we hadn't yet told her about all of the Daemoni attacks. But they probably wouldn't have made much of a difference. The next Amadis daughter would always remain a top priority, and the pendant housed the stone I needed in my possession to ensure Tristan's fertility. Although it wouldn't guarantee a daughter, I would definitely never conceive Tristan's baby without the stone. The Angels may or may not have instilled the faerie stone with additional qualities, but if they had, the Daemoni could possibly turn it against us, making it a weapon. We needed the pendant, but we hadn't been able to find it or the vampire-bitch who had stolen it until two weeks ago. Who knew when we'd find her again?

"Alexis, I will need you to take further risks now. We need that pendant," Rina had said. "It will be our top priority. You and Tristan will lead the operation, and I will give soldiers to assist."

Mom and I had exchanged a glance, but said nothing at the time to Rina. The matriarch had been returning to her authoritative self, which was good, but she didn't have the full story then. She hadn't known about the increase in Daemoni attacks or that our soldiers were already stretched thin. We hadn't wanted to bring up all of the Amadis deaths until Rina's health improved.

Now, only a few days later, we could no longer avoid that discussion.

"Who else?" Rina repeated.

Mom didn't need to answer. The memories others had shared with me flashed through my mind, and I passed them on to Rina. My grandmother closed her eyes, and the teacup rattled in the saucer as she watched the gruesome images of the fights Adolf and Shihab had been in with the Daemoni. Fangs flashed and blood splattered as limbs and heads were severed from bodies. Wolves, cougars, and lions transformed into human bodies as they died on the battlefield. Some of the German and Arabian troops had fallen with their leaders in the violent battles. Then more abhorrent visuals played of the Daemoni attacking Armand and his people as they tried to gather intelligence for us. My own memories of the funerals on the cliff also flashed for Rina, and I could feel her despair deepen with each one.

"The last one we sent to the Angels, before Lilith, was Armand's second-in-command, last month," Mom finally said.

I had liked Armand's second a lot—much more than the French vampire himself who had been one of Tristan's primary accusers last fall. His second had been a female were-bear and a much better leader than her boss. I'd only met her a couple of times, but admired her kind heart and tough demeanor. Hers was the only funeral, until Lilith's, where tears had stung my eyes.

I'd shed no tears for Adolf, the German werewolf who had also been one of Tristan's adamant accusers. Yes, he was

Amadis, so I probably should have felt some remorse, and I supposed I did. A little. But only because we needed every last soul. I certainly held no personal affection for him beyond that.

"The rest of the Amadis are busy, but doing fairly well," Mom added. "The Daemoni are focused on Normans."

"How many are they infecting?" Rina asked as she shakily placed her cup and saucer on the nightstand next to her. "How bad is it?"

Mom shook her head. "We aren't sure of exact numbers, but enough that Normans are taking notice. Some smaller countries have closed their borders completely, blaming the mysterious deaths and disappearances on foreign terrorists. It's only a matter of time before leaders begin considering more drastic measures. If the Daemoni continue their current rate of attacks, or God forbid, increase . . ."

Mom trailed off as Rina rubbed her finger and thumb against her closed eyelids. I took her other hand and pushed more Amadis power into her. She squeezed my hand in return.

"This is too much for you, Mother. You need to rest," Mom said.

Rina stopped rubbing her eyes and glowered at Mom. "I apparently have been resting for eight months while the world falls apart around me. Do you truly believe I can sleep right now?" She shook her head. "Continue. How many have we converted?"

Mom sighed and took a seat in the chair by Rina's bed. She leaned forward with her elbows on her knees and her hands clasped together. "Not enough. Not many at all. Our safe houses aren't empty, but we don't have enough conversion specialists to be more aggressive with the Daemoni's victims. Charlotte has been doing what she can. So have our others. But you, Alexis, and I have the strongest Amadis power, and, well . . ."

Rina gave me a sideways glance and looked back at Mom.

"You two have been here with me rather than out there helping."

Accusation laced her tone, but what did she expect? She was family. Besides, she was the matriarch. We weren't the only ones who needed her.

"The Amadis need a matriarch, that is true," Rina said. "But we have a line of succession. If I had not made it—if I still do not make it—we have you, Sophia. The infected need you more than the people need me."

Mom opened her mouth, likely to protest, but Rina didn't let her speak.

"That is knowledge for you to remember for the future. At the moment, however, I understand the predicament. Alexis is newly turned. She needs to be trained in the art of conversion. Or have you been, darling?" Rina turned her eyes on me. I shook my head.

"As you said, we've both been here the whole time," Mom said.

"I did try with Lilith, but . . ." My eyes stung again at the thought of Lilith. I cleared my throat. "But I failed."

"Alexis, darling," Rina said, "you did not fail. Lilith's soul is safe. I made sure of it before returning."

My mouth fell open. We'd all thought Rina's grunts when she'd first come out of the coma to be nonsense, perhaps a muttering of her last memory before she went down.

"You mean . . ." I stammered.

"The Angels took her soul, yes. I'd been holding the connection to the Otherworld for her, and when Lilith finally accepted your power and moved on, I was able to let go. You did well." Rina tilted her head as she seemed to study my face more closely. "This explains your exhaustion, however. Your low power levels."

"What do you mean?"

"Your Amadis power is low for you, Alexis. You have tried to do too much."

I shrugged. "I had to. I had to help Lilith. And you . . . you . . ." The tears came against my wishes. The emotions I'd been trying to hold inside for days burst through. "Oh, Rina, I'm so sorry I doubted you before. You always take care of us, and I had thought . . . I had thought . . ." I couldn't admit now the blame I had put on her for betraying Tristan and me, of keeping our daughter from us, and calling me a liar about it all. I'd been so wrong, so very wrong about her. "I'm so sorry, Rina. It's my fault you were even hit."

Rina withdrew her hand from my clasp, and I couldn't blame her one bit. She'd probably blocked the ugliness between us from her mind, and now I had brought everything flooding forth again. What a miserable excuse for a granddaughter I was. I squeezed my eyes shut and stopped the sobs. I had no right to cry.

Both of Rina's hands wrapped around mine. "Darling, I do not blame you."

"Nobody does," Mom added.

I shook my head, denying it. Sure, I had revealed the true traitor, but both Kali's spirit and Martin's body were gone, so who knew if it was really over? And when I did reveal the truth, Kali had thought Rina shared the sorceress's thoughts, resulting in the matriarch's coma that had thrown the entire Amadis into a downward spiral.

"Considering what I have heard about the events in that council room," Rina said, "I am very proud of you, Alexis. You did what needed to be done."

"But at what cost? You're my grandmother! I hurt you before the trial even began and then to see you . . . so . . ." I trailed off again, the fear of Rina dying choking me as it had done nearly every day since she'd been hit. "I was so worried," I finished lamely.

I mentally kicked myself in the shins. I'd been waiting so long to apologize and that was the best I could do?

"Alexis, darling, everything occurs for a specific reason. Do not fret anymore. Worry is a waste of energy, and you obviously have little to spare." She withdrew her hands from mine once again. "In fact, I do not want you sharing your power with me anymore."

"But you need—"

"What I need, darling, is for you to have your full powers. Have you been meditating? Spending time alone? Allowing your body to absorb the power from the island as I suggested three days ago?"

"I've tried," I said. "I've sat on the beach. Even did some more writing."

Rina nodded. "I have noticed you scribbling in a journal while you sit with me as I rest. A new story?"

"Not exactly new. It's my story—mine and Tristan's. I've filled three books and am finally about done. Well . . . caught up to now, anyway."

The itch to write again had nearly consumed me within the first week of sitting with Rina and Lilith. Holding them with my left hand allowed my right hand to be free—not exactly good for banging on a keyboard, but fine for old-fashioned writing. I'd started what I'd thought would be a journal, but it really came out more as a story, deeper than the one in my history book because my thoughts intertwined with the actual events.

"If you would like, you may keep the filled books in the Sacred Archives," Rina said, a twinkle in her eye. "The island and the writing have not helped, no?"

I shrugged. "I think they have. I feel more rested . . . sort of."

Rina studied my face for a long moment. "Of course. You need your family. You need to be with Tristan and Dorian."

"I do miss them," I admitted, trying to mute the desperation I truly felt. My heart *ached* with longing for them. "But I'll be fine. You and Mom need me here. Besides, it's only been ten days." Ten days, three hours, forty-two minutes to be exact . . . but who's counting?

"That is settled. You go home immediately."

My jaw dropped. *Am I that transparent?*

"*Yes, you are,*" Rina said in my head.

I frowned. *Really, I'll be fine, Rina. Please, let me stay here with you and Mom.*

"*You will not be fine. You will be useless to us if you continue as you are.*" She spoke her next words aloud. "I may never fully recover, and in the meantime, the Amadis need us. All of us. As does humanity."

"Which is why we need to help you regain your strength," Mom said.

"Sophia, it is too late for me." Mom and I both gasped, but Rina shook her head and let out a little chuckle. "No, no. That is not what I mean. The Angels visited me often while I was unconscious, but no, they did not share any plans for my impending death or ascension. I only mean that you have done as much as you can for me. I believe I am as well as I am going to be."

Mom and I exchanged a glance. If this was Rina's best ...

"You continue giving me Amadis power, and I can feel it coursing through my veins, but I am not regenerating as I should be, no?"

Neither Mom nor I could argue with her.

"I know this. I accept it. The two of you need to accept it, as well. It is time to move on. To move forward." She repositioned herself against the pile of pillows, straightening her back to sit up to her full height. Her eyes narrowed as they looked into Mom's and then into mine. "It is time we prepare for war."

Only two mornings later, Ophelia came into Rina's suite as I once again protested my departure.

"Ms. Alexis, the jet is ready and waiting for you," the elderly witch said.

I scowled at Rina. "Are you sure about this? I hate leaving you and Mom here."

"Honey, we'll be fine," Mom said from a desk in the corner that she'd set up so she could work while still being close to Rina. "We've been doing this for a long time."

"Preparing for war?" I asked.

"Not so urgently, but, yes, that is what we do. Rina and I can manage things from here. We need you out there, serving your purpose."

"My purpose is not going home to sit on the beach and relax," I argued. *Who in their right mind disputes that?* I wouldn't have a year or two ago, but now we were on the brink of war.

Mom folded her arms over her desk. "How many times are we going to discuss this?"

"I just don't get it. There's so much going on, you need every bit of help you can get, and you're sending me *home*? To do *nothing*?"

"We're sending you home to recuperate. The sooner you do that, the sooner you can be of help to us."

"Alexis, darling," Rina said, "there is much we need you for. But you are useless to us in your current state."

Hmph. As if Rina should be talking. She still couldn't get out of bed for more than thirty minutes at a time without exhausting herself.

"I am surrounded by people who love me here," Rina said. She couldn't usually listen to my thoughts as easily as everyone else's so it must have been written all over my face.

"So am I," I countered.

"Not the two whose love you need most," Rina said. "Go home, Alexis. We will be putting you to work very soon, do not worry. We will need a new safe house to start with, and eventually, I will need you to oversee conversions in the entire Western Hemisphere, since Sophia will be here, and I will need Charlotte elsewhere. Most importantly, I will need you and Tristan to recover the stone."

Mom rose from her chair, came over to me, and took my hands into hers. She ducked her head so her eyes could catch mine. "See? There's a lot you'll be doing. But first, you need to be at your best."

"Darling, simply by leaving the Amadis Island, you are doing something for us," Rina added.

With a quiet groan, I gave her a nod of resignation. This part we'd gone over many times already. We hoped that when I left the island and the Daemoni saw both Tristan and me out of the Amadis' direct protection, they'd lay off the norms and focus back on us. That had been their ultimatum before, so hopefully it still stood. We also hoped Vanessa would be too tempted to come after me and would abandon her game of hide-and-seek. In other words, I'd be bait, and although it could become dangerous, the role felt passive when there was so much going on. At least now I knew Rina had other plans for me, too.

But still, my first and primary orders were to *rest*. Because I was useless.

After two days of arguing this, however, I knew by now Rina wasn't going to budge. So I reluctantly said my goodbyes to her and Solomon, Ophelia, and even Julia, then flashed with Mom to the island's runway. A small private jet sat outside the hangar, the steps down, waiting for me. A figure moved from the cabin to right inside the entrance.

"You need an escort," Mom said, laying an arm over my shoulder.

I already knew this, for the same reason I wore my leathers and had my dagger and knife on me—just in case. I had secretly hoped Tristan had returned to serve the role of protecting me, but the figure standing at the top of the steps was definitely not my man. Not any man, actually— admittedly, after Tristan, I'd hoped Owen would have been there. That would have been an even bigger and greater surprise. Before my heart plummeted too far, however, Charlotte moved closer to the edge of the doorway and waved. I grinned for the first time in days, happy to see her face.

Mom turned me toward her and placed a hand on each of my cheeks. A small smile curved her lips, but didn't reach her eyes.

"Charlotte will be working with you again, but I wish it were me. I wish things were different. I've been waiting for this time since you were a little girl." She pulled me to her in another hug as I tried to figure out what she meant. "But we each have our duty, and mine, for now, is to be here with Rina. So you take care, listen to Charlotte, and get some rest. Then I promise you'll have more than enough to do."

"Love you, Mom," I said into her ear as I squeezed her tighter.

"I love you, too, honey."

And as she held me a little longer than what seemed natural, I felt she knew the truth of something ominous coming. The world would be very different the next time we saw each other. After all, everything that had happened in the last year or so had been only the beginning.

"Ready for more training?" Charlotte yelled over the scream of the engines as I sprinted up the steps and threw my arms around her.

"It's so good to see you!" I gushed. "How are you doing? Are you holding up? Have you heard from Owen? Where the heck is he? Where have *you* been, anyway?"

"Whoa," Char said, giving me a squeeze then extricating herself from my embrace. "We have plenty of time for Q & A."

She led me into the main cabin. I'd only been in the

Amadis jet once, and I'd been unconscious then. Julia and the so-called Martin had brought us all here after we found Lilith and Bree in the Florida Everglades. Every other time I'd traveled to and from the island, we'd needed to make a big performance—sinking the famous author's boat right after the *Ang'dora,* and then ensuring the Daemoni knew when Tristan and I had left the Amadis Island and its protection. This time, however, Rina didn't want the Daemoni aware of my departure until I was good and ready—well rested, in other words.

The main cabin looked like a living room, with a beige leather L-shaped couch, cushy chairs, and tables. It could easily seat ten people. Charlotte gave me a brief tour, showing me the two bedrooms, a medical suite, and a full kitchen in the rear. The jet was piloted by a vampire whose blond buzz-cut backed up the claim that he'd been a fighter pilot in World War II, and a wizard with strawberry blond dreadlocks served as his co-pilot.

"If something goes wrong, a mage in the cockpit can keep the jet airborne for a while," Char explained. I nodded with understanding. Owen's magic had powered the tiny plane we'd used to escape Australia. "He also keeps us cloaked and shielded."

We took our seats on the couch, and I watched out the window as Amadis Island shrank and then disappeared once we broke through the force field that kept the island invisible. As we lifted into the clouds and the scenery below was whited out, I looked at Charlotte, and my heart squeezed. I didn't know her true age—at least ninety, I figured—but she appeared to be in her mid-thirties. Or, at least, she had when I'd first met her.

Now she reminded me of how I'd looked right before the *Ang'dora,* when Tristan had been gone—a perma-frown creating lines around the corners of her mouth, her sapphire eyes tight and distant, her straw-colored hair short now and sticking out all over the place, as Owen's often did. The shock and anger of learning about the real Martin had consumed her. She'd thrown herself into her work, unrelentingly pursuing the Daemoni, jumping into every fight even when Mom had ordered her to stop. Mom and I both knew why, though. Char searched for answers.

Charlotte explained that Owen tried to do the same. They both wanted proof that Kali still existed. What worried us all, though, was that while Char sought revenge, we weren't aware of Owen's intent. After learning his life had been a total farce, he'd cut himself off from us so thoroughly, we didn't know if he'd ever return. If he thought he somehow belonged with the Daemoni now. For all we knew, the fight a couple of weeks ago could have been for show, or perhaps his attempt to prove something. The thought of losing him to our enemy sucked the breath out of my lungs.

"I wish I could give you better news," Charlotte said, "but at least we know Owen's alive and free. Otherwise, we would have heard about it by now."

"Right." I sighed. She sounded like Mom and Tristan with their *no news is good news* bit. "So, uh, what kind of training will we be doing?"

I needed to change the subject. We'd spent the last two hours talking about Owen and her, but mostly Owen, and I couldn't take any more. Training was a positive action, a way to move forward and actually *do* something.

"Well, first, you'll be resting," Char said, and I rolled my eyes. "I need to do some work around the States, anyway, before we can get started."

"Started with what?"

"Conversions. That's your next objective."

CHAPTER 4

"I have to warn you, though," Charlotte continued as she looked out the window, although only ocean and sky could be seen. "And you better keep this to yourself, but I'm not as good at it as I used to be. Probably all this anger I've been harboring."

"Maybe *you* need to rest, too," I said. "Build up your own Amadis power."

She made a face. "Resting doesn't get anything accomplished."

"Heh. Exactly what I said."

Char ignored that statement and dove right into the theory behind conversions, explaining that we needed to push the Daemoni's evil energy out of the subject and replace it with the goodness of our Amadis power. I already knew this part.

I'd tried to do this with Sheree, the were-tiger Owen had found in Key West and brought to the beach house the night I went through the *Ang'dora*. I hadn't been strong enough to help her then and had nearly killed us both. Fortunately, Rina and Mom had arrived in time to take over. They'd moved her to the Atlanta safe house, where the conversion was completed.

"So once the dark power is removed and they're stabilized, they have to go through healing and training in our faith, our methods, and our way of life," she explained. "You know—no biting or eating people, no turning norms, drinking only donated or animal blood, using magic only for good. Eventually, they should be able to live on their own and become a contributing member of society—ours and the norms'."

"How long does it take for them to get there?"

Char shrugged. "Depends. How long they've been Daemoni, how much they believe in the Daemoni philosophy, their capacity for love, which the Daemoni try to eradicate, and other things—they all have an impact on how long it takes. Some can live among the norms after several months. Others are never ready. They have to stay immersed in the Amadis culture because they're too easily tempted when on their own."

And there were some who chose to live as loners instead. Such as Jax, the were-crocodile who isolated himself in the Australian Outback rather than having to constantly fight the urge to eat people.

"And my role is to replace the dark energy with my Amadis power?" I asked.

"Yep. Once they're stabilized, if you're not already at a safe house, they'll be taken to one where they stay for the remainder of the conversion."

I cringed. "They're locked up?"

"Sort of. It's like house arrest. You have to understand—if they're exposed to norms before they're ready, the consequences can be deadly. But you've stayed at a safe house. They're not quite a third-world prison."

True. Mom and I had lived at the safe house in Northern Virginia throughout my pregnancy with Dorian and until he and I were both strong enough to move on. The "house" was actually a mansion, offering everything a person could need or want. I hadn't cared for the luxuries at the time, but if all the safe houses were so nice, I could see that a new convert should be pretty comfortable.

"So how come only a few of us can do the first phase of the conversions?" I asked. "I mean, I get why Mom, Rina, and I are stronger, but take you and Owen. Why do you have enough Amadis power to do it, but he doesn't?"

"Part of it is being born Amadis. I've never had Daemoni influence, never lived among them. That's why vampires can't administer this part of the conversion—they've had Daemoni power, even if only for a short time after they were infected. Same with converted shifters. Those born into the Amadis might have strong enough power, but converts usually don't."

"But Owen's not a convert. He's never had that influence, either."

"Well, that we don't know now, do we? We have no idea how Kali was subliminally influencing him." Her lips puckered, and her nostrils flared for a moment, but then she seemed to gather herself. "The other part is about focus. Martin—or Kali—focused Owen's talents, power, and ability on fighting and protecting. I'm strong in those areas, too, since I'm a warlock, but I spent much time learning how to build and use my Amadis power. Martin never allowed that for Owen. Owen had shown signs at an early age that he'd make a good protector, so he didn't need to be strong in the conversion aspect because the one he protected would be. At least, that was Martin's excuse. Perhaps we know now he had other reasons, as well."

He wouldn't want Owen's Amadis power to completely extinguish his Daemoni energy. I didn't dare say this aloud. The thought of Owen having Daemoni power was too much, and I wasn't about to tick off Char even more by voicing something so . . . unbelievable.

"So any mage born into the Amadis can do conversions, if they've learned to use their Amadis power?" I asked instead.

Char nodded. "For the most part, yes. But not all mages are strong fighters, and the process usually begins with a battle."

"Ah. So you're saying I'll be out in the field fighting?" I wasn't sure about this idea. Not that I was afraid or didn't want to help in this very important way. I just didn't like the thought of leaving Dorian as much as would be required. He needed my protection.

With that thought, the excitement to be headed home finally hit me. I'd felt so guilty leaving Rina and Mom, Rina especially in her poor physical state, but deep down, I really did want to go home. Not to rest, though. To make sure my son was protected, kept hidden away from the Daemoni's reach. Of course, Tristan was there, the best protector of all, and also Sasha, the lykora, but the mommy in me couldn't help feeling the need to be there myself.

A while later, as land had come into view on the horizon, the pilot's voice came from the overhead speaker. "We have a situation in Key West. We've been ordered to stop."

Charlotte frowned and studied the screen of her phone, then pushed her hand through her hair as she swore under her breath.

"Alexis, when we land, I need you to stay on the plane," Char said as we began to descend over the string of islands that made up the Florida Keys. "In fact, I want you in one of the bedrooms, and don't come out until I say."

Now she had me seriously worried. "What's going on?"

"A couple of injuries, but looks like we might have a new addition."

"A convert? We're starting already?"

She shook her head. "Yes, a convert, but no, not for your training. Not yet. I'll have to take him to Atlanta."

"But can't I help?"

"You can help by staying safe." The warlock's eyes narrowed at my pout. "Alexis, I'm serious. I can't be worried about you with all the Daemoni in Key West. To do my job and get us all out safely, I need to know you're here on the plane, okay? The pilots will stay with you. Tristan's already been contacted, and I'm sure he'll be there shortly after we land, if he's not already. Everything will be okay—as long as you stay on the plane."

"Right. Got it. Stay on the plane." I gave her a reassuring smile, ignoring the painful jab that even she, who had trained me in combat, believed I was useless.

She managed a small smile as relief flooded her eyes. She tapped a message on her phone screen and then tucked the device into a pocket. "Thank you. And if you really want to help, keep tabs on the thoughts of people around me and tell me if we're in any danger."

Now I gave her a real smile. "I can do that."

Rather than landing at the commercial airport, we hit ground on a runway at the Naval Air Station, which I found comforting. I hadn't learned all of the politics between the Amadis and the rest of the world and hopefully wouldn't need to for a long time, but if the U.S. military gave the Amadis special clearance, that must have meant we had inside connections with some pretty important people. Charlotte flashed off the plane, and the pilots climbed down to the tarmac to keep watch. I tracked Char's mind signature while reaching out to all those nearby, a sense of foreboding running a chilly finger up my spine. I couldn't believe what I found.

Nearly every mind signature was Daemoni. Four Amadis were with Charlotte here on the Naval base, which was otherwise empty, as if abandoned. Only a handful of norms were scattered throughout the island. I scanned minds, skipping around from head to head, occasionally dipping deeper into their thoughts, and discovered the horrible truth. Except for a few tourists who were trying to figure out why everyone seemed so strange, the only other norms in Key West were not only fully aware of the Daemoni, but they served as volunteer blood donors and caretakers of the evil creatures. The Naval Station wasn't being friendly to the Amadis—there was no one left to *be* friendly. Those sailors who refused to be turned had become the main course of a Daemoni feast.

"Oh, no," I choked, although no one was on the plane to hear me.

Charlotte, I called out. *Hurry! They . . . they've taken over. The Daemoni have taken over all of Key West!*

"*Just listen for trouble,*" she said, her mental voice tight.

I hated listening to the Daemoni's abhorrent thoughts, so I skimmed the surfaces of their minds, going deeper only when I felt the need to. There had apparently been a fight with our soldiers who were now with Char—some of the Daemoni were still riled up and rallied for another attack.

As I scanned, I found myself unintentionally slowing down on those signatures belonging to vampires—my subconscious searched for Vanessa. It had been a couple of weeks since we'd seen her in Greece, and no one had reported any subsequent sightings. She could have easily made it here, one of her favorite stomping grounds, and then gone back into hiding among all the Daemoni.

I didn't find her mind, but as I found two more vampires, the signature of a norm practically screamed with fear. I zeroed in on it. A young woman had been pushed against the wall in an alley, the vampires pawing at her, one tall with white-blond hair. Not Vanessa, but close enough—Victor, her brother. Hating what I had to do but having no choice, I jumped into his mind, knowing I'd want to scrub my brain with a wire brush when I was done. I took in the view from his perspective and found a very familiar scene.

Victor! I mentally shouted at him. He froze, and his fear spiked with the unexpected voice in his head. Under other circumstances, I would have laughed. *It's Alexis. Surely you've been told about my telepathy.*

He growled. "*Get out of my head, bitch!*"

Not until you let the girl go and tell me where Vanessa is.

"*Fuck off!*"

I sighed. *Just cooperate. You can't make me leave, and I can make your mind a living hell. Worse than it is already.*

The bastard basically shut his mind down by closing his eyes so I couldn't see through them anymore and mentally singing some horrible ballad, drowning out every other thought. For a moment, I believed maybe he was smarter than I gave him credit for, but he couldn't carry it on for long. As his hands remained on the girl, his thoughts kept traveling in disgusting places.

Shit. I couldn't let him hurt her. Knowing his hands were still on her sent a chill up my spine. Yelling at him in his head wouldn't do any good, but I'd promised Charlotte I'd stay on the plane. That I'd stay safe. Going solo into the heart of Daemoni-infested Old Key West wasn't exactly keeping that promise, especially with my Amadis power so weak. I wrapped my hand around my dagger, reminding myself that I wasn't unarmed. A warm surge shot into my arm.

"*You have other powers, stronger than anyone's.*" The strange voice in my head again—the same one from the little town where we'd seen Vanessa and Owen.

Who are you? I demanded, though I feared the answer. What if she was only another part of me, meaning I was losing my mind again?

"*The first daughter to handle this dagger. The only one able to, until you.*"

So I *was* losing my mind. My dagger had belonged to Cassandra, the first Amadis daughter, and had been given to her by Andrew the Angel—over two-thousand years ago. Since the Angels only talked to the matriarch, the voice in my head couldn't be real.

"*It is me, Alexis. I am—*"

A girl's cry, though only in my head, drowned out anything else the voice said, and I refocused on Victor's mind. The girl screamed again as his hand pushed between her legs, and his lust, both sexual and blood, soared, feeding off of her fear. *Oh hell no.* I couldn't stand by, knowing what they would do to her.

"*Be strong, Alexis. I am with you.*"

I hoped Char would forgive me as I flashed away, thankful the co-pilot had dropped the shield around the plane so the Amadis could flash onto it when they were ready. I told myself I wasn't listening to some strange voice in my head, but was only doing the right thing for the Norman girl.

I appeared in the alley off of Duval Street and nearly gagged. The place reeked of evil, the Daemoni presence so freaking heavy. Evening had nearly fallen, shrouding the place in darkness, and I could sense them everywhere—on front porches of old houses, on the sidewalks of Duval Street, at the bars, and in the restaurants, barely bothering to hide their true selves. They mingled with the few tourists and conspired with the locals.

My heart rate instantly spiked. Maybe coming here alone wasn't such a great idea after all.

"*You came for the girl. She needs you. And I told you, you are not alone.*" I tried to push the voice away, but unfortunately, I couldn't silence it. "*Take care of the girl, Alexis!*"

As though she gave me a mental kick in the ass, I ran my thumb over the amethyst in the dagger's hilt, revealing the silver blade, and withdrew it from its sheath at my hip. Feeling another surge of power from it, I ran and lunged at the trio. I landed on Victor's back, and he yelped with surprise. His friend immediately ran off, but I didn't care about him as long as he left the girl alone. Victor, on the other hand, had something to tell me, whether he wanted to or not.

He squirmed and bucked, trying to throw me off, but I

held on tightly, my thighs gripping his waist and my arms around his shoulders. His hand grabbed my wrist, and if he squeezed any harder, he'd pulverize my bones into powder. The pain loosened my grasp, and he flipped me over his head. Right before I'd slam to the ground, I twisted in the air and landed on my feet, facing him. He lunged at me without thinking about it first, and I moved barely fast enough to dodge his punch. He fought with instinct, no thoughts for me to hear before he acted, and I wasted precious time parrying his blows. When he swayed off balance after a missed punch, though, I made my own move and landed again on his back, this time holding the silver blade against his neck. He froze.

"That's a good boy," I said, still hanging onto him. I peered over his shoulder at the girl who'd been paralyzed with fear during our brief fight. With long dark hair and dark eyes, tall and thin, she reminded me so much of Sheree. I thanked God I'd been able to stop the attack on her. "Go. Now! Get whoever you came here with and go far away from this place."

Like Sheree had done so long ago, the girl finally scrambled to her feet and stumbled down the alley. Victor made another attempt to throw me off. The blade slid across his skin, and he grunted from the contact with the silver. He froze again.

"Your sister's right. You really are an idiot, aren't you?" I asked.

"Get the hell off me," he growled.

"Answer a question for me, and I'll think about it."

"You already ruined my dinner. I have nothing to tell you."

I pressed the blade harder against his throat. He whimpered. "I just want to know where Vanessa is."

"I don't know." Victor stiffened even more under my muscles, but I hadn't done anything to cause it.

"I suggest telling the truth," Tristan said from behind us. My chest felt as though a wide belt had suddenly loosened its tight hold on me, and I took my first real breath since leaving the plane. I was no longer alone.

Tristan moved around to the front of us, his palm facing out toward Victor's chest as he stood several yards away—far enough that if he flashed, Victor couldn't follow his trail. Overcome with happiness to see my beautiful husband in person, I grinned, fighting the urge to jump into his arms, because if I did, Victor could flash away, and we wouldn't be able to follow him. The look he gave me in return was murderous.

"I *am*," Victor managed to get out between stiff lips. "Haven't seen her in months."

Really? I'd always thought they were inseparable—I'd never seen them apart. Except . . . the last time we saw her . . . I tried to remember if Victor had been among the Daemoni on the Greek island, but I hadn't inspected their mind signatures closely enough. *Doesn't matter.* He surely had to at least have an idea of where she hid, and there was only one way to find out.

A mental shudder ran through me as once again my mind made its way into Victor's icky head. If he knew where Vanessa was, though, he had no thoughts about her now. But then he accidentally recalled a memory—a very recent one—of Vanessa standing in a dark alley similar to this one, she and a blond guy in each other's faces, their noses only inches apart. A very familiar blond and not Victor himself. In fact, the vampire hissed at the memory.

What the . . . ?

Tristan raised an eyebrow at me. I gave him a slight shake of my head. *He doesn't know where she is.*

"*Let's go then.*"

To the plane?

"*No, I told Charlotte to take off. Go home.*"

With a nod, I sprang from Victor's back and landed next to Tristan. In a flash, we appeared in our garage, which gave us a few moments before we were bombarded by an eight-year-old.

"Victor was telling the truth?" Tristan asked, his voice harsh. I stopped myself from throwing my arms around him when I saw sparks of anger in his eyes.

"Um . . . not exactly. It hasn't been months since he's seen her, like he said . . . in fact, it was only last week in Key West. But get this . . ."

Victor's memory, now my memory, played in my mind, and I shared it with Tristan. Vanessa had turned from the blond male in the alley to look at Victor. She lifted her lip in a snarl, and her musical voice warned Victor to lay off.

"He's *mine*," she hissed, and the memory faded.

"She was with *Owen*," I said with disbelief. But I couldn't decide if seeing them together shocked me more, or if the vision of him tilting his head, as if *offering* his neck to her, did.

"That's . . . unexpected," Tristan agreed. "At least we know he survived it."

"We know nothing, Tristan. She could be slowly sucking him dry, and he's letting her. Victor was pissed she wouldn't share him and all the power in his blood."

"She doesn't exactly have a reputation for sharing," Tristan muttered, which reminded me of the last time I'd heard her declare someone as hers—me.

Only, I had to admit, there was something different about the way she said it this time. Murder filled her voice when she spoke of me. Something else, something just as passionate yet different, colored her tone when she spoke of Owen.

"Oh, shit! What if he's letting her kill him on purpose? What if he's suicidal?"

"Nah," Tristan said, but he stroked his chin as if he wasn't so sure. "No," he said more firmly. "Besides, Vanessa won't kill him. He's too valuable. It'd be more likely that she'd infect him. Or perhaps convince him that he's already Daemoni because of his ties to Kali."

Exactly my fear. "He'd rather be *dead* than be a vamp or any kind of Daemoni. We need to find him. And if he's converted, we need to save him."

"And if he doesn't want to be saved?"

"Don't be ridiculous," I scoffed.

"Alexis, that's part of preparing for your role. You need to be able to face that possibility."

"We're talking about Owen, though. He doesn't really want to be part of them."

"You have no idea what's going through his mind right now."

I put my fists on my hips. "You're wrong. I *do* have an idea. I know what it's like to find out your sperm donor is evil. I don't know what the physical ties are between him and Kali, but he has her magic. He was essentially raised by her without knowing it."

"So it's a little different than finding out someone you never knew is your enemy. Owen might handle his news differently than you handled yours."

"He can't *want* to go dark, Tristan. Not Owen!"

"And if he does? Can you kill him if it comes to that?"

I turned my back on him and crossed my arms over my chest.

"We can't let it come to that," I said, then I strode out of the garage and headed for the house.

Tristan's hand clamped on my shoulder, and he spun me around. "We're not done yet."

But apparently we were, for the time being anyway, because Dorian's voice rang from inside the house, and the backdoor flew open.

"Mom's home!"

CHAPTER 5

I rearranged my mental focus and put myself in Mom mode right when a not-so-little boy came sailing at me. Using his own special skills, he slowed in mid-air to avoid a collision—he was already big enough that he could have easily bowled me over. I wrapped my arms around him as he embraced my neck.

"I told you I'd come home," I said. "Did you miss me?"

"Lots! But Blossom's been here and she does everything for me. And she's made cake every day! I think I want to marry her. Is that okay with you, Mom?"

I chuckled. "Isn't she a little old for you?"

He shrugged. "Nah. And she's beautiful." He paused. "But so is Heather. She's younger. Maybe I'll marry her instead."

I knew Blossom—the cake-baking witch with blond hair, big eyes and a spell-enhanced chest, who had become a good friend—but I didn't know Heather. The name rang some kind of bell in my mind, but I couldn't immediately place it.

"Who's Heather?" I asked him.

"She's been helping Dad and Blossom. She's here right now." Dorian tugged at my hand to pull me inside, but my

50

feet remained planted outside the door. I looked over my shoulder at Tristan.

"Heather?" I asked.

His angry scowl transformed into a guilty grimace. Jealousy's green tentacles tried to slither around my heart, but then the image of a handwritten note appeared in my mind, a letter I'd received right after the trial, signed by Heather. She'd been the girl whose dad I'd punched in the nose ten years ago, and a few weeks later, he'd driven his car into Mom's bookstore. She'd written me to ask for my help, believing that her sister Sonya, who had stalked me, the author, had become a vampire. *Ah, shit.* I wasn't in the best mental or physical state to take this on.

"Sorry," Tristan muttered. "I should have given you some warning. She was sitting on the front step the day Dorian and I arrived, and she hasn't left since."

I drew in a deep breath and exhaled slowly.

"Come on, Mom," Dorian said, still tugging on my arm. "You're letting the bugs in."

I reluctantly crossed the threshold and into my home—the place I'd lived in for only a few months and had been gone from twice as long. It didn't feel quite like home at the moment. Especially knowing my two men had been here earlier with the two women sitting at my dining table. Well, one woman and one girl. The unfamiliar one, with shoulder-length, brown hair and blue eyes, couldn't have been more than sixteen or seventeen years old.

"Hi," she said with a little wave of her hand and a wide smile that showed nearly all of her pearly whites. "I'm Heather."

Before I could get a word out, Blossom sprang out of her chair and threw her arms around my neck. "Alexis! It's so good to see you!"

Then she jerked out of my arms and started mumbling apologies for her behavior as she dipped into a curtsy.

"Oh, stop that," I growled, grabbing her arm and pulling her into a hug. She let out a joyous laugh.

"Don't worry, Heather's all right," Blossom whispered in my ear. "I've been watching her."

I gave her a squeeze of appreciation.

For some reason, I'd expected Heather to immediately jump all over me about helping her sister, but she didn't. Rather, she acted quite mature for her age, making small talk about my trip and how she and Dorian had spent the day. After a while, she and Blossom left.

"I thought you said Heather hadn't left since you've been here," I said to Tristan after we put Dorian to bed, grimacing at the accusatory tone of my own voice.

Was I reading too much into the fact that she finally decided to leave once the wife came home? She certainly had a crush on Tristan, the way she looked at him. But was there more than that? Sure, Tristan was *way* too old for her, but then again, he knew how to downplay his age and come across much younger. I'd been only eighteen when he came looking for me, and Heather seemed quite mature for her years. *Ugh! Stop being petty! Totally different situation.*

"Don't worry—she'll be back tomorrow." His annoyed tone reassured me.

"You don't like her?"

"She's a good kid. She's been really helpful with Dorian. But she's, well, very persistent."

"Persistent with what?" *Ugh.* There it was again—that tone of suspicion.

A smile danced on his lips. "About her sister."

"Oh. Right. Of course." I nodded. "She didn't say a word of it to me, though."

"Because Blossom threatened her life to give you time to settle in." Tristan came up to me and lifted my chin with his thumb. His eyes were alight, the gold dancing beautifully, a stark but nice contrast to how they'd looked earlier. "Do I sense a little jealousy, *ma lykita?*"

I leaned forward and pressed my forehead against his chest, unable to look into his eyes. "Stupid, I know. I feel weird in my own home, I guess. Like it's not even mine. And being back in the real world after so long on the island . . . I just want to get back to normal."

"Normal?" he asked with curiosity as he wrapped his arms around me.

"Heh. Yeah," I said. "Whatever that is."

Except having his arms finally around me was the best normal I could ask for. I pressed my hands against his ribs and slid them around to his back, pulling him closer, wanting to eliminate the final millimeters of space between our bodies after the thousands of miles that had separated us for the last two weeks.

"I'm so glad you're home," he said, his voice thick.

"Me, too," I whispered, my hands wandering southward to the hem of his shirt, and underneath. His muscles tightened under my touch. "Does this mean you're not mad at me anymore?"

A low growl rumbled in his chest, but he didn't let go of me. "We'll talk about it later."

"But Char and the rest got away safely, right?"

"Yes, no thanks to you. Or me, since I had to go searching for you."

Before he changed his mind and decided to talk about it now, I lifted his shirt to his shoulders and ran my mouth across his chest. The growl turned into a hum of pleasure as I made him forget his anger with me. In a flash, we were in our room, and my jacket and Tristan's shirt were tossed to the floor.

"You're so damn sexy in that," he said, his heated gaze traveling down to my breasts that nearly spilled over the top of my bustier as they throbbed with need.

In one swift move, he grabbed my wrists, lifted my arms above my head and shoved me against the wall as he planted his mouth on mine. His tongue pushed its way in and moved urgently, hungrily, leaving me breathless and weak-kneed. He brought my hands together over my head and clasped my wrists in one of his hands as the other trailed shocks down my arm. I squirmed under his touch, and he pressed harder against me, grinding his pelvis into mine. My thighs quivered, ready to open up and let him in.

"Do me a favor and stay right there," he murmured against my lips. I nodded.

He stepped backward, and my arms began to slide down the wall, but his hand returned in an instant, holding them up.

"Right there," he said.

"Um . . . okay."

What was he doing? If he wanted to play our favorite game, he could have held me in place with his power. I wasn't about to ask, though. I could either cooperate or ruin the fun. No way would I ruin the fun.

It hadn't just been two weeks, but over eight months since we'd truly been able to be together the way we preferred. Being in the woods on Amadis Island, with so many creatures who could easily encroach into my telepathic range, wasn't nearly the same as being home where I could truly let go of *all* my inhibitions. Any nearby humans wouldn't understand that I blasted orgasmic feelings into their heads, and so far anyway, Dorian had no clue, as if his child's mind blocked it out.

So I stood there with my arms crossed high over my head, trying not to squirm too much from anticipation as Tristan knelt before me.

After removing and discarding my boots, his hands went to my hips and his lips to my stomach. As he kissed the exposed skin between the bottom of the corset and the top of my pants, his fingers slipped under the tight leather and slowly slid to the button. Then his hands pushed down, taking my pants with them, and his mouth followed close behind, kissing and sucking my inner thigh, the inside of my knee, my calf, all the way to my ankles. I pulled one foot free from the tight leather and then the other, and he pushed my pants to the side. Then he placed insanely high, hot pink stilettos in front of me. I raised an eyebrow.

"Humor me," he said, his voice husky, as he slipped the shoes onto my feet, raising me several inches higher.

He rose to his full height, his eyes never leaving my body, now clad in only a black leather bustier and five-inch heels. He cocked his head, and a slow smile spread across his stunning face. Then he reached out and undid the top buttons of the corset, freeing my aching breasts.

"Hmm . . . that's what I'm talking about," he murmured.

"You like?" I asked with a small smile, enjoying the power I had over him.

"Very much." His smoldering eyes lit a fire in my belly. Well, the fire had already been lit, but now it blossomed into a heat that was both pleasurable and agonizing at the same time. My muscles clenched as if he were already inside me.

"Your turn." I glanced at the bulge in his pants.

"Don't move," he said with a grin, then he proceeded to unbutton his pants and slide them down torturously slow, teasing me the whole time.

But at some point, he must not have been able to stand the torment himself, because he was suddenly naked and pressed against me. One hand held my wrists again and the other grasped my jaw as he kissed me deeply with a desperation I felt all the way to my toes. His hand slid from my face down my neck and glided slowly to my breast. His fingertips trailed circles of current around my nipple as they spiraled their way in. By the time they reached the tip, his mouth was pulling my other breast in. His teeth grazed one nipple as his fingers pinched the other, stretching them both long and tight. I moaned and arched my back, pushing my breasts against him, begging for more.

His mouth moved to my other nipple and licked, sucked, rolled, and bit as his free hand moved down my side, to the back, over my bare butt. He pulled my hips into him as he pressed his erection against my belly. The heels made me nearly the right height to match us up.

"Ah, Lexi," he groaned against my breast, "I need you."

"Take . . . me," I panted.

In response, he spun me around so I faced the wall. His hands grasped my hips and pulled them back, forcing me to lean forward. He massaged my butt and my thighs then pushed my legs outward.

"Oh, god," he moaned, and he slid inside me from behind. I cried out as he pushed deeper in, slowly until he filled me completely. "You feel . . . so . . . *good*."

He took my wrists in one hand again and held them to the wall as his other caressed my breasts, then splayed across my stomach, holding me still as he thrust in and out. His fingers inched downward until they touched the nub of raw nerves, and a jolt of ecstasy shot through me. I succumbed to the first wave of an orgasm. He continued to move back and forth, in and out, each stroke harder, deeper, faster, and wave after wave wracked through me until I could barely stand on my shaky legs.

He pulled out and freed my arms, and I turned around. I pressed my hands to the sides of his face and pulled him closer for a kiss, all wet and sweet and tangy. His hands glided over my hips and to my butt, and he lifted me. I wrapped my legs around his waist, and he entered again. But after three magnificent thrusts that sent me to the verge of another orgasm, I realized this could be a mistake.

"We'll knock the wall down," I gasped.

With me in his arms and my legs still around him, Tristan moved backwards to the bed. When he hit the mattress, he fell back, putting me on top. His chest was hard but smooth as I pressed my hands on it and rocked my hips, feeling him pulse inside me. I rode him hard, making him groan and pant, until he bucked against me and then suddenly sat with me in his lap.

He twisted us around and laid me on my back, then pounded into me with hard, beautiful thrusts. I covered my mouth to muffle the scream of pleasure from the deep penetration. My back arched on its own, and his mouth latched onto my breast, his tongue flicking over my nipple and then caressing it as he sucked. I closed my eyes, losing myself in the bliss, and met his rhythm with my hips. But right when I was about to explode again, he growled.

We both froze. My eyelids flew open. His face twisted in a mix of heated passion and . . . agony? Then I saw what I hadn't seen in so long—a flicker of flames in his eyes. *What the hell?* Before I could even finish that thought, the spark was gone.

He closed his eyes and exhaled the breath he'd been holding. He still throbbed inside me. I flipped us over, wrapped my hands over his forearms and pushed them against the bed, holding him in place as I rode him again, looking into his eyes the whole time, mind-sharing everything I felt right now with him. His eyes filled with love. And intense desire. And then rolled back.

"Oh, *fuck*, Lex," he groaned as he came inside me.

We silently lay in each other's arms afterwards, not mentioning what might have happened. I told myself *nothing* had happened. It was the heat of the moment. *He loves me.* I felt his love flowing from his warm, strong embrace now. At least, I thought I did. Once he drifted off to sleep, it really came pouring out of him. And that bothered me. Why would he be inhibited while we made love? Afterwards, when it was only him and me, basking in the beautiful moment we'd just shared?

Something was changing between us. Hadn't we already been through enough?

Tristan was right about Heather. She knocked on our door bright and early the next morning, which wasn't a bad thing because it distracted Dorian from the fact we'd broken our bed. Again. We'd also left an indentation in the drywall from my head and torso, and Owen wasn't here to fix it all for us, forcing me to make an embarrassing request of Blossom.

"So where did these come from?" I asked Tristan as I picked up the stilettos to put them away before going out to greet Heather. I certainly never owned shoes with these kinds of heels. "Did you pick up a new hobby of women's shoe shopping while I was gone?"

He shrugged casually, but his face remained smooth. "I guess you could say I've developed a new fetish."

I stared at him for a long moment, not knowing what to think or say, but mostly fighting hoots of laughter at the thought of big, powerful Tristan—*Mr. Beautiful*—browsing the women's shoe section. But if this was really his new thing, I didn't want to laugh in his face. He could develop worse fetishes.

"Um . . . well, okay . . ." I stammered.

Then he was the one to burst into laughter. "Joke, *ma lykita*." He pulled me into his arms and whispered against my ear, "Just like any part of you, I'd rather see your feet naked."

I sagged against him with a bit of relief. I couldn't help the thought of there being something wrong with the "ultimate warrior" having a thing for women's shoes.

"So where did they come from?" I asked, the shoes still dangling from my fingers.

"Blossom."

The sense of relief disappeared faster than a warlock could

flash. *What the heck were Blossom's sexy shoes doing in my bedroom?* I stiffened in Tristan's arms.

"She said she accidentally bought the wrong size, and she thought you might like them," he explained.

"Seriously?" I asked with a forced chuckle, trying to cover up my idiotic reaction. What was up with all the unwarranted jealousy? Sure, Tristan had been acting strange lately, but not in a way that made me suspect his faithfulness to me. But something had apparently crawled under my skin and gnawed on my nerves. Perhaps the depleted Amadis power made me so cynical. "She thought *I'd* like *these*? To wear around town or something?"

Blossom knew me better than that—flip-flops or combat boots were the only things that went on these feet. Then again, this was Blossom. She'd probably bought them for the same purpose we'd used them for: in the bedroom.

"Yeah, I didn't think you would, but, well, a guy can't help but wonder how his girl would look in those." He finished with a wink, and my brain glazed over.

He took the shoes from my hand and tossed them into the closet before giving me a kiss that made me forget everything. Then he took my hand and pulled me out to the kitchen.

Blossom must have given Heather a serious threat, because the girl still didn't dive immediately into the subject of her sister. Rather, she showed up at our house every day for a few hours and watched Dorian for us while Tristan and I took care of Amadis business, which mostly consisted of finding and purchasing (on behalf of the Amadis) a mansion to serve as the new Captiva safe house. But every day before she left, she'd mention something about her sister, or vampires, or the Daemoni, or the Amadis. This went on for a few weeks, and although I could have called her out—I already knew what she wanted from the letter she sent me—I was buying time.

I needed to follow orders and rebuild my Amadis power before making any promises that I could help her. And even fully rejuvenated, I didn't know if I could keep such promises. The best way to help Heather and her sister, if she was indeed a Daemoni vampire, was to convert her. But I knew too little about the process of conversions, and Charlotte hadn't started my training yet. I'd hoped the warlock would be here by the time Heather stopped circumventing the issue, but I ran out of time. She finally popped the question—specifically asked for my help—one day as we sat on the beach, watching Dorian ride his skim-board over the low waves of the Gulf of Mexico.

"Hold on," I said. Up until now, I'd simply listened to Heather's remarks and comments with little acknowledgement, but I could avoid the subject no longer. I had questions of my own before I answered hers. "Before we really get into this, how do you know all these things about us? You're not supposed to."

She was a norm. Someone had to have disclosed our secrets. She gnawed on her bottom lip and watched her fingers as they weaved in and around several yarn anklets decorating her foot. She always wore a bikini under her tank tops and shorts, and with her sun-streaked hair, natural beauty, the friendship bracelets adorning her arms, and all of those anklets, she looked like the typical beach-town local teen.

"It's your fault," she finally said, looking up at me. "Yours and Tristan's. Mom came home every night for weeks swearing that she knew her new clients from somewhere but couldn't figure out how. And then the day after the sale finished, she completely forgot she'd told me anything about you and only said you two bought a house from her. But I saw you once when you stopped by her office to drop something off, and I recognized you immediately. Because of you, my dad stopped beating the shit out of my mom. You don't forget the faces of the people who finally scare away the real monster in your life. Well, not unless someone wipes your memories."

I cringed—she'd guessed what Owen had done to her mother.

"But that doesn't explain how you figured everything out," I said, avoiding her accusation.

"Look at you. You're like . . . *exactly* the same as you looked before. Well, not you. You're a lot more . . . well, more everything. Prettier, sexier, stronger. But still you, as if you're frozen in time. And my sister . . ." She drifted off, her mind going somewhere else as her fingers returned to twisting in her anklets. When she spoke again, her voice came from a distance. "She looked almost the same as the day she disappeared, too, but it'd been four years. She'd barely been nineteen then, and she should look older now. At least different. Instead, she just looks . . . paler. Her hair's exactly the same—same cut and everything. She'd told me once, after reading your books for the sixteenth time, that she wished she could be a vampire. Then one day, not too long after you got the restraining order against her, she said, 'I know they're out there. I'm going to go find them.' And we never saw her again."

Guilt tugged at my heartstrings. I hadn't personally obtained the restraining order. My publicist had because Sonya seemed to be a crazed fan, with a little too much emphasis on the "crazed." She'd never bothered me, though, and perhaps if that restraining order hadn't been issued, Heather wouldn't be sitting next to me, asking for my help.

I swallowed the lump in my throat before encouraging her to go on. "But then you did see her . . ."

"Yeah, I did. The first time I saw her was nearly two years ago, and I totally freaked. I couldn't believe it, and even convinced myself that I saw wrong. When I looked back to be sure, she was gone. A few weeks later, I was at the skate park with some friends, and I saw her again, and that time I approached her. She told me I didn't know what I was talking about, she didn't know me, and I'd better leave her alone if I wanted to live. But something in her eyes, Alexis . . . she wanted to tell me something. She looked so . . . *scared*." A tear slid down Heather's cheek as she stared out at the horizon. "I had to *do* something for her. There had to be something that I *could* do. I stalked her for a while, following her as best as I could, but keeping my distance because she's, well, pretty effin' scary now. Some of those vamps aren't very smart or secretive, especially lately. It was so easy to creep on them and listen to their conversations. They lie all the time, even to each other, but I learned some things that were true, too. Like last summer when they were pissed at not being able to attack some kind of colony on Captiva. Because of *you*. And Tristan. They were so scared of you guys!"

"That must have piqued your curiosity."

"Hell, yeah, it did. How could these vamps be afraid of *you*? I mean, my asshole sperm-donor was, but he was only human." I couldn't help but chuckle at the term she used for her dad—the same thing I called the guy who fathered me. She went on. "So I knew you were different, but you didn't seem the same as the vamps. I didn't get too close to them, but I didn't have to. They felt all wrong. Bad vibes. And when I'd been close to you in the office that one time, you felt right. *Good*. But I knew you had to be something not quite human."

I stared out at the water as I let her story sink in. How was this possible? How could she detect anything different about me, unless she wasn't a norm herself? But I knew she was—I could feel her humanity all over her.

"Blossom says it's because of my open mind," Heather said, startling me. I didn't think I'd shared those thoughts with her telepathically, but when she continued, I realized she'd gone down the same train of thought as I had. "How I can feel the difference between all of you and us norms, as you call us. I got that open mind from you, you know."

"Me?" I asked as I pushed my toes into the sand.

"You and your books. Sonya and I talked all the time

about how it could all be real. But I'd never want to *be* an evil vamp. I just prayed, if they *were* real, angels would be, too, and they would protect us."

So Rina and the council had been right about my books. They opened people's minds to the possibility that so-called fantastical creatures existed. I'd been so worried this would drive people to seek out the Daemoni to become a shifter or a vamp, as Sonya had. But apparently, at least as many readers could be like Heather, strengthening their faith, which would protect them against the Daemoni's increasing attacks. My guilt lessened. A hair.

"Anyway," Heather continued, "after we moved to Sanibel, I rode my bike to Captiva almost every day for a while, and as soon as I got my license, I'd go and watch my sister, too. It didn't take long to figure out there were two groups and which side you were on. And then I thought, 'They can help me. They can help me get Sonya back.'"

CHAPTER 6

a long moment passed before I realized the girl waited for my response.

"Heather," I said, "I really *do* want to help you, but honestly, I don't know what can be done. Sonya *chose* this, which meant she was willing to give up her soul to be a vampire."

"But she *hasn't* yet. She hasn't lost her soul. I see it in her eyes. I think she realizes she's made a huge mistake, but doesn't know how to un-do it." The girl turned to me, and tears filled her blue eyes as they pleaded with me. "Blossom says if there's any hope at all, you can save her. I know there's hope. I *have* to believe that!"

I pulled her into my arms and smoothed her hair as she cried. My decision was made. She needed me. She needed our help. And I owed it to her and her sister.

So a few weeks later, Heather, Tristan, and I took a ride in Tristan's new toy—a shiny black Ford F-250—to spy on a nest of Daemoni vampires in Fort Myers Beach. The mission was two-fold: try to get a feel for Sonya and learn what we could about Vanessa and my pendant. A simple reconnaissance trip. Yeah, right.

Heather spotted Sonya and a redheaded female vamp leaving the condo they shared with others from their nest, and we followed them as they walked down the main road and made their way to the crowds of tourists. August was one of the slowest months of the year, but there were still plenty of tourists around. Perhaps because Key West had earned such a dangerous reputation lately. The way Sonya and her companion hungrily eyed the norms, Fort Myers Beach would soon be gaining a similar rep.

The two vamps easily found their prey in a dark parking lot behind a bar.

"Hey, two on one, huh? I'm down with that," said the middle-aged man covered in tattoos as we crouched behind a car on the far side of the lot. I lifted my head up enough to see the vampires man-handling the guy. "Whoa, whoa, whoa. I like it rough, too, but easy now."

"*We can't let them attack*," Tristan said, and I nodded. "*You stay with Heather. I'll take care of it.*"

But by the time he finished his sentence, Heather was already sprinting across the parking lot.

"Sonya, no!" she screamed. "Don't do—"

A wail of pain cut off the girl's words.

"*Go, Alexis!*" the voice, the one I refused to believe belonged to Cassandra, screamed in my head.

Tristan and I blurred to the site to find the guy gone and the redhead squatting over Heather's splayed out body, blood pouring from a cut across the girl's cheek. With a thunderous crash of Sonya's body against hers, Red was thrown off of Heather. The two vampires rolled around the parking lot, fists flying at each other.

"She scared away our dinner," Red shrieked as she freed herself from Sonya and jumped to her feet.

"She's my *sister*," Sonya yelled back, springing to her feet, too.

"Not anymore. Now she's just a meal."

Sonya lunged at the other vampire. She never made it across the three feet that had separated them, though—Tristan appeared between them, and she slammed into his hard body. He caught her arm in one hand and reached out to grab Red, but she took one look at him and disappeared with a *pop*.

Only to reappear with three others.

No exchange of pleasantries ensued. They immediately moved in for the attack. I uncloaked my dagger and yanked it from my hip, swinging it as a little blond female flew at me. The blade sliced across her forearm, and she screamed from the silver's burn, but didn't relent. She charged me again, along with a short guy with orange hair. I shot her with electricity and pushed Amadis power into my dagger as the blade slid between his ribs. He let out an ear-piercing scream then disappeared. The blonde began to turn a sickly gray, purple smoke rising from her skin, when something knocked my arm, breaking the current.

"That's enough, Lex," Tristan murmured. "You can't kill her."

The blonde flashed out of sight as my arm fell to my side. All of the others had disappeared, too, except for Sonya and a tall guy with a dark crew-cut, both of whom stood across the lane of cars from us.

"Go on," Sonya said to the guy, nodding her head toward the road.

"Sonya—" he said, and the tone of his voice sounded as though he had some kind of authority.

"I need . . . to do this. Please," she said. They eyed each other for a long moment, and something seemed to pass between them, some kind of unspoken message. He disappeared before I had the thought to maybe "hear" what they were thinking.

Having some faith Sonya wouldn't attack us on her own, I dropped to my knees next to Heather and pressed my fingers to her neck. Her pulse came nice and strong. She must have hit her head when she was thrown, though.

"Is she okay?" Sonya asked.

"I think so," I said.

Sonya crossed the lane and stopped abruptly with a gasp as she took in her sister's condition.

"Oh, my god. What have I done?" She fell to her knees, scooped Heather's unconscious body into her arms, and rocked the girl as she sobbed. "Heather, I'm so sorry. You shouldn't be here. What have I—" She stopped suddenly, as if frozen. The next instant, Heather was on the ground again, and Sonya stood on her feet, staring at her sister with horror in her red eyes, her hand clamped over her nose and mouth. "The blood. The *blood*. Oh, god, don't let me . . ."

My eyes darted to Tristan to silently ask for a little help with the vampire, but his expression stopped me. He appeared to be waging some kind of internal battle. *Tristan!* He snapped out of it and looked at me with dark eyes. *Help Heather.* He stared for a confused moment, then finally gave a slight nod and moved to the younger girl's side.

"Sonya," I said, slowly rising to my feet and moving toward the vamp, one hand out in precaution, the other on the hilt of my dagger. "Be strong. You don't want to hurt her, right?"

She stared at me with wide eyes, the same blue as her sister's, and shook her head.

"No, don't let me," she whispered behind her hand. Then her eyes changed, glowing bright red as her worried expression morphed into anger. Her voice was no longer a whisper, but full of venom, stopping me in my tracks. "How could you *do* this? How could you bring her here? It's too dangerous!"

"*I* brought *them* here," said a hoarse voice at our feet, and we both looked down at Heather, still cradled in Tristan's arms. He'd healed the cut on her cheek.

"How could you be so stupid?" Sonya demanded. "I told you to stay away from me. You have no idea the monster I've become!"

And if I hadn't already believed it, I knew right then her soul could be saved. After all, you don't worry about someone's safety if you don't give a rat's ass about them. She still cared. No, more than that. She still *loved*.

"*Help her*," not-Cassandra whispered.

"Sonya," I said, taking another step closer to her and slowly reaching my hand out for her arm. She hissed at me, and her fangs slid out, but I refused to back off. "I *do* know what you think you are. But you're wrong. I sense good in you."

"Don't touch me," she snapped, shrinking away from my hand. She'd apparently been warned about my electrical touch or about the pain of the Amadis power. Probably both. "*You* did this. It's all your fault!"

I cringed at the accusation, but nodded. "I know. I accept that. But I want to make it better. You know I can, right? You know I can help you?"

She shook her head violently, and her dark hair stuck to the tears running down her cheek, reminding me of her mother a decade ago when her father had struck her in the park by the beach. "You won't help me! You'll *kill* me."

"Do you want to live like *this*?" I asked Sonya, throwing one hand toward Heather at my feet and the other in the general direction of her nest. She didn't respond, but her answer came loud and clear in her thoughts: *No!* "We can help you. The Amadis can get you out of this. We can show you a better way to live."

Sonya's blue eyes flew from me to Heather, back and forth several times. A multitude of emotions stormed across her face as she remained in the grip of indecision.

I think she'll come with us, I said to Tristan. He didn't

respond, and I peered at him again. He stared right at me, his eyes hard. *Tristan?*

He blinked. His eyes softened. Sort of. Again, a battle seemed to rage just under the surface, but his only coherent thought came as a growl. "*This wasn't the plan.*"

So you want to leave her here? I asked with disbelief. What was going on with him?

Heather's hands gripped Tristan's arms as she struggled to sit up. "Do it, Alexis," she implored. "Do what you need to, now, tonight, I *beg* you!"

The girl's pleas pulled at my heart, but what was I thinking? Her hopes were already flying, but I'd only disappoint her. I had almost no experience with conversions. We had a safe house, but no staff to manage it. Whose lives would I be risking by bringing our enemy there with no one but Tristan and me to babysit her until we had help for the conversion? We couldn't dare leave her alone. And what about Dorian? What if something went wrong, and she got to him, then whisked him away? Could I risk my son's life like that?

"*You cannot think that way, Alexis. You are an Amadis daughter.*"

Not-Cassandra was right, and this was my purpose—defending souls such as Sonya's. She deserved this from me. They all did, but especially Sonya, because I felt somewhat responsible for her being in this position in the first place. I couldn't turn my back on her when she needed me so badly. Helping her was my duty, and I'd find some way to do it and keep Dorian safe at the same time.

"*That is right. You just need to trust yourself.*"

Let's do it, Tristan. He blinked at me again, as if he didn't understand. *Now, while we have the chance. Go on. Do it!*

Right when I was about to reach over and smack some sense into him, he shook himself, gave me a strange look, then lifted his hand. He blasted his power at Sonya, knocking her out. The vampire dropped to the ground, and Heather screamed.

"Shh!" I clamped a hand over her mouth. "It's the only way to get her to Captiva. She'll be fine." The girl fell silent, but I felt obligated to add, "Well, as fine as we can hope for under the circumstances."

Because, really, who knew if she'd be fine? Under my unskilled care, we could both be dead by tomorrow.

Tristan scooped Sonya into his arms, and Heather, still feeling a little shaky, climbed on my back before we sped to Tristan's truck. As he unlocked doors and gave orders, I kept my mind's eye on the signatures all around us, scanning for any Daemoni who might try to stop us. Tristan climbed in the backseat of the truck with Sonya, ready to paralyze or knock her out again if she came to. Heather sat in the front passenger seat, and I cursed as I drove the big-ass truck out of the parking lot and onto roads that seemed to be way too narrow for the extra-wide tires. I hated driving the truck. But so far, so good—no one followed.

At least, until we were halfway across the bridge connecting the island to the mainland.

A red Corvette zoomed up next to us, and a yellow Hummer roared up behind us. The blue light of a mage's spell hit the side of Tristan's truck, and Heather screamed. I cursed that Owen wasn't here to shield us.

"Floor it!" Tristan ordered, and I pressed the gas pedal as far as it would go.

Another spell hit us, rocking the truck on its wheels. We left the bridge, the red brake lights of a car in front of us shone, and I jerked the steering wheel to the left, jumping onto the median to pass the little car. The Hummer and the Corvette stayed with us. I pushed the truck as fast as it would go.

"Red light," Heather whispered, then her words came out in a shriek. "Alexis, red light!"

I eased off the gas, but Tristan yelled, "No! You have to go through it. They're right on our ass."

Besides the Daemoni in the car and the Hummer, I sensed no nearby mind signatures on the roads this late at night, but my heart still raced as if trying to match the speed of the truck as we flew through the intersection. My hands gripped the steering wheel so hard, my white knuckles practically glowed in the dark.

"Turn right at that light up there," Tristan said. "Let's try to lose them."

"But the Corvette's in the right lane. I'll have to cut across it."

"Exactly. They won't see it coming. Just get far enough ahead of them."

"Oh, dear God, stay with us," I muttered, *and you, too, Cassandra, if that's really you,* I added as I floored the gas pedal again, shot ahead of the red sports car, and made the hard right turn at the last minute. I swore two wheels came off the ground as Heather's head slammed against the window. The Vette's tires squealed as it made the turn, the Hummer right behind it.

I glanced in my rearview mirror to see the Hummer pull into the lane of oncoming traffic, up to the side of the sports car. They drove side-by-side for a moment, then the car slowed down, and the Hummer sped up. I caught the driver's thoughts as he approached.

"They're going to hit us!" I screeched right before the Hummer banged into the truck's bumper. I gripped the wheel tighter, trying not to lose control. They slammed into us harder, and the wheel tried to jerk away from me.

"Right," Tristan barked. "Now!"

I made a sharp right, running over the curb. The Hummer followed in my tracks.

"I can't do this, Tristan. I don't know how to drive like this."

"You have to, *ma lykita.* Just do as I say."

"I don't even know where we are!"

"Stay calm. Panic won't—"

The Hummer hit us again, pushing the truck into the other lane of traffic. I yanked the wheel barely in time before hitting an oncoming delivery truck, but that overcorrection sent us careening toward a light post. I slammed on the brake, probably not the smartest thing to do. Our rear end began fishtailing, and the Hummer spun a one-eighty to miss hitting us.

The next thing I knew, Tristan's hands were on the wheel, regaining control before we crashed. Without taking his eyes off the situation outside, he somehow maneuvered himself into the driver's spot and me onto the center console. I scrambled to the backseat, not even trying to figure out how he'd switched places with me. Not caring, because already I felt safer. With a couple of strategic turns, he'd outdriven the Daemoni and lost them completely. We all let out a collective breath of relief as he pulled onto a quiet street headed to Captiva.

"You start driving lessons tomorrow," Tristan muttered.

When we turned onto the road that would take us to the causeway to Sanibel, Sonya moaned next to me. Her eyes slowly opened. Her hand went to her throat.

"Thirsty," she groaned.

Heather turned in her seat to look at her sister. Her eyes widened with alarm.

"Thirsty," Sonya said again, more insistently this time, her eyes locked on the only norm in the truck.

"Take care of her, Alexis," Tristan said.

Before he could explain, Sonya threw herself toward Heather. I caught the vampire just in time and wrestled her back to her seat.

"What do I do?" I asked, struggling to keep the vamp pinned down.

"You'll have to stab her," Tristan said.

"*What?*"

"With your dagger. Right in the heart."

"No!" Heather and I both shrieked.

"Dammit, Alexis, do it! You won't kill her. You *know* that."

"Why can't you—" *Use your power*, I was going to say, but he caught me off.

"Because I might hit *you*."

Sonya thrashed under me, and now her eyes locked on *my* throat. *Crap.* If she drank any of my powerful blood, all hell would break loose. My heart slammed against my rib cage as I drew out my dagger. I pulled in a deep breath as I lifted it and blew the air out as I plunged the blade down, squeezing my eyes shut at the last moment.

Heather screamed.

Warm and wet splatters peppered my face.

Sonya fell limp, her eyes staring at me without seeing. After three tries, my hands shook so badly, I finally managed to push her eyelids closed.

We zoomed through the toll plaza, and I was thankful for the SunPass we had to automatically pay the toll. I could only imagine what a booth attendant would think if they got a good look at the truck, inside and out. At some point when this all settled, Tristan would be pissed.

With shaking hands, I wiped the blood off my face, then retrieved my cell phone and scrolled through the numbers until I found Charlotte's. Just my luck that she didn't answer.

"Char," I said to her voicemail, my voice trembling as much as my hands, "I have a problem and . . . uh . . . could really use your help. We . . . um . . . we can get started on that training any time now. Like—*right* now."

I pressed End and stared out the window at the darkness underneath us as we crossed the bridge to Sanibel. Heather sobbed, and I reached up to smooth her hair, but she jerked away from me.

"It's all my fault," she cried. "I shouldn't have . . ."

"Shh. She'll be okay," I said. "We'll take care of her."

She looked at me with a swollen, wet face, trying hard not to let her eyes drift toward her sister, who sat limply behind Tristan with a dagger in her heart. "Are . . . are you sure?"

"Yes, this is what we do," I said, hoping I sounded more confident than I felt.

Tristan stopped in front of our house. "Take care of her, Lex. I'll take Sonya. Meet me there when you're done."

"No," Heather said, shaking her head. "I'm going with her."

"You can't," I said. "This . . . you don't want to be there. Trust me."

"I'm not leaving her!"

I slid out of the truck, opened the front passenger's door, and grasped Heather's shoulders. "Please don't fight me on this. It could get really ugly, and Sonya won't want you to see her like that. If you love her at all, let her be for now."

Her eyes flitted to the backseat, and immediately returned to me as if she regretted looking back there. She probably did. It was a gruesome sight. With obvious reluctance, Heather half-slid/half-fell out of the truck and into my arms. I walked her to the door of my house, and Tristan took off.

Blossom, I thought as I stood outside my house, watching Heather go inside. I didn't have time or the energy to go in and try to pretend everything was normal on behalf of my son. The witch appeared outside with me, and I told her what happened.

"Crazy," she said. "Are you sure you're up to this?"

I shrugged. "I have to be, don't I? If Char arrives—"

Blossom squeezed my arm. "I'll send her right over. Don't worry about a thing here. I've got Dorian *and* Heather taken care of."

"Don't let her out of your sight," I said, worried about Heather's mental and emotional state.

"I promise."

With a nod, I flashed to the courtyard of the new safe house, one of the oldest mansions on Captiva that the Amadis had procured. The main part of the mansion faced the beach with the island's main road running between the estate and the sand. From the street, the mansion appeared to be two stories tall, with a grand stone staircase leading to the front door. In back, however, was a courtyard with a pool and the first "floor" was an outdoor kitchen for entertaining. What you couldn't see from the road were the two perpendicular wings that connected to each end of the main house and another wing in back, creating a nearly perfect square. The rear, right corner, however, was open, where the driveway entered a parking area.

The kitchen, a dining room, rooms for gathering and entertainment, a conference room, and offices were part of the main house. Five guest rooms made up the right wing, and two master suites and a smaller room were in the left wing. The rear wing was meant for live-in staff, but I called it the dungeons.

Once I'd signed the purchase papers on behalf of the Amadis for the safe house, new shipments arrived almost every day to furnish the mansion. But not only standard furniture. Besides regular beds, dressers, and sofas, the shipments included hospital beds with silver restraints, thick iron chains coated in silver that Tristan had to bolt into concrete walls, and a variety of medical equipment. Rina, Mom, and Charlotte together had been making preparations for my training and my new role, but so far, the safe house had no live occupants. Until now, anyway.

Tristan's truck sat in the driveway, and he was pulling the vampire out of the backseat when I appeared.

"My poor truck," he muttered as he carried Sonya inside, and something about the way he said it made me want to chuckle.

"I think it could use a good detail," I said, stifling another giggle with this understatement of the year as I rushed to the house to open the door for him.

Neither of us cared about the truck, of course, but this little exchange was some kind of way to make everything that had happened tonight less real. Or perhaps more real. After staring death in the face several times and still not believing everyone had survived, we needed a moment to ground ourselves in the stupid little things before carrying on with more life-and-death decisions.

We took Sonya to a guest room in the right wing, and Tristan laid her down on the bed, then began cuffing her wrists and ankles. Only when she was secured did he pull the dagger from her heart. Several beats pounded in my chest as we waited, and I began to wonder if we'd made a big mistake. What if she didn't wake up? What if the silver had been too much for her? She was a relatively young vamp, maybe too weak to survive such an assault. Except I knew better—the only way to truly be rid of a vampire, regardless of how young, was to burn the body.

As if my self-confirmation had been her cue, her eyes flew open as she let out a gasp, and she immediately started thrashing against her restraints. Tristan's palm flew up and she stopped, paralyzed. Only her eyes moved, wide and wild, like a trapped animal.

"I'm doing what I can," he said quietly. "You know my lack of experience with conversions, my love. This is all you now."

He actually had more experience than I did, considering he'd gone through it himself. But he didn't have the Amadis power to execute a conversion—his strengths lay elsewhere. Such as keeping Sonya still so she didn't hurt herself or me.

I swallowed and nodded. My eyes studied Sonya, who stared at me with nothing but terror in her face. *I can do this.*

I've started it before and hopefully Charlotte will get here in time. I took a step to approach the bed.

My heart jumped at the sound of running footsteps echoing behind me. Had I not locked the doors? Did the Daemoni find us already? I spun around and moved into the hallway, hand up, ready to throw lightning.

CHAPTER 7

"You're worse than your mother, always getting into things too big for your little self." Char's voice came out of the darkness before the rest of her did.

A familiar face framed with long dark hair and topping a tall, thin body came up right behind Charlotte.

"Sheree?" I asked with disbelief. She grinned, and I was amazed at how much it lit up her face. The last time I saw her, she was lying on death's doorstep. She looked so radiant now.

"Rina thought you'd be happy to see her," Char said to me. "Sheree has turned out to be an excellent faith-healer. She'll take over when we're done."

Char pushed past me and into Sonya's room, taking in the scene of the tied up vampire with a bloom of crimson staining her top. The warlock shook her head with obvious disapproval. "Looks like I got here just in time."

"Sorry," I muttered. "I wasn't sure what to do, but we couldn't abandon her."

"Of course you couldn't. You did the right thing. So . . . let your training begin." Charlotte moved to the bed and wrapped her hand around one of Sonya's and told me to do the same.

"I'll, um, show myself around," Sheree whispered from the doorway, and I sensed her slip out of the room.

"Push your Amadis power into her and remind her of love," Char instructed. "Rina uses her telepathy, and it helps a lot. Use yours to share images the patient can relate to. Then you need to get her to state her desire to convert."

I started talking to Sonya in hushed, soothing tones, as Mom and Rina had done with Sheree.

"Sonya," I said, "I want you to think about Heather, okay? Focus on Heather, your little sister. You love her, right? You still feel that?"

Her mouth clamped with fear, Sonya blinked once, which I took for a *yes*. I pushed an image of Heather into her mind.

"She loves you, too," I said. "She's waiting for you, so you can be together as sisters again."

I didn't think it possible but Sonya's eyes widened even more, white showing all the way around her irises. Her whole body trembled as though she tried to fight Tristan's paralyzing power.

"We can't be sisters again! I'm a *monster*," she yelled.

"Shh, calm down," Char said soothingly. "Don't worry about that right now. Just think about how much you love her. How you would do anything for her."

The vampire's body slackened.

"One step at a time, Alexis," Char said. "And don't forget the Amadis power."

Sonya's reaction had caused me to slacken my power without realizing it. I pushed it into her hard, and her body tensed again as she screamed.

"Sonya, do you want this?" I asked.

"It hurts," she shrieked.

"I understand. If you don't want it, I can stop." I eased back on the power.

"No! Don't." She panted. "Please, don't stop."

"So you do want this?" I asked again.

"Yes. I want this."

"You have to state it," Char said.

"I want it. I . . . want . . . to be . . . Aaaaah." She screamed again, as if it hurt her to say the word. "I want . . . to be . . . Aaaamaaadis. I . . . don't want . . . to be . . . evil."

Her eyes rolled up into her head, showing how much saying those words had drained her.

"Why?" Char persisted, and I remembered Mom had asked Sheree the same thing.

"Convince us," I said, mimicking Mom's next words.

Sonya whimpered. Her eyes refocused on us. "Because I love my sister. And I don't want to hurt her. I don't want to hurt anyone anymore. I . . . I . . . I made a big mistake. I should have never asked for this."

Her last words were barely audible as her voice trailed off. Tears streamed down her cheeks.

"If you listen to her thoughts, you'll know if she's sincere," Char told me, and I opened my mind to allow her to hear Sonya as well.

"*I'm no better than our father. Worse even.*" Her regret and despair gripped me. Char nodded.

"*Now we get serious,*" the warlock said. "*Push. Hard.*"

I gathered all the Amadis power I'd been building inside of me for the last couple of months and pushed the ribbon of energy down my arm and out my palm into Sonya. Char's eyebrows pulled together, and her eyes tightened as she did the same. Sonya started shaking and convulsing against Tristan's power.

"Let go, Tristan," Char said through gritted teeth. "We need her loose. Alexis and I can handle her."

Out of the corner of my eye, I saw Tristan give Charlotte a doubtful glance, but he eventually lowered his hand. Sonya whipped about for a few minutes, but I was physically stronger than I'd been with Sheree and could hold her down. Eventually the convulsions stopped, and her body went limp.

And then I felt the evil energy building inside her. Memories of the last time we did this and the consequences flooded my brain.

"Get out, Tristan," I ordered.

He put a hand on my shoulder and squeezed. "I'm not leaving you."

"Get out!" I nearly yelled this time. "I'm not letting you take it again."

I wouldn't risk the chance of the evil power leaving Sonya's body only to find a new home in him as it had done before. Granted, freshly escaped from the Daemoni's clutches for over seven years and implanted with dark magic, he'd been what Rina had called an open vessel at the time. He had practically welcomed the evil energy inside of him. But no way would I jeopardize that happening again. He'd been acting too weird lately as it was, especially when we were around the Daemoni.

"Go," Char said, backing me up. "You're not helping, and Sheree can use you. She'll need help gathering supplies."

Tristan wrapped his arms around me and pressed his lips against the top of my head for a long moment. The full strength of his love finally flowed out of him while awake, boosting my power. *Maybe he* could *help.* I let the thought pass, though, not wanting to have to go through again what we did last year.

"Call me if you need me," he murmured.

"I don't know what that was about, but you can't waste your energy arguing," Charlotte said after Tristan left.

"When I tried to do this with Sheree, I took in her Daemoni energy, and Tristan took it from me because it almost consumed me."

"That was before your *Ang'dora*, right? You and your power should be strong enough now to eradicate the Daemoni energy. There should be no transfer this time. Unless—oh, bloody hell. Here we go."

Just as the words came out of her mouth, I sensed what

she did. Sonya felt as though she might literally explode with the dark energy building inside her. The color in Charlotte's face drained, and the muscles and tendons in her neck pulled taut as she strained against the power. I tightened my grip on Sonya's hand and pushed goodness into her with every bit of force I could muster.

A shriek of pain pierced my ears. Sonya's body bucked and writhed, and it was all I could do with my full strength to keep the vampire on the bed. A long string of profanities flew out of her mouth punctuated with more screams as visions of her life as a vampire flashed through her mind.

Then all at once, she fell calm again. Seemingly unconscious.

Char rubbed her forehead against her arm, mopping off the sweat. "That was the first wave."

"How many waves will there be?" The evil energy still swirled within Sonya, perhaps not as strong, but definitely still there.

"As many as it takes until the evil power is gone. Everyone's different."

"So we're in for an all-nighter."

"Yep. Probably longer.

"I'm so glad you're here. I have no idea what would've happened if I'd tried this by myself."

"You'll be able to do it solo once you learn the basics. Number one rule: don't let yourself wear out. That's where trouble comes in."

"That's what you were about to say before? There should be no transfer of energy unless . . . ?"

"Unless you're drained. But don't worry. It shouldn't happen with you." She rested her head against her shoulder as her hands remained stretched out to grip Sonya's forearms, maintaining skin-to-skin contact. "You have more Amadis power than any of us, including Rina. You just need to know what you're doing. Are you seeing the visions?"

"Of her past and her victims? Yeah. I hate them. All that death and darkness." I shuddered. "Do you ever get used to them?"

"Me?" Charlotte chuckled. "I don't see them. Only Rina can, so I assumed you could, too."

"Really? Huh." I thought about this for a moment. "I could share them if you want."

"Ugh. No, thanks. I see enough of what they do in real time."

Wave after wave crashed over Sonya, each hit weakening both her and us. Tristan sat with me in between, sharing his love to boost my power before each round. But I always made him leave when I felt a new wave coming on. In case I wasn't powerful enough. Once morning came and brought the sun, Sonya's energy diminished considerably, and we began to make true progress.

"They're weaker during the day, especially the young ones," Charlotte said as Sheree wiped a cool, wet cloth across the warlock's forehead and the nape of her neck. "It's always better to try to start this in the early morning. Unfortunately, since the Daemoni prefer to come out at night, that's usually not possible."

When the room began darkening again with dusk, Charlotte's cell phone rang. Sonya's body had given up its fight a long time ago, so Char had no problem leaving me alone with her, pumping Amadis power into the vampire's depleted veins, while she took the call.

"I need to go to Galveston," she said, reappearing only a few minutes later.

The urgency in her voice rang my alarms. "What happened?"

"Daemoni went on a rampage. Our people were able to take in some of the bitten and turned, but too many for them to handle alone."

"Anything I can do?" I asked, though I already knew the answer. Still too much of a novice, I was pretty useless.

"Hmph. Someday soon, it'll be your job to take care of these things, but for now, it's mine. You just worry about Sonya here." She ran her hands over our patient's arm and then her forehead. "You feel that?"

I nodded. "There's still a trace of Daemoni power."

"Right, and there will be for a while, probably months, maybe longer. It takes time and faith-healing to eradicate it all."

"And she won't be completely good until then, right?"

Charlotte cocked her head, her sapphire eyes piercing into me. "Alexis, after last fall, you know as well as anyone that not anybody's completely good, including the Amadis. We're all basically human, after all. We all have good and bad within us. Has Owen ever told you the Legend of Uri and Duff?"

I shook my head.

"Well, I don't have time to give you the children's version I used to tell Owen. I'll have to keep this short, and then I need to go." She returned to her chair by Sonya's bed and leaned toward me on the other side. "According to history, a few generations after the Ancients created the sorcerers and sorceresses, one of the younger mages decided she wanted to experience sex with a human, so she seduced one and became pregnant. The child obviously didn't have the same amount of magic as she did, but he was still quite powerful. Other members of the youngest generation saw opportunity in this child—they could create a whole new race that could serve them while never being powerful enough to overcome them. Power breeds paranoia, and the mages were extremely paranoid, especially when the Ancients created the vampires. The mages decided their new race needed to be physically strong and fearless, even against the vampires if ever needed, so they agreed they would only mate with the stoutest, toughest, and meanest human warriors."

"The race they created was the warlocks," I said.

"That's right. With powerful magic and the bodies and aggressiveness of warriors, we were bred to fight, although at the time, there wasn't much fighting going on except with each other or to pick on Normans. So I guess in their boredom, the warlocks mated with humans and over time the weaker witches and wizards became a third mage sub-race.

"Anyway, Cassandra came along and created the Amadis, and now we get into the Legend of Uri and Duff. Cassandra and her group had stumbled upon Uri and Duff in the bluffs of Scotland, arguing with each other. They had been seeking out the Amadis to be converted, but only Uri was completely committed. Duff was tired of being a slave to the sorcerers, but he wasn't quite sold on going over to the other side. After all, he said, the Amadis were created to fight the Daemoni, and if he converted, he would lose many of those qualities that made him a strong fighter—such as anger, aggression, and bravery. He thought becoming Amadis would make him weaker.

"Cassandra tried to convince him otherwise, but Duff wouldn't believe her. So she said to him, 'Fight one of my warlocks, and we shall see who is weak.' And he said, 'I do not know the strength of your warlocks, so this may not be a fair test. Uri here is an equal match to me, so after you convert him, I will fight him and prove that I am right.' Duff hung around during Uri's conversion—he really didn't want to go back to the Daemoni—and a few months later, Uri was ready for the match.

"All of the Amadis gathered around to watch. You have to remember, Uri and Duff were among the first generations of warlocks. We've lost the ability now, but at that time, they could pull some energy from their immediate surroundings to feed their power, like the sorcerers do. Uri had the Amadis surrounding him, feeding him their positive power, but Duff had no dark power to draw on."

"So Uri won and Duff converted," I guessed.

"Yes and no. Uri won, but, unfortunately, Duff's energy had been so drained that Uri basically one-shot him, and he dropped dead."

A laugh burst from my lips. "What a horrible children's story!"

Charlotte chuckled. "It's a fabulous story. It's become legend among the Amadis warlocks. But that's not the best part." She leaned farther over the bed, practically laying on Sonya's sleeping form. "Afterward, Cassandra made a speech to all of the Amadis and said, 'We all must remember that there is a Uri and a Duff inside each of us, battling for domination of our souls. The one who will win is the one you give your energy to. It is your choice. May you choose well.'"

I nodded with understanding. "So does that mean there will always be a trace of Daemoni power in the converted? Is Sonya as close as she's going to get?"

"No. There's a difference between the Daemoni's evil power and the darker side that's in all of us. The Daemoni energy *must* be eradicated. We're not talking about norms who do bad things here. Supernatural creatures with even a shade of that power are too dangerous for humanity's sake—and for their own." Charlotte glanced at her phone, stood, and looked down at Sonya's still body. "I need to get going. She'll probably be out of it for a while, so you have time to get some rest. Then, keep sharing your power regularly and let Sheree do her thing."

The were-tiger appeared in the doorway at the mention of her name.

"You have blood?" Charlotte asked Sheree, and the shifter nodded. "That's the first thing she'll need when she wakes up. Alexis, you need to always have blood ready when you're working with a vamp."

"Try not to use blood from another vamp or shifter, though," Sheree added. Her face scrunched as if she'd sucked on a rotten lemon. "Bad side effects."

"Their first several feedings after the conversion should really be normal animal blood," Char said as she made her way to the door with me on her heels. "Anything else could be too strong, and you really want to bring them back gradually. Eventually, they can handle donated mage blood. But, well, when it's an emergency, you use what you have on hand." Char turned to look at me over her shoulder. "Even your own, Alexis."

I hurried up to her side. "Mine? Yeah, probably not a good idea, from what I've heard. Not if we're going for a slow recovery."

Char shrugged. "Sometimes you do what you have to do. Just be prepared if you ever have to, especially the first time. Your mother's had a few horror stories, so I can only imagine what your stronger blood will do." When we reached the front door of the mansion, she turned to me. "You'll be fine. Whatever you do, no more conversions until I return. Sonya is young in vampire years, so she's relatively easy. A good start for both you and Sheree. Neither of you are ready for someone stronger, though. Not on your own. If you get in a similar situation, call me before you do anything. Okay?"

"Of course," I said, already convinced I wasn't ready to fly solo.

She glared at me, and I could see her thoughts on her face without tapping into her mind: *I know you, and you're your mother's daughter. I don't trust you one bit.* I couldn't blame her after I'd abandoned her in Key West. And brought Sonya here with no warning. Oh, and ditched her son on another occasion to face the Daemoni. Then there was the fight to protect the werewolf pack, too, which I kind of jumped into without thinking, bringing her son into it with me. Sheesh. No wonder she didn't trust me.

"Promise?" she demanded. "No matter what. Stay out of trouble, okay?"

"I *promise*," I said as sincerely as possible.

"Why do I bother asking for it?" She shook her head. "I've always admired your spirit, Alexis. We need it. Just remember —there's a line between moxie and recklessness." She gave me a quick hug. "I'll be back as soon as I can. I'll be gathering a team to bring here, too, so it may be a few weeks. Don't hesitate to call me if you need anything."

"We'll be fine," I said, hoping it was true.

As exhausted as I felt, I couldn't fathom how she had the energy to go straight to Texas and do everything all over again, only with more people. I could sleep for days.

"My son. My bed. You. That's all I want right now," I said as I leaned against Tristan's side. Sheree had assured me the vampire would be unconscious for quite a while and they would be fine at the safe house, so I flashed home to find Tristan waiting up for me. He'd come home a few hours ago, after Sonya had survived the worst of it.

"My pleasure," Tristan murmured as he tightened his arm around me and led me down the hall to our room.

But first, I went into Dorian's room and lay down with him. I curled my body around his, my heart aching at how long his body was now, at how big he was getting, but loving the moment of being able to still hold him against me. It didn't last long, though, not long enough for me anyway.

"Mom, go to your own bed," he complained sleepily as he rolled over. "I'm too big to sleep with you now."

What happened to my little boy? I watched him sleep for a few more minutes, appreciating that his face remained round and youthful, at least in sleep. As my mind started drifting to dark thoughts of what his growing up meant, I forced myself to go to my own room, where I snuggled with the man who would never push me out of his bed, though he already breathed evenly, fast asleep.

I tossed and turned. My mind kept tumbling over Charlotte's story about Cassandra's parable, my dagger that once belonged to the first daughter, and the voice that talked to me—claiming to be Cassandra herself—encouraging me in every dangerous situation I'd encountered recently. But why, if the voice really was hers, would she talk to me now? Of course, I'd been safe on the Amadis Island for several months, never finding myself in a dangerous situation, never putting on my leathers or using my dagger. So was that it?

Did we have some kind of connection through the dagger? I'd only had it for a few days before tucking it away in the closet for so long. Had actually wielded it only twice—while fighting on behalf of the wolf-pack when the Daemoni attacked their campground and during the trial. Neither time had I been frightened of the risk.

So was Cassandra really talking to me, trying to reassure me when I needed it, or was it only my own inner voice? Or was I losing my mind?

I slipped out of bed, grabbed my phone, and went down the hall to the reading nook, where I curled up in the window seat and called Mom. It was mid-morning on Amadis Island, so I didn't have to worry about waking her up.

"I don't mean to be rude, honey, but I'm about to meet with a few of our remaining council members," she said.

"I just have a quick question for you," I said, not wanting to go into detail anyway, in case I sounded crazy. "Have the Angels ever talked to a daughter besides the matriarch?"

"No, never. They keep their involvement in our world to a minimum. Why?"

"Um, nothing. Sorry to bother you."

"Wait a minute." She paused, and I sighed. She was feeling out for the truth. "Cassandra, huh? Well, keep in mind a couple of things. One, we don't know if Cassandra—or any of the ascended daughters—actually became Angels. They might serve the Angels or work with them, but we have no proof that we become a full-fledged Angel when we leave this realm. That's an Otherworld secret, and not even I can determine the truth about it. Second, you are unique, Alexis. Precedence means little when it comes to you. And third, you're not crazy. You are brave and incredibly powerful, and maybe you're still discovering exactly what that means."

"You can tell me all that, but can't feel the truth about the voice in my head?"

"I would say that's something the Angels want you to figure out for yourself because I'm not feeling anything, one way or the other." The sound of something covering the microphone on Mom's end followed by muffled voices came through the line. "I'm sorry, honey, but I have to go. Trust your instincts. Maybe that's what you're supposed to learn from this."

I hung up feeling more lost than ever. I considered the idea of retrieving my dagger and trying to reach out to Cassandra, but I didn't think that would give me answers now. After all, if my subconscious wanted me to believe I heard Cassandra when I needed a spirit boost, it certainly would be trying now. I couldn't trust myself.

And in that case, how would I ever know for sure?

CHAPTER 8

"*E*verything fixed. Your bedroom and everything in it look brand new," Blossom announced as she came into the bare living room.

Although she'd been coming over to repair our bedroom nearly every morning for three months, I still blushed as I smoothed the last piece of blue tape across the windowsill.

"Thank you," I said as I rose to my feet, my face burning. "Again."

"Why are you so embarrassed? If I had a sex life like yours, I'd be telling the world. Of course, I'd have to do it from my phone or some other way since I wouldn't be able to walk. He must be amazing, to get so crazy almost every night."

I couldn't help the giggle that escaped my lips. "Better than amazing."

She shook her head. "Intelligent, powerful, gorgeous, *and* a sex god? So not fair you get it all in one."

"I know, right?" I said, loosening up, then I struck a silly diva pose. "But so does he. There's a reason they say we're made for each other."

She laughed, then eyed the two jugs of paint on the floor near her feet. "So were you planning to do this by yourself?"

I shrugged. "Sure. Why not? Tristan's busy wiring toys over at the safe house, but I'm ready to work on our own house. It's time to make it a real home."

"Toys?"

"Yeah, networks, entertainment systems, intercoms, that kind of stuff." I rolled my eyes. "I guess it'll all be convenient, but the boy is way into his toys."

"Ah. Well, need some help?" the witch asked, glancing around the room. "I mean, I could have this done in no time with a few flicks of my wand."

I chuckled. "Thanks, but I need something to *do* before I go stir crazy. Using magic won't solve that problem."

Blossom nodded. "I so get that. I could use something to do myself."

"Then if you don't mind doing it the Norman way, it'd be fun to have your help." I picked up a drop cloth, shook it out, and let it fall over the floor. Blossom followed my lead, and in a few minutes we had the floor covered.

"So now what?" Blossom asked after she brought the rest of the paint and supplies from my car while I retrieved a ladder and set it up.

I recalled the instructions the guy at the hardware store had given me. "The paint goes in those pans, then you roll the roller in it until it's covered. You paint a big M on the wall and then go across it to fill it in."

"Sounds easy enough."

We each set about filling our own pans and painting our first Ms into big squares of a pale aqua blue.

"Pretty color," Blossom said as she worked.

"Tristan wouldn't let me paint it purple, so I thought I'd go with airy, beachy colors." I looked over at Blossom to see how she was doing—about as well as I was, which wasn't saying much. She stopped and tilted her head to the side as she stared at the wall.

"I don't think these rollers will reach the edges," she said.

I smacked my forehead, wet paint smudging from my hand to my head. Great. By the time this was over, I'd probably have more paint on me than on the walls. "Oh, crap. I forgot. The guy said something about cutting in with a paintbrush first."

"What guy?"

"The guy at the hardware store who taught me how to paint."

Blossom turned to look at me, her mouth open. "Wait. You've never painted before? Not even your own room?"

"I've never lived anywhere long enough to bother. Have you?

"Yeah, but not *this* way." Blossom burst into laughter. "We're the blind leading the blind. This is going to be so much fun!"

"Well, how hard can it be?" Worst case scenario: the room turned out looking as though a two-year-old painted it, but Blossom would be able to fix it, and hopefully before Tristan saw. Otherwise, I'd never hear the end of his teases.

"So why do you need something to do?" I asked from the top of the ladder as I did the cutting-in while Blossom rolled the paint. The witch usually kept busy baking cakes, creating new spells, and spending time with the vampire-barista on Captiva.

"With the tourists and snowbirds gone for the summer, there's not much business for my cakes. It'll pick up in the next couple months as they start coming down, but I haven't decided if I'm really up for making all those cakes this year." As usual, Blossom's mind and mouth were speeding along. "I guess I'm getting a little bored with it. And I haven't come up with any spells or potions lately. I feel like I *should* be working on my magic with everything going on, but I can't focus."

"And would that have anything to do with Eduardo?" I teased.

"Ugh. Eduardo can bite my ass. Well, not really. I don't want him biting any part of me anymore." Blossom shuddered. "I'm so not talking about him. We'll leave it that he's quite lacking when it comes to treating women well. So, anyway, I've just been feeling antsy. Jittery. Maybe because of all that stuff going on with the Daemoni, and I feel as if I'm being a big coward by sitting here on this beautiful island, doing nothing. Maybe it will get better when we have a real safe house with more than one measly occupant. How's Sonya doing anyway? Have you heard anything from Charlotte yet? Any news on when she'll be coming back? It's been a couple months already. Is that why *you're* so antsy?"

And just like that, Blossom had our conversation turned in a whole different direction.

"Sonya's still in early recovery mode, which means she's more like a zombie than a vampire, pretty much doing nothing but listening to Sheree's lessons. Charlotte's busy with all the other safe houses, which are staying pretty full with the Daemoni attacks. They're definitely trying to build an army."

"And we do the same, which takes away from their numbers, right?"

"Right. So Charlotte's working her butt off, and all the other safe houses are so full, they can't spare any team members to join me down here. I can't help them, though, because I'm not experienced enough, but Char's too busy to train me. It's a catch-22." My annoyance rose, causing my brush to slip and paint a streak of pale aqua on the white ceiling. I swore to myself. "I supposedly have all this power, but I'm completely useless."

Blossom murmured something under her breath, and the blue streak on the ceiling disappeared. "So why don't you go into the field?"

I sighed. "You know me. I can't leave Dorian for that long. Besides, Rina says Tristan and I are only to leave here to retrieve the pendant since we have no protector. But still, the stupid vampire bitch plays her game of hide-and-seek."

Over the last couple of months, Blossom had watched Dorian a few times while Tristan and I tried to find Vanessa in her normal hangouts, but if she were anywhere around, we couldn't draw the vampire out from her hiding spot. I thought she would have given in by now, too obsessed with killing me to stay away, but she either had more self-control than any of us gave her credit for, or she was distracted by something even bigger and better than we could imagine. Which was a pretty scary thought, considering the last time we knew of her whereabouts, Owen had been with her.

I still hadn't figured out that whole situation, and I tried to follow everyone's advice not to worry—"he can take care of himself"—but my heart still ached for him. His voicemail greeting changed every now and then, which meant he was at least alive and kicking. I called or texted him daily, hoping this might be the time he answered. He hadn't answered yet. I began to believe he truly hated me for what I'd done to his father.

"Yeah, it all pretty much sucks," I said. "At least if I had a team here, I'd feel like I was somehow helping the cause." A thought occurred to me then. "Blossom, you were born into the Amadis, right?"

The witch looked up at me as she finished the last patch of our first wall, a strange expression on her face. She seemed to ponder whether to tell me something, but then, after a deep breath, she let it all spill.

"Sort of. I was never part of the Daemoni, if that's what you mean. My father—sperm donor, as you'd call him—was a Daemoni wizard who raped my Norman mother. Aunt Sylvie, his sister, had converted to Amadis years before, and she found out about my mother, took her in until I was born, then changed her memories so she thought she'd miscarried, and sent her on her way."

"Wow," I breathed. "How horrible."

"Yeah. Rape is pretty common among the Daemoni. Sick bastards."

A thought needled into my brain, and my stomach clenched. *Had Tri*— I immediately pushed the thought away. I didn't know if I ever wanted that answer.

"How awful that you never knew either of your parents, though," I said. "Why did your aunt do that to you and your mother? *How* could she do that to you?"

"Good intentions, believe me. If my father found out he'd gotten my mother pregnant, he'd come after me, knowing I'd have magic. He would have killed her and raised me Daemoni, and Aunt Sylvie wouldn't allow that. Yeah, I'm a result of a really effed-up situation." She shrugged. "But Aunt Sylvie loves me, even when she's annoyed at my screw-ups. She and the rest of the coven raised me well."

I climbed down the ladder and moved it to the next wall, then returned the conversation to the idea I'd had. "So did Sylvie ever teach you to use your Amadis power?"

"In case you couldn't tell when you met her last year, Aunt Sylvie isn't big on getting involved like that. She and her coven prefer staying out of the limelight."

"Hmm . . . is it something—"

"Hey, Mom!" Dorian yelled as he ran into the living room, Sasha right on his heels.

"Hey, little man," I said. "Watch out for the wet—"

Too late. Sasha's tail swished across the wall we'd just painted, leaving an ugly streak in the paint and a pretty blue tint on the tip of her white tail.

"Um, maybe you two should go to your room," I said.

"But I wanted to show you what I taught Sasha. Will you watch?"

I lowered my brush and nodded. With a big smile, one I'd give anything to see the rest of my life, my son proceeded to kneel down on all fours. The lykora, looking like a normal white dog at the moment, stood next to him, both of their butts toward Blossom and me.

"Ready, Sasha?" Dorian said, and Sasha bobbed her head. "1 . . . 2 . . . 3."

They both let out the loudest farts I'd ever heard. Dorian howled with laughter as he rolled on the floor, and Sasha danced circles around him, barking and wagging her tail with pride.

"I taught her how to fart on command!" Dorian gasped with glee, as if that was the best and funniest trick ever.

Speechless, I looked sideways at Blossom, whose body silently quaked as she held her hand over her mouth.

"Boys," I whispered, shaking my head, and unable to keep it in any longer, we both doubled over with laughter, joining Dorian's hoots.

"Sasha, that is so unladylike," I admonished the lykora as I wiped my eyes.

"She's not a lady, Mom. She's a dog! And the best one ever." Dorian threw his arms around Sasha's neck, and she returned his love with a tongue up the side of his face. "Mom, I think our guy in our book needs to have a pet dragon."

"A dragon?" I asked, confused. He referred to the children's story we were writing together. The book would probably never get published since there was no Amadis purpose for Rina and Mom to pull their strings with their contacts, but it gave Dorian and me something to work on together. He enjoyed that part of his language studies, but his comment came out of the blue. "Why not a dog?"

"Duh, Mom. Because a dragon can fart fire!"

Blossom still hadn't stopped giggling, and this idea made her crack up harder, sending Dorian and me into hysterics again, too. Dorian abruptly quieted.

"Mom," he said, and my laughter stopped immediately at the serious tone of his voice. "What's wrong with Sasha?"

The dog stood at the window now, her nose pressed

against the glass. Her all-white fur began to show shades of her lykora stripes. Dorian hurried over to see what she saw, but the hair on the nape of my neck already began to rise.

"What's out there?" I managed to ask over the lump in my throat.

"Two babes getting out of a taxi," Dorian said. "They have funny hair, though. One's blue and the other's purple."

I blurred to the window. *Crap. Crap, crap, crap.*

"Dorian, you need to go to your room now. I'm sure you have more studies to do," I said, kneeling down to stroke Sasha's back. My fingers grazed over knobby ridges where her wings would come out, and her baby powder scent filled my nostrils, stronger than usual with her heightened awareness. "It's okay, girl," I whispered.

"But I want to meet the pretty girls," Dorian whined.

"Maybe later," I said absently, watching the faeries as they paid the cabdriver. "Now go."

I picked up Sasha and whispered in her ear. "Protect."

She bounded out of my hands and trailed Dorian down the hall to his room. The faeries had never done anything to hurt us—had in fact helped us more than once—but they couldn't be trusted. The only faerie we could trust completely was Bree.

"Should I get Tristan?" Blossom asked, standing next to me at the window.

I considered it for only a moment. "Nah. I need to be able to take care of things on my own."

Blossom peered at me with doubt. "Faeries, though? Are you sure?"

I nodded. "What's the worst that can happen?"

"You don't even want to know." She shook her head. "I'm staying, though. I'm not leaving you alone with them."

The doorbell rang, and Blossom accompanied me to the front door. The faerie sisters beamed beautifully, both dressed in halters, short-shorts, and four-inch-high wedge sandals, looking like models ready for a shoot on the beach.

"Hey, Alexis!" Lisa, the blue-haired faerie, exclaimed, her southern drawl pronounced. "How ahr yew?"

I blinked. "Um, fine, I suppose."

"Not happay to say us?" Jessica asked, a fake pout on her lips painted the same lilac color of her hair.

"Oh, no, of course not. I mean, it's always good to see you," I stammered. I stepped back from the door. "Please, come in."

The faeries pushed past Blossom and me as they sauntered inside and down the hall, their heads bobbing to and fro as they unabashedly scrutinized my house worse than a mother-in-law.

"We're painting," I said, as if the mess didn't make it obvious. "It'll dry if we don't keep going, so if you don't mind . . ."

I led them into the half-painted living room where they both stood off to the side since I'd removed all the furniture.

"Um . . . I don't think I have any tea. Would you like some water?"

"Water will do," Jessica said.

"No lemon, though," Lisa quickly added with a stunning smile.

They each sank down onto the covered floor as I went into the kitchen to fill two glasses with ice cubes and water.

"So what's up?" I asked as I handed the glasses to the faeries, trying to be calm and casual.

"Well, aren't y'all business?" Jessica said with a giggle.

I picked up my paintbrush and dipped it into the pan. "Somehow I doubt you're here for a girls' night out."

Lisa's face lit up. "Oh! Wouldn't that bay so much fun?"

"Oh, yeah," Jessica agreed. "Alexis, you should totally go out with us some time."

"Um . . ." *Crap.* What had I gotten myself into? I couldn't imagine these two in a club full of single men. Utter chaos I didn't want to be a part of. "Maybe sometime. But that's not really why you came, though. Is it?"

"Oh, of course not. We do have a few things to discuss." Lisa looked over at Blossom, who had resumed painting, and back at me.

"Blossom can stay," I said. "She pretty much knows everything. I trust her."

The words came out of my mouth before I realized what I was saying, but I knew they were true. Blossom had proven herself trustworthy time and again.

Jessica cocked her head as she studied Blossom. "Huh. Are we seeing the beginnin's of your council, Ms. Alexis?"

My face heated. The idea of needing my own council when I became matriarch seemed so far off that I'd never considered it. Rina's council was largely made up of those she'd known the longest, those she trusted more than anyone. I supposed Blossom was that to me. Maybe she *would* be part of my council.

"I guess we'll see one of these days," I finally said as I climbed the ladder and looked down on them. "But let's focus on right now. Did you find Owen?"

The faeries exchanged a significant look. Lisa spoke first.

"We did. We tried to distract him, as you requested when we were on Amadis Island, but he was, well . . . we didn't have the same effect on him as we used to," she said cryptically.

"What does that mean?" I asked.

"He wouldn't cooperate," Jessica said. "We tried to have a little fun with him, but in the end, we couldn't get him to return to the Amadis."

"Well, I know that much already because, obviously, he's not here, and you are. So where is he?"

Out of the corner of my eye, I saw the faeries exchange another look, then shrug.

"Not our place to get involved anymore," Lisa said. I fought a groan of exasperation.

"Then why are you here?" I demanded, flipping my hand out. Paint spattered off the tip of my brush, and the faeries jumped to their feet and moved backward a few paces, out of harm's way.

Lisa put her fist on her hip. "We're here to collect. You owe us."

I turned on the ladder to stare at them with my mouth hanging open. "But you just said you failed."

Jessica's pretty lips lifted into an ugly grimace. "We didn't fail. It's not our fault he didn't cooperate. We went out of our way, did everything we could at your request, and now you owe us."

"But you didn't deliver!" I protested.

"You dare *deny* us?" Jessica snarled, and I pulled back, not realizing I'd been leaning halfway off the ladder toward them. "Don't be stupid, young one. You do *not* want to ignore faeries calling on your debt."

Lisa placed a hand on Jessica's arm. "Relax, little sister. Let's tell her what we want first. She'll come 'round."

I narrowed my eyes. Maybe repaying them wouldn't be so bad. "What do you want?"

"Well," Lisa began, "if y'all haven't figured it out, Kali the sorceress is still alive and well. Her soul had found its way off Amadis Island and into a new host. A young, redheaded Daemoni witch."

I shifted on the ladder, mostly to fight the shiver trying to make its way up my back. "And?"

"We want her soul," Jessica said bluntly.

My eyebrows popped up. "Seriously?"

"It's not right, what she can do, moving herself from body to body. It puts everythin' off balance, and those in the spirit realm require balance."

"So you want me to *convert* her?"

The faeries laughed.

"Oh, no," Lisa said. "There's no hope for her soul! We want her soul in *our* possession, so we can take it to the Otherworld and leave it there."

"And how would Alexis do that?" Blossom asked.

Out of nowhere, a small, ceramic jar with a tightly sealed lid appeared in Lisa's hand. "Trap it in here. You'll have to kill her physical host—or at least disable it as you did with Martin —and when her spirit rises, trap it inside."

"Wait—disable Martin? Is he still alive? The real Martin?" I asked. Maybe that's what had Owen so preoccupied.

"That is an answer we cannot give. Not part of our problem," Jessica said.

I cocked my head. "But Kali is. So you can tell me if she's what Owen's looking for."

Jessica rolled her eyes. "Possibly. At one time anyway."

"So why don't you ask *him* to do this?" Blossom asked. "I'm sure he'd be more than happy to."

"He *does* owe us for bringing Bree to Amadis Island, but we don't trust Owen or his motivations right now," Lisa said, then she turned her gaze on me, to drive home her point. "We don't feel confident that he'd follow through."

I snorted. "Of course, he would. I'm sure there's nothing Owen would love to do more than take that bitch down."

Lisa's eyes remained locked on mine and something sparked in them. "Don't be so sure, Alexis. Arrogance is dangerous."

"What does *that* mean?"

Jessica grunted her annoyance, and stood. "I'm bored. Let's get out of here, sis."

Lisa nodded. "Ya know how to repay us now. We're not goin' to give ya a deadline. We don't need to. The longer that unnatural thing remains in this realm, the worse it is for the Amadis. So you don't wanna delay too long."

Lisa set the jar down, and the thing was small on the vast

floor, but its purpose made it larger than life, consuming the entire space.

"But don't ignore us either," Jessica warned, her eyes full of menace. "Y'all don't need the faeries' wrath with everythin' else y'all got goin' on."

"It's for everyone's good," Lisa said. "Just as much yours as it is ours. Say? We're really not so bad now, are way?"

I didn't answer, but simply stared at the two at a loss for words. They wanted me to capture Kali's soul. Capture a soul! How on earth or any other realm would I do that?

Jessica's expression changed completely to her friendly, shiny self. "Let's do that girls' night out sometime. You pick the date and place and give us a call."

Lisa made a face. "But not South Beach. That place has gone to hell. Literally."

"What do you mean?" Blossom asked. "It's been a while, but I go there all the time."

As usual, the faeries didn't give us a straight answer.

"Ask your new vampire friend," Lisa said to me. Then both faeries disappeared without so much as a *pop*.

CHAPTER 9

"What is it about South Beach?" Sheree asked when Tristan and I arrived at the safe house one morning the following week. When we both served up a bewildered expression, she continued. "You two and Blossom have said something about it lately, and now Sonya's been talking in her sleep about South Beach. It's like the topic of some mysterious conversation, and I feel left out."

I looked up at Tristan. "Oh, that reminds me. The faeries hinted that Sonya knows something about South Beach that we might find interesting."

"Well, she keeps saying Vanessa's there," Sheree said, making a disgusted face as if the vampire's name tasted bad on her tongue. "At least, that's what it sounds like."

Tristan shrugged it off. "She must still be a little delusional. Not quite right yet."

Sheree shook her head. "Oh, no. Actually, she's been pretty lucid. But I haven't asked her about it myself—I didn't think it my place to. She's awake, though. Go see for yourself."

I needed to sit with the vampire anyway and feed her my power, so Tristan followed me to her room. Sonya sat in bed, watching an extremely popular vampire-romance movie on

TV. She picked up the remote and muted the sound when she saw us.

"Ridiculous," she said with an eye-roll. "But I guess it *would* suck to look like a drug addict who rolled around in bat shit every time you stepped into the sun. Becoming a little weaker than normal doesn't seem so bad in comparison."

"Um . . . *what?*" I asked, bewildered. I took her hand, ignoring her usual flinch. That lingering bit of Daemoni power still made her scared of me.

"Bat shit sparkles," she explained. "And their make-up is so bad, they could be poster children for a rehab center. Especially that one." She pointed at the screen. "After all those shots of ripped wolf-boy, he looks sickly. Makes even this vampire swing for the other team."

I stared at her for a long moment, surprised at how lucid she was. Only days ago she'd been little more than a zombie, and now she ranted and cracked jokes. Inappropriate ones, perhaps, but jokes nonetheless.

"Well, at least you don't fry in an inferno, either," I managed to say, trying to keep her talking.

"True," she admitted. "Funny how all the books and movies get some things right, but can be way off base with others." She squinted her eyes at me. "Except yours."

"Yeah, well, I had help by someone close to the source, my mom. She slipped me suggestions when she read, correcting the few things I had wrong, making them sound like really good ideas to me. All those other writers were only given bits and pieces, or went off others' canon."

"Funny how the truth makes your stories so much more believable. You seriously didn't know you were practically writing non-fiction?"

"The stories are still fiction," I corrected her. "Just the characters were truer-to-life than I knew at the time."

"Well, I love your books," Sonya said. She looked over my shoulder, as if noticing Tristan for the first time, and if vampires could blush, I'd swear she did. When she didn't look away for a long moment, Tristan cleared his throat, breaking the silence.

"We have a question for you," he said, "if you're up to it."

Her mouth tugged as if she fought a smile, though nothing funny had been said. I knew how she felt—the man had that effect on everyone of the female persuasion. Thankfully, he still had that effect on me.

"About Vanessa," Sonya said, and she smiled for real now. "My physical strength may be weak, but I still hear extraordinarily well."

"Do you know where she is?" I asked.

She finally tore her blue eyes away from Tristan and looked back at me. "South Beach, as Sheree said. I've overheard you talking about her, so I guess it's been on my mind. I've always had a problem talking in my sleep. Anyway, last I heard, Vanessa was in South Beach."

Tristan shook his head, doubt filling his eyes. "That was a few months ago, though."

"The day you confronted me," Sonya said, "and brought me here. She'd been at our nest the night before, and our leader—that guy in the parking lot?—he said she wanted some of us to go to South Beach to serve her."

"That doesn't make sense," Tristan said. "Vanessa seeks the limelight. She'd never purposely go to a place filled with models and celebrities. The same reason she avoids New York and Hollywood."

"Unless she was put in charge of a new nest," Sonya said.

Tristan stroked his chin as he peered at the vamp. "That *would* feed her ego. But why another nest? There are several already in Miami."

"Lucas wanted to grow the Daemoni presence over there. It's part of his big plan. Miami, especially South Beach, has lots of prime candidates for turning, and with all that gourmet food there, they taste extra special," Sonya added with longing.

As soon as she realized what she'd said, she covered her face with her free hand. "I'm not supposed to think that way anymore, am I?"

"It takes time," I said, pushing more power into her.

The vamp clenched her jaw—I'd never realized she'd still be in such pain from the goodness—and breathed through it until she could speak again.

"So Vanessa actually *wanted* to be the one to start this nest?" Tristan asked.

"She has clout in the Daemoni for some reason, and she probably wanted South Beach because it's close to you guys."

"So why doesn't anyone claim to have seen her?" I asked.

Sonya sighed, our questions wearing on her limited patience. "Look, I'm just telling you what I knew three months ago. But if one of your most wanted was scheming something, would you have her out in the open all the time or kept hidden? I don't see *you* out there fighting."

The girl—vamp, whatever—had a point. Tristan nodded again, confirming this was a good possibility.

"So when do I get to see my sister?" Sonya asked.

"When you stop flinching every time I touch you," I replied. As long as she had the reaction to goodness that she still did, I wasn't risking Heather's life.

Sonya nodded and then sighed again, this time with sadness rather than frustration. "Probably a good idea."

"You guys are always going somewhere and leaving me on this stupid island," Dorian complained that evening when I mentioned a trip to South Beach to Tristan. I thought our son had been too engrossed in his video game in the other room to have heard me, but he'd suddenly appeared in the kitchen with us. "When do I get to go somewhere?"

"Where do you want to go, little man?" I asked.

His eyes lit up. "Busch Gardens! No, wait . . . Universal Studios and Harry Potter World. Heather says the roller coasters are scary, but I don't believe her."

I looked at Tristan, and he shrugged. "*Daemoni hate the whole vibe of family, love, and wholesome fun at amusement parks,*" he said silently. "*As long as we stay with him the whole time, I don't see why not.*" He turned to Dorian. "How about next weekend?"

Dorian fist-pumped the air. "Yes! Can Heather come? I can't wait to see her scream her head off."

Before we could answer, he bounded to his room, and the door rattled in its jamb as he slammed it with a little too much enthusiasm. I shook my head. His one and only friend was a teenaged girl. I didn't know who I felt more sorry for—Dorian or Heather.

I looked up at Tristan. "And South Beach?"

His grin dissipated. "I don't know, *ma lykita*. Sonya's answers made sense, but what I know about the Daemoni—"

"What you *knew*," I corrected. "They're initiating war now. Things have changed."

"Okay," he conceded. "Then what I know about Vanessa— she couldn't stand to lay low for so long."

"Maybe she hasn't. Maybe our people haven't seen her because we don't go to South Beach—"

"For good reason. The Daemoni have always been in control there."

"If we want to find Vanessa, we're going to have to take the risk. I don't think we have a choice, Tristan."

"I don't like it. You would have heard something from someone about this already. We've been all over the state."

"But if she's in Miami, why would anyone anywhere else be thinking about her? Or maybe they sense my presence and keep their minds focused on other things, knowing I'd be listening. I mean, since Kali is definitely still alive, I'm sure she's told them all about my telepathy."

Tristan paced the area between the kitchen table and the island. "And the way she messed with the council members' minds . . . she may have found a way to make others block their thoughts from you, at least temporarily."

"Or . . . maybe Kali's even been around, working the magic for them." Which meant maybe I could catch her and meet the faeries' demands.

Tristan stopped in front of me and leaned against the counter. "Okay, we'll go. But only on reconnaissance. Not only about Vanessa, but to see if Kali's there and up to something."

"I'd sure like to catch her, though. Not just for the faeries, but maybe it would bring Owen home." I sighed, missing my protector even more than usual when we were planning a mission. "I guess we're going by ourselves again?"

He took my hands and pulled me to him. "I've said before that we can call on other Amadis. I'm sure Trevor would come for you."

I grimaced. Trevor the werewolf *might* come for me—he did respect that I'd fought for his wolf-pack and said he'd fight for me any time—but I really didn't trust anyone besides Owen enough for these clandestine missions. Although I preferred to have my protector with us, Tristan and I had done fine so far on our own. Besides, we didn't need a shifter with us. We needed a powerful mage.

"And I've told you before how I feel."

"Then it's only you and me again. Which is why we're only getting close enough to *listen*. It's a big colony there, and we're not starting anything with them. Not even if we see Vanessa." He lifted my chin with his thumb and forefinger and pierced me with his gaze. "Understand?"

I nodded.

"No fighting," he said. "Promise?"

Sheesh. Was I really so compulsive that everyone required my sworn word? Wait. I already knew that answer.

"Promise," I mumbled under his stare.

"And *I* promise, if we do find Vanessa, you *will* get to fight her—just not when we're by ourselves and outnumbered." He leaned forward and planted his lips on mine, sealing our promises with a luscious kiss.

As soon as we appeared in the dark alley, I knew something was wrong. For 11 p.m. on a Friday night in South Beach, there weren't nearly as many mind signatures as I'd expected, and those that were around were either holed up deep inside buildings or weren't Norman. We crept down the alley that emptied onto Lincoln Road, which wasn't really a road. The street was permanently blocked off for pedestrian traffic and gatherings, with trees, benches, and even bars where vehicles would normally be. Cafes and shops lined the sides of the street. All were empty.

Where is everyone? I asked Tristan. From what Blossom had told me, the area should have been bustling.

"*Don't you feel that?*" he asked in return.

The dark magic? Yeah. Is it keeping everyone away?

"*That's what I'm thinking. Let's go.*" He took my hand and led me in a flash.

My boots sunk into soft sand, and the rush and crash of waves sounded from several yards behind me. Far in front of us but easy for my eyes to see was a street with three-story hotels and condos lining the far side, restaurants and bars on their ground floors facing the street and beach.

"*Ocean Drive,*" Tristan said. "*People should be overflowing the restaurants and sidewalks.*"

Blossom had explained that, too. In South Beach, people lived on a different clock. She'd told me about the restaurants on Ocean Drive with their outside seating and aspiring models standing at the entrances with menus, trying to get passersby to come in and eat dinner—at midnight. Her description had been so clear, I could actually see it now: colored lights brightened the art-deco buildings' fronts; twinkling mini-lights illuminated the shapes of palm trees; neon signs glowed blue, green, and pink; and beautiful, tan women in stiletto heels and tight, colorful dresses that barely covered their goods draped over men handing them umbrella drinks. I could even hear their laughter and Latin music pumping from the clubs, and smell the exhaust of traffic.

But the image disappeared as quickly as it'd come. Tonight, there were no people. No traffic. No music. The only sound and smell came from the ocean behind us, the salty air filling my nose. Now I understood what the faeries had meant.

The place was a dead zone.

Tristan suddenly stiffened, and at the same time, I felt the waves of malevolence undulate over me. My head jerked to look up at him. Sparks flashed in his eyes. His face was hard as stone.

"*This way*," he said between clenched teeth, taking my hand and leading me in another flash before I could say a thing.

He didn't take us far. I could still smell salt on the air and hear the ocean in the distance, echoing down the streets and off the buildings in the otherwise eerie silence. We stood in the middle of a wide boulevard, and a street sign half-a-block down read Collins Avenue. More hotels and condos with the funky curves and lines of 1940s-era architecture surrounded us. Their first-floor nightclubs, though now empty, were illuminated in pastel colors, contrasting with the dark magic that pressed all around me, making my skin feel tight and my bones heavy.

I felt as though we'd stepped into another, surreal world of apocalyptic ghost towns.

A tingle ran up my spine, and I fought the shiver that wanted to throw it off. The hair on my arms stood on end. My lungs and heart held still, as if my body was afraid the slightest movement would bring Satan himself.

A rattling noise echoed down the road, making me jump. My heart had forgotten its need to stay silent and now raced loudly and painfully against my ribs. Though no wind blew, a plastic bag swept past my feet, the city's version of a tumbleweed.

I slowly exhaled. My heart began to quiet—

HOOOONK!

The horn blared right behind me, and cars, taxis, and buses appeared from nowhere, congesting the street where we stood. Life suddenly teemed around us as people filled the sidewalks and loud music resonated out of nightclubs. A bus barreled right toward us, and Tristan and I leapt, hitting the curb at the last moment. He grabbed my hand and pulled me out of the way, into the mouth of another alley. When we turned toward the bustling street, it was once again deathly silent and empty.

"What the *hell?*" I whispered, taking a step forward and leaning out of the alley. I jumped back as the world filled again with sights and smells and a cacophony of noise, right in front of our eyes. And when it fell silent again, I saw it—a wavering in the air similar to those produced by cloaks. It was all just an image, projected by a faerie or a mage to feel real.

Again, the world came to life, but I saw through it this time. The colors, the sounds, the smells were no longer as vibrant now that I knew they weren't real.

"*Something's wrong. Let's get out of here,*" Tristan said as he moved toward the street, but a streak of silver in the corner of my eye caught my attention. A white-blonde head ducked around the rear of a building at the other end of the alley. I grabbed the hilt of my dagger and prepared to run.

"*Be ready to fight!*" possibly-Cassandra warned, which I didn't understand. Although I'd promised Tristan no fighting, if I caught up with Vanessa, I didn't plan on having tea and a chat. I was already prepared to fight, so why the pep talk? I swept my thumb over the amethyst in my dagger and unsheathed it.

"Alexis!" Tristan growled, but I didn't wait and took off running, swinging my dagger at my side.

Vanessa's mind signature disappeared, though, and at the same time, a big, burly man dressed all in navy blue stepped out of a dark pool of shadows and into my path. I skidded to a halt, surprised to find a Norman out after all we'd seen, and annoyed that I'd once again lost the vampire-bitch.

"What are you doing down here?" his booming voice demanded as he swung his Billy club in one hand, his other hand on the butt of his gun.

Is he real? I asked Tristan, cloaking and sheathing my dagger, in case he was. The cop certainly looked and sounded and *felt* real. Tristan didn't say anything, and I looked over my shoulder at him. He stood where I'd left him, thirty yards away.

"This is no place for tourists," the cop said as he came closer. He lifted the club to point at the street behind us. "Get on your way now. The party's that way."

He *was* real. Real and Norman, and he saw what the Daemoni wanted him to see—his city bustling with partiers as usual.

As I began to back up, closing the distance between Tristan and me, a woman appeared right next to the cop and grabbed him in a chokehold.

"That's all right, officer," she drawled against his ear, "we'll take care of this."

Her mouth clamped onto his neck. I'd never forget his blood-curdling screams.

As if those shrieks called them like a siren's song, several Daemoni vampires came out of the dark nooks and crannies of the alley. I blurred to Tristan's side, but we were surrounded.

The cop's body sagged to the ground, already drained.

"We can't exactly advertise that there's any trouble in this fabulous playground," one of the vampires said, waving his white, long-boned hand in the air to indicate the city. He was shirtless and wore skinny jeans, showing off the lean muscles that wrapped his thin frame. His narrow hips swung with a feminine stride as they all sauntered toward us. "Glamor, dark magic, visions . . . whatever you want to call it . . . keeps the norms happily oblivious. Of course, you two can see right through it."

"So glad of you to join our fun," another said.

We're flashing, right? I asked Tristan, though the answer seemed pretty obvious. Unless he'd changed his mind about fighting, we had no other choice but to leave.

Good thing I didn't immediately flash without waiting for an answer, because he didn't reply. Again. With annoyance, I peeked up at him out of the corner of my eye, while still trying to keep as many of the Daemoni in my line of sight as possible.

What n—? I started to ask, but his eyes silenced me.

Flames filled them. Just as they had in the past when evil had been trying to overtake him.

I dipped into his mind, but his thoughts were an incoherent ball of anger. I couldn't make sense of them, but hoped he was ready to fight so we could get the heck out of here. Because the Daemoni had come too close—close enough to follow our flash trails.

Using my greatest advantage, I opened my mind to hear everyone's thoughts. Vanessa and Kali were the last things on their minds. The taste of my blood was first. I bent my knees, leaned onto the balls of my feet, and slid the silver blade out of its sheath once again right as the first vampire made her move.

So much for no fighting.

"*I'm here with you!*" possibly-Cassandra said, her voice full of inhuman strength.

They all rushed at me at once. I punched and kicked,

twisted and flipped, knocking two out instantly. Hands grabbed at me, and I swiped my blade out. Someone hissed as the silver made contact with skin. Their numerous thoughts became too frenzied for me to keep track, and I had to rely on my other senses and fighting ability. And more power than I'd ever felt before.

I spun out of another's grip, and faced a female with fangs bared. I stifled a cry when their sharp points pierced into my shoulder, and zapped her with an electric charge, sending her backward several yards. Only to have another lock me into a chokehold as someone else charged at us.

My hands latched onto the iron-like forearm against my throat as I brought my knees to my chest, then kicked out at the charger. He flew back, too. With a forward lunge, I bent forward, flipping the vampire over my shoulders. He landed on his knees, and I swept my foot up, kicking him in the underside of his chin. His head snapped back, and he crumpled to the ground.

I couldn't even catch a breath as two more vampires grabbed me. Fangs dug deep this time, right into my neck, and I couldn't contain the scream. I wailed out loud as I pushed both electricity and Amadis power out of my body before the vamp had a chance to suck. They screamed louder than me and disappeared. I shot electricity at the last one in my sight, and he flashed away, too.

Hands out and ready, I spun toward Tristan to help him.

He just stood there. Just *stood* there.

Had he already fought his share off? He sure didn't look as though he'd been fighting. In fact, he didn't look like he had moved from the spot I'd left him in when we were attacked. Did they go after him? But even if they were too scared of him and left him alone, surely he would have helped me. Right?

His eyes, still bright with fire, stared down the alley, not even noticing me. His face twisted and contorted as though he fought something invisible, though his body didn't move at all.

In his head, I found . . . chaos. A red haze enshrouded his warring mind, garbling his thoughts into a hot mess. I caught only a few coherent words such as "hate" and "kill," and louder than the rest, "*NO!*"

"Tristan?" I said warily as I swiped my fingers against the tingling sensation at my neck. They came away wet. I looked at them, surprised to find them coated in crimson. My hand flew to the wound and pressed down to staunch the flow. "Tristan! Let's get out of here!"

I needed him to snap out of it so we could flash. But he ignored me.

"*More! Be ready,*" Cassandra warned again.

The smell of my blood must have been a beacon. Every vamp in the vicinity must have picked up the scent. They blurred at me down the alley, from the rooftops, from God knew where. A dozen of them, at least.

I hoped the wound would close on its own because I needed my hands to fight. Again.

Tristan! I screamed in his head as I fought off the attackers.

I kicked, hit, and lunged again, but my movements were slow compared to theirs. Their hands were on me, their fangs slicing across whatever skin they could reach. My head collided with someone else's, sending stars across my eyes. I turned and cartwheeled, swinging my blade out, returning every gash they gave me.

Tristan, I yelled again. *I need you!*

His head finally snapped toward me. His eyes lit up brighter, as if he just now realized what was going on right in front of him.

A little help, please?

He leaned forward as if to lunge, as if to finally fight. But then he stopped. Frozen in place again. Rage swept over his face, and again he seemed to be fighting something unseen without actually moving. It looked as though he *couldn't* move.

I didn't have time to figure out his problem. I was already

losing my ground. The wounds left by the vampires' fangs bled freely, sending them into a shark-like frenzy.

"*Keep going, Alexis,*" Cassandra said. "*You can do this.*"

The only thing I had left, though, was to pull on all the Amadis power I had within me and blast it outward.

The energy exploded from me like a bomb.

Vampires shot through the air and landed with sickening thuds. When they didn't move, I seized the opportunity. I tried to run to Tristan, but it was more like I stumbled. I hurt all over. My head throbbed, and my pulse thundered in my ears. But I had to get us out of there.

"Come on," I said, latching onto his arm. Rather than embracing me, he simply glared at me with flame-filled eyes. "Tristan, come on. Get us out of here!"

He still didn't move. I wanted to flash away, to go home, and let him help me heal. But he couldn't have been more uncooperative. He may as well have been in a different world. I didn't know if he'd follow my flash, and I certainly wouldn't leave him. So I tugged on his arm, pulling him toward Collins Avenue, with no idea where to go from there. At least he moved. Not smoothly. Definitely not normally. But he didn't resist.

After we rounded the corner and made it half a block, my body gave out.

"Tristan, please," I begged. "Snap out of it."

I fell into the doorway of a clothing store, pulling him down with me. He looked at me with eyes as blank as the mannequins' faces in the windows. His thoughts remained elusive. I slapped him across the face. His eyes tightened a hair.

"Help me, damn it!"

But it was too late. A blue light flashed at us, shattering the glass door we leaned against. Magic. Mages were coming for us this round.

CHAPTER 10

*D*amn. *Damn, damn, damn.* I had no strength left to fight them, and who knew what was wrong with Tristan, but he sure couldn't do anything to help us.

"Tristan, we have to flash away. Can you at least do that? Please?" I begged.

His face remained vacant. Another light, this one red, shot at us from a different direction. Barely missing Tristan's leg, it blasted a chunk off the concrete block of the store's wall.

"We have to get out of here. Flash with me. Now!" I threw my arms around him in a bear hug and held on, but he didn't flash.

"*You take him,*" not-Cassandra said, and now I knew it couldn't be her. The idea was impossible. No one could flash with another person except Tristan. I'd disappear without him, and in his state of mind, who knew what would happen to him?

Cloaked figures came out of the shadows down the street to our left, their hands and wands pointed at us. And then more wearing Norman clothes came from the opposite direction. They also aimed at us.

I wiped what I thought was sweat from my forehead, but

the back of my hand came away red. With this much blood leaking from various fang wounds, the mages would soon be joined by the vampires and probably shifters, too. The thought of fighting them all made my head swim. No. Injuries made my head swim.

My vision faltered. I was slipping away fast.

Tristan, I called out with my mind. *Please, help me. If you don't snap out of it, we're going to die.*

No response. I zapped him with electricity. His body jolted, but he finally looked at me with more awareness.

I'll die here, Tristan. Help me!

His head tilted a notch. Did he hear me?

Please, baby, I begged, *I need you.*

The flames in his eyes darkened. Or maybe that was my vision.

"*You* can *do this,*" not-Cassandra said. "*Trust in me. Trust in yourself.*"

I had no other choice but to try. With every ounce of energy I had left, I squeezed Tristan tightly, concentrated, and flashed.

We appeared on the driveway in front of the garage of our own home, lying on our sides. The thud of our landing must have snapped Tristan out of his trance.

"Did you do that?" he asked with surprise, but I had no idea. And I couldn't answer.

Help me, I whispered in his mind.

He finally looked at me, actually *saw* me, and horror filled his eyes.

He dragged me into his arms and held me tightly. "I'm sorry, *ma lykita*. I'm so sorry."

"Just help me heal," I croaked against his shoulder, barely hanging onto consciousness.

He went to work, using his mouth to close those wounds that weren't closing fast enough on their own and apologizing between each healing kiss. Then he held me close again, rocking me like a child while we sat in the driveway. His guilt felt tangible, wrapping around my body, flooding into the cells of my skin, nearly suffocating me.

But when I asked him what happened, his mouth clamped shut, and he only shook his head. Whatever had overcome him in that alley, he wasn't ready to talk about it. If I'd felt better, I would have demanded answers that very moment, but I was too tired to care. The eastern sky was beginning to lighten with dawn and after being awake for nearly twenty-four hours and surviving a brawl with the Daemoni, I needed sleep before answers.

I had many sleeps and still no answers.

"Why won't you tell me what happened?" I asked for at least the hundredth time over the last three days since the fight in South Beach.

A full moon shone through the window and bathed our bed in a silver glow, creating a contrast of light and shadows on Tristan's face as he lay on his back and stared at the ceiling. I lay on my side and stared at him. Remorse flooded out of his being, as it always did when I raised the subject of that night. His jaw muscle twitched as he scowled silently.

I placed my hand on his shoulder. His body went rigid. I squirmed closer to him, snuggling against his side, and murmured in his ear, "You know I forgive you, right?"

He placed a stiff hand on my knee, though he still stared at the ceiling, unblinking. "You shouldn't."

"I'm your wife. I'll forgive you if I want to. But I should know what happened, so we can be sure it doesn't happen again."

His jaw tightened once more. "It. Won't. Happen. Again."

"How do you know? How can *I* know?"

"Because I promise. I promise that you and I won't be

facing the Daemoni by ourselves again. I promise you won't be leaving this island any time soon. I promise to keep you safe, which means finding you a better protector than myself."

"That's ridiculous," I scoffed. "No one's more powerful than you."

"The most power doesn't necessarily make one the best protector," he said, and added with a tone of disgust, "as we have seen."

"Tristan, that wasn't about *you*. Something happened—"

In a flash, he stood at the bedroom door, a hand resting on the jamb.

"Even if you don't value your own life, Alexis," he growled, "I do. You mean too much to me, so drop it."

And with that, he was gone.

I flopped onto my back with a groan and listened as Tristan made his way through the house, out the backdoor, and down the stairs to the beach. *What does he mean, I don't value my own life? And what does that have to do with anything?* I sat up in bed and watched out the window as his moonlit silhouette moved through his Aikido routine. When it became apparent he wasn't returning any time soon, I slid my hand between the mattress and box spring and pulled out my dagger.

In the moonlight, I studied the elegant lines of gold and silver that weaved around the hilt, and my finger caressed the intricate design cut into the blade's center.

Cassandra? I felt silly as soon as I thought her name, and considered putting the dagger back and stuffing away this insane idea with it.

"*I am with you,*" the now familiar woman's voice said.

I pressed my lips together. *You're really Cassandra? THE Cassandra?*

She chuckled in my mind. "*Yes, dear. It is me.*"

How do I know? The dagger warmed in my hand. I almost snorted. *Is that supposed to be some kind of ghostly sign?*

"*Call it what you like, but know that you and I are the only two daughters with the ability to wield this Angel's dagger. It has been sitting in the Sacred Archives for two millennia, waiting for you to come along. Katerina knew this dagger would be yours and had it prepared for you even before anybody else knew the blade would be your best weapon. It is because you have the genuine power—the same power as me. We are connected, dear.*"

I closed my eyes, wishing they could pull forth her image, but even when they couldn't, I definitely felt her within me. Well, a warm power flowed in my chest that I assumed to be her.

Is that why I've been so good at fighting? Are you helping me?

"*Not exactly, dear. The power is all in you.*"

Even bringing Tristan with me when I flashed?

"*The power is in you.*"

Did she know how to say anything else?

Then why are you here? Why are you talking to me?

"*Because sometimes you need encouragement. Sometimes you need guidance to accomplish your purpose for the greater good. I come when you need me.*"

Thank you? I said. I didn't mean for it to sound like a question, but part of me still doubted the reality of this exchange.

"*Sleep well, Alexis.*" Her presence receded, although I wasn't done with the conversation.

I knew better than to push her, though. If our connection was anything like the matriarch's with the Angels, she would communicate only when necessary. Too bad. She could have answered a ton of questions, such as what was wrong with my husband. But I supposed I had to figure that out myself.

I slipped the dagger under the mattress, and looked out the window. Tristan was still outside, working off his guilt. With a sigh, I lay down and tried to sleep.

Another week passed with no progress. Tristan's guilt only grew, and as it did, he became quieter and quieter. I felt him drifting away from me, on a tiny raft in the immense ocean of his regret. Nothing I said broke through to him, and the urge to invade his thoughts had grown into a looming monster, although I'd sworn to him many times I'd never do so without his permission. I was *this* close to breaking that promise.

One October morning I finally slammed my coffee mug on the table. The sharp crack reverberated around the kitchen, and Tristan's head snapped up, his attention diverted from the business website on his laptop.

"I've had enough!" I declared. "This is ridiculous. We have a mission, and we can't accomplish it if you won't let me leave the island."

"Find your protector and you can go," Tristan said, his tone dismissive.

I wasn't about to let him blow me off, though. Not this time. "You know damn well that I've been trying to find Owen, regardless of your stupid ultimatum, but that's beside the point. You and I need to work together, so you need to get over this. I'm alive. I'm fine."

"No thanks to me."

I groaned. "Tristan, we were in a bad fight. Things aren't always going to go our way, but we can't let it stop us if we're to serve our purpose, do our duty, all that jazz you and the rest of the Amadis are always talking about. We made it home, and that's all that matters. Besides I *am* alive thanks to you. You healed me, remember?"

He flipped a switch, going from blasé to an explosion of anger in a blink. He shoved the laptop to the side.

"You should have never been that hurt!" he bellowed. "I should be able to protect you. I should have fought by your side, but I didn't."

My voice rose to match his. "And why not? If we can figure out what happened—"

"There's nothing to figure out, Alexis."

"So you *know* what happened?"

His eyes glanced at me then narrowed as he stared at the wall in front of him. His voice dropped to a low growl. "I know what I felt, and that's enough."

I waited for him to continue. He didn't. "And? What did you feel?" I pressed.

No answer. Seconds ticked by.

"Damn it, Tristan, tell me already! Do I have to go in and find out myself?" I threatened, tapping my temple with a finger. He looked at me with a challenge in his eyes. "Well, what do you expect when you won't tell me—share with your wife, your *partner*—what happened? You were a statue, surrounded by Daemoni but not fighting, and flames filled your eyes like before, when the monster inside you was trying to take over. But that monster's supposed to be dead. So you need to tell me—is it still there? Have they found a way to revive the monster? Because if so, we need to figure out—"

"It's not the monster," he finally said. "You don't have to worry about that."

Whew. That was a relief. And more information than I'd been able to pull out of him for weeks.

"Okay, then what is it?"

"Worse."

"How can it be worse? If we beat that thing, we surely can beat this . . . whatever it is."

He shook his head. Then he rose from his chair, as if to leave. "I'm not—"

My eyes grew wide. Anger overcame every rational thought. I lunged across the two yards separating us and shoved my hands into his chest. Hard. He fell over his chair and landed on his butt. He looked up at me, his mouth twitching with either his own anger or a smile. I wasn't sure. I didn't care.

"The only thing you're *not* doing is leaving," I seethed. "Or bowing out of this discussion like a coward anymore. You're going to tell me what happened. Or what you felt. Whatever it is that you *do* know."

I crossed my arms over my chest as he stood once again. He leaned close to me, all traces of any smile gone. His voice came out low and deadly. "You *don't* want to know."

I leaned forward, too, and looked up, our noses only inches apart. "Yes. I. Do."

He rocked backward on his heels and crossed his own arms. His eyes narrowed. "Fine. You want to know what I felt? I felt *hatred*, Alexis. Murderous hatred."

I sucked in a breath, more at his icy tone than his words. Very slowly, I exhaled and tried to relax my shoulders. I already knew this; I'd seen the anger in his mind that night. "Okay. Well, the Daemoni were there. Of course you did. Why is that such a big deal?"

He spun away from me, and his arms flew out with exasperation, one hand barely missing my jaw. He let out a groan and grabbed his hair in his fists. He turned back to me with a peculiar wildness in his eyes. I didn't understand the problem. Did he really think I'd judge him for hating our enemy? I mean, sure, Amadis weren't supposed to hate, but I really doubted he felt true hatred. He was beyond that. We both might feel intense anger and extreme dislike to the point that it could *almost* be hatred, especially during a fight, except . . . he wasn't fighting . . .

"Not toward *them*!" he roared. "Toward *you*! I hated *you*."

I involuntarily stepped backward, my butt hitting the granite counter, and stared at him with eyes wide enough I thought they might burst from their sockets. My lungs felt as though all the air had been sucked out of them.

"Me? You . . . hate . . ." I stammered. Then I shook my head and even chuckled, though the sound came out more like a cat choking on a hairball. "Of course not. It *was* the monster.

The monster is back, Tristan. That's how you'd felt when we first met, remember?"

He put his hands low on his hips. "It's not the same. It's not the same beast. It's worse."

I reached out for his arm. He took a step away from me, as if afraid of my touch. "Why do you keep saying it's worse? Because it's really you? You . . . hate me?"

"No! Of course not. But don't you get it? Something else *made* me feel hatred toward you. Made me see you with different eyes. Something external, and I couldn't control it. Not like the beast. That was *inside* of me—" he pounded his chest with a fist "—where I could restrain it. This . . . this was different. And extremely dangerous."

My mind went over the scene in South Beach. "But you *did* control it. You fought it. I could see it on your face."

"I was resisting the urge to join in the fight—to attack you myself."

"But you beat it."

"And it was nearly impossible!" His voice had risen again. He caught himself and lowered it. "They're using dark magic, Lex. Very strong dark magic that gave me this overwhelming desire to hurt you. To kill you."

"Wait. They're not . . . I mean . . ." I stammered as I processed the meaning of his words. "What you're saying . . . they're *controlling* you?"

Hard hazel eyes glared at me for a long moment, before he said, "Yes. They were that night."

"No," I whispered, shaking my head in denial. "It . . . They can't . . ."

"They have."

Some kind of maniacal laugh escaped my throat, but I really wanted to scream. To cry. To *punch* something.

"*Why?*" I asked, my voice shaking as I tried to fight the anger from overwhelming me. "Why can't they leave you alone? Are we going to have to deal with this shit the rest of our lives?"

Now my voice had risen, approaching the scream I tried so hard to hold back. Tristan didn't answer me, but his expression said it all. Of course, they'd try everything possible to get their warrior back. Why did this even surprise me?

I inhaled a few deep, cleansing breaths, trying to calm myself. I pushed off the counter and paced the kitchen a few times.

"How exactly?" I finally demanded, sharper than I intended.

"We're talking dark magic. They have all kinds of weapons they could use, but my guess is a mage must have created some kind of connection to me. An extremely powerful mage to be able to wield this kind of dark magic."

I stopped pacing and turned toward him.

"Kali?" I asked. She certainly had motivation. And if it was her, I had no problem following through for the faeries. They were right—I'd want to satisfy their request just as much for me and the Amadis as for them.

"Possibly, but she's not their only sorceress."

"Well," I said, squaring my shoulders, "then we find out and go after them."

He grimaced. "And there you go again, acting before you think."

I scowled. "What does that mean?"

"You're reckless, Lex. You see someone who needs rescued, and you charge like a bull. Only by luck are we and anyone else you get involved even alive."

I crossed my arms over my chest, feeling defensive. "Not luck. Might. And power." Remembering Cassandra's words, I added, "And I do it for the greater good!"

He stepped over to stand in front of me, his eyes paralyzing me with their intensity as he placed his hands on my shoulders.

"Listen to me, just this once, Alexis. Do it for the greater good, because if you're dead, so are a hell of a lot of people." He waited for me to acknowledge my understanding, so I nodded. "If we go out there, only the two of us, they can take control of me again. And now that they know how close I was to breaking, they'll be able to overcome me next time. And you know who my first target will be."

I cleared my throat. "Me."

"Right. Eliminate my weakness. So you can*not* be as reckless as you've been anymore. Understand?"

I pressed my lips together and nodded, knowing that would appease him. But somehow, I had to figure out a way to cut their connection with my husband. Again.

He pulled me into his arms, and I leaned my head against his chest, glad our fight was over and that he had told me the truth.

"It seemed as if they were waiting for us, didn't it?" I asked, relieved to finally be able to talk about that night. This had been bugging me for nearly two weeks. "As if they knew we were coming?"

"They've likely been waiting for us for some time. They surely know by now that we need the pendant, and we'll come after it."

"And Vanessa's totally been taunting us. She played hard to get in South Beach. Sonya said she'd been in Fort Myers Beach the night before we were there and might still have been. She toyed with us on the Greek island. But any other time, our people can't find a trace of her anywhere, as if she disappears from the face of the earth."

Tristan hummed in agreement. "She loves her games."

"Crap, Tristan. That *has* been her game, hasn't it?" I pulled back enough to look up at him. "Tease us with the pendant so we'll chase after it, while the mages are in the background figuring out how to connect with you. How are we ever going to get the pendant if we can't go near them?"

"We hope Owen decides to come back, or that Sophia finds you another protector."

"I don't want another protector." I frowned. "I want Owen or you. Other than you two, who else can protect me better than myself?"

He narrowed his eyes, but a small smile played on his lips. "That's the kind of thought a reckless and cocky warrior would have, Lex."

"Sorry, but it's true," I said with a shrug. I leaned back against him. "I still don't get why you kept this from me. Did you really think I'd believe *you* hated *me*?"

He pressed his lips to the top of my head. "I couldn't control myself, *ma lykita*. You could have died, and I would have stood there like an idiot, maybe even helped. How am I supposed to live with that? How was I supposed to tell you that without losing your love and trust?"

I looked up at him and lifted my hand to his face. I brushed my fingers across his cheekbone. "You should know me better by now. It will take a lot more than Daemoni magic to make me stop loving you."

"Unless that magic kills you. You can't love me after you're dead."

"Wanna bet?" I asked as I leaned up on my toes to press my lips against his. "Death will not part us. You won't get off the hook that easily."

He tightened his hold on me and kissed me. "Let's not find out any time soon, okay? Don't go off and do anything stupid."

Making no promises, I shut him up with a long, deep kiss accompanied by roaming hands and his hardness growing between us.

"My eyes! My eyes!" Dorian yelled from the kitchen doorway, and we broke our embrace with alarm.

CHAPTER 11

*M*y heart resumed beating when it became immediately obvious that Dorian was fine. Physically anyway.

"Ew! That's so nasty," he said, wrinkling his nose at us.

Tristan smiled. "Kissing your mom? I have to disagree." He pulled me back into his arms.

"Gross, Dad!" Dorian covered his eyes and made gagging sounds. "Don't ever do that in front of me again."

Tristan and I shared a grin and reluctantly let go of each other.

"So, Aikido today?" Tristan asked, focusing on our son.

"Sure," Dorian said as he took out a bowl and a box of cereal. "Are you coming, too, Mom?"

I thought about what needed to be done at the safe house. With no new guests yet, there really wasn't much. I wanted to paint the reading alcove in our own home, but Blossom was busy today, and I definitely needed her (magical) help after our last painting disaster. And I could use a good workout—I'd been pretty lazy since the fight in Miami.

"I'm in," I said.

"Do we get to spar, Dad? Can I spar you?" The enthusiasm

in Dorian's voice held an edge to it, as if he wanted a little revenge on Tristan for kissing his mom.

"You need to beat your mom first," Tristan said.

Dorian groaned. "She's too hard to beat! I wish Uncle Owen was here. I bet I can beat him now."

He dove into his usual questions about Owen—where was he, why hadn't he been around, etc. At least it wasn't his other favorite subject: the unmet promise of going to Universal Studios. He'd been as persistent about it as he'd once been about getting a dog, but after what we saw in South Beach, we weren't about to take him off-island yet. We'd only be able to put him off for so long, however, before having to tell him a flat-out "No."

"We've looked into the situation at South Beach," Mom said on a conference call between her, Rina, a few council members, and Tristan and me. This was our last meeting before the Christmas holidays, barring any emergencies, which were becoming such a norm we'd soon have to change the definition of what constituted an emergency.

Tristan and I sat side-by-side in what had once been a formal dining room that we'd converted into a conference room, with a polished cherry-wood table, six black leather executive chairs, all kinds of outlets for laptops and other technology, and a conference-call pod positioned between Tristan and me. Thanks to Tristan, we probably had the most technologically advanced safe house in the Amadis. If he had his way, he'd have gone to the others to outfit them like ours, and we'd be holding a videoconference right now, rather than the outdated telephone one. Everyone else on the call was either on the Amadis Island or in their home offices around the world.

"It's bad, isn't it?" I said, leaning closer to the pod. "I can't believe they've overtaken such a populated area, and the norms are oblivious to it."

"Well . . . that's the thing," Mom said cryptically. "Galina, would you like to explain, since you're the mage overseeing this?"

I pictured the silver-haired female warlock who'd earned my trust during last year's trial when she defended us against those controlled by Kali. Her Russian accent was barely noticeable when her voice came on the line.

"Yes, of course," she said. "Alexis, we have sent a team of mages to investigate your report and found the Miami Beach area to be heavily populated with Daemoni, including newly turned, but we did not find it under siege as you and Tristan described. The situation there isn't even as bad as Key West."

Tristan and I exchanged a look.

"Your team must have seen what the Daemoni wanted them to," Tristan said.

Galina cleared her throat. "Actually, we believe *you* two saw what they wanted you to. You have reversed what they actually did. What you thought was reality was their projection, while what you believed to be their projection was reality."

"You think the sudden appearance of traffic, people, and sounds was reality breaking through their image?" I asked.

"Yes," Galina confirmed. "They wanted you to believe they had captured South Beach. The situation is not good, but it isn't as bad as you were made to believe."

"And how do you know that for sure?" I asked, doubting their theory. The empty streets, the vacant buildings . . . that all seemed so *real*, while the thriving city simply didn't. "Wouldn't I have heard something in their thoughts? Sensed the people around us?"

"It takes powerful magic to accomplish what they did, but it *is* possible. My team sensed heavy levels of dark magic, still strong even days after your incident. Which would explain, also, how they could protect the truth from your telepathy."

"The Daemoni have, how do you say?" Rina started, pausing for a moment. "Upped the ante? Is that right? They are pulling out their big arms."

"Guns," Mom corrected. "They're pulling out their big guns."

"Right," Rina said. "This is what I mean. They are no longer holding anything back, but are using their darkest magic and most powerful weapons. We must all raise our defenses even higher. We cannot have their sorcerers gaining control of us. They *will* try, however. Be prepared. All of you."

Tristan and I exchanged another look. We hadn't told them the full story of what happened at South Beach. No one else knew that Tristan hadn't fought alongside me. Guilt had nearly led him to confess when we briefed them on the night's events during the last conference call. He'd almost blurted it out, but I'd "accidentally" disconnected the call. I thought his behavior had been a fluke at the time and refused to give anyone a reason to doubt his loyalty again. He opened his mouth now, but I shook my head. I poised my finger over the "end" button on the pod, ready to drop the call again if he said anything.

We already know what Rina said is right, and the others believe her, so you don't need to confirm it, I told him. *There's no reason to raise their suspicion of you again.*

"Tristan and Alexis, any progress on finding the stone?" Mom asked.

"Vanessa's disappeared again," I said. "I caught that one glimpse of her at South Beach, but no one's reported any sighting or other news since. Even that night, she didn't join the fight, but disappeared completely from my range."

None of her fellow vampires had thought once about her, either, which I found pretty weird, considering she was supposed to be leading the new nest there, according to Sonya. Maybe things had changed since Sonya had been with the Daemoni, and Vanessa wasn't part of the South Beach nest anymore. But then why was she there? And why did she leave when she had to have known there'd be a big fight? If she knew they'd be taking control of Tristan, wouldn't she have stayed to watch him kill me? To help him and try to make him hers? We were missing some important piece about their plan. Either that, or it was much bigger than simply eliminating me, the youngest Amadis daughter.

"Please continue your search," Rina said, and she started to add something, but broke down in a coughing fit, which eventually led to the call coming to a close. I sighed as I hit the "end" button. Rina wasn't supposed to be sick. Not anymore. The fact that her condition hadn't improved since I'd left hurt my heart.

"I should be there with her, helping her," I said to Tristan as we sat back in the cushy chairs.

"It'd probably be safer for you," Tristan agreed.

"So should you. Maybe you can heal her."

He shook his head. "My powers won't help her. It's deeper than a physical illness. Besides, someone needs to stay with Dorian. I'm sure they won't allow him back on Amadis Island."

I chewed on my lip. "Rina would be pissed if I came to the island. She wants me out here, helping the cause and finding the stone. 'Serving my purpose.'" I wiggled my fingers in the air to mark the quotations.

"Well, you're not going anywhere right now to find the stone."

I lowered my head onto my hands on the table. "It's not as if we have any leads anyway. But still . . ."

Potentially aid my grandmother's recovery or serve my purpose for the Amadis—how could I choose between those? I knew what Rina would want me to do—serve the Amadis as a whole and not worry about her personally—but what she desired and what was right weren't necessarily the same thing. Especially when I didn't seem to be doing much for the greater good of the Amadis anyway. And wasn't helping the matriarch as important as anything else? On the other hand, Rina wasn't the only person who could serve as matriarch, but retrieving the stone was certainly necessary to ensure the Amadis would continue to exist and even *need* a matriarch.

My internal debate—which I apparently had been sharing with Tristan because he'd nodded at all the right places—came to an end when Sheree knocked on the door.

"Can I talk to you?" she asked me.

Tristan rose. "I need to get home for Dorian's math lessons, anyway." He kissed my forehead. "See you later?"

"Of course."

Sheree took a seat across the conference table from me and folded her hands on top of the wooden surface. Her leg bounced under the table, her knee hitting the lip each time.

"I've been talking to my mentor in Atlanta," she said. "About Sonya. He keeps telling me everything I tell you—conversion takes time, she's progressing normally, and so on. But she's kind of in a unique situation, so we had an idea that could be her breakthrough."

I leaned forward at the excitement in her voice and the light in her eyes. "Go on."

"Well, since Sonya has a family member who knows about her, someone she obviously cares for a lot, we thought if we let her talk to Heather at least on the phone, that could help her. I mean, normally new converts are supposed to be totally isolated from norms until they're completely converted and ready, but normally we don't have anyone to talk on the phone with, either. I mean, we can't exactly call our families and friends from our old lives. Not when we're supposed to be dead. But Sonya does have someone who knows what she is, and a phone call couldn't hurt and—"

"Whoa." I held my hand up, happy to try anything that could help Sonya. Maybe communication with her sister would lift her spirits. Sometimes her mood swings gave me whiplash, so an attitude adjustment, especially a positive one such as this, would be a godsend. "Your idea is a great one. Let's give it a try."

Sheree let out a little squeal. "This will be the best Christmas present! Sonya will be so happy."

I smiled. "Heather will be, too. And, if all goes well, maybe it won't be long before they can finally see each other in person."

We both stood and left the conference room together, Sheree still babbling on about her idea.

"I don't know why we didn't think of this sooner," she said as we crossed the marble-floored foyer, past the ginormous Christmas tree Sheree and Blossom had decorated, to our offices. "I guess we thought she was doing fine, and it never occurred to us to do something extra, especially something so out of the ordinary. I mean, no one gets to see or even talk to their family *ever*, not after they're turned, well, except those who go back to eat their families. Even when we're converted we can't, because, you know, that would freak the family out. So I guess it had never occurred to us."

"Um . . . Sheree?" I said, as I stood at my office door. My knowledge of the faith-healing part didn't compare to hers, so I'd been nodding and humming when appropriate, and she hadn't even noticed that I'd stopped. She was already several steps farther down the hallway when she turned to me. "I'm going to get some work done, okay?"

She smiled sheepishly. "Oh, right. Sorry about the babbling. I was a little excited."

I didn't have a lot of work to do—only a bit of paperwork and ordering supplies for the safe house, such as animal blood. Sonya wasn't ready for anything stronger, but maybe if Heather could help, we'd finally be able to get her onto donated blood, and maybe, even, get her out of the safe house. Of course, then what would we do? Sheree and I would practically be out of a job.

"Some kind of delivery arrived," Sheree said from the doorway of my office, making me jump in my chair. I'd been so involved in my online research of the most recent murders and missing persons—evidence of more Daemoni attacks—that I hadn't heard her approach. "They're really old and kind of neat looking, so I'm not sure what they are. Maybe something for Christmas?"

"I'm not expecting anything. Not like that, anyway." Sticking to my childhood traditions of handmade gifts only, we hadn't ordered any Christmas presents. I massaged my eyes, then glanced at the clock and sprang from my seat. "Oh, crap! I'm late for Dorian's English lesson, and I promised we'd work on the book today."

Sheree hopped out of my way as I rushed into the hallway. "What about the delivery?"

I waved my hand at her as I ran for the backdoor. "I'll check it out tomorrow. Just put it in my office."

I hurried outside, jumped in my car, and drove the six miles home. I could have flashed, but in the interest of maintaining Norman appearances as much as possible, I didn't want to leave my car at the safe house. I expected to find either Tristan still working with Dorian on math or Dorian impatiently waiting for me. Instead, I found them in a heated discussion.

As soon as I walked through the door, Dorian pounced on me. "Heather's mom is taking her to Universal Studios this weekend, and they said I could go, too, but Dad won't let me. Tell him he's wrong, Mom."

Ugh. No way would I risk Dorian's life to go to an amusement park, especially unprotected. I didn't care what Galina's people had said about South Beach. The Daemoni were out in full force.

"Sorry, but I have to agree with Dad."

"*Why?* That's so not fair! You and Dad won't take me, so why can't I go with them?"

"Well, um, we *want* to take you, Dorian, but—" I clamped my mouth shut at his expression. His face scrunched up, and his shoulders sagged. He didn't want to hear any more excuses.

"Forget it," he muttered. "You guys never have time for me."

He slumped into a kitchen chair, crossed his arms over his chest, and stuck out his bottom lip. Tristan and I exchanged a glance, both of us feeling guilty. No matter how much we tried to make time for Dorian, it never felt like enough.

"We have time right now. You want to go skim-boarding?" Tristan said.

"Nah. Don't feel like it."

"Wanna spar with me?" I suggested. "Maybe you can beat me this time."

"Yeah, right. I'll never beat you until I'm big like Dad."

"Video games?" Tristan asked.

"Heather's coming later to play with me."

"We're supposed to be working on our book today, anyway," I said. "But if you don't want to do that, we can read something."

"Bor-ring." Dorian yawned.

I began to grow annoyed with his attitude, especially when he'd always had fun working on the book. He was just being obstinate. "We obviously have time for you, Dorian. We're always doing these things together. So what do you want to do now?"

His toe scrubbed at the floor tile. "You already know. I want to go to Universal and ride the roller coasters. Why can't I go with Heather?"

I pressed my lips together. "We can't allow it, Dorian. End of discussion."

"See," he yelled, jumping from his seat, a ball of angry fire. "You never let me do anything!"

I jerked back as if he'd slapped me. I'd never seen my son

behave this way. "Dorian Stefan! You're acting like a spoiled—"

Tristan cut me off. "Dorian, Mom and I really want to be the ones who take you, and we will soon. But not if you keep acting like this. Be patient, son, and we'll go. I promise."

"Whatever," he grumbled, and he stomped out of the room.

"How can you make that promise when we can't deliver?" I demanded with a hiss through clenched teeth. "That's what started all this, why he's acting like such a—"

"He's acting like this because he's nearly nine years old, almost a pre-teen, and his one and only friend is a seventeen-year-old girl."

"Heather's not a brat."

"Not in front of us. But you know she's probably overly dramatic about how bad her life and mom are when there aren't any adults around. That's how teens are. It's one constant I noticed while observing them all those years before approaching you."

"So what do we do about it? He needs other friends, obviously, but who? And what good will that do if all preteens —oh, no! Tristan, he's nearly a *teen*." The sudden realization crashed down on me like a ton of bricks. "Puberty . . ."

"He has a few years yet."

"Not enough! Look how fast time flies. He'll be . . . *gone* . . . if we don't figure something out."

Tristan handed me a tissue for the tears welling in my eyes.

"I can't lose him," I said, my voice thick. "It'd be like losing you all over. Only worse. He's my *baby*. I couldn't live through it."

He came around the kitchen island and wrapped me into the warmth and comfort of his arms.

"You'd have to live through it, *ma lykita*. I'd need you by my side to beat the living shit out of everyone who tries to keep us from getting him back. We'll find a way to break the curse, and if we don't, they'll all be dead by our hands anyway."

I drew in one more shuddering breath, and then nodded against his chest. I straightened my back and swallowed down my fear and worry.

"Of course. If the Daemoni is annihilated, then Dorian has no reason to leave us." Feeling at least a little better, I looked up at Tristan. "But first, we have to get the stone, and how can we possibly do that if they'll control you if you go near them? I mean, I'm assuming it's a distance thing, right, since they're not controlling you right now?"

"Yes, that's my conclusion." He stroked a hand down my hair. "We'll figure it out."

That night, as we were about to head to bed, Tristan's phone rang, indicating a text message. And then mine echoed it. I glanced at my Caller ID to see if the text was worth answering, and my breath caught. I practically shrieked like a little girl. "Owen!"

CHAPTER 12

*T*ristan read the text aloud: "Did you get my delivery? I thought I'd hear from you by now."

"Sheesh," I said. "We haven't heard from him in ages, and that's how he greets us? And *he* thought he'd hear from *us* by now?"

I would have given the guy some electric-shock therapy if he were here.

"I guess your eight hundred previous texts don't count," Tristan muttered. "Do you know what delivery he's talking about?"

"Must be what came in today. Sheree told me about it when I was leaving, but I didn't think anything of it."

Tristan typed out a response. His phone rang immediately.

"Yep, that's it," Owen said through the speakerphone as soon as Tristan answered the call. I was so happy to hear his voice, I bounced on the balls of my feet like a child. "Didn't you read the note right inside? The one that said, 'call me before you open the bags'?"

"First of all," I began, "what do you mean you thought you'd hear from us by now? We've been trying to contact you for over a year, Owen. Over a freakin' year! And then you

141

disappear with the damn Daemoni, and you don't have the decency to at least text back and say, oh, I don't know, 'Hey, I'm alive.' Do you have any idea how worried I've been? And now you call up like nothing's wrong, asking about some delivery with *nothing* to indicate it came from you, our long lost friend and my so-called *protector*."

The line remained silent. *Oh, no. Did I scare him off?* It'd been so long, and I was so thrilled to hear from him but angry, too, that I'd forgotten the circumstances that had caused him to leave. When I'd just taken out the person whom he'd thought had been his father.

"Ouch," Owen finally said. "So-called, huh?"

Whew. "Yeah. So. Called. Because you're not here protecting me, are you?"

The sound of his throat clearing came over the line. I could picture him running a hand through his blond hair. "Right. Yeah. I guess I deserve that."

"So are you coming back? Or did you decide to send us some fancy souvenirs from all the places you've been in the last year while we've been worried sick about you?"

Owen chuckled but even through the phone, it didn't sound humorous. "I guess you could call the contents souvenirs of a sort. Not what you're thinking, though."

"What's going on, Scarecrow?" Tristan asked, apparently hearing the same dark tone I did.

"Just, uh, wait until morning to open them. That'd be the best time. And don't let anyone else open them, okay? It's really—" A loud clamor sounded in the background. "I, uh, gotta go. Catch ya later."

"Owen," Tristan and I said at the same time, but no reply came. The phone's screen showed *Call ended.*

"What happened to him?" I asked, throwing my arms in the air. "Do you think he's okay?"

"Scarecrow can take care of himself," Tristan answered as he headed for our bedroom with me on his heels.

"I can't believe him," I groaned. "After all this time . . . that's all he says. What do you think the delivery is?"

Tristan shrugged. "We'll find out in the morning." He lifted his eyebrows at the look I gave him. "Owen said wait until morning. I'm sure there's a good reason for it."

"Fine, I won't be *reckless*," I said as I plopped onto the bed. "But it'd better be good, since it didn't sound like he's coming here. Which is probably in his best interest right now, because I swear I'm going to kill him if I ever see him again."

The next morning I couldn't get out of our home and to the safe house fast enough. We found the delivery in my office, and I stared at the two beautiful wood-and-leather boxes for a long moment. Each about three feet long and two feet high, they resembled old-fashioned travel trunks, piquing my curiosity even more at what could be inside. The intricate carvings in the wood, the leather adornments, and the ornate silver latches made me think they must have come directly from Amadis Island. But what would Owen have sent from there? And why him, when he hadn't been there for so long? Or had he? He didn't tell us where he called from.

Tristan and I knelt side-by-side in front of one of the trunks, the one with a number 1 scratched into the lid. The other one showed a number 2.

"Guess we open this one first," Tristan said. He jiggled the latches but they didn't budge.

"Don't tell me he put some kind of spell on them and forgot we couldn't counter it," I muttered.

"No. He knows what he's doing." Tristan studied the lid of the trunk for several minutes, ignoring the impatient tap of my fingernails on my leg. Finally, with deliberation, he touched three of the carved designs as if in a certain order. The latches popped open. He grinned. "Scarecrow and I have our ways."

I shook my head as Tristan opened the lid. Black velvet lined the interior, at least what I could see of it. A tray sat across the top of the trunk, hiding the contents below. A folded piece of paper lay in the tray.

Let me know when you get this. Take to a 'safe' place before opening the bags. And be sure to open them in the morning light. Tristan, you'll know what to do. Owen

"Well, we don't have to call him," I said, lifting the tray to reveal two leather bags. "What does he mean by 'safe'? He sent them to a safe house."

I pulled back the drawstring top of one of the bags to take a peek.

And screamed.

Tristan pushed my hand away and slammed the trunk closed.

"Did . . . did you see . . . ? Was that . . . what I think . . . ?" I couldn't get the words out as the thought of what I'd just seen sucked the air out of my lungs. *It can't be. It can't be. It can't be.* Surely I didn't see what I thought I had. My eyes had to have been messing with me. I mean, I'd only caught a quick glimpse before Tristan had shut it out of sight.

"Yeah, I saw," Tristan said through a clenched jaw. "We can't open these here."

His tone and implication made my stomach roll.

"Alexis," Sheree said from the doorway.

Tristan sprang to his feet and jerked me up with him, but my trembling legs could barely hold my weight. With a hand on my waist, he walked me to the door, as if he didn't want Sheree inside, near the trunks. *Was it really . . . ?* I swallowed down the acid that had lurched into my throat.

"Um . . . are you okay?" Sheree asked, her voice distant beyond the rush of blood in my ears.

I tried to look at her, but I couldn't see her face past the image of the black bag and the smooth, white—I blinked and shook my head, trying to erase it from my mind. It didn't go away, but danced around like a ghost only my eyes could see.

My lips parted, but no words came out. My tongue stuck to the roof of my dry mouth.

"What's going on?" Tristan asked, his tone sharp.

"I, uh, wanted to talk to you about Sonya, Alexis." She paused but I still couldn't answer, so she went on about something having to do with Sonya and Heather and a phone call. "It went really well, did wonders for her, and I think she might be ready for an in-person visit."

Her voice stopped again, and I looked at her without really seeing her. She apparently waited for me to say something. My hand drifted to my temple and massaged, as if that would make the vision go away.

"We can talk about it later," Sheree said, her eyes tightening with worry as she stared at me. "You look like you're about to be sick."

"Later's a good idea," Tristan said, speaking for me again.

Thankfully, Sheree left us, and only then was I able to let out the breath I'd been holding since Tristan first opened the trunk. The breath felt good in my tight lungs, so I tried deep breathing while closing my eyes to center myself, but on the back of my eyelids I saw my hand reaching inside the trunk, opening the bag and then the . . . *No! That's not what it was.* It couldn't be, because Owen would never, ever send us such a thing in a million years. Would he?

"We need to move them," Tristan said. My throat remained too dry and constricted to answer, so I simply nodded.

He raised his hand, and one of the trunks lifted into the air. I swore I heard the contents inside shift and rattle. My imagination ran wild about what could have caused that sound—if it'd even been real—and I bit my tongue to stifle another scream. With a hand that shook worse than a recovering drug addict's, I lifted the other trunk with my own power and followed Tristan out of the room.

We'd put Sonya in one of the five guest rooms in the right

wing, so, purposely avoiding Sonya's wing and Sheree, Tristan took us down the left side. We passed the two master suites, continued to the end of the hall and turned right into the rear wing. Three bedrooms and a bathroom were back here, most recently used by the previous owners' nanny, live-in maid, and chef.

I called this wing the dungeons, not only because it was the remotest part of the mansion, but also because Tristan, following Mom's instructions, had bolted heavy silver chains to the concrete walls and attached silver cuffs on their loose ends. The rooms were furnished similarly to the others, with beds, nightstands, chairs, and table lamps, but the chains on the walls and the carts in the corners housing medical supplies made the rooms anything but homey. Instead, they felt as though we'd somehow merged a hotel room, a mental facility, and a torture room in the cellar of an old castle.

The eerie environment didn't help the foreboding feeling in my stomach.

We took the trunks into one of these rooms and set them on the floor. Tristan closed the door, then grasped me by the shoulders. The look on his face told me I'd really seen what I thought I had. My body began to tremble again. Or perhaps it had never stopped.

"*Ma lykita*, it's okay to be afraid," he said softly, looking into my eyes, "but I need you to be brave. You remember the definition of courage, right?"

My head bobbed once. Not only had he and Charlotte pounded their definition into me while I trained back on Amadis Island, but we also drove it into Dorian's memory every time we worked with him.

"Feeling fear, but doing what's necessary anyway," I whispered.

"Right. I need you to be courageous, because you need to see this. It won't be the last time you'll come across something like this, and there's a chance you won't be in a safe place next time."

"Then it really was . . . was a . . ." I tried to swallow but my throat refused to cooperate. ". . . a person's hand?"

He nodded. I felt all the blood drain from my face.

"Oh, dear God." No way did a person fit in that trunk, not whole anyway, which only meant . . . "*Holy hell!* Who is it? Is the rest of him in these trunks?"

In answer, Tristan lifted the lid of the first trunk and pulled out the leather bags. With a solid determination I could never muster, he withdrew the hand, which remained attached to an arm, and I knew immediately it didn't belong to a "he," but to a "she." The skin was whiter than snow.

"A vampire?" I whispered.

"Remember, that to kill a vampire, you must cut it up and burn the pieces. If you don't burn them . . ." Tristan pulled out the other contents of the bags from that trunk, laying out another arm and the top of a naked torso with perfect, full breasts. The pieces, all of them rock hard, started trembling in place, as if the floor under them quaked. Then . . .

"Oh. My. God." I threw my hand over my mouth.

The body parts were *moving*. Moving! The sound of stone scraping across the ceramic tiles screeched like nails on a chalkboard as the pieces inched across the floor on their own volition. They slid toward each other, as if each one was magnetically pulled to the others.

Tristan fingered the top of the other trunk to unlock it and lifted the lid. He pulled out more bags, these containing hips and butt, thighs, calves and feet, and placed them near the rest, the display representing a morbid piecemeal of a human form. Somehow in my daze, I pulled a blanket out of the closet and was about to throw it over the naked female's chopped up body.

"Wait," Tristan said, holding his hand up to stop me. "You have to let it finish first."

He stood and turned his back to give the . . . the thing . . . privacy. He pulled me into his arms but I couldn't tear my eyes away from the macabre scene. Each white, stony body part made its way to the others and latched on with a sick, sucking sound like shoes pulling from mud. The body melded itself back together until it was whole. Well, almost whole.

"Where's . . . where's her head?" I whispered. The form ended at the shoulders with only a stub for a neck. The whole thing began to vibrate, quivering on the floor as if it knew it was missing a vital part but didn't know where to find it. My own body shook, and my voice came out as a shriek, escalating with hysteria. "She doesn't have a head. Where's her head? Oh, my god, it's not here! She doesn't have a head, Tristan!"

A faint *pop* sounded, and suddenly Owen stood in the corner of the room. His eyes immediately went to the body on the floor, and he nodded in appreciation.

"Last piece," he said, holding up another leather bag, a round object the size of a basketball shaping its bottom. My stomach churned again.

I couldn't respond. I couldn't squeal my happiness at seeing him. I couldn't scold him for his gruesome delivery. I couldn't do anything. I simply stared in a daze as he moved toward the snow-white vampire. His body came between us, thankfully blocking my view as he pulled the . . . *Oh, god, the head* . . . out of the bag.

But I did catch a glimpse of the hair.

My eyes trained in on the long, silky locks as my brain processed what I'd just witnessed and what I saw now.

Long, silky, *white-blond* hair. The newly re-formed vampire let out a long sigh—and even it was musical.

I gasped.

"No. Fucking. Way."

CHAPTER 13

My mind tried to decide whether to thank Owen for capturing Vanessa or to demand from her where my necklace was. My body didn't wait on the decision, but acted on its own. One moment, I stood in Tristan's arms and peeked around his shoulder. The next, I had the vampire-bitch by the upper-arms and slammed her against the concrete wall.

Her head flew toward mine with a head-butt, but I blocked it with a hand in her face. Of course, this meant loosening my hold on her body, which she took advantage of. She did a spin-and-duck move under my arm, freeing herself completely from my grasp. I swung my leg in a roundhouse that pounded into her ribs, but she caught my foot before I could kick her again. I flipped out of her grip and lunged at her. We flew into the steel medical cart and crashed to the floor, medical tools and supplies clamoring around us. She grabbed my throat, and her ice-blue eyes held mine as she punched me in the cheek. I zapped her with a shot of electricity. She pulled her knees under me and shoved me hard with her legs, and I flew backwards like a ragdoll. My head and back cracked against the wall.

The pain stopped me for a moment, and I closed my eyes, bracing for the impact. She should have been on me instantly. We had to have been moving in a blur before, and she had her chance now. I opened my eyes and prepared to grab onto her thoughts to know her next move as electricity sparked along my fingertips.

But the vamp wasn't making a next move.

She couldn't. Owen stood in front of her, blocking her out of view, but I could tell he gripped her upper arms. Okay, she *wouldn't* make a next move, because the vampire was definitely stronger than the warlock and could have broken free from his grasp if she really wanted to.

"You *promised*," he snarled at her.

"I was only defending myself," she said, her voice dripping with false innocence.

Defending herself? Yeah, right. But as I thought about it, I couldn't deny that every one of her moves had been in self-defense. Except . . .

"Choking and punching are *offensive* moves," Owen said.

Vanessa's glare cut over his shoulder at me, and I took a step toward the two of them, my fists still balled at my sides. She shrugged as she looked me in the eyes. "Yeah, well, I've been wanting to hurt that pretty face of hers for years. I couldn't help it. One last hurrah and all that."

Tristan stepped forward with a growl of warning to the vampire. I'd have to remember to thank him later for not interrupting our fight. I just wished we could have finished it. Instead, after being absent for so long, Owen suddenly decided he had to do his job. Only . . . I cocked my head. Despite his accusation of her, he sure stood as though he protected *her*, not me.

Vanessa's eyes flew to Tristan at the sound of his warning, and I hoped she'd start calling him lover boy and proceed with her infatuation with him. I needed the excuse to pick up where we left off. But she didn't. She was standing there naked with one of the hottest bodies on the planet, an ideal opportunity to flaunt all of her perfection, and run at the mouth about what he was missing out on. But she didn't. Her eyes didn't have that usual spark of lust when she saw Tristan. And she actually looked as though she *hid* behind Owen.

"Can I get some clothes or at least a blanket?" she asked. And she was modest? *Vanessa?* What was going on here?

With a swish of magic, Owen lifted the blanket I'd dropped earlier and wrapped it around her.

"What the hell?" I finally demanded.

Tristan crossed his arms over his chest. "I'd like to know the same thing. What are you up to, Scarecrow?"

Owen turned to face us, but kept his body in front of Vanessa's and angled, as if prepared for an attack. By me. Tristan must have noticed, too. He cocked an eyebrow.

"You know, the 'so-called' part of being my protector, I'd only said that because you were gone," I said. "Not because I thought you actually abandoned me. You're supposed to protect *me*, Owen. Not our enemy."

"*You* don't need protecting," he said. "Not right here or right now, anyway."

"And she does?" Tristan scoffed, nodding in Vanessa's direction.

Owen's sapphire eyes hardened as they looked at me. "As long as Alexis can't control herself, yeah, she does."

I sucked in a sharp breath. Tristan took another step forward and leaned in closer to the warlock who was supposedly his best friend.

"She *is* our enemy, Owen. How did you expect Alexis to react? What in God's name are you even thinking, bringing Vanessa in here like this?"

"She was completely defenseless when she got here."

A chill ran up my spine at the memory of the beautiful, crazed vampire-bitch in white pieces only minutes ago.

"She's weak now," Owen continued. "She needs blood.

And she needs your help."

I laughed. It sounded deranged, maniacal. "*What?* Have you lost your mind? Why on earth would we help her? She wants to kill me!"

"I told you." Vanessa's musical voice came out from behind Owen's back. And something about her tone, about the implication that she knew how I'd react better than Owen did, pissed me off.

Owen ignored Vanessa, though. "She has something you want. You have something she wants."

"We don't negotiate with the enemy," I said, crossing my arms over my chest.

"She doesn't have to be your enemy. You two have a lot in common, you know."

My eyes bugged. Red hatred seeped into my vision. My pulse flooded in my ears as the anger built up. But I managed to bite back all the profanities I wanted to slew at my so-called friend and protector.

"Chain her up until we figure out what to do with her," I said through clenched teeth.

"*What?*" Vanessa shrieked. Her eyes went wide as they took in the silver cuffs at the ends of the chains hanging on the wall. Tristan lifted his hand, and Vanessa's body rose several inches off the floor.

"Alexis," Owen said, his voice harder than I'd ever heard it, "this isn't necessary. Will you just listen to me?"

I spun on him and narrowed my eyes. I practically spit my words at him. "She has *nothing* I want, and she will *always* be my enemy. And I'm beginning to wonder if you are, too."

I heard the cuffs clamp around Vanessa's wrists and ankles as I stomped out of the room. The sound of her wails—not so much of pain but more of indignity—followed me down the hallway. So did Owen and Tristan.

"You need to shut her up," I snapped back at them.

As I rounded the corner to the left wing, a hand landed on

my shoulder and spun me around.

"She wouldn't be screaming if you'd unchain her," Owen said, but at the same time, his hand flicked, and her shrieks suddenly stopped. I didn't know if he actually silenced her or blocked the sound from leaving the room. As long as Sheree and Sonya didn't hear her—and I didn't have to listen to her—I didn't care about the how.

"And why would you even think we'd do such a thing?" I said, glaring at him. "Her ultimate goal has always been my death. Really, Owen, whose side are you on?"

His eyes flicked to Tristan and back to me. He didn't answer my question, but denied everything about Vanessa instead.

"She won't kill you. That's not what she wants. Not now." He looked away from me and cleared his throat. He shoved his fists into his pockets, then finally returned his gaze to me. "She doesn't even want Tristan anymore. She has a, uh, new . . . interest . . . obsession. Whatever you want to call it."

I stared at the warlock, trying to decode his meaning. What could finally pull Vanessa's attention away from Tristan and me? According to Tristan, she'd been chasing him for over two centuries, desiring him to be her boy-toy. She *hated* me and had wanted me dead before I was even born. She pursued these goals with the kind of single-minded determination that doesn't simply disappear without good reason.

Owen's gaze jumped about from the wall behind me to the ceiling and to some point down the hall, as if he avoided looking at me. And then I knew. Not *what* distracted her, but *who*.

"You've got to be kidding me," I said with a hollow laugh as I rocked back on my heels. Owen finally looked at me, and a pink tint crawled up his neck and face. "*You?* She's obsessed with *you* now?"

His face reddened even more, confirming my statement.

"But you don't feel—never mind, don't answer that. Of

course you don't." I shook my head in disbelief. "Well, I guess that's somewhat of a relief."

"Hardly," Tristan said. "Just because she isn't after me at the moment doesn't mean she won't still try to kill Alexis. Or both of us. She *is* Daemoni. Tell me again what exactly you were thinking by bringing her here, Owen."

"Yeah, what could she possibly want from us?" I asked, already knowing what we needed from her. My angry claim that she didn't have anything we wanted was a lie. She didn't have it on her naked body now, but she knew where the faerie stone was. Would she really exchange it for something from us? What could she want in return? Owen? "You're your own man, as you've shown us for the last fifteen months. That's up to you, not us. Or . . . wait, if you made some kind of deal sacrificing yourself—"

Owen shook his head. "No. I'm not that self-sacrificing at the moment."

I tilted my head at his tone and meaning. We were definitely dealing with a changed Owen. He didn't elaborate but returned to the subject of Vanessa.

"*She* wants to make the sacrifice. She's been talking about it for a while . . . months, actually . . . has been *begging* for me to bring her to you."

"She wants us to kill her?" Tristan asked.

Oh, dear God, I thought. A suicidal vampire? Thing was, we *couldn't* kill her. As much as I'd wanted to on the surface, I knew I couldn't do it unless she was trying to kill me or someone else. Which she hadn't been earlier—she really had been defending herself for the most part, definitely not doing anything to jeopardize my life. There was still hope for Vanessa's soul. I could feel it; I've always felt it every time I was around her.

"No, not that either," Owen said. "She thinks . . . she really wants . . ."

Why did he have such a hard time voicing what Vanessa

wanted? Before he could manage to say it, a squeal came from the other end of the hallway.

"Owen!" Sheree sprinted down the corridor and threw herself at the warlock. She wrapped her arms around his neck. "My savior! I was hoping I'd get to see you soon."

Owen's mind tugged at mine. "*She can't know about Vanessa.*"

Of course not, I agreed.

"Hey, Sheree." Owen returned her embrace and spun her around, acting as though everything was peachy-fine. He pulled back and seemed to drink the shifter in with his eyes. "Lookin' good."

She blushed and grinned. "Thank you. I owe it all to you."

And I knew that tone, the same one she used when talking to Tristan, but huskier with a heavier layer of flirt. She started chattering away about how much her life had changed since he'd saved her from the Daemoni and how appreciative of him she was, until I finally cleared my throat. Sheree looked at me with chagrin and dropped her head, almost in a bow.

"Sorry, Alexis," she said. "I just wanted to let you know that Sonya's begging for more blood, even though it's not really time yet. What do you think?"

"Sonya?" Owen probably recognized the name from when he accompanied me on book tours. Sonya, Norman at the time, hadn't been a real threat, but my publicist had been told Owen was my bodyguard, so she'd notified him of the "stalker."

"Oh, Owen, you have to meet Sonya," Sheree gushed. "She remembers you and has been dying to meet you. Come on." She tugged on his hand, and Owen willingly followed her down the hall.

"*Owen*," I said, tossing my hands out in a what-the-hell gesture. He looked back at me and shrugged, as though he were completely helpless against Sheree. "We're not done here!"

"He'll only be a minute," Sheree said. "I promise."

I sighed and waved my hand in the air with resignation as I watched them saunter down the hall. As they turned the corner into the main house, I caught Owen's hand move out of hers so his arm could lie over her shoulder instead.

Great. First Vanessa. Now Sheree. Owen was on a roll. But at least I liked Sheree, and her interest in him made perfect sense. She probably hero-worshipped him. After all, he'd saved her from being nearly beaten to death. By the vampire in the room down the hall.

And Owen wanted us to *help* the vamp with something? He *was* out of his mind.

Sheree will totally freak if she finds out Vanessa's here, I silently told Tristan.

He agreed as he took my hand and led me into one of the master suites, all the way into the bathroom, the room farthest from the hall, shutting doors along the way. He tapped on his forehead, and I tuned into his thoughts.

"*Too many vampires who might be able to hear us*," he explained, and I nodded. "*Do you have any ideas what Vanessa wants?*"

No, but I'm sure you do. At the moment, though, I'm more worried about Owen. Do you think . . . The thought felt like a boulder in my throat, blocking my air. *Do you think he's left us? The Amadis, I mean? I never would have thought it possible but . . .*

"*He* is *acting odd, isn't he?*"

Definitely not our usual Owen, I agreed.

Tristan shook his head. "*I honestly don't know, Lex. I trust him for the moment, but this stunt he's pulled . . .*"

You can't help but wonder. I nodded, completely understanding.

I *wanted* to trust Owen. But I struggled to do so, especially when he'd brought Vanessa, of all people, right here to the safe house, of all places. Of course, maybe he thought he was doing us a favor so we could get the stone back. And he *had* taken precautions to make sure she couldn't really hurt me. Even during our fight, either he or Tristan could have jumped in if I could no longer handle her myself.

But he'd also defended Vanessa. Protected *her*, not me.

"*You'll have to listen to his thoughts to know where his loyalties are,*" Tristan said.

Ugh. I hated the idea of breaching his privacy, especially when he knew I could and trusted me not to. Of course . . . *He'd be sure to think the right thoughts while he's around me.*

"*Then you'll have to do it when he doesn't think you're around. Preferably when he's with Vanessa.*"

I grimaced, wishing we weren't having this conversation. This was *Owen*, not Julia or Armand or anyone else I could never trust. I just hoped when he finished flirting with Sheree he'd return and give me good reason to believe in him again. To trust that he remained on our side.

But when he finally returned and found us back in the hallway where he'd left us, I didn't get the warm-and-fuzzies. In fact, what he had to say only convinced me that perhaps Kali the sorceress and her antics had gotten to him. Somehow she'd made him think he wasn't Amadis anymore and put him up to bat for our enemies.

"So back to Vanessa's *sacrifice*, as you put it," Tristan said, picking up where we'd left off before Sheree's interruption. "What does Vanessa want that doesn't include killing her? What *were* you thinking, bringing her here?"

Owen's eyes squinted as he scrubbed his hand through his hair, then he heaved out a breath.

"Why else do you bring the enemy to a safe house?" he finally asked. "What do they want when they come here?"

I stared at him for a long moment as his words sunk in. Then I waited for him to clarify a different meaning or even to laugh and say, "Kidding." But he just looked back at me with an even sapphire gaze.

I snorted. "Oh, please. You've seriously fallen for that?"

Tristan didn't take it with such good humor. In a heartbeat, he had Owen by the collar and pinned against the wall. "You may have been right about Sheree, but *Vanessa*? You honestly expect us to believe her?"

"Yeah, I do," Owen said. "*I* believe her."

"Then you're an idiot." Tristan gave Owen a shove before letting go and turning to pace the hall. His hands clenched into fists, and the muscles of his forearms bulged against his rolled-up sleeves. "It's a set-up. There's absolutely no way that bitch would ever want—"

"Then you can believe *me*," Owen cut in.

Tristan spun back toward Owen and roared, "*Can we?* Because you haven't done a damn thing to prove it, Scarecrow. In fact, you're doing a damn good job proving that you've changed sides. Because that—" His hand flicked in the general direction of Vanessa's room. "That's bullshit, and you know it!"

"It's not," Owen yelled back, bowing up and leaning toward Tristan, his own hands in fists. I'd only ever seen him stand up to Tristan once and that was about me. This . . . this was unbelievable.

I stepped in front of Owen and put my hands on his chest, trying to get him to back down.

"Seriously, Owen," I said, "I don't know where this came from, what you've been doing all this time, and what you've gotten yourself into, but this . . . You can't get any more Daemoni than her. I mean, we're talking *Vanessa*, the biggest bitch of all Daemoni bitches."

A growling sound came from Owen's throat as his eyes shot daggers at me. "You have no idea, *princess*. No idea about any of it. But I can tell you that I never would have asked for your help if I had a choice. I need you. Vanessa needs you, and you can't, as an Amadis daughter, turn her down. Vanessa truly *wants* to be Amadis."

CHAPTER 14

*M*y head spun. Nothing made sense, and everything was so overwhelming. Owen's sudden reappearance after being gone for so long. The arrival of the trunks containing body parts. Watching a vampire put herself back together from chunks. And then to see it was *Vanessa* . . . and, most astonishing of all, to hear she wanted to be *converted*? Never in a million years would I have expected this.

I mean, when I envisioned the Daemoni, Vanessa took front and center in my mind, overshadowing the rest of them. Although I logically knew Lucas led the army, I had never met him, and Kali-slash-Martin had only represented the enemy for the short time in the trial room and had become a faceless entity since then. So to me, Vanessa was the face of the Daemoni. Because she'd always been in the lead, at least where Tristan and I were concerned. Always on the prowl, always on the attack.

Except . . . the last couple of times I'd seen her, she didn't attack. Others had, but not her personally. And besides those sightings, she'd been in hiding, pretty much the whole time since Owen had been gone.

"You and Vanessa . . . you've been together all this time?" I asked Owen.

We'd gone through several rounds of Tristan saying the vamp tried to fool us all to get in close for the kill, and Owen swearing up one side and down the other that she was sincere. They'd get so loud in their arguing, I was surprised Sheree didn't come running, but realized Owen must have magically muffled us, just as he had Vanessa. But the arguments took us nowhere. None of us had even said a word for the last ten minutes. We needed to get off the stupid merry-go-round and uncover the truth.

"Not the whole time, but . . . yeah, for a while," Owen said.

"And what? You think she's so in love with you, she'd really give up the only life she knows?" Tristan asked, sarcasm dripping off each word.

"Well," I said, with a thought, "that could actually be her motivator. She does go to any lengths to get what she wants."

Tristan shook his head. "She *lives* for the Daemoni. She'd die for them."

"You don't know her like you think you do," Owen said quietly, and once again, the one-eighty of his allegiance felt like a slap in the face.

Tristan's expression turned to stone, and I worried he'd get in Owen's face again. But he simply narrowed his eyes and rocked back on his heels. "I knew her for over two centuries."

"You didn't *know* her," Owen countered. "You never took the time to. You ignored her as much as possible, treating her like nothing more than a pesky wasp."

"So now you've been around her for a few months and think you know her so well? What about the past decades witnessing the carnage she left? What about what she did to Sheree, who would have died if you hadn't rescued her? What she's done to Alexis? Have you forgotten all that so quickly?"

Owen broke his gaze from Tristan and looked at the wall.

His lips pursed together, and his brows drew down, creating three lines between them.

"No, I haven't forgotten that," he said in a near whisper. But then his eyes hardened as he turned them back to Tristan. "But I also haven't forgotten how you used to be, either. She can change. Like you did."

"You're so gullible," Tristan snapped.

"And you're so arrogant! What makes you think you're the only one who can change?" Owen demanded. "We get new converts all the time. You're not some unique specimen. Not in that way anyway."

"I already admitted I was wrong about Sheree. I'd been suspicious then because of everything going on at the time. But *Vanessa*? She's the poster girl for the Daemoni!"

"Just as you were once the poster boy!"

With that, the merry-go-round wound up again as they went in circles about Vanessa pulling the same scheme Lucas and Tristan had with my mom, back when he'd been Seth, and Owen defending Vanessa and her desire to change. Although I couldn't help but agree with Tristan, I stayed off the ride. But finally I could take no more.

"All right, all right!" I nearly yelled to be heard over their debate. They both shut up. "This is stupid, and it's getting us nowhere. She has to proclaim her desire to change as part of the process, and I'll be able to read her mind to know if she's telling the truth. If not, we'll have plenty of protection to overcome whatever scheme she has in mind. So you two . . . just stop, okay?"

Neither of them responded, too proud to give in.

"*Okay?*" I insisted.

Finally, Tristan barely lifted his chin to me in subtle agreement.

"I don't like it, you being that close to her," he growled, "but I'll be there if you need me. And so will your *protector*.

Right, Owen?" He bumped Owen's shoulder with his own as he came to stand by me. "*Right,* Owen?"

Owen gave us both a hard glare before heading for the door. "You won't need me," he muttered.

My jaw dropped, and tears pricked my eyes. He may as well have stabbed a knife in my heart and left me for dead. *What's happened to him?*

Tristan shook his head slowly. "He's right. We don't need him. Charlotte will be here if we need a warlock."

Owen stopped in mid-stride and spun around. "No. Mum can't be here."

"But she'll be so *pleased* to see you," I said, my tone burning with acid, "especially like this." I flipped my hand at him and all his un-Owen-ness.

"She can't be here," Owen repeated, nearly pleading. "None of the council. Not Sophia or Rina, either. Nobody can know Vanessa is here. Not even Sheree or Sonya or anyone else."

I cocked my head. "Owen, I can't convert her by myself."

"You *have* to. She's too high-profile for anyone to know what she's doing. No one can find out until it's done, after it's too late. Why do you think I brought her here? To you?"

"What? You think someone's going to tattle off to the Daemoni that Vanessa's converting?" I asked.

"That's exactly what someone might do, and guess what happens next? Guess who shows up here to get her back?"

I shook my head. "Owen, I can't . . . I mean, I don't have enough experience with the first phase, and I've never even done the second part."

"But you know *what* to do, right? What better way to learn than trial by fire?"

My breath went out in a huff of exasperation. Owen had always enjoyed pressing me to my limits to see what I was capable of, but he really had no idea what he asked of me now.

And if he did, then he didn't care what happened to Vanessa or me. So much for being anyone's protector.

"Look," I said, "I vowed to your mother I wouldn't do anything without her. There's a reason she made me make the promise. Owen, seriously, you can't trust your own mom?"

"Well, let's see," he said, his voice regaining that hard edge, "I trusted my own dad and look what happened there."

I opened my mouth to argue—as if Charlotte was anything like Martin or Kali—but decided not to. Part of me couldn't blame him.

"It's a moot point," Tristan said. "Alexis is *not* doing this on her own. The little bit of experience she has is with young ones. Vanessa is a whole different game—out of her league right now."

My hackles raised. "Her? Out of my *league*? Ha! You think I can't handle the old hag? Well, I'm pretty sure I can take her on if she tried anything. In fact, I already have, just a little while ago, remember?"

Tristan gave me a look. "That's not what I mean. This is different, and you know it."

"But she has taken on *you*," Owen said to Tristan. "And you were a lot worse than Vanessa ever was."

Tristan pursed his lips together. He wouldn't argue this point because he credited me with saving him when he'd first returned to me with the Daemoni's dark magic implanted in his soul. I kept my mouth shut. Mom had originally converted him, so what Owen referred to wasn't really my doing. But what could be worse than what Tristan had fought then? Than what I had helped him beat? Surely, if I could handle him and all his power, I could handle the vampire-bitch who'd still managed to keep her soul for more than two centuries.

I straightened my back and stuck out my chin. "Owen's right. If I could do what I did with you, especially right after going through the *Ang'dora*, I can do this."

Tristan narrowed his hazel eyes at me. "And break your

promise to Char?"

My shoulders sagged as my puffed up manner deflated. That was the kicker. I sincerely didn't want to break my promise to Charlotte, not again. I wanted her to trust me, but at this rate, she never would. I wanted Mom and Rina to trust me, too, to know they could count on me to do the right thing.

But . . . wasn't serving my purpose the right thing? Owen was certainly right about that—I couldn't refuse Vanessa. If she honestly wanted to convert, I *had* to do this for her. And sooner rather than later. Although part of me enjoyed it a little bit, I knew keeping her chained up like that for long wasn't the "right thing." How much longer until Charlotte could finally get here? Six months had already passed since her last visit.

I wished I had my dagger on me. I wanted to talk to Cassandra.

"Well, while you sit there and contemplate the future of the world, I need to go check on the subject at hand," Owen said as he once again headed for the door. "Don't take too long to make up your mind, unless you want either a dried up corpse on your hands or a dead were-tiger."

My head snapped up. "What?"

He stopped one more time, but barely turned. "I brought her to you weakened on purpose. I haven't given her blood yet —on purpose. But she's starving, and we can't leave her like this forever. I *won't* leave her like this for long at all. Understood?"

He didn't wait for an answer, but strode down the hallway and around the corner to the wing where Vanessa probably still screamed bloody murder. I looked at Tristan.

He leaned against the wall and explained. "If he feeds her, he'll not only strengthen her, but since he'll be giving her his own blood, he'll be giving her magic, too. Powerful magic. She'll be able to do things we probably don't want her to do."

"But we have animal blood—oh. Sheree will notice."

Tristan nodded. "But if we wait too long to feed Vanessa, she won't make it through the conversion. She'll either die or dry up, and it'll take our whole supply of blood to refill her. But it's Vanessa we're talking about. She has too much self-preservation to simply let herself die."

Crap. I understood now and knew that we really didn't have much time. Because Vanessa wouldn't simply lie back and take the conversion if she was starving. She was still evil. She'd attack. I had the best blood for her and probably Tristan did, too. But if she was too scared or weak to fight us, she'd go for Owen or, worse, Sheree. And from Owen's comment, he seemed pretty confident she wouldn't attack him. Once she drank, she'd be a lot more difficult to contain for the conversion. Worse yet, if this was a trick and she attacked and strengthened herself, the whole village, the whole island and Sanibel, too, would be at risk.

I cursed Owen for putting me in this situation, but, at the same time, I understood the lengths he'd gone through. He'd carefully planned this to ensure I'd say yes and to force me to move quickly and on their terms, but he'd also done what he could to make it as safe as possible for me. Right? Well . . . unless this was all part of the set-up . . . unless *he* was part of the set-up and they were reviewing their plan of attack right this very minute.

I turned to Tristan and he opened his arms. I walked into his embrace and drew on his love and strength.

"You knew the best solution all along," I mumbled against his chest. He didn't answer, but he didn't need to. "So why did you insist on arguing?"

"Just because I know the best answer doesn't mean I like it," he said. He paused for a long moment, then added, "Besides, this is a decision you need to make. You deserve a choice in the matter."

I sighed. "I don't really have a choice. As much as I *want* to hate her, as much as I have in the past, I'm Amadis and can't turn her away. I won't let her suffer any longer than she already has. This really is the best time for all of us."

"If they're even telling the truth. You know what you need to do."

I hated invading people's private thoughts, and Rina had taught me to use my gift responsibly, which meant only when necessary. But I had to know, and, really, this *was* necessary, not simple curiosity. So I found Owen's mind signature in the next wing and took a quick peek into his thoughts.

Get out of my head, Alexis, he silently growled at me. I cringed as I immediately let go of his mind.

"*Owen's* telling the truth," I said to Tristan. If Vanessa was tricking us, Owen was completely unaware. I gathered that much before he kicked me out.

"And Vanessa?"

I sought out for her mind signature, but it was distorted, and I couldn't hear her thoughts. Only muted screams. The shield Owen put up to block out the noise apparently muffled her thoughts, as well. Either that or her mind was completely focused on yelling her head off.

I shook my head. "Won't know until I get in there with her. But first, I want to see Dorian. Just in case . . . you know."

"You can't think that way, my love."

My shoulders lifted in a shrug. "I can't help it."

"You're running out of sunlight."

"I only need a few minutes. An hour. Then . . . we'll do this."

We found Dorian in the family room at home, sitting on the floor and playing some kind of war video game with Heather. Sasha sat between them, closely watching the screen and growling every time Dorian groaned when his character died, as if he himself had been hit. Tristan slipped away to his man-cave to check on a few financial things before we "disappeared" for the next day or so, but I stayed in the family room and watched the kids for a few minutes, basking in their normalcy after this morning's surreal events, until Blossom sauntered out of the kitchen.

"What are you doing here?" I asked with surprise, and my nose twitched with the sweet smell of a cake baking.

She wiped her hands on a dishcloth before giving me her usual hello hug. "I was kind of lonely, and we were supposed to hang out this weekend, so I came over a little early." I sagged in her embrace. "You have something going on, don't you?"

Guilt curled its fingers around my heart. "A, um, mission, yes."

"No worries. We'll do it another time."

I hugged her tighter before pulling back and giving her an appreciative smile. "What kind are you baking today?"

"Your favorite," she said with a teasing grin.

"Chocolate and raspberry?" I licked my lips. "Is it done yet?"

She laughed. "You'll have to wait until after you eat your dinner tonight, young lady." When I made a face, she said, "You won't even be home for dinner?"

I led her into the kitchen so we wouldn't be overheard. "Something's come up. Owen's back—"

She let out a squeal, but I held my hand up.

"Shh. I don't want Dorian to know yet. I don't know how long he's staying." I waited for Blossom to nod her understanding. "Anyway, Owen brought us, um, some information that we need to check out. If all goes well, we should be home tomorrow night, but it might not be until the next day. Can you—?"

"Of course I'll take care of Dorian."

She watched me as I began pulling out sandwich makings for an early lunch. I wasn't really hungry myself, but having lunch together gave me a reason to pull Dorian away from the game and spend time with me. And if I could manage to get anything down, it'd probably be good—I'd need the energy.

"There's something I've been wanting to talk to you about," Blossom said, and I didn't miss the careful way she spoke. I looked up from the bread I'd been smearing with mustard. "Dorian's been talking about his ability to fly a lot lately, and I had an idea. Actually, part of it was his."

"Uh-oh," I muttered as I went back to my task.

"Wait. It's a good one, actually. He said he thought you were unfair to not let him practice—these are his words, not mine—because if the bad guys ever tried to get him, he'd be able to get away."

I nearly dropped the knife with shock. We'd warned him once that bad men might want to take him, but I didn't know we'd actually scared him this much—enough that he'd been thinking about how to defend himself. *Crap.* Had I gone too far? Well, a little fear was good. You couldn't have courage without it. No fear, especially for the Daemoni, was just plain stupid.

"So you think it's a good idea?" Blossom asked, and she saw on my face that I'd missed something she said. "A cloak. I'm able to cloak him—I've done it before, remember? Then he could practice right outside. I know you're teaching him Aikido and other ways to defend himself, but if he could fly away, no one could even get him in the first place."

"Um . . . I don't know," I said. "I'll talk to Tristan about it."

"I'm strong enough to cloak and even shield him, if that's your concern. I mean, mine aren't a level five like Owen's, and I can't leave a permanent shield or cloak, even if there are other mages around to keep it up, I have to be close by for my temporary ones to stay in effect, but they aren't bad at all. Good enough to where I've done a level—"

"Hold up," I interrupted. Something she said in her rambling caught my attention. "Do we have *any* mages in the colony who can do a permanent shield?"

"Only Owen, now that he's back. The colony's never

needed one before, though. But honestly, I'm not sure if the other mages would share their power with Owen to keep a permanent shield up. They're all pretty wary of him. They're finally coming around to you and Tristan, especially knowing there's a safe house they can flee to if necessary, but they're not sure what to think about Owen, since you know, his dad and everything . . ."

She finally trailed off and took in my expression. What my face said, I had no idea, but it had probably paled. The safe house really needed a permanent shield, especially with its new VIP occupant. Perhaps the colony hadn't attracted Daemoni attention before, but Vanessa's disappearance might have them searching everywhere, including here. And if Owen took off again . . .

"Surely the local mages would keep a permanent shield up over the safe house, even if Owen was the one who put it up in the first place. Wouldn't they?" I asked. "Whatever they think about Owen, we'd only need them if he wasn't here anyway. And it's a *safe* house, after all. If they want to feel safe there, they have to help."

"Oh, they'd do the right thing when it came down to it," Blossom said quickly. "I was only saying that some people have lost a little trust in Owen. I'm sure they just need to see him again, be reminded of what a great guy he is."

I harrumphed at that. Owen *was* a great guy, but I wasn't so sure about his intentions anymore. One thing was for sure —he needed to stick around at least long enough for his little present to fully convert. We needed his shield.

Blossom gave me a questioning look. I waved it off as I took the sandwiches and a bag of chips out to the family room, made Dorian turn off the game, and we all sat on the floor for a picnic. He complained that it was too early for lunch—he'd eaten breakfast only an hour ago—but when I told him Tristan and I were leaving for a couple of nights, he agreed to at least sit with us. Being a boy with food in front of him, he quickly forgot he'd said he was stuffed full of cereal and dug into a ham sandwich.

After a few moments of silence as we all chewed, Heather reached for a handful of chips and somehow a piece broke off, flew in the air, and hit Dorian square in the forehead. They stared at each other for a long moment, but Heather couldn't keep her face straight, so Dorian picked up a whole chip and threw it at her head. Another moment of silence passed before they both busted out laughing, and the next thing I knew, chips were flying across the room. At least, until Sasha started catching them in her mouth in mid-air, then their game became how high they could toss a chip and Sasha could jump to catch it.

"Lex, we really need to go," Tristan said from the doorway, grimacing at the mess.

I'd been so engrossed in watching the kids play, I hadn't heard his approach or even noticed Blossom had gone to the kitchen after her cake. With dread, I rose to my feet and called Dorian over to me.

"I'll see you in a couple days, okay, little man?" I said as I wrapped my arms around him and held him tightly.

"And then we'll talk about Universal again?"

Wow. He really wasn't letting that one go.

"We'll see." I squeezed him tighter and kissed him on the head, which I couldn't help but notice came up to my chin now. "You guys clean up this mess. Don't leave it for Blossom."

"Sure, Mom. Love you."

"I love you, too, little man." I picked up the lykora next and nuzzled my nose into her neck, inhaling her sweet scent. Then I whispered in her ear, "Take care of him, Sasha."

Heather followed us to the door, obviously having something to say. "Thank you for letting me talk to Sonya today. It meant the world to me."

I forced a smile for her. "Thank *you* for being such a good friend to Dorian."

She gave me a real grin. "You sound like it's a chore—"

"Well, he's not exactly your age."

"No, but he's awesome. More mature than most kids his age and a lot more fun. Those Norman kids are so boring to me now." She managed to pull a small, but real smile from me. "So, um, do you think I'll get to see Sonya soon?"

I frowned. "I'd hoped so, but . . . uh . . ." I looked up at Tristan, lost at what to say. Sonya would surely be telling her that we'd considered an actual visit. With Vanessa in the house and no telling how this could turn out and how long she'd be there, I wasn't about to make any promises.

"We told Sonya it might be possible soon," Tristan said, "but we don't know how soon. Alexis and I have some important Amadis business to take care of, but we want to be there. Just in case."

Heather's eyes widened at the implication, and she nodded with understanding.

"Thanks again," she whispered, lifting her arms from her sides awkwardly, then she scrambled off, back to Dorian and their mess.

Once we returned to the safe house, I made a stop in my office to retrieve my dagger. Wearing it 24/7 felt over the top and a little ridiculous with my typical attire of shorts and tank tops, but I did try to keep it close by in case of emergencies, so in my office when I was at the safe house, or under the mattress when I was home. I wanted it on me now, though, if anything, for Cassandra's extra power.

"*You can do this*," she whispered in my mind, sounding like Rina. "*You will be fine.*"

I strapped the holster around my waist, then rubbed the amethyst to make the dagger disappear. The weight felt funny on the elastic waistband of my shorts, but I'd have to deal with it. I hoped Cassandra was right. I certainly felt comforted about the foreboding task ahead with Cassandra's presence within me.

CHAPTER 15

*a*s I left my office, I mentally called out for Sheree.

Can you hold the fort down here for the next day or two? I asked her when she responded. *Tristan, Owen, and I have a mission we need to do for Rina.*

I hated lying to her, but I had no choice. And in the end, it *was* for Rina and the Amadis, because I was simply serving my purpose and adding to our army. At least, if everything went the way I hoped it would.

"*Of course. Going out of town? Does this have to do with the trunks?*"

Um . . . no and yes. I'll tell you all about it later.

"*Don't worry about a thing here. But I can't wait to hear. Are we going to have a new patient? I'm getting a little bored . . .*"

Heh. Her wish would be answered, but if she knew *whom* our new patient was, she'd be eating her words, I was sure. At least she wouldn't be bored anymore.

I don't know. Which was true, because I didn't know if I'd end up killing Vanessa instead of saving her. But even if the vampire survived, it'd be a while, probably a long while, before Sheree could learn the truth. I had no idea how we would keep that secret from her. *But don't get your hopes up. I don't expect to be seeing Charlotte.*

There. That should help. She knew I wasn't to proceed with a conversion without Charlotte's help, so she'd never suspect. I hoped.

The hallway that led to Vanessa's room felt dark and ominous, as if we really did traverse the dungeons of an ancient European castle rather than a mansion on the beach in bright and sunny Florida. I projected my own fear into my surroundings, of course. The sense of impending doom shaded the walls and floor in a somber gray, although golden sunlight poured through the banks of windows at each end. The nearly non-existent shadows outside meant it was almost noon—we'd already wasted precious hours of sunlight and even the slightest bit of weakness in our patient would help.

The door to the vampire's temporary accommodations was closed, probably to keep out said sunlight. She must have heard our approach, however, because it swung open from the other side. Owen hurried us in and closed the door quickly behind us. My eyes adjusted to the true darkness of the room immediately.

The heavy curtains were drawn tight, completely blocking out the sun. A single lamp was lit on the bedside table. Vanessa leaned limply against the wall, practically hanging from her shackled wrists. Owen had magically fashioned a tunic out of the tan blanket to cover her nakedness, for which I was grateful. I was almost surprised she wasn't shrieking about its ugliness, as well as the braces on her limbs, but she'd apparently exhausted her energy. She had to know we'd entered the room, but her eyes remained closed, and her face had never looked so vulnerable.

"Vanessa," I tried to say, but nothing came out except a croak. For some reason, it occurred to me that I'd never called her by name to her face. I cleared my throat and tried again. "Vanessa?"

"What?" she mumbled without opening her eyes.

My brain had such a hard time processing this scene—how soft and helpless my worst enemy was before me. How much she trusted me and didn't even try to put up any kind of defense in case I attacked. We could have killed her with one swipe of my dagger and a fireball from Tristan's palm, yet she showed no fear. No, she wasn't fearless. She was without care. As if she wanted to die.

Don't be a fool. It could all be part of her plan. My internal warning bells sounded. I couldn't take her for granted, not for one moment.

I latched onto her mind signature and worked my way into her head before I prompted her thoughts. Her mind was open, relaxed, though I could feel a thread of fear in its deep recesses. But her prominent thought was discomfort.

"Owen says you want to convert," I said to bring up the subject in her mind.

"Yes," she murmured, and her face remained calm even as her thoughts ran wild. "*He said she'd do it, but I don't think so. How could she accept me as one of her own? She should have killed me by now. Why hasn't she? If she doesn't convert me and doesn't kill me, Owen will have to. I can't ever go back now. Never!*"

Her thoughts sounded sincere, and I sensed nothing to contradict them, but I wouldn't know the real truth until we began. I just didn't want to begin.

"You'll have to declare it," I said as I made my way slowly around the room, running my fingers over the velour upholstery of the wingback chair Owen sat in, straightening the throw pillows on the unused bed, smoothing down the curtains as if to be sure not a crack of light came through. I didn't have this time to waste, but the thought of touching the vampire made my insides squirm. Vanessa's lips parted, as if to say something, but I stopped her. "Not now. Not yet. In a moment."

I was within touching distance of her now. I only had to reach out with my arm and place my hand on her skin to begin. She sensed my closeness. Her eyes fluttered open, and she stared at me with a faraway look.

"Do what you need to do," she said.

"It's going to hurt," I warned.

Her head moved slightly in a nod. "Owen told me it would be horrible. But this is what I want."

"Are you sure?" Again, I was delaying. Her answer didn't matter until I was feeding her Amadis power, when she'd actually feel in her soul everything her decision meant.

A single tear rolled down her cheek. Her voice came out in a weak whisper. "I want to be loved. Not hated."

Something happened in my chest. To my heart. A tiny crack opened. For her, for this vampire who'd always tried to kill me, who I'd sworn to kill by my own hands. An opening to allow my innate enemy in. A lump formed in my throat as the warmth of Amadis love and power flowed through my body. For some reason, this one statement from Vanessa affected my natural instincts more than anyone I'd worked with before, except Tristan. More love and goodness than I could hold built within my core, about to explode its way out. If I didn't maintain control, this could be disastrous.

Well, I might just love you to death. Then we'd both get our way.

I almost chuckled at my own thought, until I saw the look on Vanessa's face. She showed more fear at this moment than I'd ever seen in her before. More than when I'd almost fried her in Australia. More than when Tristan turned his power on her. She sensed the energy I was about to unleash and feared it.

But she also showed resolve. At this moment, she exemplified the definition of courage.

"Do it," she whispered.

I pulled in a deep breath, braced myself for the immense pain I knew would come, and lifted my hand to her.

Oh, god, oh, god, oh, god. Please, Angels, I beg for strength.

The thought of touching Vanessa—*Vanessa!*—in any way besides a punch or a kick scared the crap out of me. Or perhaps it was the growing power that scared me so much. I'd never felt this way before. As though something within my core *wanted* to reach into her soul and grab it, heal it, change her to be more like me. My heart jackhammered against my ribs. My chest swelled with so much power . . . so much *love!* And I didn't understand it.

Why? Why did she, of all people, make me feel as though this really was my purpose? Why did something within me want this so badly when a big part of me wasn't even positive *she* wanted it? When my brain screamed *trap, trap, trap?*

My hand shook in midair, following my brain's orders to stay away. *Don't do it*, my mind said. *Love thy enemy*, my heart countered.

"*Reach out to those who need you most*," Cassandra added.

But I didn't have to reach out to Vanessa.

No longer able to contain the power within the confines of my corporeality, my body exploded. At least, that's how it felt. The energy of love and goodness erupted like a volcano, shooting out of me and pouring directly over Vanessa, a soft light bathing her as the lava of my power drenched her body.

Her ice-blue eyes popped open wide and so did her mouth, but no noise issued forth. She looked more shocked than anything, and I probably mirrored her expression. Where was the pain, for either of us? Why didn't she spasm and convulse as the others had? Why didn't I feel . . . anything? The only sensation I had was that of Tristan's and Owen's eyes staring at us in awe.

"Vanessa," I whispered hoarsely. Her stunned gaze fluttered toward me. "Say it now. Declare your motives."

Her eyes locked on mine. "I want this. I want to be Amadis."

"Why?"

"I want love," she said flatly, as if nothing could be more obvious. As if the words didn't come out of the most hateful mouth I'd ever heard speak. But somehow what she said made as much sense to me as it obviously did to her. "I want to love others. I want to be loved. I want to be the person I am meant to be. Not who everyone else thinks I am." She whimpered, but still, not in pain. Not physical pain, anyway. Fat tears rolled down her cheeks as her head dropped, and her gaze broke from mine. "Nobody knows the real me. Only Owen has seen through my façade."

I shook my head. "God knows. He sees your heart."

"Not Satan," she moaned. "He's caused all this. His deceit, his lies . . . he caused all this pain I've suffered for so long."

"No, not Satan. The true God. You must accept our God as yours."

She lifted her head and looked at me again. Conviction swirled in her eyes as they held mine.

"I do," she whispered, and I didn't have to read her mind to know she meant it. Her desire for light and love to enter her heart was palpable.

Without any warning, my body launched itself at her. I wrapped my arms around her and held her tightly against me.

And with the collision of good and evil energies finally came the intense pain.

The dark energy within her was so much greater and so much more powerful than I'd ever felt before, even with Tristan. Our high-pitched screams tangled together into an eerie song. I hung onto her in a death-grip as our bodies convulsed against each other's in a freakish dance. Tristan or Owen must have released her arms from their shackles, because they were suddenly around me, holding on as if I were her life preserver. Which, at this point, I probably was.

We collapsed to the floor, and the clash of the opposing powers rocked us back and forth. I pushed my Amadis power against her Daemoni energy, and it pushed back. Hard. The iciness of the evil slid into my veins, but I willed the warmth of love to melt it, boil it, evaporate it. But just as I felt warm again, more ice prickled its way in. I fought it, again and again and again. The darkness only seemed to strengthen.

Tristan said—or perhaps simply thought—something about night. Had that many hours already passed? Nightfall would explain the increased struggle. If the sun had set, the Daemoni power in Vanessa would no longer be at its weakest. So I gathered my own strength and willed it into her, fighting, fighting, fighting.

Until I could fight no more.

What did Charlotte say about becoming too drained? I couldn't remember now. My brain was too fuzzy. Something about being drained of my energy was bad. Very bad.

I closed my eyes as I tried to focus on the goodness still within me and share it with Vanessa. Visions that weren't mine appeared in my mind. Images of corpses, pale faces with vacant eyes, savaged throats . . . Vanessa's kills. With each flash of an image, she experienced a mix of remorse and glee. And then there was only blood. Blood *everywhere*. I felt her thirst, her present need to feed, her desire to feed on me.

No! I tried to yell at her, but it came out weakly. *Vanessa . . . you're stronger . . . than . . . the desire. You . . . can . . . fight it.*

I felt her try, felt the thirst diminish a bit. Then a somewhat familiar vision popped into my mind, although I saw it from a different perspective—Vanessa's. We'd just flashed into the fight at the beach house right after I'd gone through the *Ang'dora*, and Vanessa got her first look at me after the change. Anger and hatred boiled up within her again, mirroring her feelings back then, but more than anything she felt envy. And not only because of Tristan.

"*You have everything!*" she'd thought. "*Everything! How do you get it all and I get nothing? I was supposed to have it all! ME!"*

Her current feelings escalated to nearly pure hatred, and her mind filled with various ways to kill me. I fought back, pushing what Amadis power I still had into her, pulling the evil energy away from her. But my power was weak and the Daemoni energy too strong. The ice stabbed into my veins again.

The next thing I knew, I no longer held Vanessa in my arms. My head came back to the darkly lit room to find Owen holding her instead, securing her limbs tightly against her convulsing body so they wouldn't flail. I was across the room, in Tristan's lap, his arms around me.

"No!" I jumped to my feet, away from him. "Don't you do this! Don't you take the power."

"I'm not, my love. I'm not." He reached up for my hands. "I'm giving you what you need."

The energy of his love flowed through my hands and up my arms. When I didn't feel a pull, as I did when he'd tried to leech the Daemoni power out of me before, I relaxed and let him pull me back into his lap. He wrapped his arms around me again and pushed his love through every place where our skin touched. Under different circumstances, I would have been tearing our clothes off for the increased skin contact.

"Is it working?" he asked after a while.

"Yeah," I murmured with my eyes still closed as I continued to picture his naked body against mine. Even the thought of it seemed to build my power even more, so I had a good reason for the naughty vision.

"Good. She needs you," Owen said, and the image vanished. I reluctantly opened my eyes.

"Patience," Tristan told him. "You insisted on Alexis doing this by herself, so she needs to go slow. I won't let this kill her." When Owen opened his mouth, Tristan added, "Either of them, if we can help it. But you know my choice if one needs to be made."

Owen stared at us long and hard, then finally muttered, "Let's hope we don't have to choose."

Vanessa's seizures had died down, but she began to moan.

"Seth," she cried, tears seeping between the lashes of her closed lids. Tristan's old name wasn't a cry of desire, though, at least not in a lustful way. Longing filled the sound, and deep sadness. The image came to me clearly.

Through her eyes, I watched from a distance as Tristan took hold of my mom's hands. He gazed at her face with complete trust. Her lips moved, and her voice traveled to our vampire ears: "You're sure this is what you want?"

Tristan nodded. And then they both disappeared.

"No!" Vanessa cried. "Don't leave me! Take me with you!"

Probably unintentionally, she shared her intense feelings of abandonment, loneliness, loss as "her" Seth went with my mom to be converted. "*I want to go, too,*" her mind whispered. But then her anger overwhelmed her once again. Anger at Seth and even more at my mother for taking him away . . . and for leaving her behind. Why would Mom leave her behind, though? If Vanessa really wanted to convert way back then, why wouldn't Mom do it? Vanessa's thoughts answered for me: she wasn't ready to voice it aloud then. She still hadn't been sure that's what she wanted. So instead, she let anger and hate rule her life for another thirty years. That was her comfort zone.

I went to her again and took her out of Owen's arms and into my own. Another wave of pain engulfed both of us, but not quite as bad as before. As our energies fought, her memories continued to fill my mind, as though we moved backwards through her life. More kills, more dead faces, more blood.

And then . . . in Vanessa's mind, we sat with a familiar person draped across our lap, holding his shoulders in our left arm, his head lolled back on a limp neck and his white-blond hair falling to the sides. Victor, Vanessa's brother, wore what seemed to be the fashion of early Victorian London, and he was dead. Tiny streams of blood leaked out of two puncture-wounds on his neck, and the taste of it lingered on our tongue. Regret combined with the thrill of revenge filled Vanessa's thoughts as she gazed at her brother.

"How dare you!" yelled an icy male voice, the owner unseen in our vision. "Don't let him die! Turn him!"

Vanessa had changed her own brother? I couldn't believe what I was experiencing, but I could feel the truth coming from her.

A wave of pain wracked through us both, and the vision disappeared. We rode the crest, and as it receded, more memories flooded back. We lay on a bed in a room with brown, stone walls, where shadows danced from flickering candlelight. Or perhaps our vision made the room flicker as pain roiled through us. Not current pain—at least I didn't think so—the sensation was dulled by time. Vanessa's breaths labored in our lungs, and we felt weak, so weak. "*I'm dying*," she thought, convinced of it.

Then we must have been lying on a bed as another familiar face loomed over us—that of the vampire who had demanded I stop writing, the one I thought had been my own character Claudius when I had believed he was only a dream. But we weren't dreaming now. We were remembering.

"Your weakness is abhorrent! Now you will be strong and more suitable," said the same voice that had ordered Vanessa to turn Victor rather than let him die. The vampire standing over us hadn't spoken, though. The sound had come from our right.

Our eyes drifted over to a man's silhouette standing at a window. His back was to us as he stared into the blackness beyond, but Vanessa knew him, knew him well. Her father? No, I didn't think so. But somewhat of a father figure. At least, he might have been, but as the vampire's mouth clamped onto her neck, she only felt hatred toward the man at the window. He was taking everything she ever wanted away. She would have rather died.

With the renewed anger and hatred, the Daemoni power boosted once again. We fought it together, but Vanessa weakened to it quickly. I gave her all the goodness I could muster, but I, too, began to drain again. And once more, I found myself back in the present room, shivering in Tristan's lap.

"I'm s-so c-c-cold," I stammered between chattering teeth. The Daemoni power had come closer to overpowering me than I'd realized. Tristan rubbed his hands up and down my arms, trying to warm me. "K-k-kiss. I need-d-d a k-k-kiss."

I tilted my head up to lift my face to his, and his mouth pressed gently to mine, then harder as our lips separated and our tongues danced. Yes, exactly what I'd needed. The love was so much more powerful and so much more direct through the kiss than through the skin. He kissed me long and deep, and I pulled in his goodness.

"Don't take it," I said to him when we'd finally broken apart, knowing he'd understand what I meant.

"I won't," he promised. "The sun will be rising soon. It should become easier."

I remained in his embrace until we felt the evil power weaken in Vanessa from the sun's appearance outside. Then I sucked in a breath, let the Amadis power build up again, and went back to the vampire's side.

Vanessa, I spoke into her mind. *Do you remember love?*

A new image popped into my mind—Tristan's face. But he looked a little different and it took me a moment to realize I saw him through Vanessa's eyes for the very first time, over two hundred years ago. Her heart swelled, and she knew she loved him at first sight. I squelched the jealousy creeping into my own heart and focused on my patient.

That's right, I said, my inner voice shaking. *Remember love.*

But the Daemoni power fought back, and suddenly we were upset again. Seth had just rejected us. *"But we're* supposed *to be together,"* Vanessa cried silently as he walked away without a backward glance. Our heart ripped apart into pieces, shards cutting into our soul. But then resolve mended our wounds, and determination to have him filled us. Her desire grew into more than love and lust, but into a selfish need to prove herself right. I didn't understand what that meant, but knew, as the evil power started building again, I needed to get her back on track.

Love, Vanessa. Think of love—those you've loved, those who have loved you.

I thought it worked as an image of teenaged Victor filled our thoughts. Both he and Vanessa were pre-vampire now, yet . . . not completely human. What were they, if not Norman before they were changed? A question I couldn't worry about now.

Vanessa had loved her brother, and I refocused my thoughts on him, but I also felt jealousy in her, especially as Victor turned and joined a man who was only a foggy figure at the fringe of our vision. As he turned, I thought it could have been the same man who'd been at the window, calling her weak and allowing her humanity to be taken away. A white-blond ponytail hung down his back, just as one trailed down Victor's. The man draped an arm over Victor's shoulder as they sauntered off, leaving Vanessa to feel abandoned, outcast, lonely, crying in the corner of a cavernous room with the only light flickering from torches on the wall. She only wanted to be loved and included, but neither of them seemed to care, strengthening my belief that the man probably wasn't her father. Perhaps a sperm donor, but not a father. Not to her, anyway.

Vanessa felt the hurt and jealousy again, feeding the evil energy. The Daemoni power within her took on a new urgency, growing stronger and more intense. I built up my own power, readying myself to fight it. *This could be it. Final battle coming soon.*

Vanessa's thoughts lost their cohesiveness. Images of living in a castle mixed with the wonder of being brought to live there dissolved into earlier memories of a crumbling cottage that had once been their home. The vision of a pretty woman's face—their mother?—filled our minds now, and I knew Vanessa did love her.

That's right. Focus on love.

A high shrieking sound pierced my ears as the evil energy protested, building and growing, becoming a gigantic dark cloud enshrouding Vanessa, trying to fill the entire room. The air froze around us, the chill seeping into my bones.

I'd been right—this was it. The final battle for Vanessa's soul.

CHAPTER 16

That's right, Vanessa. Remember love. You can be loved! You can love again!

Vanessa's mom or caregiver or whoever she was spoke sweetly to her, and although I couldn't hear the words, I encouraged Vanessa's mind to latch onto the kind voice. I focused on my own love, my goodness, the Amadis power within me, creating that bubble inside me and growing it until I could contain it no more.

Vanessa shrieked as the evil energy exploded from her, and I cried out, too, as my Amadis power burst from me once again. The powers collided and fought around and inside us. Vanessa's body trembled and quaked and seized in my arms.

Fight! I screamed at her. *If you want this, you'll fight it. And you'll win! Let goodness win, Vanessa. Release the darkness. You can do this!*

And she fought. Even as she drew on my power, my heart swelled with pride and conviction. My soul burst with love for her, for her determination, her perseverance to overcome what had dwelled inside of her for so long. I pushed as hard as she pulled. And we were winning. Winning! The Daemoni energy warred against us, but the Amadis power was stronger.

But she kept pulling with vehemence, strengthening her goodness with mine, until I had no more to share. And still, she tried to pull more, eagerly lapping it up like blood, draining me as if she were feeding off me. In some distant corner of my consciousness, which was fading quickly, I felt a stream of love pushing into me.

Tristan? What was he doing? I was still connected with Vanessa. The powers were still battling it out. If he held on, if the energies . . . *Shit*. What did Charlotte say would happen? I still couldn't remember. Bad, though. Very bad.

The clashing energies suddenly withdrew and separated. They each built up, two clouds, one black and the other bright-white, growing, churning, intensifying. Electricity charged through every cell of my being. And as if they actually had minds and planned the assault, the energies charged at one another.

The crash of the collision pierced my ears, and the pain rattled my bones.

Vanessa screamed. So did I.

Then I lost it. Lost everything. I had no more to give, no more to keep me in the battle.

Everything fell silent. Went black.

Then gray.

Then muted sounds. Heavy breathing. Sobbing. Whimpering. A soothing voice trying to quiet another.

My consciousness slowly returned. I lay on the floor. No. On Tristan's lap. His face came into focus above me, his eyes filled with concern.

"Is it over?" I asked, my voice a hoarse whisper. He nodded. The relief lasted only a moment as the memory of Charlotte's warning shot through me. If I allowed my energy to be drained during a conversion, the evil energy would be transferred, not eliminated. And Vanessa had drained me. I bolted upright. "Oh, no! Did you take it? Did you take the dark power?"

He shook his head. "No, my love. I'm good."

"Owen?" My head twisted, my focus shooting across the room until it landed on him, with a very limp Vanessa in his arms.

He shook his head, too. "I'm fine."

I studied Vanessa's face—relaxed, even more beautiful in its serenity.

"But it worked?" I asked.

"I feel no evil energy left within her," Owen said. "Not even a trace."

"*Really?*" I couldn't believe it. Six months since her conversion, Sonya still had traces of Daemoni power. And she'd only been Daemoni for a few years. Sheree said that was normal, that the residual energy could linger for months or even longer. How could Vanessa be eliminated of it already? I crawled out of Tristan's lap and over to Owen and Vanessa to see for myself. I pressed my hand to Vanessa's chest, over her heart, and assessed her.

Owen was right. Not a trace. I had done it. I'd converted Vanessa. Freakin' *Vanessa*!

"*You did well,*" Cassandra said softly.

Thank you, I told her.

"*It was all you, Alexis. You and the power you've been given.*" With that, her presence disappeared.

To be one-hundred-percent positive the vamp wasn't hiding anything, I tapped into her mind. The voice of the woman from her vision—the one I'd told her to latch onto and remember—floated through her thoughts:

"*Hidden daughter of enemy and ally will offer strength and valor to the worthy. Yet first, she must unite with son of power and war. Only when together will they anchor victory over foe.*

"*That's your prophecy, Vanessa. Don't let anyone convince you otherwise.*"

Vanessa's eyes fluttered open at the sound of my gasp, and

she looked at me without focus then up at Owen above her. Her gaze sharpened, and she clawed at her throat.

"So . . . thirsty," she croaked, and all three of us—Tristan, Owen, and me—stiffened for a moment. Then Owen stretched out his arm, obviously planning to give her his wrist.

"Wait!" I said. "Do we really want to do that?"

Owen eyed me. "She needs to drink."

"But your blood is too powerful."

Owen glanced at Tristan and back at me. "It's the weakest blood here. We have no other options, do we?"

I grimaced. "Yes, we do. Let's do this right."

"Sheree will notice missing supplies," Tristan said.

"I know, but too bad. She's going to find out sooner or later anyway." I stood, a little too quickly—pinpricks of light danced across my vision. I, too, was still weak. Tristan caught my wobbly frame and sat me down in the wingback chair.

"I'll get it," he said, and he disappeared.

I didn't know how Sheree would take Vanessa's presence, now that the vampire was nearly converted. Sure, she had much faith-healing to go through, but I was still amazed that she held no trace of Daemoni power. She was less Daemoni now than Sonya. So maybe Sheree would feel that and forgive the vampire for her past. After all, forgiveness was part of being Amadis, and she knew that as well as anyone. It was part of her teachings. And if *I* could forgive Vanessa, hopefully Sheree could, too.

In less than a minute after he'd flashed, Tristan opened the bedroom door and slid inside, two bottles of animal blood in his hands. Owen lifted Vanessa and carried her to the bed, while I pulled the bedding back. He took the bottles from Tristan, twisted the lid off of one, and held it to the vampire's lips. She drank greedily, pulling long draws without even tasting them. At least at first. As she finished off the first bottle, her body lurched, and her hand flew to her mouth, as if to keep the blood from spewing out.

"That's *disgusting*," she said.

"I told you the rules," Owen said.

"I know, but *ugh*."

"You feel better, though, right?"

She made a face and took the second bottle. After a full-body shudder, she drank that one down, too. Then she finally turned her blue eyes on Tristan and me. And they were as icy as ever.

"Is there a reason you're still here?" she asked.

My eyebrows shot up. "Excuse me?"

"Was I not clear? What the hell are you still doing here?"

"Vanessa," Owen warned.

"What? I'd just like a little privacy for a while," she said, sticking her bottom lip out in a pout and making her eyes big, as if feigned innocence could excuse her rudeness. "I feel like I've been ripped apart and put back together—oh, wait. I *have* been, remember? You *chopped* my body up into pieces. Chopped me up! Do you have any idea what that's like? And then to put myself back together . . . And my *insides*. Gah! All this Amadis power in my body . . ." She shuddered again. "I'm so fucking sorry if I need some time to get used to it."

I swallowed down what I wanted to say and simply nodded. "I could use some rest myself, but one thing. Where's my pendant?"

Vanessa's eyes darted away from mine, and she shrugged. "I don't know."

"You don't know?" I echoed without an ounce of belief. I peeked into her mind, which focused on the fact that she had nothing to her name now, not even clothes on her back, let alone the pendant.

She looked back at me, straight into my eyes. "I. Don't. Know."

Owen? I reached out to the warlock. *Did you get it?*

He pursed his lips. "*I looked for it, but couldn't find it in her*

189

stuff. She'll tell us eventually. Give her time, and she'll come around, Alexis."

"Weren't you leaving?" Vanessa snapped.

Again, I bit my tongue, holding back a few choice words for both of them, and moved for the door. When Tristan stood to leave with me, Vanessa's eyes watered, and I thought she would beg him to stay. But her gaze flicked away, and she stared at the wall for a moment, then looked at Owen. The tears disappeared as a small smile formed on her lips. I didn't want to see anymore. I flashed out of the room, only to go as far as my office, blinking against the late-afternoon daylight flooding through the windows, a shock after the near darkness of Vanessa's room.

"I thought eliminating the Daemoni power was the hard part," I said to Tristan as soon as he appeared. "But she still has a lot of bitch left in her, doesn't she?"

"Faith-healing should help . . . but I doubt you'll ever get rid of all of it. That's just who she is."

"Great. And I barely have a clue of what I'm doing with this next phase. I kind of wish I could ask Sheree for help."

"I'm right here," the were-tiger called from the other side of the closed door.

Ugh. Sometimes I still forgot how good everyone's hearing was. I waved my hand, and the door opened. I couldn't help the smile that broke on my face—I often forgot I could move things with my mind, too, and the coolness factor never became old. Sheree grinned back at me.

"So?" she asked. "How did it go?"

"Um . . ." I looked at Tristan but he simply looked back at me, no help at all. "Sort of good, I guess. I'll be pretty busy for a while, though . . ."

My thought went unfinished when Sheree lifted her nose in the air and sniffed, then made a face mixed with disgust and surprise. She came closer to me and sniffed again. Her eyes widened with alarm. "*Vanessa?* You found her?"

Crap. Crap, crap, crap. "You can smell her? Her specifically?"

She wrinkled her nose. "You never forget the stench of someone who almost killed you for fun. At least, this shifter doesn't."

Which meant she'd eventually detect the vampire's scent in the safe house. The only reason I could figure that she hadn't smelled Vanessa in the trunks was because of Owen's protection on them. Or maybe chopped up body parts lost their scent since they were no longer an actual being? I fought the shudder that tingled my spine at that thought. I could soak my eyes in bleach and still never rid myself of the image of Vanessa putting herself back together.

"Yes, we found her," Tristan said. "Owen did, anyway, and she's actually—"

I couldn't let him say it, not yet. She'd have some kind of stressful reaction to the news, and I wanted to be there for her completely. I didn't know how Charlotte could do back-to-back conversions, but they drained me, and right now, I was too exhausted to be the friend Sheree deserved.

"She's incapacitated," I interrupted. "For now anyway. We had a pretty rough fight."

Sheree nodded. "No wonder you look so bad. Sorry, but you look like you could use some rest and regeneration. You'll tell me what happened later?"

I gave her a weak smile. "Yeah, of course." *No matter how badly I don't want to.*

Tristan called me out after we arrived home and were in our own bedroom. "You know it's better to tell her before she finds Vanessa on her own."

"I know," I said as I fell backwards on the bed, too tired to hold myself upright any longer. After further thought, I moaned and covered my hands with my face. "I should go back and tell her, shouldn't I? I just wanted a little rest before—"

Tristan leaned over me, moved my hands off my face, and placed a finger over my lips. "Rest, my love. I'll take care of it."

"Don't . . . tell . . ." I drifted off.

I awoke still fully clothed at 12:22 a.m. to Tristan sleeping next to me and a tray on the nightstand. After my eyes adjusted to the darkness, I slowly sat up and placed the tray over my lap, finding a bottle of orange juice sitting in a small bucket of ice, a bunch of grapes, and a roll of Tristan's handmade sushi in a container kept cold with an icepack. Judging by the size of the ice cubes and the chill of the icepack, he hadn't been asleep for long, so I let him be while I quietly ate the dinner he'd prepared for me. My mind remained relaxed and open, finding only Dorian's sleeping signature. Tristan must have relieved Blossom of her babysitting duties.

As I placed the tray back on the nightstand after finishing, Tristan rolled over, throwing the sheet off of his upper body. His arm slung over my lap and his fingers slid under my thigh in an embrace although he still slept. My fingers traced over his muscular forearm and then up, admiring the contour of the mounds and dips of his bicep, tricep, and shoulder. Even in sleep, they were rock-hard. My groin tightened, and although I really wanted Tristan to wake up, he'd already done so much for me and deserved to rest. So I carefully slid out of bed and padded to the adjoining bathroom.

Enjoying the peace of the middle of the night, I lit candles around the bathroom rather than flipping on the overhead lights. I turned on the faucet for the separate tub and poured a generous dose of bubble bath into it, but while it filled, I stepped into the shower to wash my hair. I had just rinsed out the conditioner when Tristan joined me, very naked and very hard.

A smile threatened to break across my face as I looked at him with innocent eyes. "I didn't mean to wake you."

His lips danced with his own smile. "I'll never complain about being woken to this."

He pulled me into his arms, pressing our naked bodies together. His love flowed through the skin-to-skin contact, and I pulled on it, needing this for true regeneration. I tilted my face up toward his, and he bent down to deliver an amazing kiss that spread warmth throughout my body. Our tongues flicked and danced together. I pulled on his bottom lip with my teeth, and he returned the gesture, sucking a line of desire from every nerve of my body. On their own accord, my hips ground against him.

Our mouths stayed locked together in a mind-numbing kiss as our hands slid along our wet bodies, exploring and playing and teasing. As the water rained down, I made my way over his chest and abs, licking and sucking the rivulets as they slid down his skin, until I was on my knees. I took him in my hands and then my mouth.

"Ah, Lex," he moaned pleasurably as my tongue and hands caressed him and my mouth sucked.

As much as he obviously enjoyed it, he didn't let me play for long. His hands grasped my waist and lifted me to my feet. After another kiss, he used his power to raise me up until my belly button was at his eye level. He moved me against the wall, gripped my thighs, and pushed my legs up and open. He looked up at me with a devious smile before his gaze traveled down my body. His eyes smoldered as they took me in, and he licked his lips, igniting a fire within me at the anticipation. He kissed and sucked and nibbled the insides of one thigh from hip to knee, making my body quake with need, and when he started at the other knee and worked his way in, I thought I'd die from the torture of waiting one more second for his mouth to reach its final destination. And then it did, and I whimpered with the first lick. His lips and tongue and fingers moved in unimaginable ways, bringing wave after wave of orgasm crashing over me.

"I want you . . . inside me," I finally panted, the need for him to fill me overwhelming. But he didn't obey until I came once more.

Then he released my thighs and his power over me, and I skimmed down the wall until I reached the right place, then slid onto him. We both moaned as his inches filled me. Then we were all animal, savage, thrusting and bucking and slamming against the shower walls. Twisting and flipping and clawing at the tiles until our minds shattered and the raw passion consumed us, leaving us trembling against each other on the shower floor.

Not until we turned the shower faucet off and still heard water flowing did I remember the tub. Bubbles spilled over the side, but the damage wasn't too bad. Good thing it was an extra-large tub. After draining a few inches and mopping up the floor with a couple of towels, we sank into the water together. Tristan leaned against the back of the tub, and I sat between his legs and leaned against him. We lay there peacefully, candlelight dancing around us, until the last bubble disappeared, my energy replenishing with his undying love.

Yet it still wasn't as strong as it should have been.

When we arrived at the safe house the next day, we found Owen sitting in Sonya's room, visiting with the vamp and Sheree. Sheree practically sat on his lap, while Sonya's expression exposed her own hunger for Owen. Maybe it was only his blood she desired—she didn't exactly love the animal blood any more than Vanessa did—but I didn't think so. What was I going to do with him? With all of them?

Withholding a few names I felt like calling Owen, I shook my head and told Sheree I needed to meet with her in an hour.

"What does he think he's doing?" I muttered to Tristan as

we headed for Vanessa's wing. I needed to take care of the vamp before I could do anything else, such as spill the news to Sheree. "He just leaves his charge all alone to go flirt with those other two?"

"Scarecrow's got his mojo back," Tristan said. A grunt of annoyance escaped my throat. "I thought you wanted him to find a girlfriend."

"One, Tristan. *One.* Not three. And two of them are spiritually unstable and when the other sees who she's competing against, she might become mentally unstable." I groaned with frustration. "He shouldn't be playing with their minds and hearts like this Especially since *he's* the one who brought Vanessa here. He should be focused on her. She isn't exactly pleasant when she's jealous."

"No. And if she has second thoughts—"

"She won't have second thoughts," I said automatically. "Not about converting."

"You're sure?"

I thought about why that reply had come to me so easily, why I was convinced she really wanted this and didn't do it only to make Owen happy. Well, obviously, converting didn't lock Owen down into any kind of commitment, and I still wasn't sure which side *he* was on. He seemed to care enough about Vanessa's desire to change to make it happen for her, but for *her*, not for him. Which made me question his motives even more.

But Vanessa's motives? They'd come clear to me through her memories. She'd lived lies all of her long, miserable life, including the biggest lie of who she really was—under all the evil and innate bitchiness, she really just wanted love and acceptance. I hoped, once she felt those two things through the Amadis, she'd open up and tell me more about her life. I had so many questions about what I'd seen, and I knew she'd barely scratched the surface of what dwelt within her.

"I'm positive," I said to Tristan as we reached Vanessa's

door with two more bottles of blood in hand. We stopped to listen, but the room on the other side remained silent. I whispered, "Maybe we shouldn't bother her yet."

"You already have," she said from inside, her normally musical voice marred with annoyance. "May as well come in, especially if you have blood for me. I'm parched."

I drew in a deep breath, made a here-goes-nothing face at Tristan and turned the knob on the door. From her seat at the top of the bed, she appraised Tristan with her eyes, obviously still liking what she saw even if she'd finally given up on the idea of the two of them together. Her little smile turned into a smirk when she looked at me, but when Tristan held up the bottles of blood, her face twisted with disgust.

"Ick. Not again. When do I get *real* blood? Owen said I'd get mage donor blood."

"First, we rebuild your strength gradually to make sure you're ready for that much power," I said.

She smirked at me again. "Still afraid of me?"

I crossed my arms over my chest. "I haven't been afraid of you for years."

Well, not even two years, since I'd gone through the *Ang'dora*, but those were details.

Tristan opened a bottle for her and held it out. She stared at me a long moment and tilted her head. The look in her eyes seemed to change—she knew and appreciated that I'd stand up to her—then she took the bottle and drank without further comment.

"So," she said after finishing the first bottle and setting it on the nightstand, "what are these rules I have to learn? Let's get this over with. The sooner I can get out of this room—" she glanced at the shackles chained to the walls "—the better."

I frowned, now feeling badly about the way I'd treated her. No, she was no Mother Theresa right now and probably never would be, but she was definitely a billion times better than she'd been before, and I'd tried to beat the crap out of her and then strung her up like a prisoner in the middle ages.

She grunted. "Don't get all soft on me now. I *am* still a monster. Don't worry about that. I just want to get out of here and get on with my new life." She gave me a broad smile about as sincere as a politician's promises.

Tristan rubbed the back of his neck. "I don't know how soon you can do that, but we'll see about getting you into a more normal bedroom soon."

"We have some logistics to still work out," I said, as I moved the winged back chair around to the side of her bed. "And first, you have more work to do."

She gave me her full attention, those icy blue eyes piercing me. "Like what?"

CHAPTER 17

I wanted to start by ordering her to tell me where I'd find my pendant, but that would have been selfish. Although retrieving the stone remained a top priority, Vanessa's soul and well-being came first. Owen was right—she needed time to adjust—so I forced myself to be patient and snuffed out my burning curiosity.

"Like you have some sins to repent for," I said, making my voice as kind as possible although her snarky attitude brought the worst out of me.

Vanessa rolled her eyes. "Oh, please. Is this like a 12-step program those Norman idiots do? Can't I just move on with my new life and forget the past?"

"First of all, watch how you talk about the norms. They're our friends. *Your* friends now." I reached out to grab her hand, ignoring her eye-roll. "And sorry, but it doesn't work like that."

"What are you doing?" she shrieked as she jerked away, her back pressing against the headboard as if she tried to become part of it.

My heart had jumped with her sudden movement and now pounded a little too quickly. "You need a boost of Amadis power."

"And you have to hold my hand? Can't Seth do that? Or Owen? Where the hell is Owen, anyway? Did he abandon me already?"

"Skin-to-skin contact is more direct and best. *Tristan*— that's his name—doesn't have my power and neither does Owen. And no, he hasn't abandoned you." I kept the "not yet anyway" to myself.

She looked down at my hand still lying palm up on her bed and hissed. "You only want in my head."

I pressed my fingers to my temple, trying to push back the annoyance and impatience. "I don't have to touch you if I wanted in your head. But believe me, I won't be jumping in there if I don't have to."

Somehow, this made her flip a switch. "I don't believe you! Where's Owen? This isn't what I asked for. You're keeping him away from me, too, aren't you? Not satisfied with just one man? You need both to yourself, you selfish little slut?"

Tristan leaned over her, his expression threatening. "That's enough."

Her eyes widened, and then she started screaming. "Owen, you fucker! Get your ass in here! They're gonna kill me! *Owen!*"

"Stop it! He can't even hear you," I yelled over her shrieks. But she didn't stop. *Vanessa! Shut up! He's muted your room, so he can't hear you.*

She fell quiet at my silent words and stared at me with fear-filled eyes. She drew her knees to her chest, clapped her hands over her ears, and started screaming again and rocking back and forth. "Stay out of my head! Stay out! Stay out!"

I threw myself against the back of the chair and closed my eyes. What was I going to do with her? Thankfully, the door flew open, and Owen came to her side. His presence calmed her down.

"What did you to do her?" he demanded, shooting an accusatory look at me.

"I'm trying to *help* her," I said through clenched teeth, "but she won't exactly let me."

"Owen?" Sheree's voice called from down the hall. "Where'd you go? Oh, my God. Oh, no! Owen? Owen! Are you okay?"

Before any of us could react, Sheree already reached the doorway. Her eyes went wide as saucers as she took in the vampire in Owen's arms, and then they began to change, her pupils elongating and her irises yellowing. Her fingers had already lengthened into claws by the time Tristan wrapped his arms around her and carried her away.

"Take care of her," I told Owen, flipping my hand at Vanessa while I hurried after Tristan and Sheree.

I followed them as he carried Sheree into another room down the hall, where he released her, then backed away several paces in case she exploded into a tiger. Her mouth bulged open with her growing teeth and fangs, and she bent over, placing padded hands that were nearly paws on her knees. She panted, more in a beast-like way than human, and a soft whimper, almost a mewl, escaped with each exhale. After several moments, though, the claws retracted, and her large paws shrank into human hands. When she finally looked up at us, her face had returned to normal, but her body trembled— with the effort of fighting the change or with anger, I wasn't sure. Probably both.

"*What* is she doing here?" she demanded as soon as she could speak. "You're keeping prisoners of war here?"

I bit my lip and shook my head.

"So what's going on?"

I looked at Tristan, and he stared back at me. *Well?* I wanted to ask him. He'd been so gung-ho on telling her yesterday, but now his tongue suddenly didn't work? *It worked perfectly well last night.* My body warmed all over, and heat crept up my neck. I frowned at that random thought, but he took my expression the wrong way. When he opened his mouth, my hand grabbed his and squeezed to stop him. Although I'd looked to him for help, I knew that *I* needed to do this, not him.

"Vanessa, um . . ." My mouth struggled to form the words. "She, well, wanted to convert. That's what she's doing here."

Sheree stared at me with wide, brown eyes for a long moment, then she burst out laughing, doubling over with the fit.

"Now that's a good one!" she chortled.

I simply watched her until she realized I was serious. She sobered up immediately.

"Vanessa? Amadis? Are you *sure*? No. It's probably a trick. It has to be!"

I shook my head. "That's what we thought at first, but it's already done. Well, at least the first phase is. She really did want this."

Sheree stared at me again then at Tristan, then looked around the room, as if still expecting a camera crew to show up. I knew exactly how she felt. She must have finally decided she wasn't being punked, because she dropped her butt to the bed and rubbed her long, thin hands over her face.

"Vanessa . . ." she muttered to herself. "Who would have ever thought?"

She took it better than I'd expected. I thought she was entitled to an all-out fit or to issue ultimatums that the vamp leave or she would. But, of course, that had been foolish of me. Sheree's heart was bigger than anyone's.

She finally looked up at me. "And you did it yourself?"

"Had to. No one can know she's here. The Daemoni—"

Her eyes grew even bigger than they'd been before. "They'll want her back. I was nothing to them, but Vanessa . . . they'll come for her."

I nodded.

"We have to keep this quiet as long as possible," Tristan

said. "Until she's fully converted so it's too late for them to do anything when they find out."

"That's why you weren't going to tell me?"

I shifted my weight and stared at my feet. "Sorry. That's what I wanted to talk to you about, but I should have told you sooner. I was a little tired last night."

"I'm sure you were," Sheree muttered. She looked up at Tristan. "No wonder you called me last night and told me to stay close to Sonya. Alexis didn't really hear anything suspicious in Sonya's mind, did she?"

Tristan grimaced. "As far as we know, Sonya's the same as always. It was an excuse to keep you away from the back wing."

Sheree examined her fingers, chose one, and began gnawing on a nail. She'd once told me she kept her nails short because when she shifted, her claws would be less dangerous. They'd still appeared plenty lethal to me when they'd come out a few minutes ago, but whatever.

"Vanessa's a mess," the shifter finally said. "How bad was the first phase?"

"Not bad, actually," I said. "I mean, not great, of course, but not even as bad as Sonya's."

She leaned forward. "Really?"

I lifted my hands in a shrug. "She'd been wanting this a long time. That's all I can figure."

"Well, this next phase may not go so smoothly. Based on what I heard and saw for that brief moment . . ."

"You're right. She's a mess."

"She's scared of your telepathy, Alexis," Owen spoke up from the doorway. "She knows you were in her head during the conversion."

I turned to look at him. "Not really. Not on purpose, anyway. The visions I see—that just happens during a conversion. I can't control it when everything's so intense."

"Doesn't matter whether you meant to or not. She's

freaked out. She doesn't like that you, of all people, know her inner thoughts and worst memories."

My head dropped, and I stared at the floor once more, unable to argue with that. In fact, once again, I felt badly for Vanessa. Nobody would want the person they disliked most to know those things.

"It's part of the process," I said, looking back up at Owen. "I mean, what we still need to do. She has to confess and repent before she can move on."

"I'm only saying it's going to be difficult to get her to cooperate, especially with you."

"Well, she needs to get over it! I'm the only one who can do this, remember? You didn't want to involve anyone else."

Owen's eyes flitted over to Sheree.

"Oh, no," I said, stepping in front of the shifter as if to protect her. "You agreed not to drag her into this. In fact, you insisted we leave her and everyone else out of it."

From behind me, Sheree put a hand on my shoulder. "I'll help. If you need me, I'll do it."

Owen opened his mouth, and I feared he would accept her offer.

"No! It's not fair of us to ask this." I turned around and looked up at Sheree. "You don't need to do this, not after what she did to you. There's no reason to put yourself through this."

Sheree's eyes softened. "Forgiveness is part of the process, Alexis. Part of *my* healing. I'd do this just as much for me as for her."

I searched her face, looked deep into her brown eyes as if they could show me what was really in her heart, which might be different than what was in her mind. But I didn't need to delve deep, didn't need to listen to her thoughts. Her feelings were right there on her face. She was not only certain about this but was also pretty adamant. I let out a breath of relief. I couldn't help but feel better that I wouldn't be alone in this. With a reluctant sigh, I nodded acceptance of her offer.

So Sheree and I at last had more than one patient to work with. It took some time, but when Vanessa finally trusted that I wouldn't listen to her thoughts any time I felt like it, she relaxed a bit and eventually allowed me to sit in on her faith-healing sessions with Sheree. I pumped Amadis power into her, and she listened to Sheree intently, but when it came time to act, she refused.

"Vanessa, you're doing great," Sheree said one day, a little over a month after the vamp had shown up in those trunks. We sat in our usual positions—one of us on each side of Vanessa's bed, my hand over the vampire's. "You really are. But if you're going to heal completely, you have to confess and repent."

Vanessa pulled her hand from mine and folded her arms over her chest. Her eyes stared at the window across from her bed, and she didn't say a word.

"You can't leave here until you do," I said.

She scowled. Then she finally turned her head to look at Sheree, as usual ignoring me. "I've been working on it. Just . . . privately. I don't need anyone but God knowing my business."

I had a feeling she meant she didn't want *me* knowing, so I stood up. One pair of warm, brown eyes and one pair of icy, blue ones looked up at me. "I don't have to be here for it. Whatever helps."

Vanessa rolled her eyes. "Oh, please. It's not all about you. I don't want any of you to know all the things I've done in the past. This life is gonna be hard enough without everyone's judgments."

"It's not our place to judge," I said. "If it were, you wouldn't be here."

Sheree threw an annoyed glare at me before turning to our patient. "She's right—the Amadis don't judge, I mean. Our place is to help you reclaim your soul so it can be saved, and then simply to love you. After all, pretty much everyone in the

Amadis has committed some of the worst sins and crimes imaginable."

"Except little miss perfect," Vanessa sneered, her hand twitching toward me.

"I thought this wasn't about me," I retorted. After another warning glance from Sheree, I cleared my throat and added, "*Nobody's* perfect. Not me, for sure. And we already know you've murdered, lusted, envied, stolen . . . I'm sure the list goes on."

Vanessa hissed at the accusations but didn't deny them. "Why don't you confess for me, if you know so much?"

I rested my hands on my hips. "I'm just saying that we're not stupid and God isn't blind. The thing is, you're *here*. That means more than anything you've done in the past. We've already forgiven you, Vanessa. Don't you get it?"

"If everyone knows, including *God*, why do I have to confess?"

"Because *you* need to know," Sheree said. "You can't repent if you don't know what you're repenting for."

Vanessa looked out the window. "Like I said, I've been working on it on my own."

We let it go that day, but a week later, Sheree tried again. Vanessa gave us the same response.

"It's between God and me," she said. "I won't do it with you, so forget that idea. But you know I'm serious. You know I want nothing more than to put this all behind me and never think about it again."

Sheree and I exchanged a look, both of us at a loss. We couldn't force Vanessa to voice her sins to us. We could only do so much for her, and beyond that, this was like most things in life—she'd get out of it what she personally put into it. If she really wanted to heal her soul, she couldn't avoid this step, whether she did it with us or without.

"As long as you know what needs to be done so you can move on," Sheree said with resignation. Then her tone perked up. "Once you get through all this, do you want to change your name, like Tristan did?"

Vanessa's eyes snapped toward Sheree's, and she cocked her head, as if considering this idea for the first time.

"No," she finally said. "I always thought my name sounded kind of like a combination of valor and strength. It doesn't mean that, but maybe that's why it was given to me. Maybe I'm still being stupid, but valor and strength—they have a special meaning to me." She must have read my expression that I was impressed, because she added, "Yeah. Believe it or not, I have values. What the fuck of it?"

I withheld a snarky retort and smiled sweetly instead. "What do you value now, Vanessa? Do you value the Amadis?"

She narrowed her eyes with suspicion. "I'm supposed to say *yes*, but I feel like you're setting me up."

"No, I'm not. I'm hoping you really do value us all. You're one of us now, right?"

"That's what I'm doing here, isn't it?"

"Of course," I agreed. "So you understand all that it means —that the Daemoni are now your enemy?"

Her eyes flickered, and she swallowed before nodding. "When they find out what I've done . . . that I'm with you . . . they'll kill me."

"But we'll protect you. We're always here for you. At least, that's the plan. But you're a vampire, which means you'll likely outlive most of us. The future of the Amadis is *your* future."

She chuckled but without humor. "I get where you're going—you need the fertility stone. I can't believe I let you lead me through all this BS."

"It's not BS," I said. "If we don't have the stone, we don't have a future."

"Well, let's hope someone figures something out, because I can't help you. I don't know where it is."

"Did you lose it?"

She groaned with exasperation. "I haven't seen it in

months, okay? In fact, the last time I saw it was before I saw you and Se—Tristan in South Beach. End of story."

She hadn't exactly answered my question about losing it, and she'd learned, probably from Owen, to focus her mind on mundane subjects when she thought I might be poking around her mind. Right now she thought hard about the color of the tile in her room, whether she would call it toffee or coffee-with-cream or flesh. But her intense efforts to avoid thinking about the stone meant she hid something. So *did* she lose it? Or did she know exactly where it was but had some reason to keep it from us?

"Can I be alone now?" she asked. "I have some talking to do with God, right?"

With a shake of my head, I strode out of the room, my work done here for the day. Sheree followed me out.

"I think she's telling the truth," she said as we walked together toward my office. "About working on it on her own. She's made too much progress otherwise."

"Every time I assess her, her Amadis power is stronger, so there's no doubt." I opened my office door, and we both entered the elaborate room.

"I feel her strength, too," Sheree said as she stepped up to the front of my oversized, cherry-wood desk as I walked around it. "So . . . uh . . ."

She picked up a ceramic bowl Dorian had made for me when he was in kindergarten and studied it as though it might have come from another planet.

I sat in the leather executive chair, folded my hands on the desk, and eyed her, feeling all boss-like. "You're stalling. Spill it."

"Well, I know you postponed the whole Sonya-Heather thing because of Vanessa and not knowing if she'd freak out on us and go on a rampage. But she's doing so well. You just said so yourself."

I already knew where this headed, so I nodded. "Vanessa's

probably more harmless than Sonya. You think Heather should come for a visit?"

Sheree put the bowl down, then wrung her hands as she looked at me sheepishly. "I promised Sonya I'd ask you. Of course, she can't leave—I don't trust her out of the safe house yet—but I think it would be safe if Heather came here. With you and Tristan in the room, too, of course," she quickly added.

I leaned back in my chair. "You still think seeing Heather will help her make a breakthrough?"

"She's in a better mood every time they talk on the phone. The effect is temporary, but maybe seeing her, being with her . . . maybe even getting to hug her . . . with all that, we might see more lasting effects."

"Well, then, I guess we give it a try."

Sheree's face broke into a big grin. "She'll be so happy about this! This could be it for her, Alexis. She really does need this."

The way she practically bounced out of the room and down the hall toward Sonya's wing made me think of Tigger, and I giggled. But then the weight of it all pressed down on me. I crossed my arms on my desk and lay my forehead against them. What if we were wrong about Sonya? Or Vanessa? What if I was putting Heather's life at risk?

A longing to talk to Charlotte, Mom, or Rina suddenly overcame me. I wished they could be here to provide guidance. I'd managed to convert Vanessa and run this place, though barely occupied, without them, but I often felt so alone. Tristan helped where he could, but ultimately, the decisions were left up to me, and so many of them felt like life-or-death. So many lives in my hands. And this was only a tiny hint of what I'd have to face when I became matriarch. *How does Rina do it?*

I lifted my head enough to rest my chin on my arms, and my gaze swept over my office. When we first purchased the mansion for the Amadis, I'd thought I should decorate my office like Rina's, with a solid but elegant wood desk, lots of bookcases, and a fancy seating area, hoping the look would grow on me. But it hadn't yet, and I seriously considered redecorating in purple and black zebra stripes. At least something more *me*, because, although it looked like Rina's space, the wisdom and sophistication it represented hadn't rubbed off. Not yet. I wondered if it ever would. *Will I ever be the leader Rina is?*

Without lifting my head, I reached out with one arm and slid my cell phone from the corner of the desk to the space in front of me and stared at it for a long moment. The temptation to call my mom nearly overwhelmed me. It was almost midnight on Amadis Island, not terribly late. Surely she wouldn't mind a call from her daughter at any time of day or night. But what would I say? That this was too much for me to handle on my own? That I needed my mommy? Of course, then she'd want to know everything going on, and since there's no point in lying to her, I'd have to tell her about Vanessa and converting her by myself, defying all of their specific requests, let alone betraying the people here who trusted me with their safety. No, I couldn't call my mom, not even to hear her voice. She'd know immediately something was wrong.

So I picked up the phone with a sigh, sat up straight, and called Heather instead.

CHAPTER 18

"Telepathy, huh?" Heather asked me as she sat on the couch in my office and stared up at Tristan and me.

I'd never told her about my gift before because even our kind, who knew the ability existed, had issues with it. Vanessa served as a prime example. But Tristan had pointed out that we could use it to our advantage during this supervised visit.

"I'm not going to listen to your every thought," I said, "but if you feel frightened or simply uncomfortable, you can silently tell me."

She squinted her eyes as she considered my suggestion. "Because if she knows I'm afraid, it would upset her."

"She'll smell your fear as soon as you feel it," Tristan said, "and yes, she'll feed off of it. But if you don't panic, it'd be a lot easier to get you out of there. If you feel at all that you don't want to be there, silently tell Alexis."

"Okay," she said simply. "Now, can I see her?"

Tristan and I flanked her sides as we took her to Sonya's room, where Sheree waited outside the door. I'd wanted Owen there, as well, but we'd decided he'd better stay with Vanessa, just in case she caught a whiff of Heather's human scent and freaked out. Sheree stepped inside and closed the door for a minute or so, then opened it wide.

Sonya sat on her loveseat, dressed in street clothes and a smile. Heather lurched forward, as if to run to her sister, but caught herself.

"It's okay," Sonya said, her grin widening as she spread her arms open. "I promise not to bite you."

After a moment's hesitation, Heather ran into her older sister's arms. They laughed and cried and talked at the same time, overjoyed to be reunited. I couldn't help smiling myself, and a peek out of the corner of my eye caught Tristan grinning, too. With everything we'd been through with Sonya —the ups and downs, the mood swings, the worry that she'd never complete the conversion, and the more permanent concern that she may never be able to live in Norman society again—this made everything worth it.

They chatted on and on, sometimes pulling Sheree, Tristan, and me into their conversation, but mostly reminiscing about childhood memories. Sheree eventually made herself comfortable in the chair by the bed, and Tristan and I shared the chair by the loveseat, me in his lap. We talked and laughed, not realizing how much time had passed.

"*Alexis!*" Owen's voice called into my mind.

Yeah?

"*Sun goes down in an hour. Things could get bad fast.*"

It's going really—

"*Sonya's not the only vampire in the house.*" If the words didn't alarm me, the warning in his tone did.

I jumped out of Tristan's lap. "Sorry, girls, but time's up."

Heather looked up at me with puppy-dog eyes. "Just another hour. Please?"

"Or two?" Sonya asked.

"Maybe I could stay for din—" Heather stopped herself as she realized what she was about to say—or possibly offer. Her hand flew to her mouth, and her eyes grew wide as Frisbees.

Sonya laughed. "I don't want *you* for dinner!"

"No, but we're taking no chances," I said. "Sunset isn't far off."

And that was so the wrong thing to say.

Heather understood the exact meaning of my words, and, with no warning, her fear spiked. Sonya's nose twitched, and her face became stone at the scent. Her hand went to her throat, and her eyes changed, growing deadly serious. Tristan and I both moved, grabbing Heather by the arms and pulling her away from the vampire, but then Sonya exploded into laughter.

"Kidding!" she screeched.

We all froze and stared at her for several loud heartbeats, then Heather burst into a fit of giggles.

"You . . . were always . . . so good . . . at getting me," the younger girl gasped, doubling over. "I'll never forget . . ." And completely relaxed again, she delved into a story from when they'd gone camping with their grandparents.

"*Alexis,*" Owen called out again. "*Seriously. If you don't get that norm out of here now—*" His voice went from mental to audible, but since our minds were connected, I still heard him. "Vanessa! Relax!"

Oh, crap! Through Owen's eyes, I saw Vanessa blurring around her room in an angry maelstrom. The warlock knew powerful magic—he'd restrained Tristan for hours, after all—but again, I'd take no chances with Heather.

"Now!" I barked, grabbing Heather's upper arm once again and pulling her back toward the door. "Sorry, but no time for goodbyes."

The effect I'd had on Heather before was nothing compared to now. The sour smell of pure fear filled the room.

"Get her out of here," Tristan shouted even as I dragged Heather out of the room.

I glanced over my shoulder at them. Sonya, fangs out and eyes glowing red, pushed against Tristan and clawed at his shoulders as she tried to get to her sister. As if Heather wasn't already afraid. As loudly as her heart pounded now, every vampire and shifter on the island would hear it. Tristan paralyzed Sonya, but a feral growl still rumbled from her chest, and her upper lip curled in a snarl. Sheree rushed to us and helped me get Heather out of the house and safely away from both vampires.

"I'm so sorry," Sheree murmured as we deposited a trembling Heather into the passenger seat of her own car.

"Don't," I said, shutting the car door and hurrying around to the driver's side. "It's not your fault. Don't blame yourself."

"But I—"

I held up my hand. "You suggested what you thought best, but I made the ultimate decision. Now get inside and see who needs you more. My bet is on Sonya."

I couldn't believe I'd said that, but it was true. Perhaps by willingly giving her soul up to become immortal, she'd sealed the deal for herself. Or perhaps we weren't trained well enough to do what we needed for her. With that thought, I couldn't help but blame Charlotte and mom and Rina, too, for this fiasco.

I jumped into the driver's seat, fished Heather's keys out of her purse, and drove her back to my house. Blossom and Dorian were just setting the table for dinner when we walked in. By now, Heather's fear had dissipated, replaced by anger. She spun on me as soon as I closed the backdoor.

"What was that all about?" she demanded. "One minute we're having a good time, and the next, you're dragging me out of the room."

"I'm sorry," I said, trying to ignore the stares from Blossom and Dorian, who both stood on the other side of the kitchen island. "I had to get you out of there, though."

"Why? She was fine! You freaked out for nothing. You could have at least let us say goodbye."

"It wasn't for nothing, Heather." I wanted to tell her the

truth about Vanessa being there, too, but I couldn't for everyone's safety, including hers. "You have to trust me. I did everything for your best interest."

"Whatever," she huffed before turning on her heel and heading for the family room.

"Don't walk away," I said to her back.

"You're not my mother. Don't tell me what to do."

I stared after her in shock. She'd never spoken to me—to any of us—like that before. *She's a teenager. She's hurt. She misses her sister.* I looked at Blossom, who looked back at me, and Dorian, who stared toward the door Heather had left through.

"Let's eat," Blossom said with a smile too big to be real. "I made lasagna."

The three of us had barely dished out the food and begun eating when Heather decided to join us. She ate quietly at first, probably embarrassed by her outburst, but eventually joined in the conversation. By the time she left for home later in the evening, she was over it all. She didn't even ask me when she could see Sonya again. That made me sad for both of them.

Tristan arrived home much later, and I sat at the table again, watching him eat lasagna at ten o'clock at night.

"So if you got them both settled down, what took you so long?" I asked after we updated each other on everyone's status. As expected, Vanessa had calmed down quickly, and Sonya took a little longer. Like her sister, now she held contempt for us for cutting the visit short.

Tristan swallowed the bite he'd been chewing and took a swig of wine. "I had a couple of beers and a talk with Owen. We're taking a trip to South Beach."

"South Beach?" I asked, bewildered. "Wait. Oh, no, you're not. You're not going anywhere near there and the Daemoni!"

"It's not as bad as we'd thought, remember?"

"I don't care! It's bad enough. Do you *want* them to take control of you?"

"Of course not. But I'll have Scarecrow with me this time, and he can shield and cloak me. They'll have no idea I'm even there."

I gnawed on my lip as I considered this—a much better arrangement than what Tristan and I had when we'd gone. "I still don't like it. Why do you even need to go?"

"Vanessa had a place in South Beach when Owen met up with her again, before, well, before he brought her here."

Although Tristan had tried to avoid bringing up the gruesome memory, my stomach clenched at the reminder of Vanessa's arrival and what Owen had done to her. I just couldn't imagine my Owen—my sweet, protecting, *normal* Owen, anyway—slicing her into pieces.

"What do you mean when he met up with her *again*?"

Tristan shrugged. "I guess they've had an on-again-off-again thing going for a while. That memory you'd seen of Victor's—they were on then. But Owen left for a while and Vanessa went back to the Daemoni, tried the South Beach gig but her heart was elsewhere."

"You mean with Owen?" My nose wrinkled as my mind tried to visualize them together. The idea of them as a couple was still too absurd for me to accept. Obviously for Owen, too, since he still flirted with every female in sight.

"With Owen. Maybe with the Amadis, too. You were right —she'd been wanting this for a long time, but she had a hard time convincing Owen that she meant it. He didn't bring her here on a whim, Lex. You need to cut him some slack."

"I know," I admitted as I stared at my hands in my lap. "I worry about him, though. I'm glad you had a chance to talk to him. Does he hate me?"

"Of course not. But I think he's having a hard time figuring out how to handle you. A lot has changed with both of you since the trial last year."

I sighed, feeling bad for my behavior toward Owen. I loved him like a brother, and I'd let my frustration with his choices get the better of me, rather than showing my unconditional love.

"So," I said, "why on earth do you two need to go to South Beach? What's so important at Vanessa's old place, assuming her stuff is even still there? I mean, we've bought her new clothes. If she needs anything else, we'll get it, too. Everything's replaceable. Nothing warrants this risk—"

"Except your pendant."

"What? *Really?* Did Vanessa finally admit to having it? Did Owen find out where it is?"

"No, but we're going to search her place. We'll go in undercover, find the pendant, and get out as fast as possible," Tristan said before he took another bite of pasta.

My excitement deflated. "But Owen told me he looked already."

"He said he tried to look, but didn't have time to go through everything. He thinks, as possessive as he's seen her with it in the past, that since she didn't have it on her, she must have hidden it somewhere obscure. She wouldn't take the chance of someone else finding it."

"She's definitely hiding something," I agreed, and their plan started sounding better to me. "You're all right with Owen? I mean, you trust him?"

"With my life, Lex. I know he's different than he used to be, but he's still Owen."

"Then you trust him with mine?"

He placed his fork on his plate, crossed his arms on the table, and leaned closer to me. "You're not going."

"Why not? You need my telepathy."

"No, we don't. We don't plan on coming into contact with anyone."

"Yeah, well, plans go awry, remember?"

"You're not going, Alexis. For once, don't argue with me."

"I can't just sit here, waiting for you to return. I'm not doing that again! Last time you did that to me, you didn't come back, remember?"

He grimaced. Then he reached his hands across the table and took hold of mine. "You promised me you wouldn't be reckless anymore. I need to know you're safe here and that Dorian is, too. Besides, someone needs to stay, in case anyone comes sniffing around for a long, lost vampire. Or two."

"Then you stay, and I'll go with Owen. It's not me the Daemoni are trying to control."

"Sonya and Vanessa need *you*, my love. Owen and I can't do what you can for them."

I stared at him for a long moment, but no further argument came for me. My breath huffed out with resignation. I would be left behind. Again.

The following week, I paced my office at the safe house, my hand twisting and pulling at my hair. Giving themselves plenty of daylight to work with, Tristan and Owen had left at dawn this morning and said they'd be home within a few hours. Winter's early dusk was only an hour away now, and they still weren't back.

"This isn't good," I muttered to Sheree, who sat on the couch, chewing on her nails. "There's no way it should have taken this long."

"Think positive, Alexis. They're virtually unbeatable, right? I'm sure they're fine."

"But they're not invincible." My voice had risen several octaves with the panic growing in my chest. I couldn't stop thinking about the last time they'd left me for enemy territory, when Owen had come back but Tristan hadn't. My chest tightened, and tears pricked my eyes. "They shouldn't have gone, not by themselves, what were we thinking? I should have never let—"

I froze. The agitated mind signatures appeared on my mental radar at the same time crashing and banging echoed down the hall from the main part of the safe house. The shifter and I exchanged a look, and then I was gone. I blurred to the foyer and skidded to a stop in the doorway of one of the common living areas. My heart stuttered at the scene.

Owen and Tristan were apparently in a standoff.

Tristan's arms wrapped tightly around his own torso as if bound in an invisible straightjacket, and murderous flames filled his eyes. He growled and thrashed about, throwing his body at Owen, who dodged each attack. Tristan's body kept hitting the walls and crashing into furniture, destroying everything in his path. Owen circled him, his hands up, working his magic against Tristan.

"What the hell is going on here?" I demanded.

"He's flipped a freakin' switch!" Owen answered while keeping his full attention on Tristan.

As if noticing me for the first time, my husband turned his enraged eyes on me, growled again, and threw himself at me. But I didn't duck away. Instead, I wrapped my arms around him and rolled with him, doing my best to diminish the impact for both of us. The Daemoni obviously had control of him—which meant distance was no longer a factor—so I pushed my Amadis power into him. He didn't react as expected.

"That won't work!" he snapped, but I couldn't tell if he mocked me or actually tried to help.

Tristan! I yelled into his mind. His body calmed. It trembled violently, but he no longer fought me. Again I tried sharing Amadis power.

"*It's not Daemoni power doing this,*" he said. "*It is . . . but . . . not in me.*"

The strain in his mental voice scared me. He could barely fight off whatever controlled him.

Just don't forget you love me and I love you. No matter what. You don't want to hurt me. You don't want to hurt anyone here.

He nodded. His body relaxed even more. But as soon as I released my embrace and moved to get up, he started thrashing about again.

"*You lie! You're a lying whore,*" he silently yelled.

My head snapped back as if he had physically smacked me. *What are they doing to him?* He moved as if to attack me again, but Owen held him back with magic. The muscles in the warlock's neck and shoulder strained with the effort, so I raised my own hands and did what I could to help. I didn't have Tristan's power to paralyze, but I could control objects to a certain extent, almost to Owen's level. We couldn't back off in the slightest, though, because Tristan could easily overpower both of us if he wanted to.

"What are we going to do?" I asked Owen.

"We can't hold him like this forever. I can bind him to the fridge again," he said, reminding me of a similar situation two years ago at the beach house in the Keys, right after I'd gone through the *Ang'dora*.

I shook my head. "I can't do that to him again. Besides, this is different—"

"Yeah, he's not only after you this time. He seems to hate all of us."

Sheree appeared in the doorway, and Tristan's body jumped against our power, trying to lunge for the were-tiger. Owen and I were able to hold him back, which told me Tristan fought the impulse, too. If he'd given the attempt his full potential, we'd never been able to hold him off.

"Get out," I yelled at Sheree before she got hurt. She simply stood there with wide eyes. "Go!"

Her eyes snapped to me, then she scrambled off.

"We can't do this forever, Alexis," Owen said. "Decide."

Decide? Decide to tie my husband up? How could I do that?

The smell of burning flesh interrupted my thoughts. My eyes bugged at the sight of smoke rising from Tristan's sides.

"What's he doing?" I cried, though it was obvious—he was shooting himself with fireballs.

CHAPTER 19

"Owen, make him *stop*," I shrieked. "Do something!"

Owen flicked his hand, and Tristan's arms jerked away from his body and lifted to his sides so that now he looked as though we were crucifying him on an invisible cross. A lone fireball fell from his hand to the tile floor, no power behind it. Without looking away from Tristan, I stepped forward to stomp the flames out. Tristan's flesh stopped sizzling. Through the holes burned into his shirt, I noticed his skin already healing.

"All right," I croaked around the lump in my throat. I couldn't believe what I was about to say, but I couldn't let him hurt himself or anyone else. "If we put him in the shackles in one of the rooms, can you shield it or something so he can't flash out of them?"

"Sure, but will the chains hold him?"

"He installed and tested them himself, so let's hope so."

The fire in Tristan's eyes had died by the time we had his wrists and ankles locked in shackles in the room next to Vanessa's, but mine burned even more with tears.

"I'm sorry," I whispered, taking a step toward him.

He shook his head. His voice came out low and hoarse. "Don't be. It's necessary."

I reached out to touch his shoulder but he jerked away as far as he could, the metal chains jangling noisily against the concrete wall.

"What are they doing to you?" I asked.

He closed his eyes, and his expression became one of shame. "I don't know. They're in my head . . . or my heart. I think I'm feeling what they're feeling."

"What are they feeling?"

A growl rose from his chest. "Hate. Anger. A desire to kill. Toward you. Toward me. Anyone and everyone, actually." Another growl. "I can barely control it."

His body violently thrashed again. His back arced away from the wall while his head threw back, cracking against the concrete. His hands burned a bright reddish-orange, and I knew he must have been controlling the urge to shoot more fire.

I turned on Owen. "How did this happen? How did they get to him? You were supposed to have him shielded and cloaked!"

"I did. I . . ." He shook his head. "I don't know. Nobody was around. I have no idea how they knew we were even there."

"Did you at least find the pendant?"

The defeated look on his face told me. "We tore the place apart, but it was nowhere—"

"Alexis!" Sheree came running into the room. She stopped short at the sight of Tristan. Blinked. Swallowed. Slowly turned to me, as if trying to remember the urgent matter she'd apparently needed to share. "Um . . . someone's here. Someone's at the door! Not Amadis, but not Norman, either."

Daemoni! They've come for Vanessa. Or Tristan! Those thoughts immediately shot through my mind, but I couldn't sense Daemoni. Nothing more than the trace that still came from Sonya's room. I felt out beyond the mansion for the mind signature. Strangely familiar, but in that unidentifiable way . . . no thoughts to latch onto.

"Must be a faerie," I muttered. I looked at Owen, and he nodded.

"I'll stand guard here," he said. "Holler if you need me."

I ran for the front door, Sheree on my heels, and peeked out a side window. An old woman stood on the front steps, wrapped in raggedy cloaks. I could barely see through the illusion—a few golden strands in her hair, gold flecks in her flat eyes.

I yanked the door open, grabbed the old woman's arm, and pulled her inside. Then I threw my arms around her. "Bree! Thank God you're here!"

"You mean thank the Angels," she said, hugging me back. "They sent me."

She stepped back from my embrace and transformed into her real self.

"The Angels sent you?" I repeated, confused. I thought the Angels only communicated with the Amadis matriarch. On the other hand, as a faerie, Bree was more of the Otherworld than she was of ours, and although she'd been an outcast since agreeing to become Tristan's mother, she had closer ties to the spirits of the Otherworld, including the Angels, than the rest of us. Well, besides the connection between Cassandra and me, which remained inexplicable.

"Well, in a roundabout way," Bree said as she shook out her golden hair. "They didn't directly tell me, but I think I know what they did to the stone. Where's Tristan? Can we talk?"

I grimaced. Did I want her to see Tristan, her son, chained up and behaving like a madman? But if she could help . . .

"Um . . . er . . ." I started unsuccessfully and tried again. "If you know what they did, maybe it will help us figure out what to do. Tristan is . . . well, a bit of a mess right now."

Bree nodded, showing no surprise. "In the heart?"

My eyes widened. "Yeah, sort of. I guess that's what it is. Why?"

"Has he been near the Daemoni lately?"

"Yes. And when he came back—"

"Take me to him. You both need to know."

I led Bree, with Sheree following us, to the room where Tristan remained chained to the wall, Owen keeping an eye on him. Bree didn't gasp at the scene as I'd thought she would—as I still did even knowing what to expect—but she shook her head.

She walked over to Tristan and placed her hand on his arm. He growled, but at least he didn't thrash about as if trying to attack her.

"Do you know what's going on?" he asked, his voice rough, barely human sounding.

"I believe so," Bree said. "The faerie stone—when the Angels took it, I believe they enhanced it—"

"We already know that," Tristan snarled, clanging his chains with impatience. "We need to know *what* they did before the Daemoni figure it out."

Bree cocked her head. "You don't think they know yet?"

"If they did, you'd probably all be dead by now," Tristan answered. "They're angry and frustrated. I can feel that as if they're my own feelings, and it's *maddening*. So no, they don't know."

"Good," Bree said. "I think I *do* know, especially after seeing this. I believe the Angels wanted to be sure you know when you're loved. That you feel your soul mate's love when she is in possession of the stone so you wouldn't doubt it. So whoever has the stone . . . that's whose feelings you are experiencing."

The room fell deathly silent as this news settled in.

"So Tristan is feeling the Daemoni's emotions right now?" Sheree asked.

Bree nodded. "Whoever has the stone . . . that's what he's feeling. At least, anything toward himself or those he's around."

More silence as we continued to think about it. Tristan spoke up first.

"It makes sense." His eyes turned on me, no longer full of murder, but not exactly full of love, either. "What do you think kept me going while they had me all that time? We talked about a connection between us. And if you think about it, this unexplained anger goes back to when you first lost the stone—when Vanessa grabbed it."

I understood. We'd fought a lot ever since then, and at one point, he'd even stopped believing that I loved him at all. "You felt what she did."

He nodded, and then his chains clanged again as his body writhed in frustration, and he let out a string of profanities.

"Why is it so bad now, though?" I asked. "I mean, last time we went to South Beach . . ."

I trailed off when everyone but Tristan stared at me without comprehension. Right. They weren't aware of the full story of our trip. Well, maybe Tristan had told Owen, but Bree and Sheree didn't know. Rather than telling the whole story for them, I opened my mind and shared the memory.

"Was that Vanessa in control then?" Sheree asked afterward.

"The question is who has it now," Owen said, deflecting Sheree's accusation.

"Your trip must have created the link with a mage. Someone with powerful magic," Bree said, and Tristan nodded in agreement.

My breath caught. "Kali?"

"No," Tristan grunted. "Not that strong."

That was a bit of a relief.

"But as long as this mage has it," I said, "Tristan will

always feel what she's feeling, rather than the truth around him or within him."

"It will likely become stronger, too, the longer one person possesses the stone. The connection will strengthen," Bree added.

"Well, that's just fabulous. Until we find the stone, my husband will hate me."

"You're forgetting the worst part," Tristan snarled. We all turned our eyes on him. "If they figure this out, they'll use it to their advantage. I'll become their personal killing machine right in the heart of the Amadis. Exactly what they've always wanted." He locked his gaze on mine, and a jolt ran up my spine with the intense look in his hazel eyes. "And guess where they'll want me to start?"

With me, of course. He gave me a nod of confirmation. Instead of fear, though, anger welled inside me. *Would he ever be free of their control?* I inhaled a slow breath, then let it out even slower.

"Okay, then," I said, lifting my chin and squaring my shoulders, "we find the stone, and we get it back. Fortunately, we have a new friend who probably knows who has it now and ought to be quite helpful."

I strode out of Tristan's room, turned right, and crossed the five yards to Vanessa's door. Owen suddenly stood in front of it. I raised my eyebrows at him.

"I doubt she'll cooperate," he muttered.

My eyebrows shot even higher. "Before I agreed to convert her, you said—"

"I said she had something you wanted. A weapon. Another soldier for your army."

I didn't miss how he said "*your* army," not "*our* army." I told myself it only meant that he acknowledged my leadership position. I hoped that was all he meant.

"And as part of *my* army, she will do her duty and tell us what she knows."

"Listen. She's pretty sensitive about the pendant. She felt some kind of, well, connection to you and Tristan through it."

I rolled my eyes. "Of course, she did. Isn't that what Bree just said?"

But then the deeper meaning of what he said came to me. A connection not only to Tristan, but to me, too.

"She'd felt the love, Alexis. Projected it to herself, I guess."

I tilted my head as I studied his face. "That's what made her decide, isn't it? How she knew for sure that she wanted to convert?"

He shrugged. "I don't know. But that's what she told me when she came to me."

"Came to you where?"

He pressed his lips together and looked away. Closed his eyes for a long moment, then opened them again, but still stared at the wall behind me. "It's a long story I don't feel like reliving. But yeah, she knew where to find me."

A current of pain flowed under his words, and I had the feeling Vanessa had rescued him from something before he rescued her. And whatever she'd brought him out of, it hadn't been pleasant.

"Owen . . . ?" I placed my hand on his arm. "Are you okay?"

I tried to move into his line of sight to catch his eyes, but his gaze dropped from the wall behind me to the floor, which he scowled at. Eventually he looked at me with a smile. As fake as can be. "Just peachy. No need to worry—"

"You're lying," I blurted. "I see it on your face. You've always been there for me, Owen. It can go both ways, you know."

His left eye twitched as he brightened his smile. "I'm *fine*, Alexis. The best thing you can do for me is take care of her."

"Owen—"

His voice came out in a near growl. "Drop it. Worry about Vanessa, about Tristan, but not about me."

"Then at least tell me, you and Vanessa . . . ?" Did he feel the same way about her as she did him? He shrugged noncommittally. I tapped my finger against my temple. Understanding my message, he leaned closer to me, and his voice came out very softly.

"You really don't want to see what's in here. Trust me."

We stared at each other for a long moment, and I felt as though he tried to tell me something I wasn't grasping. The temptation to actually read his mind nearly overwhelmed me, but I wouldn't do that to him. Not about this. It was his business, and if he wanted to tell me, he would. He must have seen this in my eyes, because he straightened.

"So," he said, as if the last few minutes hadn't happened. "Vanessa. The pendant. I'm just sayin' that she might get a little . . . *anxious* . . . over the whole thing."

"Too late to worry about me, warlock," Vanessa's voice called from inside her room. As Owen opened the door and we both stepped inside, I wondered how much of our conversation she'd heard. Probably all of it. The vampire gave us an annoyed look from the chair she sat in next to the bed. "How can you so easily forget about vampire hearing? But thanks for looking out for my oh-so-precious feelings."

Owen glanced sideways at me, and I knew immediately he remembered her keen hearing. He *wanted* her to hear us. Well, not my probing questions, which is probably why he'd avoided answering them, but the part about showing that he still protected her. I shook my head at him before turning to the vampire.

"So the pendant?" I demanded, cutting to the chase. Her attitude—and Owen's behavior—had already raised my hackles. "Do you know where it is?"

"Nope," she said without a tinge of the anxiety Owen was so worried about. But she didn't expound, so I peeked into her mind, catching a glimpse of a memory of someone ripping the necklace away from her. I gasped, and she narrowed her eyes at me, realizing I'd entered her head. "They took it from you? *When?*"

She stuck her bottom lip out in a pout. "Before you came to South Beach last time. I . . . I was going to warn you then, but the local nest surrounded us, and I had to get out of there."

"And you couldn't have mentioned this all the time since you've been here?"

She shrugged. "What was the point? When I told you I didn't know where it was, I was telling you the truth. That's all you needed to know, for your own good."

"For my own *good*? Are you freakin' *kidding* me? Owen and Tristan risked their lives to go get it! Now all of our lives are at risk. You knew it wasn't at your place, and after everything we've done for you, you let them go anyway."

"Nobody asked me, now did they?"

My muscles bunched to fly at her and choke the living crap out of the bitch, but Owen grabbed me around the waist.

"Where was your vampire hearing then?" I spat at her. "Surely you heard plans, and now Tristan's like this for *no reason.*"

She held her hand out in front of her face and studied her nails. "I thought there's a reason for everything. Isn't that what you and the tiger are always preaching?"

I inhaled deeply, trying to control my anger, and shrugged Owen off of me.

"Are you going to help us or not?" I asked through clenched teeth.

"Not. Just forget the idea of getting your hands on that stone."

"I can't forget it! We *need* it. Our lives—including yours—are at stake." I stared at her, waiting for her to do the right thing, but she simply stared back at me. I rocked back on my heels. "I think you're bluffing. You know where it is."

"No, I don't. A warlock took it from me to deliver to more powerful hands, not the mage coven in South Beach."

"But if it's not there, then how did they affect Tristan so badly?"

Vanessa narrowed her icy eyes, finally showing at least some interest. She spoke slowly, deliberately. "Very powerful, very dark magic. The mages in South Beach only needed to be energized by a source of extreme power. A sorcerer or sorceress, who could be anywhere in the world."

Well, at least now we were getting somewhere.

"Kali," I said. "Is that who they took it to?"

"No, that wasn't the plan, at the time anyway. And you better hope it doesn't get to her or she to it. After Lucas and the Ancients—" she practically spit the words as if they tasted bad on her tongue "—Kali's the most powerful, most dangerous, most formidable Daemoni."

My turn to shrug. "We beat her once. She can't be all that bad."

With vampire speed, Vanessa suddenly stood right in my face, so close her breath fluttered my hair as she spoke. "In *your* house, surrounded by *your* people. And now she's pretty fucking pissed off after what you did to her. *Don't* underestimate her."

I took a step back and threw my hands in the air. "Okay. Whatever. At the moment, I don't care about her. I care about the stone, and you said she doesn't have it."

"*Yet.* She doesn't have it yet, or you'd know it. But you'll never be able to retrieve the stone now, so you may as well kiss it goodbye."

"Yeah, well, there's a bit of a problem with that idea," I said. "We don't have a choice. I'm sure you heard, with those vampire ears of yours, what's going to happen if we don't get it back."

Vanessa nodded. "Yeah, I did. Killing machine and all that."

My eyes bugged at her nonchalant attitude. "Yeah, *all that*. We have to do something, Vanessa. Just tell me where the stone is, and I'll get it myself."

She let out a dry chuckle.

"Don't you get it? You're supposed to be so smart." She shook her head in mock disappointment, then she stepped back into my space. "What Mr.-Not-in-Control-of-Himself so conveniently forgot to mention is that even if they don't figure out the value of the stone right away, they do know two things: you need it and you'll come after it."

I pulled up straight at this. *Crap. Crap, crap, crap on a crap-flavored biscuit.*

"They're using it as bait," I said.

Vanessa nodded as she looked at me with those piercing blue eyes. "So, *princess*, you can spread 'em wide or bend over. Either way, you're fucked."

CHAPTER 20

*V*anessa's crass words clenched my gut and twisted until I felt sick, not because of their vulgarity, but because of their truth. *What are we going to do?* Although Tristan had calmed down, he wouldn't let me release him from the shackles. He proved why any time someone came too close to him—he'd work himself into a frenzy, bucking and writhing against his chains and lashing out, even snapping with his teeth. I couldn't leave him like that forever, though, and if the Daemoni really gained control and he lost it completely, the chains may as well have been made of straw. He'd break right through them and have at us all he wanted. And for that to happen was only a matter of time.

But going after the pendant myself was likely suicide or worse—being captured and held by the Daemoni. Which would leave Tristan still vulnerable anyway, Dorian lost forever, and Mom and Rina to deal with the consequences. Even if I did decide to take the risk, I had no idea where to look for the stone. Vanessa refused to cooperate and share anything she might know, always telling me that keeping her secrets to herself was for my own good. But I really thought she did it to keep Owen right where she wanted him—my anger flared every time she refused, causing Owen to stand by her side, rather than mine.

My cell phone rang as I lay in the bed in Tristan's room two days later, trying to catch up on a little sleep. His head jerked up at the sound. I groaned as I blindly reached for the phone. He was peaceful when he slept. For the most part, anyway. Unfortunately, whoever had the stone didn't let him sleep much. I glanced at the number and knew I had to take the call, so I quietly slipped out of the room, feeling his glare on me the whole time.

"Hi, Mom," I answered. "Please tell me you have good news."

With simply too much going on here, I finally confessed everything to her and Rina the other night —Vanessa, Tristan, the stone, Bree's theory, the Daemoni's scheme. They praised my ability to handle things so well, but to say they were concerned was an understatement. We'd left off our previous conversation with their plans to find out if we could do anything about Tristan without actually sending out a search party for the stone.

"I'm not sure if you'd call it 'good,'" she said, "but there might be a way to sever the connection between Tristan and the stone."

I contained a whoop of joy, only because of her tone. "Sounds like good news to me, so what's the problem?"

"Well, it's possible for a mage to shield Tristan's heart and disconnect it from the stone, but it means dulling *all* of his emotions. *Everything* he feels for you and from you—"

I sucked in a breath. "Forever?"

"Nobody's sure. The shield is only temporary, but the effects can be permanent."

But he needed to know I loved him. That knowledge kept him strong, especially during times such as right now. If he didn't feel love forever, what would happen to him?

"I don't think that's an option, Mom," I said.

"It might have to be. Unless we're able to get the stone back, we might not have a choice."

"So you're forming a search party?"

Mom sighed. "Not yet. Rina has ordered me to, but I don't have anyone to spare at the moment. Char would be willing to lead a team if I asked her, especially if it brought her to Kali, but I'm afraid her emotions will override her logic. Her team would probably be okay, but I'd never forgive myself if she sacrificed herself for revenge. Besides, we need her where she is. And I don't have anyone else I feel confident about facing a possible sorcerer."

I ended the call feeling worse than I had before. Not wanting to disturb Tristan again, I looked for Sheree, but couldn't find her, so I told Bree I was going for a walk and to call if they needed me. I headed straight for the beach, kicking my shoes off and relishing the feel of the sand between my toes. The Gulf's low waves lapped lazily at the shore, the sound almost immediately soothing my nerves. The caress of the late winter sun also tried its best to relax me. Unfortunately, I found no answers written in the wet sand, no messages in a bottle to tell me what to do. And the beach wasn't enough of a distraction. But I knew who would be.

"Dorian?" I called out as I entered the backdoor of our house.

I hadn't had the pleasure of spending much time at home lately, unable to leave Tristan all chained up like an animal while I luxuriated in the comforts of our home. I never knew what I could do to repay Blossom and Heather for all the time they spent with Dorian, watching him for me, but I would have to find a way. I also needed to find a way to repent with my son himself for all the time we've spent apart.

"Blossom?" I called when Dorian didn't answer. I frowned. The house was empty. My mind felt no signatures except Sasha's. The lykora sat at my feet, looking up at me with puppy-dog eyes. *Weird*. Dorian never went anywhere without her.

Where could they be? I'd just been on the beach, so I knew they weren't there. I called the safe house. Although I kept Dorian away from the safe house as much as possible, if they'd needed something, maybe they'd gone there after I left, and we'd crossed paths. I was about to nix that idea because nobody was answering, but then Bree picked up.

"No, Dorian's not here," she said. "I haven't seen him or Blossom since yesterday."

"Did you find Sheree?" I asked as my heart picked up speed. *Something's wrong.* The frightening feeling began creeping under my skin.

"No. She's nowhere in the mansion. I can't sense her at all. Maybe she went to the store or the coffeehouse? Maybe she just needed to get out for a few."

"She never goes anywhere without telling me. What about Owen?"

Bree didn't answer at first. "I don't sense him here, either."

I told myself that was a good thing. Dorian must have been with them, and he'd be safe with them, especially with Owen. But where could they have gone? Why hadn't anyone told me? My heart rate spiked again. This didn't feel right. My finger could barely tap the buttons on the phone as I tried to dial Owen's number. No answer. I tried Blossom's. Again, no answer. Sheree's went straight to voicemail, which wasn't even set up. She rarely left the safe house, so hadn't bothered with it.

I couldn't shake the feeling that something was wrong. My throat tightened as I thought of all the possibilities. What if something had happened to Dorian? Maybe he was hurt when Heather was watching him and not knowing any better, she took him to the hospital. I shook my head. No. Heather *would* know better. Besides, Dorian could heal himself before they'd even get to the hospital, and that didn't explain everyone else's absences. I could barely scroll through the contacts on my phone, searching for Heather's number, as more possibilities shot through my mind.

He ran away, mad at us for not giving him enough attention. He'd been practicing his flying, as we had reluctantly allowed him to do, and he'd gone beyond Owen's cloak so they were all searching for him. He was bored and demanded all of them to take him to the village on Captiva for something to do and their phones were off. All of them. Maybe the batteries were drained.

But no. Those were all stupid excuses my mind created while trying to suppress the one and only real possibility: the Daemoni had come for him.

Panic wrapped its fingers around my throat and squeezed.

"Dorian!" I choked. *Oh, god, no.* I ran through the house, throwing open every single door. Sasha ran at my heels, barking. "Where is he, Sasha? Where's my baby?"

Tears flooded my eyes as I charged into his room, tripping over toys scattered on the floor. I collapsed on the unmade bed, pulled the covers to my chest, and stared unblinkingly at the wall. *What am I going to do? What will I tell Tristan? Oh, god, my baby!* Sasha cuddled next to me and licked away the tears that rolled down my cheeks.

"No, no, *no*! I can't do this. Dorian, please . . ."

"Please what, Mom?"

I bolted out of the bed. "Dorian!"

"What?" He cocked his head. "What's the matter, Mom?"

I lunged at him and swept him into my arms, lifting him off the ground and spinning in circles. I kissed him all over his face.

"What's going on?" he demanded. "Put me down already."

His annoyed tone shocked me back to reality. I put him back on his feet as my heart finally stopped racing. I took a step back, put my fists on my hips, and narrowed my eyes.

"Where on earth have you been? Do you have any idea how worried I was?" I shook a finger in his face.

"Universal Studios. Since you and Dad couldn't bother to take me, Uncle Owen, Sheree, and Blossom did."

I recoiled with the verbal smack. "*What?*"

He lifted his chin, a look of triumph all over his face. "Yep. They took me and Heather. We didn't want to *bother* you with permission."

The grief and longing fell away. Far, far away. Anger bubbled up in my chest.

"You, young man, stay right here. You will *not* leave this room until I say." I stomped out of his bedroom toward the kitchen where I found Owen and Blossom.

Blossom took one look at my face and bolted for the backdoor. "I need to take Heather home and Sheree back to the safe house."

She didn't wait for a response, swinging the door shut behind her.

"Are you trying to *kill* me, Owen?" I shrieked. "What were you thinking?"

He gave a casual shrug. "Dorian's been begging to go, and you and Tristan can't exactly take him. I thought I'd do the uncle thing and help you all out."

"You didn't ask me!"

"You were a little busy with more important problems."

"More important problems? Nothing is more important than my son. How dare you!"

"Calm down, Alexis. Everything's okay. Why are you so worked up?"

I half-expected the top of my head to literally blow off and steam to pour out of my ears, just like in Dorian's cartoons.

"Oh, I don't know, Owen, maybe because I came home to spend some time with my son only to find that he's gone. *Gone.* The son who may permanently be gone at any time. Or maybe because I couldn't get a hold of any of you, and no one bothered to tell me a thing. You didn't think I might freak out a little? And Universal Studios? *Really*, Owen? In what dimension would you think that was safe, because definitely not this one. Not with Daemoni everywhere, any of them looking for a chance to snatch him up."

He cleared his throat and dropped his head. He stared at the floor, scuffing his toe against the tile floor. "Sorry. The shield blocked the cell signals. I thought—"

"What shield?"

"I shielded the park, of course. No one was there but us."

"Except the workers, any of which could have been Dae—"

"Nope, no workers either. The park was closed, Alexis. Closed. We were completely alone, with a shield. You had nothing to worry about."

I crossed my arms over my chest. "Then how exactly did the rides run? With mag— Oh."

He wiggled his fingers in the air. "Between Blossom and me, yeah, with magic. And Dorian had a great time."

I glowered at him for a long moment. At least he'd taken every precaution possible, and my son was home, safe and sound. But still . . .

I took a step toward him, trying to get in his face, but like most people, he towered over me. "Don't. Ever. Do. That. Again. Got it?"

He lifted his chin in a nod.

"That's an order, Owen!"

He held his hands up in surrender. "Understood. Just trying to do everyone a favor."

He disappeared with that.

After a few cleansing breaths, I headed for Dorian's room.

"Are you really mad?" His voice was small and quiet as he sat on his bed, knees to chin, and backed up as far as he could go against the headboard.

I pushed a hand through my hair. "I'm not happy, that's for sure. Did you have fun?"

He shrugged. "Yeah, I guess. I wish you and Dad could have taken me, though."

"Me, too, little man. Me, too." I tilted my head. "What about the roller coasters? Were they as great as Heather said?"

His mouth pulled up in a crooked grin. "They were all right. But nothing like flying! And I can do that anytime."

I gave "the mom" look. "Not anytime."

"Right. But you know what I mean."

No, I wasn't sure what he meant. Had he been flying whenever he wanted, not just under careful supervision? Did he somehow find a way to sneak that in? Sheesh. Who was I kidding? He found a way to go to Universal Studios without my knowledge, so he could have done all kinds of things and I'd never know. Some mother I was.

But . . . wasn't that what even normal teens did? And wasn't that how their parents were—clueless of half the things their children did? *Ugh. There we go again.* Dorian wasn't a teen yet, but he was definitely growing up way too fast. I'd have to become one of those meddling parents, only I didn't have to dig around his room—I could mind-snoop, and I had no qualms about invading *his* privacy.

"You're grounded," I said. Dorian's head snapped up, and he looked at me with a face full of shock. I rarely disciplined him. I rarely *needed* to discipline him. "I don't know how many times I have told you. No matter who it is taking you, no matter where they're taking you, you always, *always* clear it with Dad or me. Understood?"

He nodded.

"Say it. Say you understand."

"I understand," he mumbled.

"Just to make sure you don't forget again, you'll have lots of time to think about it. No video games. No TV. No Heather." I waved my hand at his room. "You have all these toys and books and Sasha to keep you company for the next week."

He stuck his lip out in a pout as he stared at his comforter, obviously fighting tears. The temptation to forgive and forget nearly got the best of me. I hated this. Hated that we'd disappointed him by not fulfilling his one request sooner. Hated that someone else was able to spend the time and enjoy the thrill of taking him to an amusement park for the first time. Hated that I had to discipline him over it. But he had to understand that he could never do this again. The potential consequences were far too great.

Now, if I could only ground Owen, who'd obviously been the instigator of this little field trip.

When I found him the next day, he was serving Sonya breakfast in bed. I watched from the doorway as he poured blood into a cup and sat on the side of her bed, her eyes never leaving his face. She licked her lips, and her fingers brushed against his as they lingered on the cup he gave her. I couldn't help the snort. *Please.*

Owen looked over his shoulder at me with raised eyebrows.

"When you have a moment . . ." I said. He stood and followed me down the hall, across the foyer, to my office. He shut the door, and I spun on him. "What about Vanessa? Did you even think about her this morning? Or, wait. Yesterday was Sheree and Blossom. Today's Sonya. I guess Vanessa has to wait until tomorrow?"

He pulled back. "Vanessa has already eaten, and Sheree's working with her right now."

"Oh, wow, Owen," I scoffed. "That's brave of you. What are you going to do when they start talking?"

He cocked his head. "What's your problem, Alexis?"

I blew out a huff and then groaned. His girl problems were really none of my business. "Nothing. Nothing's my problem, except your little escapade with my son yesterday."

He nodded. "I owe you a real apology for that. I'm sorry. I wanted to do something for Dorian and something for Sheree. She's been cooped up in this mansion all the time—"

I lifted my hand up. "Don't. Just stop with the guilt trip."

"I'm not trying to make you feel guilty. Only pointing out facts."

I pushed past him, opened the door, and headed for Tristan's room. I knew what Owen said about Sheree being practically imprisoned here was right. But how could I have done anything differently? The Amadis was short on qualified personnel, which left Sheree and me to run the safe house by ourselves.

"Whatever," I muttered. "Just don't ever take my son anywhere without my permission again."

"I said I was sorry."

"Save your apologies. You'll need them for your girlfriends."

This time Owen snorted. "My *girlfriends*?"

I lifted my shoulder in a shrug. "What do you call them? Your girls? Your toys? Your playthings? Because that's all you're doing is playing with their feelings."

Owen sputtered behind me as we reached Tristan's room. My heart broke once more, seeing him chained against the wall. Bree sat in the winged back chair to keep him company —and to guard him—although it didn't appear they'd been in conversation. Tristan's head hung, his chin against his chest, as though he slept.

"You have no idea about my feelings," Owen muttered from behind me. I spun on him.

"You're right. I don't. And it's none of my business. Except someone will have to pick up the pieces of whoever's heart you break. Pick one, Owen. One. Whichever one you want, but don't keep stringing the others along."

He narrowed his eyes. "No, it's not any of your business,

but I'd think you would have figured it out by now, Alexis. The one I want—"

A growl ripped through the air from behind me, and Owen cut himself off. I looked over my shoulder at Tristan, who was fully awake, staring at his best friend with flame-filled, murderous eyes. Bree jumped out of her chair and went to Tristan. For some reason, she could touch him and he wouldn't snap at her. Maybe because she wasn't exactly Amadis. I didn't know but was grateful she could calm him.

I looked back at Owen. He'd clamped his mouth shut. I searched his face for the ending of that sentence, feeling as though I should already know it, but Tristan had distracted me. Owen's eyes looked sad as they flitted away to Vanessa's door.

"She's the one I want," he murmured. "The others are only friends, and they know it. Just like you and me."

"We're more than just friends," I said.

"Yeah, well, I haven't been much of a protector, and you're not really much of a damsel in distress."

"That's not what I mean, and you know it." What had happened to us? Where was the Owen who called me his "little sis from a different miss"?

"Whatever, Alexis." He strode over to Vanessa's door and disappeared inside her room.

I stared after him in bewilderment underlined with sadness. *Well. I'd asked for it.* I had told him to pick one, and he had, apparently before he'd even arrived here. I just really hadn't thought it so serious between them. Had really *hoped* it hadn't been so serious. I wasn't exactly jealous—I had no right to be—but the vamp wasn't quite who I'd expect Owen to fall for. Owen, who didn't exactly love nor trust vampires had become a vamp tramp, to use his own words. And love and trust were pretty vital ingredients to any relationship. Then there were the others. Did they really know they were only friends? Especially Sheree?

I shook my head. Not my problem. Not yet, anyway, and I had many other issues to contend with. Such as my poor husband. I turned to enter his room, and once again, my heart stuttered at the sight. I couldn't get used to it, no matter how many times I saw him like this, which was way too many. This couldn't carry on.

"Bree, I think we need to do it," I said quietly as I sat on the bed next to her. My heart broke as if each word were a slice right through it. "We need to sever the connection."

CHAPTER 21

*B*ree's eyes snapped up to mine and pleaded with me to take my words back. "Alexis—"

As if in response to my decision, as if the Daemoni had actually heard me—*could* they?—Tristan's body bucked to life once more. But they must not have heard me, because a wild grin spread across his face and a wicked gleam filled his eyes, which wouldn't be the expected response to losing their connection. Tristan broke out in what I assumed to be laughter, but the eerie sound would haunt me the rest of my days. The glee lasted for only a few moments as he fought the mage's control, his muscles bulging and straining with the internal battle.

"Kali . . . has the pendant," he croaked. Bree and I exchanged a glance.

"You're sure?" I asked stupidly.

Several heartbeats passed before his eyes rolled up to me, dark and full of flames. "I could practically hear her saying *my precious.*"

Before Bree or I could respond, commotion broke out in the hallway as the sound of Vanessa's door banging against the wall was followed by her voice, not so musical at the moment.

"Owen, no! Don't go. It's too dangerous," she yelled as Owen's figure strode past Tristan's open door on some kind of mission.

I ran into the hall and called after him. "Where are you going?"

"Business to take care of," he grunted, and then he was gone.

"This is all your fault, you stupid bitch!" Vanessa yelled from her room, and I had no doubt she spoke to me.

I crossed the couple of steps to her door. "Excuse me? What did *I* do?"

"You had to screw with him and make him think too hard about what he's doing here and what he *wants* to do, which is to find his father. And that means he's gone off to face that bitch Kali. He's going to get himself *killed!*"

I pulled back. "What do *you* know about it?"

"Because I found him last time. If it weren't for me, he'd already be dead."

I stared at her for a long moment, even peeked into her mind. She told the truth, though she cut me off as soon as she realized I was in her head.

Damn it, Owen! Why? I screamed and punched the wall, and my fist plunged through the sheetrock. Tears of anger and regret burned my eyes. Had I pushed him too far? Obviously, I had. And having no idea where Kali was, I couldn't follow him, couldn't apologize.

I swallowed down the emotional outburst that threatened to do more than leave a hole in the wall, and recited like an automaton what everyone had told me the first time he left. "Owen's a big boy. We have to let him go and hope he chooses right."

Vanessa huffed behind me as I strode back to Tristan's room. Bree stood with Tristan, trying to calm him, but one look at my husband's contorted face reminded me to focus.

"We definitely have to do it now," I said as I sat on the end of the bed, closest to Tristan. I leaned my elbows on my knees and dropped my head into my hands. "Now that Kali has the stone . . . she'll figure out its power sooner or later. And we can't . . ." A sob caught in my throat.

"We can't let her control him," Bree quietly finished for me, confirming my decision.

I lifted my head and looked up at Tristan, wanting desperately to reach out and touch him. His stony expression warned me not to come any closer.

"I'm sorry," I whispered as a tear overflowed and slid down my cheek.

"I'll call your mom," Bree murmured as she stepped toward the door.

"Don't do it," Vanessa said, her voice closer than it should be. I turned to find her behind us. She blanched at the sight of Tristan. Her voice came out quieter. "You'll lose him if you do."

"Don't you think I *know* that? But look at him, Vanessa," I said. "I have to do *something*."

She stared at Tristan for a moment longer then moved her eyes to me, leveling me with her steady glare. "Get the stone."

"Why didn't I think of that?" I said, hitting my head with my palm. "Oh, yeah. Because it's a trap. Remember pointing that out?"

"You would do it for him." It wasn't a question. And she was right. I would sacrifice myself to give Tristan and the rest of the Amadis a chance.

"Maybe I would if I knew how and where. All I know is that Kali has it, but not *where* it is.

"Well, I do."

I jumped to my feet. "You do? And you'll tell me?"

She studied my face. "On one condition."

"Vanessa . . ."

She held up her hand. "One condition only. I go with you."

I threw my hands in the air. "*Seriously? That's your* condition? Or, should I say, your *ultimatum?*"

She shrugged. "Call it what you want. If you want to get the pendant—"

"Damn it, Vanessa," I snarled. I flipped my hand toward Tristan. "Look at him! Are you getting off seeing him like this? Or are you so cold-hearted that you'd rather play games with me than help?"

She took a step toward me. But only one. "I'm doing you a favor. Do you really think you can get in and out with that pendant in your hand? *Alive?* I told you. They're waiting for you. They're *planning* for you. I can get us in *and* get you out. *I'm* your only hope."

Crap. She had a point. I knew nothing about what I'd be walking into, but she knew everything. Even better than Tristan would.

"No," Tristan croaked from the wall, as if he heard my thoughts. "*It's a trap. She's setting you up.*"

I nodded. I didn't know if he knew this from his connection with Kali or if he was simply suspicious, but I was thankful that he still had enough control over himself to warn me. I knew he was right.

My eyes became slits as I peered at Vanessa. "You have the nerve to blame me for Owen leaving when he only left because you told him where Kali is. That's what just happened, isn't it? You guys heard Tristan, and you told Owen. It's your fault he left."

The vampire didn't answer me, but she didn't need to. I saw the truth in her eyes. At least this much of the truth.

"Why do you think I want to go?" she finally said. I cocked my head. Going after Owen motivated her to help me? A tap into her thoughts confirmed this. And where would that leave me once she found him?

"Forget it. I can't trust you as far as—" I almost used the old cliché, but I could actually throw the vamp farther than I could trust her. I shook my head. "You're not ready. Not on any level."

She guffawed. "Scared?"

"Don't waste your breath taunting me. I'm not falling for it. Drop the ultimatum and just tell me where the pendant is."

"And you call *me* cold-hearted? You're going to *lose* him. You have no idea what will happen when they sever the connection, but I've seen what it's like when emotions are cut. He'll be a zombie, Alexis. Or worse, he'll go rogue. Is that what you want? You'll let that happen because you're afraid you can't *trust* me? *That's* cold-hearted. He's your man, though. Do what you want."

She turned and left, leaving me to stare after her. I blinked, then pushed my hands through my hair, clasped them behind my head and studied the floor as if it would reveal the answers I sought. *What do I do?* After several long moments, I lifted my eyes and considered my husband. His arms were spread out, his wrists locked in the shackles at the height of his shoulders. His naked chest barely lifted as he breathed shallowly. His bare legs were pulled out, as well, also chained. Bree had cut away his jeans days ago, leaving only scraps around the shackles so they wouldn't chaff his skin. She gave him a sponge-bath at least once a day. Something I couldn't do.

Even now, as I stood and stepped closer to him, his head jerked up, and he growled at me. His muscles went taut as he strained against the chains.

"Don't tempt me," he snarled. I reached out anyway, *needing* to touch him, missing him so much even when he was right here, yearning for even the simplest caress over his cheek. His jaw snapped at my hand, his teeth narrowly missing the tips of my fingers as I jumped back. He growled in anger—at himself or me or the Daemoni, I didn't know. He dropped his head again. "So . . . sorry," he managed to say.

I swallowed and nodded. "I know," I murmured. "I still love you."

"You . . . shouldn't. I'm broken . . . now, Lex."

"No. Don't say that. We have options."

His head jerked up, and he glared at me. "And none of them are good. Don't do it, Lex. Don't . . . do . . ."

He didn't finish. Had Kali regained control? Did she somehow know he warned me? I couldn't even fish through his thoughts. His mind was . . . black. Nothing. As if a dense curtain veiled his thoughts. His head fell to his shoulder, then rolled down, so his chin pressed against his chest once more.

"He'll probably be out for a while," Bree said. "He's been doing this a lot lately. I assume it's when whoever has the stone sleeps or leaves it behind. Tristan's more like himself, but when he realizes he doesn't have to fight, he collapses in exhaustion. That's what I've noticed, anyway."

She moved again toward the door.

"Don't call my mom yet," I said.

"I won't." She gave me a weak smile that came nowhere near her golden eyes. "I wish I could tell you what to do, but it's not my place. I don't have what you do with him. This is something you have to figure out on your own. But whatever you decide, I'll support you, and do what you need me to do." She glanced at her son with longing, then looked back at me. "You'll be okay here while I take a break?"

I nodded, glad to be left alone with him.

Tristan? I tugged at his mind once I heard Bree stride off toward the kitchen. No response. I stepped toward him again, holding my breath, but still he didn't move. With a shaking hand, I traced my fingers over his cheek. Electricity pulsed through me with the touch. I sighed. I wanted so much more. But I couldn't chance it.

What do I do? I asked myself once again. I had no one to turn to. Mom and Rina would never agree to Vanessa's ultimatum. Owen was gone. Again. *The bastard.* I immediately felt guilty for that thought, remembering Vanessa's warning. I might never see my protector again. *Hmm* . . .

Trying not to disturb Tristan, I stepped silently out of the room and over to Vanessa's. She sat on her bed, arms crossed, looking as though she'd been waiting on me. As if she knew I'd eventually bow to her ultimatum.

"You think we can stop Owen and get him back, too?" I asked.

"That's my hope."

"And you're not setting me up? Luring me right into the lion's den?"

She peered at me for a long moment. "Think, Alexis, about every confrontation we've ever had. How many times everyone else warned me about Lucas wanting you alive and how many times I said I didn't care. Because I *didn't* care, Alexis. I didn't care what they wanted. In fact, giving them what they wanted was the *worst* thing for me."

I had no idea what she meant, but I could hear the jealousy in her voice. They wanted me, and she hated that anyone wanted me, even if for horrible reasons such as my murder.

"But if you gave me to them now, I'd be out of the picture. You'd be Amadis and have Tristan and Owen and whatever else you want."

She laughed. It almost sounded like a snort. "I really don't know how you can be so smart yet so stupid. Seriously. If I deliver you to the Daemoni, I'm *no* one. The Amadis would have nothing to do with me, and I've already severed myself from the Daemoni. I may as well be dead. In fact, I probably would be sentenced to death by both sides. Besides . . ." She looked away and stared at the curtained window, as though she could see through it. Her voice came out in a near whisper. "I owe you my life, or at least the chance to have a real one. I *do* want this way of life, whether you believe me or not, and I wouldn't have it without you."

I didn't know what to say, but I could feel the truth in her words. Vanessa's gaze returned to me, watching as I paced her room, thinking over our options. They were so limited, and the longer I waited to make a decision, the more likely Kali would figure out how to use the stone. And then she would achieve the Daemoni's goal since the beginning of the Amadis. Tristan would single-handedly destroy us, their very intent for creating him.

But the Angels wouldn't allow that, would they? They had as much of a role in his creation as the Demons did. They brought him to the Amadis to serve *them*, not the Demons. So they surely had a plan for all of this. A way for us to win, to get the pendant back, to free Tristan and also to bring us another daughter. I could have retrieved my dagger and seen if Cassandra would tell me the plan, but I already knew it.

I was the plan.

I had to go in myself to get the pendant, and, if I was really lucky, capture Kali's soul, as well. And the plan included Vanessa, too, even if she was setting me up.

So what else? Who else? I couldn't go in there by myself with only Vanessa by my side, especially since I couldn't trust her. But who could be on my team? I had no one besides Vanessa. Sheree needed to stay for Sonya, who was definitely not ready to take on the Daemoni. Bree needed to stay with Tristan, being the only one who could get near him and also the only one who could hold him back. I could take Blossom, and I knew she'd jump at the chance, but even if Dorian and Sasha stayed at the safe house with Bree and Sheree to protect him, no way could I bring Blossom into such a dangerous situation. She wasn't a warlock. She wasn't a fighter. Besides, I needed a mage here, at the safe house.

Because there was one other way this could be a set-up. The Daemoni would expect Tristan and Owen to accompany me, not knowing the situation with either of them. Which meant they'd expect Dorian to be as vulnerable as ever. No, I needed Blossom, as well as every other mage in the colony, here at the safe house with as strong of a shield as they could possibly muster.

"Well? Do you have a plan?" Vanessa asked when I turned one last time, stopped, and stared at her.

I pressed my lips together, pushed a hand through my hair, massaged my temple with my fingers, and then finally said, "Nope. Sure don't."

"But you don't have a choice. You know that."

"I do know that. But what are we going to do? Just the two of us saunter in there by ourselves, pick up the stone, and leave? *You* know it won't be so easy. But there's no one else to help us."

Vanessa shrugged. "We can do it. The two of us . . . ugh, I can't believe I'm saying this . . . but the two of us would make a kick-ass team."

I chuckled. "I don't know what I'm doing, and you're barely converted. In fact, who knows what will happen when you're drowning in all that Daemoni power? I don't even know what will happen to me, and if I can't boost your Amadis power, we're both dead." I shook my head. "You're too weak."

I expected her to make a smartass retort or to even flare up with anger at that comment. But instead she looked at me with a gleam in her light-blue eyes.

"You can make me stronger than I've ever been *and* give me a powerful dose of Amadis energy at the same time." She cocked her head as if to show she'd wait for me to understand, but she didn't give me a chance, too excited about her own idea. "With your blood pumping through me, princess, we'll be unbeatable."

My eyes bugged. She had to be kidding. "Absolutely not."

"Why not?"

Why not? Because that was the last thing I needed—the

person about to betray me hyped up on my extremely potent blood. If she truly didn't want the Daemoni to have me, she could easily kill me using my own powers, and make it look as though the Daemoni had done it. I could beat her now, and even before her conversion, but not easily. With my blood in her system, she'd be too even of a match, and with the Daemoni power surrounding her, it would be too easy for her to freak out and flip a switch. I wasn't about to take that chance.

"It's too risky," I said and gave her only that last reason. "We don't know how stable you are. Besides, you've only been drinking animal blood for how long now? I'm no expert, but I'd think going from that to my blood would be about as smart as a kid exchanging milk for a bottle of whiskey."

"I can handle it," she said with a shrug, but she didn't push it further. "If not yours, then mage blood."

Yes, I'd already thought of that, too, but how? All of our stocked blood was animal. Sonya definitely wasn't ready for anything more, and Sheree didn't want to take the chance with Vanessa until someone more experienced—Char or my mom —could assess her. We had no mage blood on hand, and I didn't know the protocol for asking for it. If I asked Blossom or any of the other local mages, would they freak or did they believe it part of their Amadis responsibility? Of course, if they knew *who* would be getting it, they'd never volunteer to donate anyway. Vanessa remained a secret from the Amadis, although . . . that may not last much longer.

"*Alexis!*" Tristan's voice bellowed in my head. I rushed out of the room and into his. Madness filled his eyes as he looked at me. "*I felt shock . . . a surprise . . . a good one. I feel . . . glee . . . hope? No . . . pride.*"

My heart skittered then stopped. *She figured it out?*

"*I . . . don't know. If not . . . she's close.*"

He fell silent, and his body sagged. *Tristan?* No response. He'd passed out.

I punched the air and screamed a slew of profanities.

I was out of time. If I didn't act—and act *fast*—we could all go down. Kali and the Daemoni would win after all.

"All right," I told Vanessa as I marched into her room. "We're going."

CHAPTER 22

*B*lossom had a fit when I told her about the plan that evening, especially the part about Vanessa, since not even she knew about the vampire's presence in the safe house or the conversion. I'd felt bad about keeping the secret from her for so long, at least until I thought about her own safety, as well as that of the rest of the colony. She probably wouldn't tell anyone else on purpose, but something might have slipped unintentionally during one of her mind vomits.

"I can't believe you trust her," Blossom said when I finished laying out the plan as we sat at her little kitchen table.

Blossom's home was just like her—full of all kinds of interesting things. Bookshelves overflowed with ancient-looking books I imagined to hold spells and potion recipes, as well as various bowls and pots that looked a lot like cauldrons. More books were stacked on tables and counters. Odd shaped objects were scattered about, some with strange symbols engraved or painted on them. And more shelves held jars and jars of ingredients, ranging from human fingernails to muskrat eyelashes to a variety of herbs from all over the world.

But even with all the old books and objects and the array of organics, her house didn't smell musty or icky. It smelled delicious, as if she always had a cake in the oven. Probably because she pretty much did.

"I don't," I said, "but I have no choice."

She looked at me skeptically. "You really think she's converted?"

I rested my elbow on the table and dropped my chin into my hand. "She feels like she is, but we're talking about Vanessa. She's been lying and deceiving for so long, maybe she has some way of fooling me. But all the signs . . . she *feels* Amadis now." I sat back and waved my hand in the air dismissively. "It doesn't matter anyway. Whether or not she's fully converted, I'm out of options. I have to do this."

Blossom's mind spun through all kinds of ideas as it always does, but I had a response for everything she proposed. Eventually, she came to the same conclusion I did.

"Okay," she admitted with exasperation. "You're right. You have no choice. So how can I help?"

I gave her a tired smile. "I was hoping you'd ask."

But when I told her my idea, she freaked out.

"You want me to give her my *blood*? Are you crazy?" Her eyes bugged, and her mouth hung open.

I sighed, regretting I'd put her in this situation. "Yeah, I am. But again, no choice, remember? She needs something stronger than animal blood, and also some magical power so she can at least flash. I need her to have some basic powers."

Blossom made a face. "We'll have that connection vampires get, though. I mean, I've had it with guys, but with another girl? It's just weird. And with Vanessa? It feels wrong in so many ways."

I nodded. "I understand. I wouldn't have asked you if I had any better ideas. Would it help if you saw her?"

Blossom's shoulders sagged. "You already said you don't trust her."

"Right. It's just . . . I don't know . . . on some level I guess I do trust her. I mean, I just feel that she's not Daemoni anymore. That whatever she's planning is to serve her own selfish needs, not theirs."

"Doesn't mean she won't feed you to the wolves to benefit herself."

I rose from the table. "Of course not. I'll be keeping a close eye on her. Anyway, I don't blame you. I'll figure something out."

Blossom couldn't help her generous heart, and by the time Dorian and I arrived at the safe house just after dawn the next morning, Vanessa was stronger than she'd been in months, pumped up on Blossom's blood. The witch had also convinced a group of mages from the colony to hang out at the safe house for a few days to "practice" their shield skills. The plan was in full swing.

Bree would stay with Tristan in the farthest wing where no one would accidentally stumble upon him, and Sheree tended to Sonya while also helping Blossom as the witch bounced between taking care of Dorian and Sasha in one wing and tending to the mages in the commons room.

"Will this work?" I asked Dorian as he looked around the master bedroom suite.

"It's kind of like yours and Dad's room at Rina's," he said after examining the sitting area, the bedroom, and the bathroom, "but better. It has a TV."

"Yes, it does. You brought your games, right?"

He went over to his suitcase, packed mostly with things to do and only a few clothes. He pulled out a game console and went to work hooking it up to the television.

"Heather really can't come?" he asked as I watched him set up the game.

"Sorry. Not this time. You and Sasha will have to hang out by yourselves for a while."

He frowned. "What about Dad? I miss him."

So do I. I pursed my lips together. "I know. Hopefully he'll be home by the time I get back."

As far as Dorian knew, his dad had been out of town for the last few days.

"And Uncle Owen?" Dorian asked.

I bit back a few choice words. Dorian had been ecstatic to finally see and spend time with Owen, and now the warlock had abandoned him again.

"Him, too," I said, hoping Vanessa was right about finding him. "I should be home in a few days, and we'll all be together again, just like we used to be."

His face lit up. "That would be awesome!"

I forced a smile while the probable lie ate at my gut. For all I knew, we could all be dead in a few days. *No. Can't think like that.* I had to have the same hope I fed Dorian. Believing that I'd see him and his father very soon was the only way I could get through what lay ahead of me.

Forcing myself to my feet, I held my arms open, and Dorian walked into them.

"You listen to Blossom, okay?" I said. "She's in charge for now. You do everything—and I mean *everything*—she says, okay?"

"Even if she says let's go to Universal Studios and won't let me ask you first?"

I chuckled drily. As if that would happen.

"Even if," I said.

His next words came out a little garbled. "You'll come back, right? You and Dad and Uncle Owen? You're not leaving me for good, are you?"

I squeezed him tighter against me. "I'll never leave you, little man. Not like that. I'll *always* come for you."

And as the words tumbled from my mouth, I believed them. If nothing else, my love for Dorian would ensure I made it home, or at least, I'd die trying.

"I'd always come for you, too, Mom."

As if I wasn't already having a hard time fighting back tears. If he only knew what that promise meant to me.

"I love you, little man. You be good, and I'll see you soon."

"See you in a couple days, Mom. Don't worry about me. I'll be fine." He pulled back and gave me his stunning smile. Geez, he looked so much like his father.

I kissed him on the head, then bent down to pet Sasha.

"Protect," I ordered. Her blue tongue licked my hand, indicating she understood.

After one last kiss to Dorian, I slipped out of the suite, checked his door lock, then moved into another room to change into my fighting leathers. I tucked the little jar the faeries had given me into my little leather backpack and strapped it to my back and my dagger to my hip before going to say goodbye to my husband.

As soon as I walked into the room, Tristan's eyes slid over me, taking in my outfit.

"Don't do this," he said, barely able to lift his chin from his chest as his eyes rolled up to my face. "I'm not worth it."

"Of course you are. You are worth everything to me, much more than my life."

"Alexis—"

"Besides, it's not just for you. It's for all of the Amadis."

"You're being reckless."

"I'm doing what needs to be done!"

He growled, low at first, in protest to my plan. But then the volume increased and the sound became much more feral. His head jerked. The muscular cords in his neck strained, and he squeezed his eyes shut as he fought whatever was coming over him. His teeth gnashed, and he threw his head back. His eyes popped open, filled with flames.

"*Eureka!*" The voice cackled in my mind—a vaguely familiar one that didn't belong to Tristan or anyone else in the house. Kali's voice. She'd somehow managed to push it through Tristan and into my head. Whether she actually discovered the stone's secret or not, she wanted me to believe she had. She wanted me to come seek her out. Bait. A trap.

And for all I knew, Vanessa played a role it. But it didn't matter. If there was any chance Kali had discovered what she could now do with Tristan, I couldn't spare another second.

"Vanessa, let's go!" I barked.

The vampire called "ready" from the hallway, where she stood right outside of Tristan's door. Blossom had managed to alter a set of my fighting gear to fit Vanessa's height, and we found her some boots. The black leather pants and tank top hugged all of her perfect curves, and her white-blond hair was pulled back in a tight ponytail, mimicking my own. She stood with her hands on her hips, her head cocked impatiently to the side.

"No!" Tristan roared, his back arching again as he pulled against the chains with renewed anger—his own this time. "You'll get her killed, Vanessa. Don't take her to Hades!"

Vanessa eyed Tristan, looked at me, then back at him. "Relax. We're going to Savannah."

"Not much better," Tristan snarled, but his body relaxed against the wall as his eyes turned back on me. "Don't be stupid, Alexis."

"Nobody else can or will do this. I have to find Kali and stop her."

He broke into a maniacal laugh that wasn't his, Kali controlling his emotions again. But when he spoke, his own voice taunted me. "I dare you to try! Have a nice death, Alexis. Wish I could be there to watch."

I didn't acknowledge this last outburst, knowing it wasn't his true feelings, but silently studied his haggard face one last time, wishing like crazy he could go with me. I'd feel tons better about this trip with the ultimate warrior by my side. But, of course, that would accomplish their goals, not ours. This was the first time I was leaving for a fight without him. Hopefully not my last time seeing him.

"I love you," I said.

The way he looked at me, I knew he warred with himself,

fighting Kali's control.

"You may not feel it," I continued, "but *know* that it's true."

I lifted my hand to his face, taking the risk that he'd try to bite it off again, but I needed to touch him. It might be the last time ever. I gingerly pressed my palm against his cheek. His muscles pulled taut under my touch as he strained against the urge to hurt me.

"I . . . know . . . in my head . . . if not . . . my heart," he whispered.

"And I know you love me." He gave me no response, except what I thought might have been the slightest of nods. It was the best I'd get out of him right now. I needed that stone.

"Let's go already," Vanessa whined from the hallway.

"Take care of him, Bree," I said over my shoulder as I strode out into the hallway. "If I'm not back with the stone in time, you know what to do."

"Of course," the fae said, and I hoped I could trust her to do what was needed if I failed at this mission. Severing the connection—and all of Tristan's emotions with it—was our last hope. Our Plan B. I prayed it wouldn't come to that.

I paused in the doorway, placing my hand over my dagger's hilt.

Cassandra? Am I doing the right thing?

"*It is what must be done for the greater good. Just remember, you have the power.*"

With that, I jogged down the hall to the backdoor of the mansion, Vanessa, of all people, by my side. My heart grew heavier with each step I took away from Tristan and my son, and I couldn't help but wonder if Tristan had felt like this when he'd left me at a different safe house, pregnant with Dorian, pleading for him to stay. Same situation, but our roles were reversed now. Hopefully not the same outcome.

As soon as we were off the property and beyond the mages' shield, Vanessa took my hand and led me for the flash. I took in the smell of an orange grove right before we flashed again. This time we appeared under a highway bridge, cars zooming overhead as they crossed the river to our immediate left. Old oak trees stood nearby, Spanish moss dripping from their branches. About two miles down-river, buildings rose from the river's bank and over the land. The mind signatures from the small city weren't all clear to me, but a good portion of them were Daemoni.

"Savannah?" I asked.

"Yeah," Vanessa said, her eyes scanning the area.

"So what's the plan?"

"Well, first I need to confirm my hunch."

"Your *hunch*? I thought you knew!"

"Chill. I've been with you for the last three months, remember? There's a chance I'm wrong. I doubt it. I know them too well. But I'm not going to take you to Hell until I know for sure that's where we need to go."

She disappeared with a *pop* before I could respond. And suddenly, I was alone, far away from home, and, in fact, very close to a large cluster of the enemy.

Shit! I kicked at the dirt, and a rock went flying into the river. Well, it hadn't taken her long to show her true colors. I was so stupid. I thought she'd at least get me close, perhaps even tease me by letting my hand grasp the pendant one more time. But I should have known better. Vanessa wouldn't waste any more time on me than she needed to.

I squeezed my hand over the invisible hilt of my dagger, ready to pull it from its sheath. My feet moved in circles, and my eyes continuously studied my surroundings—the oak trees, a bush down a few yards, a large boulder jutting into the water. Tall Georgia pines tickled the sky just beyond the bank. The smells of river water, dead fish, Georgia clay, and pine filled my nose, but nothing from a living being. Still, I turned and turned, my heart pounding, forcing my ears to strain to hear anything other than my pulse.

What is she doing? What is her ambush?

I knew it was coming. Any second now. My feet moved faster, my eyes continuously scanning for any movement. Would I be able to hold my own for any time at all? How many would she bring? I hadn't been able to pick out any clues from her thoughts. Vanessa was good. Conniving, deceitful, clever enough to know how to catch me off guard.

Even now, the only mind signatures close enough to be clear were those traveling on the bridge overhead. Nobody else was nearby. I sent all of my senses out, including my telepathy. Perhaps if I could ruin any kind of surprise, I might survive long enough to flash back home.

Stupid! She was right. I could be so incredibly stupid. What was I doing standing here, waiting? Did I really think there was any chance she'd told me the truth and this wasn't an ambush? I should just flash home now. Forget about it. Come up with a new plan.

Just as I made up my mind, Vanessa appeared in front of me. Alone.

She lifted her brows at my expression, then she shook her head. "At some point, you're going to have to trust me."

I didn't move. My knees were still bent, keeping me in fighting stance, my left arm out ready to shoot electricity and my right hand still on my dagger. Seeing that I wasn't going to back down—no way would I loosen my guard so they could launch their attack when I thought the danger was over—the vampire simply shrugged.

"I was right," she said, "which means we have a long trip ahead of us."

This pulled me up straight.

"What? Where? I thought Savannah was our destination."

"Kali's not here. I didn't expect her to be—and Tristan pretty much confirmed it—but I wanted to be sure. She's in Hades."

"*Hades?*"

"It's what we—I mean, *they*—call it, a joke left over from what the Ancients and the faeries did to the Greeks. You've heard of the Taymyr Peninsula, right?"

I had. That's where they'd kept Tristan all those years. "As close as you can get to the bowels of Hell," he'd said. So that's what Vanessa meant—she really was taking me to Hell. No wonder they called it Hades.

"So you lied to Tristan about going there."

She lifted a shoulder in a shrug. "Not exactly. I said we were going to Savannah, and we did. It was the only way to calm him down in that brief moment that he actually cared about you. I didn't say that was the *only* place we're going, but if Kali was listening, it was for our own good. Why? Do you have a problem with it? Because if you do—"

I threw up my hand to stop her. If I'd known our plans, I probably would have done the same thing, which bothered me. I would have deceived my husband. *And* I was breaking a promise to him. If going to Hades, the absolute worst place I could possibly go if I valued my life, wasn't being reckless, I didn't know what was.

"Tell me your plans," I said. "*All* of them, or we go nowhere but home."

"We'll flash our way up to Alaska and then over into Siberia." She went over the path of our flashes, town by town, for the first leg. As I visualized the locations, I couldn't help but notice the short distances between each stop. "We'll take a break in Washington before crossing into Canada."

"We don't have time to hang out," I protested. "And why the short flash distances? They're wasting time."

"It's still faster than flying, and safer, too—no chance of getting caught by the Daemoni or delayed by the norms. But if that's not fast enough for you, share your blood with me, and I can flash as far as you can."

"How does that have anything to do with it?"

She let out a breath of impatience, and her tone sounded

as though she explained something complicated to a five-year-old. "It's been too long since I've had real blood, especially mage blood. I'm limited. Unless you—"

I rolled my eyes. "Yeah, nice try."

We began our trip north and west, and the shorter flash trips quickly wore on us. You'd think I'd have an easier time with the shorter distances, but the energy came from the disappearing and reappearing, not the distance traveled. And we disappeared and reappeared a lot more often than I was used to when flashing with Tristan.

By the time we arrived in the forests of Washington in mid-afternoon, my energy was low and Vanessa's was depleted.

"I wanted to follow the sun," she said as she struggled to hike the mountainside to a cave just above us, "because fewer Daemoni are out to catch us, but the daylight's too much for me. I'm too weak in this blood state."

As if to emphasize her point, her foot slipped, and she almost tumbled on top of me. I caught her before she fell and pushed her to her feet.

"We'll stay here until dark," I said, making an executive decision as we reached the cave.

She must have heard the disappointment in my voice. "I only need a short break. And maybe a small taste of your blood?"

"Haha. We'll wait until sundown, you'll find a deer or something, and then we'll go. You're no good to me if you can't at least protect yourself."

Vanessa huddled in the darkest corner and closed her eyes, but I couldn't relax enough to rest. I sat with my back against the cave wall near the opening, my knees drawn to my chin, and my dagger in hand, while my mind spun in more directions than should be possible. I couldn't help but think of Dorian and Tristan, missing them so much, and wondering how things were going at the safe house.

How was Tristan? Had Kali made a breakthrough? If so,

were Bree and the mages strong enough to restrain Tristan? If they couldn't, whatever I was doing could be pointless if I didn't get to the stone in time. I just knew once I had it in my hand, he'd be okay. I had to believe that.

So another part of my mind couldn't help counting off every second we wasted. Another second could be another life Tristan took if Kali gained complete control of him before Bree and the mages could sever the connection. This part of my brain sent signals to my muscles that kept them coiled, ready to act when I finally decided it was time.

Then there was the third part that could barely contain those muscles from springing on their own—the part that kept one constant eye on Vanessa, even when my physical eyes finally began to close. This part kept tight hold on her mind signature, ready to alert me if something twanged in her thoughts.

As the sun moved overhead and into the western sky, my head started falling, and I jerked up.

"Sleep, princess," Vanessa said, watching me from where she lay in the deepest, darkest part of the cave. "You need to regenerate."

"I'm fine," I muttered. A brief burst of adrenaline pumped through me, caused by the feeling of falling as I'd nodded off, but it quickly ran down, and my eyes began closing again. *Only an hour or two. Have to wait for the sun to set anyway.* I let my eyes stay closed, and my mind finally drifted off with images of Tristan and Dorian flickering on the backs of my eyelids.

A sting across my hand tugged me out of unconsciousness, but it was the feeling of a mouth against my palm that jerked me full awake. Not Tristan, I knew right away. The hardness of the cave floor reminded me where I was, and my eyes popped open. I squinted against the late afternoon sun shining brightly through the cave's opening to find Vanessa squatted over me, her tongue sliding over my palm.

"What the hell?" I shrieked, jerking away from her, but she held tightly to my hand. She gave it a look of longing then threw it at me.

"It's already closed up," she complained.

"What do you think you're doing? I told you. Not my blood!"

"Relax. I only got a couple drops before you healed." She licked her lips. "But damn, was it good."

The way she looked at me . . . fangs fully extended beyond her upper lip and glowing blue eyes swirling with desire . . . I tried to scoot backward, away from her, but my spine already pressed against the cave wall. At least her eyes weren't red like a Daemoni's would be—a good sign. But, shit, she'd drank my blood. I looked at my palm, and she was right, the wound had already healed, which made no sense. I couldn't heal that quickly from a vampire's fangs.

"I didn't mean to," she said, her voice small now. "You slid your hand over your dagger while you were sleeping . . . the smell was overpowering . . . I—I couldn't help it."

She stared at my blade with intense longing, and, squinting, I saw the narrow line of blood that confirmed her story. Which also explained how I'd healed so quickly. She told the truth.

"I'm hungry, Alexis. I have to—" Her head swung toward the opening of the cave as her nose twitched, sniffing the air. She disappeared in a flash.

My breath caught in my throat, and I lunged for her flash trail, but I was too late to catch it. Fortunately, my mind found her signature not too far away, about a hundred yards down the slope. She must have picked up the scent of a deer or a—

Oh, shit.

Animals don't laugh.

CHAPTER 23

Vanessa, don't! I warned her before I flashed to her location, but she was already flying at the hikers when I appeared. I slammed into her body, knocking her far off course. We flew so far so fast, the Norman hikers probably had no idea we were there or how close they'd come to being Vanessa's dinner. A tree stopped us, and we crashed to the ground.

"*Bitch! I'm freakin' starving!*" In a blur, Vanessa came at me.

No people! I threw my arms up to block her attack.

Her knuckles skimmed against my temple. I jabbed my fist up and caught her chin. Her head snapped backward, and anger filled her eyes.

"I'm a *vampire*," she said as she punched me in the jaw, making me stagger. She moved forward. "We eat people!"

"You're Amadis now. *You* don't eat people." My leg came up, and my foot thudded against her ribs. "You're better than that."

In an instant, her hands were around my throat. She lifted me off the ground.

"Your goody-two-shoes act gets so *old*," she groaned.

"Little Miss Perfect who gets everything she wants. You make me sick!"

She squeezed my throat harder. I punched and kicked her, but she didn't let go. I zapped her with electricity, which caused her grip to loosen enough for me to breathe, which was enough for me to keep fighting.

"Well, your lack of self-control gets old," I retorted as I shot another bolt of electricity at her. She jumped out of the way, releasing me completely, and the current hit a tree trunk, blowing off a chunk of bark. "Little Miss Spoiled Brat who needs to learn some self-discipline. Your sense of entitlement makes *me* sick."

"I hate you!" she screamed as she flew through the air at me.

"I hate you more," I yelled, throwing myself into her path.

"I've hated you longer!" She wrapped her arms around my shoulders, pinning mine to my body. We hit the ground and rolled several yards, before stopping against a boulder with her on top. She punched me in the face. If I were a norm, she would have knocked me unconscious. Perhaps even killed me with the force. As it was, pain shot through my cheek, and stars danced across my eyes.

"Only because you're old as dirt," I said. "What were the dinosaurs really like, anyway?"

She let out a hiss-snarl as she swung to punch me again. I arched my back and bucked her off before her fist made contact. We punched, kicked, choked, and wrestled, shoved each other into tree trunks, and rolled over the rocks and logs on the ground. Each blow brought a grunt out of the other, but we kept fighting, wrestling, and yelling profanities. At one point, I couldn't help but think how much Tristan would have enjoyed watching this.

The thought of him reminded me why we were even here. We didn't have time to be screwing around like this. I needed to end this farce so we could move on. If only my blood hadn't given Vanessa such a burst of energy. I had to wear her out before I could bring her down, and to be honest, I could only do that by listening to every thought she had before she actually made a move. But she was super-fast, even with the sun still up. My blood apparently increased her vampire speed. Finally, I got a hold of her with my legs and flipped her to the ground. She landed hard on her back, me on top of her. I shoved my hand into her face, pushing it sideways into the ground, waiting for her to yell mercy.

Then I felt it. And we both froze.

Her fangs had been out. My hand had pressed down on one. Hard enough for it to puncture my skin.

I jerked my hand to my chest as Vanessa looked at me again with intense longing.

"Please . . . Alexis," she panted. "I'm really sorry about all of this. About what I said. I didn't mean it. I'm just so *hungry*. And weak. If you won't let me feed off those hikers . . ."

My head moved side to side in a slow shake. "No, Vanessa. No people."

"Animal blood won't do it, though. We won't make it!" Her voice rose in volume with her desperation. "The mage power is *gone*. I've burned through it already. I can't even feel your witch friend anymore. Norman blood would strengthen me, but yours . . ."

She trailed off, not needing to finish the sentence. She didn't move underneath me, didn't try to get up or throw me off of her. She just lay there, looking up at me with big, pleading eyes. Was the fight in her really gone? If she had any energy left, she wasn't using it against me now when the smell of my blood had to have been driving her crazy. Despite what I'd said, she really had improved in showing self-control. Perhaps we'd both said things we didn't mean.

"A few drops of my blood gave you that strength to fight me?" I asked, truly amazed.

She nodded her head against the ground. "But it was just a tease, and it set me off."

Any more than a few drops could make her formidable against our opponents . . . or against me. Could I take that chance? Did I have a choice?

"I guess we can use that kind of strength," I finally said. "But no more fighting me, or I'll blast your ass with electricity until you shrivel into a pile of ashes and purple smoke. Got it?"

"Feed me, and I won't need to fight you."

Hoping I wasn't about to make the worst mistake of my life, I removed the backpack, unzipped my leather jacket, and shrugged it off, leaving my shoulders and arms bare, only the leather bustier covering my top half. The late winter chill of the mountains caressed my skin, probably too cold for a norm but not uncomfortable for me.

I held my wrist out to her.

Vanessa didn't miss a beat. She grabbed my arm and pulled it toward her mouth. My jaw clamped when her fangs pierced my skin. Then my blood gushed toward the wound as if it'd been waiting for such a release from the confines of my veins. After a few swallows, a strange look overcame Vanessa's face. Her light blond brows pushed together, and her eyes showed confusion, then a spark of a thought. They locked on mine for a long moment as she seemed to be considering me in a new light, then she shut them, seemingly in bliss as she fed her hunger.

I couldn't help but compare this to the one and only other time a vampire had drank from me. In our first real fight, right before I'd gone through the *Ang'dora*, Vanessa had nearly killed me. Who would have ever imagined then that I'd be feeding her purposely now? I also thought about the time when Tristan had sucked my blood. He hadn't done it for nourishment of course, but to clean a wound he was helping to heal. The feeling had been erotic, nearly bringing me to an orgasm.

In fact, that's how it *should* have felt. Solomon had confirmed the drinking of blood served as a sensual and sexual pleasure for both vampire and victim/donor/partner/whatever-the-situation-was. But I felt *nothing* now, and Vanessa showed no signs, either. I mean, she drew heartily and made sounds of contentment, but no more than anyone enjoying a delicious meal. I'd been on the brink of death last time, so I couldn't be sure, but I didn't think either of us had felt anything then. Why not?

Although we weren't exactly BFFs and despite the fight of a few minutes ago, I thought we'd moved past the true hatred. Was it my Amadis blood? Or something else?

Vanessa finally opened her eyes and pulled away. She ran the back of her hand over her lips, wiping off any blood. "You taste . . . familiar."

"Well, it's not the first time you've had me, remember?"

She ran her tongue over the bite marks on my wrist, and they closed right up.

"No, that's not what I mean. I'd thought about it that time, too, but had dismissed it. But now . . ." She shook her head, then smiled lazily, and I couldn't help but notice how she was even more beautiful like this—rosy cheeks, bright eyes that weren't full of hatred, at the moment anyway—a natural look. I swung my leg around and rolled off her, onto my back.

I hadn't realized I'd needed to lie down until I did. How much blood had she taken? Of course, I hadn't had much rest and regeneration, and I hadn't eaten since . . . well, it'd been over twenty-four hours, that was for sure. No wonder my head felt woozy.

One moment Vanessa lay on the ground next to me, and without so much as a blur, the next she stood over me, picking leaves and twigs out of her ponytail. She shrugged out of her jacket and danced around me.

"I feel *fabulous*." She let out a hoot as she spun in a circle.

I moaned, her movements making me dizzy. "I feel like crap."

She stopped and stared at me for a long moment. I grimaced at her in her tight leather pants and bustier, but not out of jealousy. Actually, I had on a nearly identical outfit and looked as good. At least, I had before our fight. Now I probably looked as bad as I felt. I only wanted . . .

"Aren't you supposed to have fed, too, by now?"

I didn't answer her. Something on her chest had caught my attention, momentarily making me forget how badly I felt. A fading tattoo . . . no, more like a scar that had healed yet not completely vanished. With a very familiar design.

"Vanessa, what's—?"

I tried to lift my hand to point, but didn't have the energy. She followed my gaze, then rolled her eyes. "Oh, that. It showed up when you converted me."

"Is it what I think it is?"

"The Amadis mark? Yeah." She said no more.

"But how? You don't get the Amadis mark from converting. You have to actually have Amadis blood—oh! *Really?*"

She shrugged. "I never knew my mother. She died while giving birth to my brother and me, but I think she was the daughter of an Amadis son. A converted daughter, no less."

"Your mother was *Amadis?*"

From what Mom had told me one night as we sat in Rina's room, Daemoni daughters were even rarer than Amadis sons. Female descendants of Jordan only came every few generations and hardly ever survived the change. Same with daughters of male descendants of Cassandra. This had been one of the reasons they weren't sure about my surviving the *Ang'dora*, since my sperm donor was a Jordan descendant. And if Dorian had a daughter, the probability of her making it past the change was virtually nil. Mom had said there were none of these daughters alive now, and there hadn't been since before her own *Ang'dora*.

"In every which way," Vanessa said. "At least, that's what I think. Like I said, never knew her, and I was raised by the Daemoni."

If this were true, why wouldn't Mom know about Vanessa? On the other hand, why would Vanessa lie about it? The Amadis mark was right there on her chest, and it couldn't be faked. She would have healed too quickly if it hadn't come from the inside.

"And your father?" I asked.

"No idea who he is." Something flickered over her face that told me she thought otherwise. "A Daemoni bastard who raped my mom and left us with a witch to live as orphans."

Another rape. Another pierce in the back of my mind—a question I didn't want to acknowledge.

Instead, I recalled Vanessa's visions during the conversion, and all of this explained how she'd not been norm before becoming a vampire. But who would turn her, if she'd already had her own powers from both sides of her lineage?

"Then why were you turned? With the bloodline . . ." My voice trailed off at her closed-off look.

"I thought you didn't feel well. Don't you eat more often than this?"

She'd opened up to me about herself more than she had ever before, but apparently she was done. Ready to change the subject.

"I *don't* feel well," I said, "but we haven't exactly had time to stop and eat."

My stomach gurgled, as if on cue. I definitely needed to eat, but unless I hunted down my dinner, which there wasn't a chance in Hades of happening, we had to move, get going to the next town. But I felt too weak to even push myself off the ground.

Vanessa squatted over me. "What do I do?"

I couldn't help the shock of seeing her face, so kind and concerned. For me. This day grew weirder and weirder.

"I don't think I can even flash," I admitted. "Not yet anyway. Just give me a few minutes. A little rest will help."

I closed my eyes for what felt like a minute or two, but when I opened them again, I darkness surrounded me. While I'd dreamt of lying in Tristan's arms once again, night had fallen. My heart hurt at the reality that I wasn't with him. With the knowledge that he and my son were so far away. I squeezed my lids shut, wishing myself to them, conjuring the image of sitting on the beach and watching the sunset while Dorian built a sandcastle by the water. The image came so clearly, I could almost feel Tristan's breath on my ear as his lips nibbled my lobe.

But, of course, when I opened my eyes, I still lay on the forest floor in the Pacific Northwest, about as far away from them that I could be while still in the Continental U.S. And tonight, we'd be traveling in the opposite direction of them. Soon, I wouldn't be in the same country, and by the end of the night, not in the same hemisphere. If everything went wrong, not even the same world. *Let's not let everything go wrong.* I let out a sigh. *The sooner we start, the better.*

I blinked a couple of times against the pure darkness of night in the middle of a forest until my vision adjusted. Vanessa was in her jacket, leaning against a tree trunk, her arms across her chest, and her eyes moving, never stopping for long in any one place. She was keeping watch over me.

A white paper bag sat on the ground between us. My mouth watered at the scent, even if it was that of cold grease. I stretched my arm out, but couldn't reach it. She nudged it with her boot, pushing it toward me.

"I hope you're not a vegetarian," she said.

"Where'd you get this?" I asked as I tore open the bag and through the wrapper around the hamburger.

"Went to town. Just over that ridge." She nodded toward

my left. "We might have a bit of a problem. I hope that burger keeps you satisfied for a while."

I was too busy eating to speak. *What's going on?*

She narrowed her eyes at the sound in her head, and spoke aloud, clearly indicating her preference. "I didn't get the full story, but the military is cracking down. Apparently, they're looking for anyone not human."

I choked on the bite I'd been trying to swallow. Vanessa had to pound me on the back to dislodge it from my throat. I'd have bruises between my shoulder blades in the morning. Well, even more than I probably already had from our wrestling match.

"They know? The norms *know*?" I asked with disbelief.

The moonlight danced off her white-blond hair, making it look silver as Vanessa shook her head. "I don't think so. I eavesdropped on a couple of guys in uniform—police, border patrol, National Guard, I don't know. Anyway, from what I heard, the norms are suspicious of our existence, but have no proof yet. There were uniforms all over the place. The guys said the borders are lined with military."

I stared at the ground and chewed for a moment as I considered this new obstacle.

"This is all part of the Daemoni's plan, you know," Vanessa added.

I squinted up at her.

"No, I don't really know. Tell me," I said before taking another bite.

"Turning norms against each other. Country against country. They'll make everyone suspicious of each other to instigate wars. Then they turn the wounded, leaving the Norman armies weak and outnumbered, and that's when they'll come out. The Daemoni. They'll come out of hiding and take control. They're taking over little cities, like Key West and Savannah, getting reading to move in on the big metros. They've infiltrated the governments worldwide. It's only a matter of time." She watched me as I shuddered. "Of course, they need to get rid of the Amadis first."

"So we need to move faster, before they get to Tristan." I jumped to my feet, hoping it wasn't already too late. "Let's get going."

"Wait, there's more. If the military is guarding the Canadian border so heavily—a border between *allies*—then something's going on. Someone's working with them, possibly more than just planting ideas in their heads. One or both sides of the border may be protected by a mage. Or certain towns might be. We might not be able to flash everywhere we need to." She peered at me in the darkness for a long moment, then blew out a breath she'd apparently been holding. "How far does your mind reach?"

"I don't know. I actually haven't tested it in quite a while, but a couple of miles last time I checked."

Her lips twisted in a grimace. "I can't believe I'm saying this, but keep it open with mine. If we try to flash into a shielded area, we'll bounce off and might not land in the exact same place."

"Sounds like an adventure," I muttered, once again wishing I could go home, be with my men, where it was safe and . . . *No. It's not safe.* You *have to make it safe.*

We flashed several times, through Canada and all the way through Alaska, with no problems. Vanessa now easily flashed place to place, going farther, pushing my normal limits, and with little energy drain. I barely caught a glimpse of each place we appeared before she popped away again, and I followed her. As we made our way up the coast of the Pacific and across the Alaskan tundra, the air became colder with each flash, and the moonlight bounced off snow and ice rather than running rivers.

We finally hit the western shore of Alaska, the Bering Strait in front of us, and an island in the distance. In one more flash, we'd be deep into Russia. But Vanessa sucked her breath in, and didn't disappear right away. I turned away from the sea and toward land, took in the scene and echoed her gasp. Rather than a vast landscape of snow reflecting the moon, several large, tan tents were spread in front of us, along with Hummers and snowmobiles. Big spotlights shone down on us, making me blink several times.

We'd apparently appeared right in the center of a makeshift military installation, and at least thirty rifles pointed at us from all directions. At least they were all norms.

"Looks like we have our proof, boys," someone said. "*Humans* don't just appear out of thin air. I knew the Russians were hiding them."

"What do we do, sir?" someone else asked, but I already knew what the first guy was thinking. I gathered him to be the commander, and what he wanted to do with us wasn't good. *Shit, fuck, damn.*

"Lock 'em up for now," he ordered, and the circle of men moved toward us.

"*Let's get outta here,*" Vanessa's voice rang in my head, just as my own thought came to mind.

Wait! No. I have an idea.

Vanessa glanced sideways at me, her eyes lit up. "*We're gonna fight them?*"

I didn't have time to lecture her about not fighting norms unless absolutely necessary. I only had a few seconds as the men crossed the fifty yards to reach us, and I needed that to share my idea, sparked by Rina's plan with my books—to expose just enough truth to ignite a little fear in the norms so they'd learn to better protect themselves.

"Don't do anything stupid now," the man in charge said as the group moved as one, closing their wide circle around us.

Show them what you have, I told Vanessa.

Her eyes flicked toward me again with questions in them, but she shrugged. "*If you say so . . .*"

In a blink, she had her jacket unzipped and her fingers were working the buttons at the top of her bustier.

What—No! Show them your fangs. Let them see what they want to see. Scare them—just don't bite.

She stuck her bottom lip out. "*Where's the fun in that?*"

"We don't want to hurt you," the commander continued as his men came dangerously close to us. "Just be good—"

I shot a small bolt of lightning out of my hand, and it hit the ground in front of the commander. All of the men jumped back a pace.

"Now, see, that was stupid," the commander said. "That's not being good."

"*We* don't want to hurt *you*," I said, keeping my hands held up, palms out, as they started closing in on us once again. Purplish-silver electricity crackled over my fingertips to give them a good show.

With fangs fully extended, Vanessa blurred around the edge of the circle, stopping a couple of times to half-lunge at the line with a threatening hiss. The men paused. She returned to my side, her lap completed in maybe two seconds, and I thought we'd shown them enough to believe whatever they'd heard. I was about to tell Vanessa to flash.

But, unfortunately for us, they were either avid fans of my books or, as Vanessa suspected and much more likely, someone had fed them secrets. Because they knew exactly what to do to protect themselves.

Shots cracked loudly through the air. A moment passed before I realized what they were as smoke trailed out of the barrels of several guns and the smell of burnt gun powder filled my nose. Vanessa's body jerked in response, and four soldiers were on top of her before she even hit the ground. From her screams, I knew immediately those were no ordinary bullets and no ordinary handcuffs they tried to clamp on her flailing wrists.

They knew to use silver, and it must have been enchanted since she was now Amadis.

For a moment that felt like minutes but probably lasted only a second or two, I watched the soldiers trying to overpower the vampire. The silver might have weakened her, but she wasn't going down without a fight—she was mad as a, well, as a vampire who'd been shot with silver. Two more men joined their comrades, trying to pin Vanessa down, while others trained their guns on her.

Had they forgotten about me? Should I use this distraction to flash away and save myself? She was a vampire. Surely she could overpower them, especially with my blood in her, and escape. Besides, she was likely setting me up anyway, leading me to my own capture or death. Perhaps this was a blessing.

Vanessa snarled and growled, and her body bucked against the captors as she tried to fight her way out. Another shot cracked the air. The vampire screamed with pain. And I had no decision. There was only one right thing to do.

"Vanessa!" I shrieked as I blurred to the frenzy. I grabbed a soldier by the jacket and threw him off, but the sounds of rifle chambers clicking into place stopped me from grabbing the next. All twenty-something guns were now trained on me. I froze, hands in the air.

They shot me anyway.

CHAPTER 24

*W*hite-hot pain seared across the back of my calf. Again in my thigh. Too shocked at first to react, two bullets hit me. I didn't wait for more. I dropped and rolled, then sprang to my feet and ran at them in a blur. Adrenaline pumped through my veins as I shot electricity at some of the men and waved my hand at others, sending them flying through the air. My fists grabbed the coats of two more men, one in each hand, and I yanked them off of Vanessa and threw them to the side. They landed with simultaneous thuds in the snow about ten feet away.

Another soldier swung his gun at me. I caught it in one hand while flipping around in an aerial cartwheel, knocking him out when my boot collided with his temple. He crumpled to the ground. I grabbed Vanessa's hand.

Can you flash?

"No!" she screamed as her body jolted from the ground just as another round of gunfire cracked through the air. The barrels had been aimed at me. Vanessa took the hits, her body wrenching with each one. She fell into my arms.

Hoping my flash with Tristan from South Beach wasn't a fluke, I held the vampire tightly and flashed. I targeted right across the Strait, to the island I had seen from the shore. We appeared—both of us—at the top of a snow-capped cliff, the sea far below us. Nobody around.

As soon as I let her go, Vanessa collapsed in a heap. The searing pain finally registered in my mind, and a scream hurled out of my mouth. I dropped to my hands and knees next to the vampire, clamping my jaw shut against more cries. The wounds healed immediately, and the pain began to recede. I blinked away the tears so I could inspect Vanessa's body. They'd only been trying to incapacitate her the first time with shots to the legs that were already healed. But three more holes patterned her leather jacket—the bullets that had been meant for me. Blood leaked from these, but not nearly as much as expected. A closer inspection showed the wounds already closing.

"I need . . . your dagger," she gasped. "Gotta . . . cut . . . these out."

"I'll do it."

"No! Just . . . give it to me."

I pushed myself around to sit next to her. My calf and thigh still throbbed, but the bullets must have only grazed my skin because I felt no foreign objects lodged underneath.

"Vanessa, you can't do surgery on yourself," I said, exposing the dagger and removing it from its sheath as I leaned in closer.

"Watch me." In one swift motion, she'd snatched the blade from my hand and had discarded her jacket. Her eyes squinted, and her lips curled in a grimace as she dug the tip into her right shoulder.

"The silver," I said, not knowing how she could stand even more than what had already peppered her body.

"A perk to being Amadis now," she said through gritted teeth as she maneuvered the dagger around until the bullet popped out. She sighed as her skin closed right up.

"It doesn't hurt you?"

"Oh, it hurts all right." She gasped as she dug the blade into her side. "Hurts like a motherfucker. But if I were still Daemoni, I'd be wishing to die to escape the pain."

She removed the bullets quickly and expertly, as if she'd done this before. I made sure to return my dagger to my side before we both collapsed on our backs.

"We should have flown after all," she mumbled as we stared at the star-studded sky. There seemed to be more stars here than there had been in the Australian Outback. And they were so big, so close.

"Yeah," I agreed. "Why didn't we? Oh, wait. Something about this way being faster? And safer?"

"Shut up," she muttered.

"Bite me," I said.

"Don't tempt me."

We lay in silence for a while, neither of us particularly wanting to move on yet.

"I think we would have been better off showing our boobs," Vanessa finally said, breaking the silence.

"Maybe." I laughed. "I can't believe that's what you thought I meant. As if . . ."

"Trust me, it works. You've been given beauty and a hot body, why not use it?"

I blinked. "Never crossed my mind, actually."

"The Angels gave it to you for a reason. Well, you get it from your vamp DNA—the Ancients gave us physical beauty to better attract our prey. But the Angels enhanced yours for a reason, right? Because norms respond to beauty. I mean, even before the *Ang'dora*, you were—"

"What?" I'd never forgotten her words when we'd first fought in Key West. "You were disgusted by me."

"Yeah, because Se—I mean Tristan still wanted *you*. And you didn't compare to *this*." Her hand flipped off the ground, waving at her curves. "How could he *not* want this?"

I kept my mouth shut, but could hear Tristan's voice

saying something about *that* not being his style, especially everything that came with it. Even now. He'd picked me.

"I'm sorry you went through all that with him," I said quietly. "I don't know what it's like to not be with someone you want—"

"Of course, you don't. You always get what you want."

"Oh, please. You think I *wanted* to be the freak growing up? To move around all the time and never have any true friends and no family that I knew of? That I *wanted* to be thrown into this crazy world with supernatural creatures that shouldn't even exist? To have my husband taken from me for seven freakin' years and to know that he may never be completely free from his creators who want nothing more than my head? That I want to someday lead an entire society that depends on every decision I make? Whose future won't exist if I don't have a daughter against all possible odds? Oh, but wait. I must have *wanted* to have a boy so I could just hand him over to the enemies and lose him forever. No, Vanessa, I don't always get what I want." I paused, then couldn't resist adding, "If I did, you would have been dead two years ago."

My rant was met by pure silence. And then a musical laugh. "Touché."

"But no," I said quietly, "I've never had my heart broken in the same way you have. And I'm sorry about that."

"Whatever. It doesn't matter now." Vanessa cleared her throat. "Anyway, there's nothing wrong with using what you've got. It'll make your life a lot easier. Men don't usually go around shooting beautiful women unless provoked. Such as *you* had us do."

I ignored her spot-on jab. "We're Amadis, though. We don't use *any* of our gifts unless there's a good reason."

"And getting out of there alive so we can retrieve the stone is a pretty damn good reason."

She was right once again. Another weird moment for the night: *Vanessa* teaching *me* how to fight like an Amadis.

"Of course, I don't recommend that with the Daemoni," she added. "Rape is one of their favorite past-times. You don't need to worry about Normans—you just proved you could handle them—but Daemoni . . ." Her voice trailed off, and then she sighed. "I can't believe I stayed one for so long."

Statements like these made me wonder whether she really was setting me up or actually helping me, especially because her thoughts and emotions always corroborated her words. In fact, as I thought about it, I couldn't remember a time Vanessa had actually lied to me. I didn't always like what she said, but at least she'd always been truthful.

Maybe she'd give me an honest answer to my question about our current topic of conversation. I couldn't bring myself to ask Tristan because I didn't know if I could stand to hear the truth from his mouth. I'd been trying to dismiss the nagging thought, telling myself I really didn't want to know, that it didn't matter because it was in the distant past. But I couldn't let it go, especially when the topic kept coming up.

"Can I ask you a question?" I finally blurted. "About Daemoni and rape . . . I think I should know . . . if Tristan . . ."

I stammered, as if my tongue didn't really want to ask the question.

Vanessa turned her head to look at me. "He never raped, as far as I know. He never *needed* to—women were practically raping him." She chuckled, though no humor colored the sound. "To be completely honest, he drove Lucas nuts when it came to anything with women and children. Seth claimed he was too much of a warrior to be bothered with them, that having anything to do with them was a waste of his time and power. He would only take on the big guys in battles because the younger ones weren't worthy. But I knew—and I'm sure Lucas knew—Seth had a soft spot. That's why I fell in love with him." She let out a sad sigh.

I gulped down the lump in my throat. "But I've seen his memories—women and children's faces . . ."

"Did you actually see him hurting or killing them directly? Him personally?"

I tried to remember the visions I'd seen on that balcony at the beach house in the Keys, when I'd been trying to convert Sheree and Tristan had taken the evil into his body.

"He burnt down whole villages. There was blood on his hands. And lots of their faces . . . the faces of his victims." Tears burned my eyes, blurring the stars above into smudges of light.

"Well, he *did* always take the credit—or the blame, whatever you call it now. But Lucas used to come back from battles completely pissed. He'd rant and rave about what a pussy the so-called warrior was for not showing his domination over *everyone*." Vanessa snorted. "And then other times, Lucas would brag about how he got to rape all the women because Seth wanted none of them." She shook her head. "Disgusting, really, to hear that from the man who was —" She paused for a moment, as if editing her thoughts. "From Lucas."

I lay in silence, letting the relief wash over me and through me, cleansing my soul from that worry.

"I mean, don't get me wrong," the vampire continued. "I'm sure he was responsible for many of their deaths. But rape and torture of women and children? That was beneath him."

I could accept that. After all, I already knew he had a dark past, including murder and other heinous acts. I'd forgiven him for it all, but still . . . somehow, knowing he didn't partake in the Daemoni's favorite past-time, as Vanessa had just described it, made me feel better. And thinking about him doing the right thing, even when he was at his worst, made me love him and miss him that much more.

"We should get going," I said, forcing myself upright.

Vanessa sat up again, too, and eyed the dried blood on my torn pant leg. "What a waste," she muttered.

My mouth twisted into a grimace. "Do you need to feed?"

"Well . . . I *was* just shot. And we have our longest leg ahead of us."

I pushed my sleeve up far enough and slid my dagger across my wrist. She only pulled a few swallows before closing the wound up with her tongue.

"That's enough?" I asked. I hoped so. My body probably couldn't handle more, especially when there wasn't exactly a Burger King or Publix anywhere around.

"I'm good. At least, I am if we can rest for a while longer. What about you?"

"Does it matter?"

She looked around at the barren landscape. "Good point."

We lay down and watched the pattern in the sky slowly shift for a couple of hours before returning to our journey.

The moon never seemed to move as we followed it over the frozen tundra of Siberia. Several hours later, we finally stopped flashing outside of a remote village near the Taymyr Peninsula. With Vanessa in the lead, we hunted the area until we took down a mountain goat, then lugged it to an abandoned cabin —if you could call the rickety structure a cabin—where we'd fuel up and regenerate. We settled in a little after midnight local time, and we would stay until sunrise. Today was the day we'd go to Hades, and we'd both need our full strength. That meant Vanessa would get another meal of me, and I'd need a sizeable amount of the goat that she showed me how to cook over a fire.

Even after being shot, my body aching from all the flashing, and my belly a little full, I couldn't sleep. And it had nothing to do with my surroundings, because when I closed my eyes, the cabin disappeared and I was home with my two men. My heart ached with longing for them. Tears seeped through my lashes. *If I make it through today, I'll see them again soon.*

I'd already decided that if we survived this insane stunt, we'd flash non-stop to the nearest airport, call Mom, and have the Amadis jet pick us up and take us straight home. First, we had to survive. And the reminder of what would come in only a few short hours sent my heart into a gallop.

"Maybe if I drink now, you'll pass out again," Vanessa suggested after a couple of hours of fighting sleep. She must have heard my heart pounding, sensed my unease. "You'll be no good if you don't rest."

Her idea worked. She drank. I ate. Then I passed out. She woke me a few hours later, the gray light of dawn seeping through the cracks in the walls. I stretched, feeling renewed and even better after eating more of the mountain goat.

"So," Vanessa said, standing at the door of the cabin, watching the sun rise from behind the mountain. "You ready for this?"

Ready to meet the enemy? Ready to face my likely death?

"Not in the least," I said, joining her.

"Well, then. Here goes nothing." She paused, then added with obvious reluctance, "Keep your mind open to me."

We went over her plan once more, then moved out. I unsheathed and exposed my dagger, ready for anything, and the feeling of power rushed through me.

I'm going to need you now more than ever, Cassandra.

"I am here as always, but you already have the power you need. Look to yourself, Alexis. The power you and I share resides in your heart and soul."

What does that mean? She didn't answer, but I felt her with me, and for now, that's all that mattered.

Wanting to avoid as many people as possible for obvious reasons, Vanessa took us the "back way" known by only the Daemoni elite. As soon as we stepped inside an icy cave, the secret entrance to the underground city they called Hades, my skin prickled and crawled. Every cell of my being, all the way to my soul, sensed that we'd entered enemy territory. The waves of evil energy strengthened as we descended down a dark tunnel carved into the earth, wide enough for Vanessa and I to walk side-by-side, but Tristan and I probably couldn't. The air grew colder the farther down we went, but also heavier, pressing down on me until I thought I might suffocate. The energy thrummed in my head, and I could easily imagine the world collapsing in on us.

"*You should have warned me you're claustrophobic,*" Vanessa said.

I'm normally not.

"*Then you're letting their dark power get to you. Just breathe.*"

I nodded and tried to focus on the fact that we'd been lucky so far—we hadn't encountered a single Daemoni yet. But then I couldn't help but think how convenient that was. Breaking into the enemy's compound shouldn't be this easy. Where were the guards? The locked gates and doors? The ear-piercing alarms to alert them of intruders? Of course, they might not need such mundane security measures. Perhaps we had already set off magical alarms, and they were just waiting in secret foxholes to ambush us.

Unless . . .

"*Wow, you have serious trust issues, don't you?*" Vanessa broke into my thoughts, already knowing where they led. "*I have the Amadis mark now. The silver didn't debilitate me. I took a bullet for your ass—three of them, actually—and I haven't killed you myself yet. When will you start trusting me?*"

But why aren't they coming? Why haven't they stopped us yet?

"*Because they're arrogant assholes. It probably hasn't even crossed their minds that anyone but their most revered would enter this way. They'd never imagine that I'd betray them. If they even know we're here, they believe what you were just thinking, that I'm leading you right to them. But you're both wrong.*"

I still couldn't help but think she was setting me up, but I repressed those thoughts, hiding them away from her. I still needed her help, and making her angry wasn't the best way to get it. I couldn't mask my racing heart so easily, but hell, we walked through the lair of my enemy. It'd be racing no matter what.

The packed-dirt floor finally leveled out as a soft light in the distance grew closer. We were almost at the end of what I was about to determine an endless tunnel. Just as the corridor widened into a large room with sconces of fire on the walls, Vanessa pulled me against the wall. Little particles of dirt crumbled away as we pressed against it.

"*Anyone?*" she asked.

Although I'd kept my mind open to mind signatures and knew there were none nearby, I mentally scanned the area again. And bit back a gasp. Two strange vibrations in my mental realm, one nearby and one several hundred yards away. My first thought was shifters in their animal forms, but no, shifters still had clear mind signatures with their human brains. These were more like something trying to be a mind signature, but not quite . . . *there*. Faeries? Possibly, but I didn't think so. It was more like they hid behind veils, as if cloaked. I focused harder, trying to break through the veils, and finally the signatures became clearer. I knew them both.

Kali, I answered Vanessa. *But that's not all.*

CHAPTER 25

J peered over Vanessa's shoulder with a small smile as the owner of the closer mind signature came around the corner, although at first, he couldn't physically be seen. When he came to stand in front of us, he removed the cloak.

Before I could do the same, Vanessa jumped at him and threw her arms around his neck.

"Shhh," Owen whispered as he extricated himself from the vampire's embrace. He tapped his blond temple, and I opened my mind for all of us, although a sense of unease prickled the back of my neck. Something wasn't right here.

Have you been following us the whole time? I asked.

"*I knew you'd lead me right here,*" he answered with a smirk.

"*And you made it!*" Vanessa said. "*When I'd told you about the village before, I never thought you'd actually find it.*"

"*I'm not stupid. I waited there, knowing Alexis wouldn't resist your offer.*"

My eyes tightened as that feeling of unease grew. *So are you here to help us? Or do you still have your own agenda?*

Owen peered at me for a moment. "*If you're here to find the sorceress, our agendas are the same, aren't they?*"

With a clear connection to his mind, I knew that's all he

thought about. Not anything about this being some kind of trick or set-up. Not from Vanessa, either. But the thought still niggled its way under my skin.

Yeah, I guess so.

If we were here only for my personal agenda, I'd do everything I could to avoid Kali and just get my pendant back. But I needed to find her to find the pendant, and besides, I had the faeries' agenda, too. If Owen felt the need to kill the sorceress once we found her, well, he'd be helping me out. My fingers traced the strap of the backpack that held the little jar for Kali's soul. The faeries must have given it some kind of protection for it to have survived in one piece after everything I'd already been through.

"*Wait,*" Vanessa said. "*Does Kali even have the stone?*"

I tried to latch onto the sorceress's thoughts and share them, but the powerful mage wasn't stupid. She knew how to block me. Which meant she knew I was here?

"*More like she doesn't trust anyone,*" Vanessa said. "*She probably shields herself at all times, especially this close to the Ancients.*"

"*She's the best place to start,*" Owen said. "*Anyone else nearby?*"

I shook my head.

Are you going to cloak us? I asked Owen.

"*It will make moving more difficult. We need to be able to see each other, especially if we get ambushed.*"

I nodded with understanding. At least, most of me understood, but a tiny part of me still suspected.

"*As long as you keep your mind open to new approaches, we'll be fine,*" Vanessa said.

Let's get on with it then.

Staying close to the wall, we crept our way in the direction of Kali's mind signature. The large room ahead was a junction of four tunnels, including the one we'd just come down. We went through the opening to our immediate right.

"*I'm not surprised this is where she is,*" Vanessa said. "*She'd stay away from the crowds.*"

From there, we blurred to Kali's location, a small room carved into the earth. A fire blazed in a grate on the far side and more sconces hung on the walls, lighting up a workbench with scattered vials, herbs, and old books with ancient-looking handwriting.

A young-looking woman with bright red hair that flowed thickly down her slender back had been sitting at the workbench, but she'd jumped up just as we'd arrived, an emerald green cloak, the same color as her eyes, billowing around her. Kali's mind signature came from this woman—the body she must have taken over now. Her snake-like eyes fell on Owen.

"I knew you'd come," she said. But rather than fear or concern, joy filled her voice.

And Owen smiled back at her as he fell to one knee and bowed his head.

"Of course," he said. "You've always been my one and only master."

Owen, stop it! I yelled at him. *She's controlling your mind.*

"*No, Alexis,*" he answered. "*This is all me.*"

My jaw dropped as Kali took two steps to stand in front of Owen, her eyes never leaving him, while Vanessa disappeared into a blur. So this was their plan? They'd both been serving the Daemoni and Kali all along? My muscles automatically braced for Vanessa's impact, but she didn't come at me. She continued blurring around the room.

"*She's distracted. Search!*" Vanessa ordered me.

I couldn't move for a moment, frozen with disbelief as Kali stroked Owen's hair and cheek. The sorceress then lifted her hand, and Owen obediently rose to his feet.

"*Hurry!*" Vanessa shrieked.

I snapped out of it and followed her lead, moving around

the room at a blazing speed, rifling through everything on the table in a matter of seconds.

"Stop them!" Kali barked, and Owen waved one hand while twisting the other in the air.

A current of air blew past me, and I slammed into an invisible wall, forced to stop, and at the exact same time Vanessa slammed into the other side. We both stumbled backwards, but quickly regained our footing. Owen's hand waved again, then he moved in between us, where the invisible wall had been, a palm out directed at each of us. Kali stood in front of us all, a wicked gleam in her green eyes.

The sorceress flicked her hand the same way I'd seen Owen do when summoning something, but nothing happened. She narrowed her eyes and did it again, but still nothing moved. She rushed over to the table.

"Where is it?" she hissed. Objects started flying through the air as Kali searched. Owen took several steps back, his hands still aimed at us, and glanced over his shoulder.

"Looking for this?" Vanessa dangled the pendant between her fingers, the ruby-colored faerie stone flashing in the firelight, before tossing it at me. My heart leapt. I could have kissed Vanessa.

As I reached out my hand to catch the pendant, Owen's wrist twisted, and the stone's trajectory changed. It landed in the warlock's hand. With a bow of his head to the sorceress, he dropped the pendant into the front pocket of her robe. My heart, which had been soaring, plummeted.

Owen, how could you? No answer but a cold, sapphire stare.

"Well done, my son," Kali said to Owen, and when he dipped his head in another bow, my stomach lurched. "Now what to do with you two? I don't appreciate thieves."

"The pendant is mine," I said. "You're the thief."

Kali's mouth turned up in a beautiful but dreadful smile. "I think I feel like playing."

She turned the heat of her full gaze on me, and a piercing

pain shot through my head, as if an icepick had been buried into the back of my skull. The agony blinded me and nearly brought me to my knees. My heart bruised the inside of my chest as it raced, but when my hand reached to my head, no weapon protruded. I clamped my mouth shut, silencing my scream, and gritted my teeth through the pain. Kali preferred mind games. *Not me, bitch.* Straining with intense focus, I eventually raised my mental shield I used to block out others' thoughts. The pain disappeared.

Thwarted, Kali's face twisted with anger, then she shot her glare at Vanessa. The vampire's mouth screwed into a painful grimace that eventually gave way to a spine-tingling scream. Her hands clawed at her chest, and blood poured over the top of her leather halter as she fell to her knees.

"Stop it," I yelled as I lunged for Vanessa. I caught the vampire in one arm and, with the other, raised my dagger at the sorceress. "Stop now!"

Kali eyed the silver blade—the one that had caused her to lose her body the last time it had pierced her—and laughed. But the blood that had been all over Vanessa disappeared as if it had never been there, and the vampire stopped screaming, though she still trembled against me. Magic had made us both believe the mirage, but I knew from my own experience the pain felt very real. Knowing the sorceress could inflict such mental agony was more frightening than if she'd physically attacked us.

"You're right. Why waste my time with you, when I can do this?"

She lifted her hand, waved it in the air, and the fire-lit room disappeared. We suddenly stood in the middle of the main road of Captiva Island with the safe house on our right and the beach on our left. *Oh no!* Tristan came barreling down the front stone steps of the mansion, shooting fire from his hands back at the safe house. The mansion exploded, its roof blowing into pieces, windows shattering, and flames jumping high in the air. With fire-filled eyes, he ran down the road toward the island's small business district, shooting more fireballs with one hand and causing trees to crash on houses and cars with the other.

The scene disappeared, and we were back in Hades.

But my heart was still in Captiva. A storm of emotions roiled through me, taking my breath away. My son. Blossom and Sheree and Sonya . . . the colony and the norms . . . Had Tristan already done all of that? Or had she just given him the orders? Either way, she'd shown that she knew the power of the stone, and it sat right now in her pocket, giving her control. What was meant for love would now be used with the darkest of purposes. *This was all for nothing. We're all dead.* But then my mind focused like a laser beam on a single thought. *Not if she's dead first.* With the hope that killing her would sever her connection with Tristan, I twisted the dagger's hilt in my hand and threw it. Just like last time, it spun end-over-end in an arc, but this time, it landed in her chest.

Kali's mouth shaped into a surprised O as her hands flew to the dagger buried hilt-deep in her chest.

"Get. Her!" she hissed, and the next thing I knew, Owen's hands were around my throat, and my feet dangled in the air.

Owen! Don't do this, I pleaded with him, staring him in the eyes as I clawed at his hands. He glared back with hard sapphires, his face straining as the grip on my throat tightened. Tears blurred my vision before falling. *Please, Owen. Don't let her do this to you. You're my friend. My protector. You're like my brother!*

"*No, I'm not, Alexis. I'm nothing to you.*"

Stop it! My lungs seized with the lack of air. *This isn't you. You give your energy to Uri, remember? Not Duff, Owen. Not . . . Duff.*

A memory of his mother flickered in his mind, and something in his eyes glimmered. Or maybe it was only one of many pops of light flashing in my vision from the lack of oxygen.

You're really . . . going to . . . kill me? I asked with the last bit of consciousness I had.

"That's enough!" bellowed a vaguely familiar male voice.

Owen let go, and I fell to the floor, on my knees next to Vanessa. My lungs drew desperately for a breath, and the air felt like razor blades slicing down my throat. When the lights stopped flashing before my eyes, I looked up to see someone new in the room, removing the dagger from Kali's chest. The sorceress gasped as the silver left her body, and then sneered at me.

"You're not so dangerous when your mommy and pussy-whipped husband aren't around, are you?" Kali asked.

"I said that's enough," the man growled at her, his voice cold and deep. "Remove the projection."

With a slight bow of her head, Kali waved her hand, and our surroundings transformed. We were no longer in a small workroom, but in a vast cavern with several other people—well, shifters—standing at its perimeter and this man in the center, just in front of us. I slowly rose to my feet, pulling Vanessa up with me, and eyed the man who had made Kali obey.

Nearly as tall as Tristan with shoulders almost as wide, he wore a black sleeveless shirt that exposed his muscular arms and black dress pants with combat-style boots. Eyes the color of icebergs looked Vanessa and me up and down, as if appraising us. Not a single wrinkle lined his face, but his goatee was snow white, as well as his long hair, which was tied in a ponytail and draped over the front of his shoulder. This had been the guy from Vanessa's memories, and with their similar features, I had no doubt he was her dad. So why had she said she didn't know her father?

"Very well done, both of you," the man said, his icy blue

eyes scanning over all of us, then resting first on Owen and then on Vanessa.

His meaning sunk into my brain and then branded my soul. *Both of you? I'd been right?* Vanessa had been playing me all along? Even now . . . all of this had been an *act?* Although I'd suspected it—even *expected* it—the betrayal of both Owen and Vanessa slammed into me with the impact of a city bus. I inhaled sharply, and my lungs trapped the air inside. My heart stuttered, shrank, became a rock in my chest.

I was never getting out of here.

"Thank you, too, Kali," the man said, waving my dagger in the air as he eyed the sorceress. "I appreciate this gift. You can go now. And take your minion. That is, if he wants to go. Maybe he wants to stay here with us?"

Those ice-blue eyes locked on Owen's now. The warlock shook his head and moved to Kali's side. At this point, I was no longer surprised. My protector had tried to kill me, after all. The bruises on my neck still throbbed.

"You're dismissed." The man sneered at Kali, as if she dared to remain any longer. "Go on! You have work to do."

And the frightening sorceress—the one who had nearly drained the entire Amadis Island of all its energy, who now controlled my husband—almost seemed to cower beneath this man. Who was he, that he could frighten even Kali? With a flourish of her hand and a breeze that lifted the hair off my neck, the two mages disappeared, leaving Vanessa and me alone with the man. Oh yeah, and with the silent shifters standing guard.

"So what do we do now?" the man asked.

Vanessa swallowed noisily, and for the first time in, well, ever, I felt fear rolling off her body. But what was she so afraid of? She'd done her job, as far as I could tell.

"Vanessa, you of all people ought to know that you can't take something from me without giving in return," he said.

Vanessa pulled up her shoulders and lifted her chin. "We've taken nothing."

He snarled at her. "I'm not a fool, child! I know what you came for!"

Vanessa swallowed again. "But we don't have the pendant. They took it back. Besides, it belongs to her. What had you given *her* in return when you took it?"

My mind spun. What was Vanessa doing? Whose side was she on?

"Her life," he said. "And, apparently, yours."

"Well, then, since she doesn't get the pendant, let her keep her life. In return," Vanessa took a step forward, "you can have me back. *Father.*"

The man made a sound that I might have called a snort if anyone else had made it, but he wasn't the snorting type.

"*Father?*" he asked as if he didn't believe she'd had the gall to call him that. "We're going to do this again?"

"I know it for a fact now. You can't deny it anymore." She took another step forward, anger overpowering the fear she'd felt moments ago, giving her confidence. Her voice came out as icy as his. "I was never good enough for you, was I? Victor was. Your oh-so-precious Victor. But not me. You were too embarrassed to call me your daughter so you denied us both. And then you made me into *this*. This monster that I am."

"I did it for your own good. I saved your life."

"No, you didn't. You took everything away from me. Everything! I wanted a family. A life. And you took it. Just like you took my mother's." Tears streamed down Vanessa's face, and I actually felt sorry for her. She surely hated each traitorous drop. And at that moment, I knew she hated him, too, and the Daemoni. That she truly had converted. That she hadn't set me up, and I could trust her.

The man smirked. "This is exactly why I did it. To make you *strong*. Invincible. But you're still so *pathetic*, it's disgusting."

It took every ounce of control I had to keep from getting involved. This wasn't my fight. Not this part. This was between Vanessa and her fa— No, not father. That was no father standing before us. He was no better than my own sperm donor. But what did I expect from the Daemoni?

He crossed his arms over his chest and looked down his nose at her. Ice dripped from every word. "What has finally convinced you? What makes you so sure you're even right?"

Vanessa jerked her head in my direction. "Her. The one you *did* always want."

My heart jumped again. She was bringing me into this after all. But why? What did I have to do with them and their dysfunctional relationship?

Vanessa smirked at the man's narrowed eyes as her tongue ran over the tip of a fang. "Her blood tastes very much like someone else's I've had. So much, that there must be a close relation. Closer than cousins. It tastes like Victor's. Like mine. And we know Sophia's not our mother, so the tie must come from you. Am I right, Father?" She practically spit that last word out. "Or, I guess you prefer I still call you *Lucas*."

My heart leapt into my throat. I felt like I had when Mom had first told me about him. As if I'd been punched in the stomach. How had I not considered that I'd come face-to-face with him while we were here? How had that not crossed my mind? And here he stood in the flesh.

Lucas. My infamous sperm donor.

CHAPTER 26

"*W*atch it, or it'll be Mr. Emerson to you," Lucas snapped at Vanessa, dropping another bombshell.

So not just Lucas, but Lucas *Emerson*! As in A.K. Emerson. Rina had given my author's pen name after *him*. *Why*? But even more jarring—if Lucas, my sperm donor, was also Vanessa's father, that meant she . . . *Whoa*. I couldn't process it all. My mind was in too much shock. I stood there stupidly, eyes wide and mouth open, no words forming in my muddled brain.

Lucas's mouth stretched into a grin as he drank in my expression. My jaw must have been hanging at my knees. I snapped it close.

"Welcome home, my daughter," he said as he acknowledged me for the first time with a tone that became suddenly warm and inviting. "I hope you plan to stay."

I took a step backwards, swallowed down my heart, and croaked, "Never."

"Ah, that's a shame. I hoped for a different answer. But I guess you are your mother's daughter, aren't you? How is that cunt, anyway? She probably thought it funny to rub your

301

books in my face by using the surname I so frequently go by. Just made me proud to be your father."

A small noise sounded in my throat as I tried not to gag. Lucas smirked again at my reaction. *Jabbing buttons. He's just trying to get to you.* I tried to control the anger clawing at my chest.

He shook his head when I didn't answer. "I guess it's not the time for a grand reunion. So let me make this clear." He stepped toward me, his icy blue eyes piercing into my soul. His warm, buttery voice became glacially cold. "You take something from me, I take something in return. It's only fair."

"As if you believe in fairness," I whispered.

"Oh, now, see, you don't even know me. I *do* believe in fairness. At least, when it's in my favor." He chuckled at his joke. "And this works in all of our favors, don't you think? You get Vanessa and I get something I want. Win-win! Isn't that what your generation calls it?"

"What do you want?" I asked, stalling for time to try to figure out how we were going to get out of here alive. Never had I wished so vehemently that I knew the best solution.

"My daughter of course."

"Then take me," Vanessa said. "I'll stay. Let her go."

Vanessa, no! I knew she really didn't want this. She was doing it for me. Vanessa, my once sworn enemy, was trying to save me.

"He'll never let us out alive. I have to try!"

Lucas eyed her, as if considering. Then he waved his hand at her, and she flew backwards, her back cracking against the earthen wall. He burst into laughter as her body slid to the floor. My heart hurt with the sound of his frigid guffaws, but not nearly as much as Vanessa's must have.

"*You're* not what I want!" he barked. "You're right—you were never good enough. And definitely aren't now." He turned back to me. "I want the daughter that actually matters. You stay, Alexis, and Vanessa can go, and I'll even let her take the stone with her. Seth will be free of us. He'll be safe, and so will the Amadis."

My head moved side to side with each promise I knew he'd break. Lies. Deceit. Their most powerful weapon.

"You wouldn't do that for your people? Your husband? Your *sister*?" And, man, did he know how to use that weapon. "How about my grandson, then?"

"Never!" I seethed.

"I'll eventually get Dorian anyway, though. He'll be, what —nine?—next month? I'll be getting him soon, so why delay the inevitable? It'd be such a great trade for you."

The anger boiled over at the sound of my son's name coming from his wretched mouth. Just that he knew my son well enough to know his age and birth date made me sick. My body moved on its own until I stood nose-to-chest to Lucas. I glared up at him.

"You lay a hand on my son, and I'll fucking kill you."

He laughed, the sound of an iceberg breaking apart. "Beautifully said. I'll have you on my side one of these days, my daughter. It's only a matter of time." His eyes flicked over to Vanessa and then to me as he combed the tip of my dagger through his goatee. "Here's what I'll do. I'll let you go as long as you take that traitorous whore with you. If you can get out of here alive, you're free."

What? I eyed him with suspicion. "You're letting us go? Just like that?"

"Well, no, not *just like that*," he said, mimicking my voice. He narrowed his eyes at me. "But I can't keep you here. Not against your will and not alive. Otherwise, Dorian might get it in his head to come rescue his mummy. And *that* just might break the curse and ruin all of my plans for you and your little family." He leaned toward me. "I need him to come to me on *my* terms, not as a self-sacrifice."

"*If he's letting us go, we gotta get out of here!*" Vanessa shrieked in my mind.

Lucas snapped his fingers and the shifters—five burly men and a woman with black hair down to her knees—instantly stood next to him. The woman gave me a surly grin.

"Let's see what you're made of. I'll even give you a head start before I set Rene, here, after you." Lucas nodded at the woman and then the others. All of them burst out of their skins, were-goo flying, replaced by five werewolves and a cheetah. He petted the cheetah's head, and she let out a growl.

Vanessa was on her feet, already tugging at my hand. "*He's playing a game. Let's go while we can!*"

But I didn't move, my eyes on my dagger still in Lucas's hand. I needed my weapon. I needed Cassandra.

"My dagger?" I boldly asked. "You've given me nothing for it in fair trade, so can I have it back?"

"I'm giving you your *life!*" he roared, all sick humor gone, replaced by the intense anger of an overpowered tyrant.

A hissing sound whistled through his teeth. The shifters crouched, ready to pounce, the hair along their spines standing on end and their lips pulled back from their saliva-dripping fangs. Vanessa wasted no more time. She bolted, pulling me with her, through the doorway and down the tunnel, the werewolves right on our heels. But not the cheetah. Lucas really was giving us a head start.

I shot electricity blindly behind us, but it sounded as though it hit the walls and not our pursuers. I glanced over my shoulder, and a wolf's golden eyes were right. *there*. I flicked my wrist, and he flew back, plowing into the others like a bowling ball. They recovered immediately.

"*Faster!*" Vanessa said. We moved so quickly, the walls became a brown blur on either side of us.

But we weren't fast enough. As we rounded the bend, claws dug grooves down my back. I stumbled, then fell face first.

My fingers fumbled for the back-up weapon I kept in my boot as long teeth scraped against my knuckles, trying to stop me. I eventually found the knife, and flipped it open while trying to roll over, but the wolf pinned me to the ground with one paw on each shoulder. Its jaw snapped near my head, its hot breath blowing on my ear. I wiggled and squirmed and finally pushed myself over. As I rolled, I plunged the knife in between the gray wolf's ribs. It *arfed* like a dog, but the wail trailed into a human moan of pain. I scurried out crab-like from under the naked man's body, and yanked my knife out of his side. I stared, mesmerized, at the blood pooling under him. My chest contracted. I'd *killed* him? Was this my first kill?

"*Alexis!*" Vanessa shrieked.

I spun to find a wolf's mouth attached to her arm and another yanking on her calf, about to pull her down. I pushed a wave of power at them, and they both flew off her, their bodies crashing to the ground. Now freed, Vanessa took off in a blur, and a second later, reappeared right where she'd been, her tongue licking blood from her lips. All of the wolves morphed back into their human forms. All of them dead.

"*Let's go!*" She grabbed my forearm and ran again. I stumbled after her at first, still in shock, but my survival instinct finally kicked in, and I ran.

The large room where the tunnels met felt so much farther away than it had been before, but we finally flew into it. And so did more wolves from all directions, blocking our way out. We had no choice but to fight.

One or two wolves would have been no problem. Even five or six or seven. But this many? And still more poured out of the tunnels. Vanessa grabbed the ones that lunged at her by the heads, snapped their necks, and flung them away like ragdolls. I blasted them with Amadis power and electricity until the putrid odor of burnt fur made us gag. But there were more than a handful to pick off one-by-one. A pack of twenty or so attacked us, jaws snapping and claws swiping.

Our fists and feet pounded at the creatures' bodies. Vanessa ripped into their necks with her fangs, and my knife sliced into their limbs and shoulders and haunches, but this smaller blade didn't compare to my dagger, and the damage was minimal. A wolf's claws raked through my hair, ripping out a clump. Other claws ripped through my leathers and into my skin. Snouts clamped down on my arms and legs and shook like a dog does with a rope, tossing me back and forth. My head smacked the wall, then the floor, then the wall again, each impact rattling my brain. I formed a bubble of Amadis power within me and pushed it outwards. They all let go.

But only for a moment. They lunged again and grabbed on to whatever part of my body their teeth found. I gathered more Amadis power, worked it into a frenzy, and exploded it out of my body. The wolves yelped and whimpered as their bodies crashed into the walls and floor. We seized the opportunity and ran again.

But something was wrong.

I thought we'd chosen the same passageway we'd come through, the one that led back to the icy cave. But that one had been long and empty, no signs of life surrounding it. As we continued running now, I sensed mind signatures up ahead. Tons of them. Way too many to fill a tunnel. Way too many to fill a cavern or even a large building. Enough for a small town . . .

Vanessa!

"*Oh, shit!*" she said at the same time. "*That's the marketplace.*"

She spun on the spot and grabbed my wrist again.

"*Hurry! Before they sense us!*"

We ran back the way we came, but before we returned to the junction, the tunnel suddenly veered off to the left when it had been straight just a moment ago.

"*Mages are changing the paths. He's messing with us,*" Vanessa said.

We passed a wide opening, and Vanessa darted inside the

room. She bent over, her hands on her knees, and looked up at me.

"We need to regroup," she said, keeping her voice low.

I leaned my butt against the wall and assumed her same position. Neither of us was out of breath, but at least for me, my heart raced, and adrenaline pumped too quickly in my veins. My pulse pounded and whirred in my head.

Then the wall disappeared from behind me, and I fell on my butt.

Lucas stood over me, and his lips turned up in a smirk. "Change your mind, my daughter?"

I jumped to my feet, and Vanessa straightened up. One glance around told me we were back in the room where we'd started.

What now? I asked Vanessa. She gave me an I-have-no-clue look. Actually, knowing her, it was more like a we're-fucking-dead look.

So Lucas really was just playing a game with us. He had no intention of letting us go.

"Did you change yours?" I asked bravely. Or stupidly. Whatever. It didn't matter anymore, if Vanessa was right. "Did you decide it's okay for Dorian to break the curse? Or that it's okay to kill me?"

Lucas grinned, exposing his perfectly straight, snow-white teeth. "See, I can't bring myself to kill you. You have too much potential for me." He tsked, and Rene the cheetah, in animal form, sauntered over to his side. "My followers, however . . ." He ran a hand down the cheetah's spine. ". . . I can't always control them."

"So you're still letting us go?" I asked.

"Like I said, if you can find your way out alive, yes. This time."

Vanessa and I exchanged another glance, then moved for the doorway.

"One more thing, Alexis," Lucas said, and I hesitated.

"Since you were so kind to return, I must offer you another deal. I think you wanted this?"

I looked over my shoulder. He held his hand out, my dagger lying across his palm. I lunged, but he clamped his fist around the blade faster than I could grab it.

"Now, now. Fair trade, remember? But I'll need more than just the garbage taken out this time," he added, his eyes flickering to Vanessa then back to me. "Seth or Dorian will do."

A dagger over 2,000 years old, forged by the Angels themselves, probably more precious than anything in Amadis history. And it was my best weapon, especially with Cassandra's power behind it, my connection to her. I needed the dagger to give us any hope of escaping Hades. I needed Cassandra's power to live through this. But nothing, not even the possibility of my own survival or even Vanessa's, was worth the lives of my son or husband.

"Not a chance in hell," I said.

"Ah, you'll regret that. But don't worry. I always get what I want. I *will* get what's mine." He glanced at his bare wrist. "Oh, sorry. Out of time. You've lost your head start."

He hissed, and instead of werewolves coming after us, Rene did.

Vanessa and I ran again, the cheetah chasing us down. I'd never run so fast in my life, but it wasn't fast enough. With a peek over my shoulder, I looked right into amber eyes. The cat roared, drool hanging from her five-inch-long fangs. Then she sprang off her back legs, and those same fangs tore into my bicep. I cried out as I spun around and slammed her with electricity.

I held the current on her, even as we ran, and the cheetah slowed enough to give us a chance. Then her footsteps behind us fell away, and I looked over my shoulder once again. The cat took off down a corridor we'd just passed.

"Where's she going?" I asked Vanessa.

We ran another hundred yards or so, then Vanessa slowed almost to a walk now that nothing chased us. Her head turned at each corridor we passed, inspecting it even as we moved on.

"To get help?" she finally answered my question. "To spring ahead and cut us off? Who kno—"

An orange streak of light blasted through the air and smashed into the side of her head. She screamed once and fell to the floor. Another streak flew at me. I threw myself on top of Vanessa's body, narrowly missing the spell that hit the wall, carving a chunk into it. Granules of dirt rained to the floor. My mind found a mage's signature down the hallway that branched off to our right, where the orange lights had come from.

I lifted my head just enough to peek. A cloaked figure crouched in a doorway. I latched onto his thoughts in time to hear the next spell before the orange light soared at us. I rolled off Vanessa, flat on my back. The light skimmed over us, singeing our leathers before hitting the wall like its predecessor. I shot a bolt of electricity in return. It hit the floor right in front of the mage, making him jump. While he reconfigured, I yanked Vanessa's body out of his path, then shot another bolt at the mage as he sent a spell at me. I connected with him and kept the current flowing in a bluish-silver arc, the air sizzling around it. But he continued shooting a series of orange lights at me. With my free hand, I pulled my knife out again and held it up to try to parry the spells. One bounced off the blade and slammed back into him. His figure sank to the ground, smoke rising from his cloaks.

I hurried to Vanessa, squatting next to her body.

"Come on, he's gone," I said, pulling on her arm. "At least, for now."

"I can't see," Vanessa whispered as she sat up, her eyes wide but glassy. She rubbed her fists into her eyes, and when they came away, panic contorted her face. "Alexis? I can't see!"

I grabbed her hand. "I'm right here. It's okay."

"It's *not* okay!" She shook off my hand. "I can't *see*. How can I run if I can't see where I'm going?" She threw herself back on the floor. "I'm dead."

"No, you're not."

"I may as well be. And you are, too, if you don't go."

"Then let's go."

She pounded her fists into the floor, leaving divots in the frozen earth. "I *can't*, Alexis. Don't you get it? You go. Get out of here."

"I'm *not* leaving you here."

"Yes, you are. There's no need for both of us to die."

I rocked backward off my heels to sit on my butt and dropped my head into my hands. *What am I going to do?* After everything we'd been through, I wasn't about to leave Vanessa behind. But I didn't know how to get out. Hell, she *knew* this place and hadn't found the way out yet. And now she couldn't see to at least try.

"You're still here," she said.

"Of course I am. I told you, I'm not leaving you."

"Then what do you plan to do, oh smart one?"

"I don't know. We can't sit here right in the open." I didn't sense any mind signatures close by, but that could change in an instant. "Do you think your vamp powers will heal your sight any time soon?"

"I'm sure. Eventually."

"Will a drink from me help?"

Vanessa lifted her hands in a shrug. "Probably. But then *you'll* be too weak to go on, and although I could, I'm not carrying your ass out of here if I don't have to."

"So we need a hiding place." I looked around, then glanced down the hall where the mage had been. "I'll be right back."

Keeping my mind open, I rushed to the doorway where the mage's body still lay and peeked inside. A small, empty room, no bigger than a bathroom, and with no fire in the sconce on the wall. Just dark enough that maybe we could hide there for a while. I hurried back to Vanessa.

"Keep your hands on my shoulders and try to see through my mind," I said, and I led her to the room.

We settled in the darkest corner, huddled together, and I gave her my wrist. When she was done, I collapsed beside her. But only for a few minutes. Several mind signatures buzzed on my radar.

Someone's coming, I told Vanessa. *Can you see yet?*

"*Not in the slightest.*" But then she straightened up. "I have an idea, though. Follow me."

CHAPTER 27

*V*anessa held her hand out in the air, searching for mine, and I took it, not knowing what to expect since she couldn't exactly lead me anywhere. But then she flashed, and I realized barely in time to catch her trail. Of course, we couldn't flash out of the Daemoni compound—that would have been too easy—but we flashed to a different part, and appeared in another tiny room that had no doors or windows, no way in or out. And treasure filled it—all gold, no silver, of course.

"Put what you can in your pockets," Vanessa said, feeling her way around.

"What is this? *Whose* is this?"

"It's mine. This is my vault. We can't stay here long, though. This will be one of the first places Lucas looks for us when he realizes they lost us. But hopefully we'll have enough time for my sight to come back."

I picked up an ancient looking gold coin. "Wait," I said, hesitating before putting it in my pocket. "Where did *you* get this stuff from?"

She shrugged. "Some I won, fair and square. Most I stole."

I dropped the coin. "We can't take this, Vanessa. It's like . . . blood money."

She groaned as she sank to the floor. "I knew you were going to say that."

I sat on the floor, leaned my head against the wall and closed my eyes. "We don't need it anyway. Let's get a little rest then get out of this God-forsaken place."

But resting allowed the adrenaline to dissipate from my system and my mind to think of more than running for my life. Everything that had happened in the last few hours pressed down on me like a two-ton beast making itself comfortable on my bruised throat and chest. The image Kali had shown us of Tristan destroying Captiva Island, and the colony and the norms with it, replayed behind my eyelids. Now that she knew the power of the stone, what had she made him do? Where would she lead him next?

Breathing became impossible as heartbreak ripped through me. I had failed. Oh so miserably failed. The Amadis, with humanity right behind it, would fall. This whole trip had been a waste of time. I'd not just miserably failed, but *epically* failed. And I would never see Tristan or Dorian again.

Or would I? I could always choose to stay here and then we could all be together . . . I remembered the vision I'd seen during my *Ang'dora*, of Lucas—I now knew the man in the snowy field—tempting me with this idea while Mom and Rina had stood on the sunny side of the mindscape, fighting for me. With the Amadis, I was guaranteed to lose Dorian, and now I'd lost Tristan, too. But as Lucas had promised, we could have it all with the Daemoni.

Was he right, or were those more empty promises? Could I stand to live this life if it meant being with the two people most important to me? Did we even have a choice, since the Amadis would be gone anyway? Grief blossomed, enshrouded me as this thought seized hold, and my mind barely registered a muffled clanging in the walls.

"We gotta go," Vanessa said. "That's Lucas digging his way in."

I shook my head, though she couldn't see me. Tears overflowed down my cheeks. "It's no use," I said.

"*What?* What are you talking about?" She sniffed the air. "Are you *crying*? Oh, for fuck's sake. You're *not* doing this. You can't break down on me now, Alexis. I have a plan. We're going to get out of here."

"But what's the point? I didn't get the faerie stone. I didn't get Kali's soul, and we lost Owen. They have Tristan, and they'll get Dorian soon enough. I failed, Vanessa! You go, but there's no reason for me to."

She reached her hands through the air in the direction of my voice. They found my face and clamped down on each side.

"Don't. Give. Up." Her voice lost its musical quality, replaced by the firmness of a mother. Or an older sister. "Don't let their evil energy get to you. It's not over until it's over. You wouldn't leave me before, and I'm not leaving you now. Not like this. I've seen you break through their dark power before to get to Tristan and that was darker than dark. I know you will find a way to reach him again. And Owen . . ." Her voice trailed off for a moment. "I don't know about Owen, but we can't lose hope, Alexis. We'll get through this."

I sniffled and scrubbed at my wet cheeks. Was she right? Could I break through to Tristan? And what about everyone else?

More noise in the walls reminded me of the pointlessness of worrying. We were trapped, anyway.

"No, we *won't* get through it. It's futile. I don't know my way out. You're blind as a bat. I can't even fight. I've failed, Vanessa. I. Have. Failed. We'll *never* get out of here."

"Don't say that. We *will*. Look at everything you've done since your change. You are strong, Alexis. You are powerful!"

I tried to shake my head again, but her grip was too

strong. "You don't understand. I lost the dagger. Cassandra's dagger. My connection to her and her power was the only reason I'd been able to do anything. It was her, not me. Her power, not mine!"

Vanessa's hands fell from my face. "What the hell are you talking about?"

More ruckus came through the walls, but I ignored it.

"Cassandra's power was driving me," I admitted. "All this time, it was her helping me. The dagger connected us, she gave me her power, and she guided me through everything. Everything! Every fight she's been there, and now I've lost her, too."

Vanessa's head tilted. "Well, from everything I've heard about Cassandra, her strongest power was love. They say she could literally love you to death. Sounds stupid but the threat works with the Daemoni, since they fear love so much. But even if it's a crock of shit, I know you and your love for Tristan, for your son, for . . . *everyone*. Even strangers. Everything you do is to protect those you love and even those you don't think you do. Like me."

I wiped at my cheeks. She was right. That's why I so easily threw myself into danger, risking my own life to protect others. But this time, everything had gone so terribly wrong. I hadn't protected anyone. In fact, my actions would probably get us all killed.

"Yeah, well, you're right. I'm stupid," I said.

Vanessa groaned. "Yeah, right now you're being really damn stupid. End the self-pity party, Alexis. Tristan needs you. Dorian needs you. The Amadis need you. So put your big-girl panties back on and get your ass out of here, then we'll figure the rest out. But you're *not* going to stay here! I won't allow it. We're all dead if you stay. *All* of us. And there's no hope for Tristan and Dorian if you don't make it. So are you going to fight for them?"

She glared at me with blind eyes, and I still felt them

piercing into my soul, forcing me to study it myself. My soul opened and bared itself to me, exposing the raw layer of nerves that contained my love for Tristan, for Dorian, for the Amadis, even for Vanessa, and strangers. All of humanity. The Angels had given me love for them all, and they all needed me.

I considered again if she was right about being able to break through to Tristan. I didn't have the stone, but did I still, in some way, have his heart? Could I stop him from doing any more damage than what he must have done already? Was our love strong enough to drive away all of this dark power? If I could find my way to Tristan and pull him back to us before he destroyed the Amadis, we could figure out the rest. We'd all be *alive* to figure out the rest.

Well, there's only one way to find out if we can salvage this mess.

I pulled in a deep breath, mentally put on my big-girl panties as Vanessa had instructed, and nodded. Vanessa gasped.

"Did you just nod?" Her hands reached out for my head. "I can see you. Sort of. You're just a big black blur, but I can see your shape. I saw it move. So you'll fight?"

Maybe her vision returning was a good sign. It gave me a little more confidence. I nodded again.

"Yes," I said. "I'll fight."

She let out a whoosh of relief. "Okay. So here's my plan. The city has two shields and two exits. One exit is through town, which we're staying far away from, and the other is the cave we came through."

"Which we couldn't find our way back to," I pointed out.

"We're not giving them time to change the paths this time. We're going to flash right to where the inner shield ends, about half-way down that long tunnel. Then we can walk through the shield and flash again to the cave, where the outer shield ends."

"But that long tunnel changed, remember?"

"They won't change it at the shield or they'd mess up its force."

I drew in a raggedy breath as I considered her plan, which sounded too simple. "And why didn't we do this sooner?"

She scowled. "Sorry. I was too busy running for my life to have a clear thought."

The clamor in the walls came closer, making both of us jump. The adrenaline spiked through my system again, and if I hadn't already decided, I knew now that I would do whatever necessary to get us out of here. My fight had, indeed, returned.

"Well, we have nothing to lose, do we?" I said.

"Nope. So are you ready for this?"

"Not exactly, but I don't have a choice. How about you?"

She waved a hand in front of her eyes and scrunched her face. "I'll be relying on you."

"Well, then, let's do it."

We clasped hands and flashed. We appeared in the forever-tunnel, both ways empty of physical bodies and mind signatures. Was this actually going to work? Were we going to get out of here alive?

"We should feel the shield about ten yards up," Vanessa said, and she was right. We walked uphill twelve of my paces, Vanessa stumbling after me with her hand on my shoulder to guide her way, before we felt the slight resistance and a buzz as we passed through the shield. "Now let's flash to the cave."

Her hand slid down my arm and grasped my palm. We flashed. And bounced. We landed on our butts.

Vanessa swore. "You're right. This was too easy. Where did we appear?"

I looked around and swore as well. "Right where we were."

"Damn it! They've blocked us from flashing."

With no other choice, Vanessa clamped her hand on my shoulder again, and I led her up the tunnel. Being nearly blind, she lacked her normal vampire grace, and we moved slowly, for us anyway. At least until I felt the mind signatures from way down the tunnel.

"They're coming," I whispered.

"Go faster," Vanessa hissed.

We picked up the speed, but the signatures were coming much faster. I took Vanessa's hand and yanked her forward, but she kept stumbling, catching herself on me, nearly pulling us both down. I wrapped my arm around her waist and practically carried her, moving as fast as I possibly could. We made better progress, but the thoughts—shifters' thoughts— were closing in on us.

Then, out of nowhere, a fork appeared in the tunnel. Three prongs that hadn't been here before. It had been a straight and narrow, boring tunnel all the way down.

I swore. "Any ideas? There's a three-way fork."

"Hmm . . . straight ahead is too easy. Right?" She obviously wasn't sure about that.

An inexplicable but strong pull made me think left. "I think this way."

"No, right. I'm sure of it." And now she did sound more confident, so we went right. We jogged as best as we could for about twenty yards and slammed into an invisible wall. "Damn! Sorry!"

We scrambled to our feet and headed back, losing valuable distance between us and the shifters. When we reached the fork, I followed my gut this time, and Vanessa didn't have much choice but to go with me. We hit two more forks, and both times I ignored Vanessa and followed instinct. The feeling went further than my gut, all the way into my heart and soul, as if they were pulling me toward freedom and safety.

The howls and barks of wolves followed us, coming closer and closer. I tried to run even faster, holding most of Vanessa's weight so she wouldn't stumble in her blindness, but her legs dragged behind us. I could physically carry her weight, but she was too tall for my short frame.

We rounded a new bend, and there it was—the light at the end of the tunnel. Literally. The bluish light of the ice cave. The floor underneath our feet confirmed it, becoming slick with ice. We were almost there, just as growls and snapping jaws sounded behind us.

We slipped and slid as we fought our way up the hill and into the icy cave, and all I could think was, *Get outside. Just get outside, beyond the boundaries, then we can flash. Then we'll be safe.* And finally, the opening, brightly lit right in front of us. But it was farther than it first appeared. I pushed my foot into the ground, determined to make it out. My boot slipped. Vanessa and I went down. Crashed onto our faces. I lost contact with her as I skidded across the ice and slammed into a stalagmite.

My vision swam. My ears rang. But under the ringing, from what sounded like a far-off distance but I instinctively knew was way too close, came the sound of claws scratching on ice. I scrambled on the slick floor, pushing myself forward. I grabbed Vanessa's hand as I passed her, yanking her struggling form with me.

"Come on!" I yelled. "We're almost there."

But after everything else, Vanessa now felt like a sack of bricks. I half-ran, half-scuttled us out of the cave, teeth snapping at our heels. We burst through the opening and out into the white light of afternoon sun. I blinked and squinted in the sudden brightness. Vanessa collapsed, too weak to go on. And out came the wolves. More than I realized had pursued us.

They launched themselves onto Vanessa, and she couldn't fight back. I blasted them with electricity and swung my knife at them, but there were too many, and I was too weak. Vanessa whimpered and moaned under the mass of fur. With tears blinding my eyes and my sensibility, my hands grabbed onto a neck, and my fingers dug into the fur as I yanked a wolf off of the vampire—off of Vanessa, off of my comrade-in-arms—and threw it to the side. But that was only one, and it came back at me before it even hit the ground.

"Hang on, Vanessa," I cried out, although, as the wolf's mouth latched onto my shoulder, I had no idea how I could save her. How I could save either of us.

We had fought with everything we had, but we didn't have enough. We were no match for Lucas and his minions. I had known all along. I had nearly given up with this knowledge. But I'd told Vanessa I would fight. And we'd been so. *close*. So close to the stone, to the sorceress's soul, so close now to escape, to winning this battle if not the war, to beating the sperm donor at his own game.

But in the end, I couldn't do any of it. Not alone when he had all these creatures at his beck and call. Hell, I couldn't even keep my own protector loyal to me. Perhaps Lucas deserved to win . . .

The wolf hanging on me went suddenly still, and I jerked from the edge of unconsciousness just as its snout released my shoulder and it fell to the ground. The wolves on Vanessa, one-by-one, went down with a yelp, too. I spun around with another shot of adrenaline, hands out and ready to fight whatever Lucas had sent after us now.

My jaw dropped. I blinked, sure that what I saw must have been my imagination. But no. Tristan still stood there. Not halfway around the world, but only twenty yards away. Big and strong and beautiful.

And the enemy.

CHAPTER 28

I didn't have the stone. Kali had control, which meant we were dead if I couldn't break through to him. Unless . . . if Bree had acted soon enough to sever the connection . . . But Tristan still might have gone rogue. Regardless of how or why he was here, without the stone in my possession, my love for him meant nothing, and his for me would be a thing of the past. He'd kill Vanessa and me in a heartbeat.

So I just stood there, not sure what to do.

Tristan's arms moved out to the side. Opened wide. "*Ma lykita.*"

The full strength of his love—what I hadn't felt in so long, possibly since the day my pendant disappeared—burst from him and washed over me. It hadn't been freedom and safety pulling me through the tunnel this way. It had been Tristan's love, even without the stone. I blew out the air I'd been holding in my lungs forever.

"Tristan!" I ran into his open arms, and he swept me up, held me tightly against him. "You're okay?"

"I'm perfect now that you're in my arms," he murmured against my ear.

"But how?"

"I felt it as soon as you had possession of the stone."

I pulled back. "But I don't. I failed, Tristan. I didn't get it back."

He cocked his head as he peered at me. "But I feel it. So strong now."

He let go of me with one arm and lifted his hand to my chest. With one finger he poked, and though he didn't actually touch me, I felt the pressure. His finger tapped a pattern, and I gasped. My necklace appeared from nowhere, hanging from my neck, and I hadn't even known it.

"Scarecrow," he whispered with a smile.

I started to shake my head. *Couldn't be.* But if not, who? How? When?

"But I saw you . . ." I closed my eyes against the vision trying to replay in my mind once again. "Kali controlled you. You . . . you destroyed the safe house . . . you—"

"Not me, my love. She showed you what she wanted you to see."

I swore under my breath. Would I ever learn to see through their projections? I'd almost given up on everything because of their deceit.

"I'll kill her," I said, meaning it with every fiber in my being.

"Not now. We need to get out of here."

No, not this moment. But soon.

Right now, I really just wanted to revel in the realization that my dream of being truly safe and in my husband's arms actually came true. But we didn't have the luxury of time for that either.

"Vanessa needs you first," I said.

Tristan released me and strode over to the limp body of the vampire. Her wounds were closing slowly, her body too weak from the sun and the shifters' saliva to heal itself as fast as normal. My throat tightened, and I had to look away as

Tristan ran his mouth over the deeper gashes, helping them to heal faster. Too bad for her that she was practically unconscious, too out of it to enjoy this.

"*Don't worry. It's not at all like I'd imagined it,*" Vanessa whispered in my mind. "*He's too much like a brother now.*"

And that's when it truly hit me: *I have a sister.*

"So," I said while I stared out the little window as the buildings on the ground below shrank away into miniatures.

Vanessa fidgeted with her seat belt. "Yeah."

With her in his arms, Tristan had led me for several flashes to a private airstrip where the Amadis jet waited for us. With the tightened security we'd already experienced, Mom had had to make special arrangements on both ends of our flight so we could avoid anyone considering us too closely. She'd also sent a couple of mages to the military installation to alter the norms' memories of what Vanessa and I looked like before we ended up on the Most Wanted lists.

Until now, Vanessa and I had been able to avoid the elephant in the room, but I'd finally broken the awkward silence.

"How long have you known?" I asked, finally looking at her. From the seat next to me, Tristan took my hand in his.

She lifted a shoulder in a shrug. "I've suspected for a long time, since I was young, really. Lucas always denied it, said we had common ancestors to explain our similar features. When we'd come to live with him when we were eleven, he acted a little like a father figure, but we were to call him Lucas. Never *father*. God forbid anyone suspect anything." She looked out the window, blinking several times. Her eyesight had slowly returned, and her brain still seemed to be adjusting. Her voice became distant. "At first, I tried to love him like the father we'd never had, but that only made him hate me more. He'd push me away and ignore me whenever possible. But Victor . . . he loved, *loves* Victor. My brother could do no wrong. Lucas had amazing plans for Victor and Seth. But never for Vanessa. Not after it became obvious the first time we met that Seth wanted nothing to do with me. The prophecy wasn't about me, so I was nothing but an embarrassment."

My gaze dropped from her face to the floor. I toed the carpet, feeling unnecessarily guilty. None of this was my fault —my mother hadn't even been born yet, let alone me—but I could now understand why she'd hated me so much. The Daemoni had believed the prophecy was about Vanessa, and when the faerie stone in Tristan's heart didn't respond, Lucas had no use for her anymore. And she must have been determined to prove them all wrong, her heart set on making something happen between Tristan and her. Then I came along, and there was nothing to prove anymore.

"So why did he have you turned?" I finally asked, curiosity getting the better of me.

Her mouth puckered. "I never really knew why he turned me. He says to save my life—our version of the *Ang'dora* nearly killed me, just like it does most of Jordan's descendants. He had me turned so I wouldn't die. But why? He hates me. He said it would make me stronger, the monster he wanted me to be. And I guess it did. I was so full of hatred—for him, for Victor, for the world. He'd given me anything I wanted to shut me up, but had taken away any chance for real happiness."

"So you turned Victor in revenge?"

"Yeah. I was newly reborn, starving, and mad. Mad as hell. And darling Victor was right there. I'd wanted to kill him and make Lucas live with that the rest of his existence. But Lucas forced me to finish the process. He would rather have Victor as a vampire than not have him at all, even if it took away any chance for Victor to lead with Seth." She looked at me with a tilted head. "Did you know we vamps aren't leadership material? At least, not of other species. They say we're too impulsive."

"Go figure," I replied, and she snorted.

"So, anyway, Lucas has hated me ever since I turned Victor. No matter how much of a monster I became for him, I was never good—or bad—enough."

I shook my head, not knowing what to say.

Tristan stroked his chin, then spoke up for the first time since takeoff. "I always thought Lucas told me just about everything, but I knew nothing about this."

Vanessa chuckled without humor. "Lucas has more secrets than anyone could ever guess. Victor never knew about the supposed prophecy until Alexis was born. The fool actually thought you two were brothers for the longest time, and Lucas let him believe it! Oh, there's worse, I'm sure. He's the best deceiver there is besides Satan himself." She looked at me. "So, yeah, our father's a dick."

"I don't have a father," I said. "And neither do you. He's just a sperm donor. Nothing more."

Vanessa nodded, and she looked out the window again. Her voice came out quietly with her next words. "But we do have a brother."

Of course. I had gained both a half-sister and a half-brother. They were twins, so no doubt about it.

I swallowed the lump in my throat and spoke just as quietly. "Is there any hope for him?"

Vanessa didn't answer at first. Her eyes glistened as she finally looked at me. "I don't know, Alexis." She shook her head. "I really don't know."

"He's not rogue," Tristan said. "There's hope."

I didn't know if he said it for Vanessa or for me or because he truly believed it, but I was thankful he did. I squeezed his hand.

"So how did you get to us so fast?" I asked him. "It took us more than twenty-four hours to get there."

His mouth quirked in a small smile. "I had a little help from Bree."

"She couldn't help us get home a little faster than this?" I asked. "I miss my son."

"You have to be faerie to cross the veil."

"You went through the *Otherworld*?" I asked with disbelief. "But *you're* not—Oh. Yeah. You are."

Vanessa snorted as she still stared out the window. "That explains a lot," she muttered. "Big, bad warrior is a *faerie*."

Tristan growled at her teasing tone. I placed my hand on his thigh.

"Be nice. She saved my butt, and she's a friend now," I said, and then I smiled. "No, she's more than that. She's family."

Vanessa turned away from the window and stared at me for a long time. Then she gave me a look that was so foreign on the face I'd hated for so long. She almost looked happy.

I let out a sad sigh myself. "I've gained a sister and a brother, but I seem to have lost the closest thing I ever had to a real brother. Owen's . . . gone."

Vanessa frowned again. "He's not gone. Not for good. We're going to rescue him, right?"

"I don't think the traitor wants to be rescued."

"Whoa," Tristan said, "back up. What's up with Scarecrow?"

"He abandoned me and went off with Kali to be her little minion."

Vanessa shook her head. "I don't think so. I think he's trying to get her to trust him. He needs to figure out her weakness before anything can be done about her."

I fingered my pendant, *wanting* to believe her, but I just didn't know. "Are you sure about that?"

"Sounds more like Owen than your version," Tristan said, which was true.

"Did he tell me that straight out?" Vanessa said. "No. But that's what I want to believe. That's what I *have* to believe."

"Well, I want to believe it, too, but that's not how I saw things," I said. "He's supposed to be my protector, and he left me in the worst situation possible. Unprotected."

"You weren't unprotected," Vanessa muttered. "I'd promised Owen I'd take care of you if he needed me to. I tried my best. But I'm no warlock."

"No, you're not. You're not trained to be a protector." Tristan put his arm across my shoulder and squeezed. "He shouldn't have left. He's dug a pretty deep hole for himself."

Vanessa blew out a breath of exasperation. "So you're not going to rescue him? *You're* going to abandon *him* now?"

"I'm just saying that Alexis may be right. Owen hasn't been himself. Maybe he's chosen what he wants."

Vanessa opened her mouth, and I braced for the list of profanities she'd spew out. But she was trying to learn control over her emotions, so she shut her mouth and scowled, diverting her attention to the clouds out the window. Tristan took my hand, stood, and led me over to the couch, giving Vanessa her space.

"I lost my dagger, too," I lamented as we sat in the corner of the L-shaped couch. I hated not having my best weapon, but I knew now that I didn't need to rely on it. Perhaps Vanessa was right about love being my strongest power. Cassandra had always said I had the power within me.

"*Yes, you do,*" her voice whispered in my mind.

My back straightened, and Tristan gave me a strange look, but I ignored him. *Cassandra?*

"*Always here.*"

But how? I don't have the dagger.

"*The dagger does not connect us. Our shared power does.*"

Then where were you before? How could you let me go through all of that alone?

"*You were not alone. I was there, but I only guide when you need me. You didn't need me, Alexis. With Vanessa's help, you succeeded on your own. And now you know your true power."*

Her presence receded again, and I sagged against the back of the couch, lost in thought. Tristan always said my biggest advantage was my telepathy, and my dagger may have been my best weapon. But what made me really powerful was something the enemy feared more than anything because they didn't understand it, and they'd never be able to steal, block, or beat it out of me.

Vanessa had been right. My power was not dark, but light. Like Cassandra, my true power was love.

"You've lost a lot, but you have me," Tristan said as he pulled me onto his lap, totally unaware I'd just had a major epiphany. He nuzzled my neck. "Feels good to be whole again. You and me."

"Yes, it does," I said, encircling my arms around his neck. "Let's hope forever this time. I'm sick of them taking control of your life."

"You and me both, my love." He kissed my jawline.

"And we have Dorian," I said, my excitement to see him growing the closer we came to home.

Tristan lifted my pendant and rubbed his thumb over the stone. "And maybe now we can have a daughter."

"I can't wait to start working on it," I said as his mouth finally made its way to mine and delivered the kiss I'd been waiting for.

My family was growing. And soon, it would be even bigger. In fact, with our daughter, it would finally be complete. At least, until we had to deal with Dorian and the Daemoni. But I wasn't going to think about that right now. It was a long way off. Right now, I was going to wholeheartedly focus on this amazing man giving me the most amazing kiss.

I lost myself in it.

EPILOGUE

By the time we landed in Florida, night had settled in. I couldn't wait to get home, and we had to avoid the authorities anyway, so we flashed right off the plane and to the island. We appeared on the beach across the street from the safe house, Vanessa's temporary home and where Dorian waited for us. My heart swelled with excitement to see my son and hold him again.

Then, after a few hours with him, Tristan and I would finally be able to enjoy some real time together. That kiss on the plane had only been a tease.

When we stepped onto the safe house's property, though, I knew immediately something was wrong. I didn't feel the little buzz of crossing through a shield. Had the mages left already? Perhaps Blossom knew we were home, and they could lower the shield. Maybe they'd done it so we could flash directly into the house. But there was something wrong with that possibility. Vanessa gasped and covered her nose and mouth with her palm.

"Everything was fine when I left," Tristan said, feeling it, too.

Vanessa shook her head vehemently, and her voice came out muffled behind her hand. "Blood. Lots of *blood.*"

"Vanessa, stay here," I ordered, my words tumbling out of my mouth in a rush as my body strained to run for the safe house. "Promise me!"

"I . . . I'll be in the water." She blurred toward the Gulf to immerse her senses in the salt water.

Tristan and I exchanged a glance, then flashed into the house.

Right into the scene of a horror movie.

A pattern of crimson splattered the wall of the common room. The bodies of the four mages from the colony lay crumpled on the floor, blood spilling from ripped-out throats and decimated wrists. Tristan blurred to each of them. Shook his head each time.

Oh, no!

"Blossom," I cried out. "Dorian!"

"Alexis?" Blossom came running down the dark hallway, her phone in her hand. "Alexis! Tristan! They're gone! Sheree . . ."

"*Sheree?*" I echoed, my voice several octaves too high.

"She's in Sonya's room. She's okay. Not great, but okay."

Tristan rushed past me for Sonya's room to help the shifter.

"Sonya?"

Blossom shook her head. "She's gone. Heather is, too. Her mom just called, freaking out. Sonya . . ." Tears leaked from her eyes as she drew in a shudder of a breath. "She . . . she did this, Alexis. We couldn't stop her. I'm so . . . so sorry."

I took the witch's hands in mine.

"It's not your fault," I said, as firmly as I could muster. My own emotional stability was on the line. This was supposed to be *my* safe house. I was responsible for it and everyone here. And now four mages were dead and a Norman missing, her life in grave danger. I sucked in a breath, trying to calm my own nerves. "Where's Dorian? He's okay?"

"I think so."

My stomach rolled.

"What do you mean you *think*?"

"He hasn't come out of the room where you left him. He probably heard the screams and hid. Sasha's in there with him."

I nodded, but the prickly feeling that something was wrong climbed up my spine. *Dear God, please say my baby's okay.* I ran across the common room and into his wing. Blood smeared the walls, and I told myself it came from the mages. *He's just hiding. He's fine.* But the blood trailed all the way to his closed door.

My hand shook as I reached out for the knob. I gripped hard as though I expected it to be ripped out of my hand. With a deep breath, I slowly opened the door.

"Dorian?" I said as I peeked in. My heart sped, hammering against my ribs. I could barely speak, my throat too constricted to let the words out. They came out in a choked whisper. "Where are you, little man?"

No answer.

Tristan appeared next to me. "Is he in here?"

"I . . . I don't know." The suite was too big to see everything from the door, but when I reached out with my mind, I only found one signature. Not human.

Before I could say anything else, Tristan took off down the hallway, throwing open other doors. "Dorian! Dorian, come out!"

I stepped farther into the front room of his suite on shaky legs, my heart not accepting what my mind already knew. My eyes adjusted to the darkness, and everything looked fine. But I knew everything was far from fine. Even with this knowledge, though, when I entered the bedroom, I gasped at the disaster area. The blanket had been yanked from the bed and the sheet shredded. Little white things littered the floor. My stomach clenched. *Feathers.* I told myself they were from the pillow. *Down feathers. That's all.*

But then more blood.

I moved around the bed, following the trail, barely able to breathe.

"Dorian?" I choked out.

My son wasn't there, I already knew this, but a small, white figure lay still on the floor.

"*Sasha?*" I fell to my knees next to her. She blinked and whimpered, but otherwise didn't move. My hands fluttered over her broken body, not knowing what to do.

"Did you find him?" Blossom asked, running into the suite and to the bedroom doorway. Unable to speak, I shook my head, not knowing if she could see me or not. Not caring.

"Is he in here?" Tristan asked, right behind her. "Ah, *fuck!*"

A loud crash sounded behind me. He must have taken in the scene.

I still couldn't speak. I just stared through the tears at the lykora, my son's protector, as she lay there. Silvery blood gushed from where one wing had been torn from her back. I blinked back the tears that insisted on falling, and a silver glint next to Sasha caught my eye. Not her blood. But the tip of my dagger.

"I always get what I want. I *will* get what's mine." Lucas's words taunted me from inside my own head.

The rest of my dagger hid under Sasha's normally white nuzzle, which was now stained crimson. She'd put up a fight. But she'd lost.

And Dorian was gone.

Tristan fell to my side, his arms swallowed me, and he rocked me back and forth, back and forth, horrible, horrible noises wrenching through his throat all the way from his heart and soul.

"Maybe . . . maybe Dorian flew away," Blossom said from

right behind us, her voice a mere whisper, "just like we taught him. Maybe he's hiding somewhere."

Grasping at this fine thread of renewed hope, I opened my mind and searched for Dorian's mind signature. I pushed beyond the safe house, forcing my mind outward, scanning through all the signatures for the only one that mattered,

past the shores of Captiva

over the sound to the other islands

to the mainland

as far as I could push my mental boundaries

but not him

not him

not him.

He was nowhere to be found.

They'd taken my baby.

Continue on for an excerpt from the next book or click here to buy Sacred Wrath. Before you read *Sacred Wrath*, you might want to read *Prophecy of the Wolves*, which introduces Sundae, who you'll see in *Sacred Wrath*. Download your free copy of Prophecy of the Wolves by subscribing to my reader group and receive other bonus and exclusive content, as well as be the first to know about new releases, sales, and special events.

GLOSSARY & CAST

A.K. Emerson – Alexis's famous pen name.

Alexis Ames Knight – Youngest Amadis daughter who is second in line for matriarch of the Amadis. Married to Tristan Knight and mother of Dorian. Youngest daughter to ever go through the Ang'dora. Her bio father is the leader of the Daemoni. Known abilities include telepathy, electricity, telekinesis, super strength, speed and senses, Amadis power.

Amadis (uh-MAH-dees) – Secret matriarchal society that serves as the Angels' army on Earth, currently led by Katerina Ames. Their purpose is to defend human souls from the Daemoni and to convert Daemoni souls to Amadis. Consist of a variety of supernatural beings.

Amadis daughters – Women of the bloodline of the original creator of the Amadis. Each daughter eventually serves as the matriarch. Currently use the surname Ames. They always have daughters, which are sometimes accompanied by a male twin. Until Alexis anyway.

Amadis power – A special power of love and light gifted to the Amadis by the Angels. The Amadis daughters receive it during the Ang'dora. Other society members are granted a lower level of power upon conversion and official acceptance into the Amadis.

Andrew – The Angel who fell from Heaven and fathered Cassandra and Jordan before eventually ascending (read about it in *Genesis: A Soul Savers Novella*).

Ang'dora – Literally means "gift of the Angels" (Ang = angels, dora = Greek word for gifts). An enigmatic change all Amadis daughters go through to receive their powers and supernatural abilities. Usually happens in middle age, after the daughter has experienced major milestones of life as a human, but Alexis went through it quite early. Until Sophia, no Amadis daughter has given birth after the Ang'dora.

Armand – French vampire on Rina's council, he oversees Amadis police force and is anti-Tristan.

Attair – Amadis warlock from Arabia who's on Rina's council and is anti-Tristan.

Blossom – Amadis witch from the Daytona coven who befriends Alexis and the guys.

Bree – Fae and Tristan's birth mother.

Carlie – Alexis's human classmate during her first year at college.

Cassandra – Half angel, half human who started the Amadis (read her story in *Genesis: A Soul Savers Novella*).

Chandra – Amadis were-tiger who sits on Rina's council and oversees the region of India.

Charlotte Allbright – Amadis warlock, Owen's mother, Sophia's best friend, new addition to Rina's council, and overall badass aunt figure to Alexis.

Cloak – A magic spell performed by mages that hides or makes invisible its subject. Often used in conjunction with a shield.

Conversion – The process of eliminating dark or light energy and replacing it with the opposite, then indoctrinating the supernatural being into the new society. The Amadis purpose is to convert Daemoni souls before they become damned, destroyed, or forever lost. However, on occasion, Amadis members will convert to the Daemoni (e.g., Ian).

Daemoni (day-MAH-nee) – Satan's servants as the Demons' army on Earth, currently led by Lucas. The Amadis enemies harvest souls to build their army. The Amadis try to stop them.

Dorian Knight – Son of Alexis and Tristan, unknown creature but currently human. Known abilities include self-healing and flying.

Edmund – Member of the Daemoni. Known abilities include flashing, super strength and speed, idiocy, and being an overall douche-canoe.

Eris – Daemoni witch from ancient times who helped Jordan create the potion that changed everything (read about it in *Genesis: A Soul Savers Novella*).

Faeries/Fae – Little is known about the fae as they tend to stay away from human affairs, as well as those of the Amadis and Daemoni. A handful do enjoy wreaking havoc in the Earthly realm, and sometimes they may even help out. They're considered Otherworldly creatures, because their world is not exactly part of Earth. They closely guard their secrets about the Faerie realm.

Ferrer – Blacksmith mage who lives on Amadis Island.

Fertility Stone – The faerie stone Bree gave Tristan when he was a young boy, embedding it in his heart with the instructions to give it to his true mate. Only when she has possession of it can he father children. The stone also allows the holder to share their emotions so he could feel his mate's love—but also the possessor's darker emotions.

Flashing – The supernatural ability to transport to another location up to a hundred miles away (give or take) in the blink of an eye. While objects can be held or attached to the body during a flash, Tristan is the only known creature who can flash while carrying another person. While both Daemoni and Amadis can flash, it's not necessarily a natural ability for all—some creatures have to be assisted by mages.

Galina – Russian warlock and a member of Rina's council, she favors Tristan and Alexis.

Hades – Daemoni HQ, an underground city in the Taymyr Peninsula of Siberia.

Heather – Human girl, Dorian's babysitter and friend, daughter of Phil and sister to Sonya.

Ian – Member of the Daemoni, converted from the Amadis. Known abilities include compensating for his miniscule junk by spilling secrets, causing problems with the Amadis, and ruining Alexis's life.

Jax – Were-croc who resides in the Australian Outback.

Jelani – Wizard from Africa who is one of Rina's council members.

Jessica – Faerie with a southern accent, calls Lisa her sister.

Jordan – Early leader of the Daemoni who sought power over all, inadvertently helping to create the Amadis (read his story in *Genesis: A Soul Savers Novella*).

Julia Acerbi – Vampire, Amadis council member, and one of Rina's closest advisors.

Kali – Daemoni sorceress who took over Martin Allbright's body

Katerina "Rina" Ames – Current matriarch of the Amadis. Known abilities include telepathy, super strength and speed, flashing, bonding souls, converting souls to Amadis, making ballgowns everyday attire.

Kuckaroo – Amadis village in Australia.

Lilith – Bree's daughter and Tristan's sister.

Lisa – Faerie with a southern accent, calls Jessica her sister.

Lucas – Alexis's sperm donor and leader of the Daemoni. Often (but not always) uses the last name Emerson.

Lykora – An Angelic being that is extremely loyal and highly protective of its master. When in hidden form, looks like a small white dog, but when in defensive mode, can grow as large as necessary to protect, has a wolf head and body, tiger stripes on a white coat, and feathered wings.

Mages – The wide classification of supernatural beings that can wield magic, including witches/wizards, warlocks, and Sorcerers/sorceresses. These general sub-classifications are based on strength of power. Some may call themselves by other names, depending on the type of magic they use, preference, or other reasons (e.g., Shamans, Druids, etc.).

Martin Allbright – Powerful warlock, Charlotte's husband and Owen's father.

Minh – Vietnamese witch council member who oversees the Asian region for the Amadis.

Norms/Normans – Normal humans.

Ophelia – Witch who serves as head of staff at the Amadis matriarch's mansion.

Otherworld – Currently unknown but seems to refer to Heaven and Hell, as well as Faerie.

Owen Allbright – Warlock and Alexis's so-called protector. Also like a brother to her and Tristan's best friend. Known abilities include shielding, cloaking, magical bindings, flashing, and pushing everyone's limits. And now a big, fat traitor.

Phillip Jones – Human wife beater, child abuser, and overall scum of the earth who drove an older orange Camaro. Heather and Sonya's father.

Rene – Daemoni were-cheetah who chases Alexis down in Hades.

Safe House – Homes, lodges, and other accommodations scattered around the world where Amadis can retreat to when under attack or when going through the conversion or transformation process.

Sasha – Dorian's lykora.

Savio – Italian were-shark who sits on Rina's council and is anti-Tristan.

Seth – Tristan's former name when he was Daemoni. The Daemoni still call him that.

Sheree – An Amadis were-tiger who'd been bitten and turned against her will by the Daemoni. She was Alexis's first ever conversion from Daemoni to Amadis. Now she helps with conversions of others.

Shield – A magic spell performed by mages that puts a protective barrier around its subject. If the subject is not also cloaked, the subject can still be seen, so it's often used in conjunction with a cloaking spell.

Shihab – Wizard from Arabia who sits on Rina's council.

Solomon – Vampire, Katerina's partner, and Amadis council member. Known abilities include being scary AF.

Sonya – Recently turned vampire, now converted to Amadis. Heather's sister. A.K. Emerson's "biggest fan" (a/k/a stalker).

Sophia Ames (a/k/a Mom a/k/a Mimi) – Alexis's mother and Amadis daughter who is next in line for matriarch. Known abilities include telekinesis, summoning and manipulating water, persuading others to do as she likes, sensing the truth of a situation, super strength and speed, flashing, converting souls to Amadis.

Sorcerers/Sorceresses – The most powerful of the mages that can boost their energy by siphoning more from the earth and everything around them. Their greed for power, narcissism, and general disdain for pretty much everyone make them loners and also not part of the Amadis.

Stefan – Warlock, council member, and Sophia's former protector. Known abilities included creating a protective shield, flashing, serving as Alexis's only father figure. Died in book 1.

Sylvie (Aunt Sylvie) – Blossom's aunt and leader of the Daytona Beach witch coven.

Trevor – Amadis werewolf and leader of the main Florida wolf pack.

Tristan Knight – Former Daemoni converted to Amadis by Sophia. Sexy AF warrior. Known abilities include shooting fire from his palm, quickly determining the best solution if he knows enough of the facts, telekinesis, paralysis, instant killing power, super-duper strength and speed, brooding with guilt, giving a girl multiple Os.

Vampires – Supernatural beings that are sustained by blood. They can also feed on fear and other emotional energy. There are vampires on both the Amadis and the Daemoni sides.

Vanessa – Formerly one of the Daemoni's star vampires recently converted to Amadis. Alexis's half-sister, Victor's twin, and Lucas's daughter. Known abilities include stirring up trouble and pissing everyone off.

Victor – Vanessa's twin brother, Alexis's half-brother, Lucas's son and Daemoni vampire who's not too bright.

Warlocks – Part of the mage classification, supernatural beings who are born with the ability to wield magic and physically endowed with strength and speed, making them excellent warriors. They are not gender specific and are on both the Amadis and Daemoni sides.

Witches/Wizards – Part of the mage classification, supernatural beings who are born with the ability to wield magic, usually using a wand as well as spells, incantations, potions, elemental energy, etc. While they can be quite powerful, their powers and physical strengths aren't as strong as Warlocks or Sorcerers. Using the term Witch or Wizard was traditionally by gender, but really is up to each individual's preference. There are Witches and Wizards on both the Amadis and Daemoni sides.

Were-creatures/animals (a/k/a Shifters) – Supernatural beings with two combined spirits—human and animal—and they can physically shift between their two forms. There is a were-creature/shifter for nearly every predatory species on Earth, and they're on both the Amadis and the Daemoni sides.

DARK POWER PLAYLIST

(The songs I listened to on repeat while writing this book.)

Never Be the Same by Red
Shadows by Red
Your Love Is a Song by Switchfoot
Cry for Help by Shinedown
Give Me a Sign by Breaking Benjamin
The Mission by 30 Seconds to Mars

ABOUT THE AUTHOR

Kristie Cook is a lifelong, award-winning writer in various genres, primarily New Adult paranormal romance and contemporary fantasy. Her internationally bestselling, award-winning Soul Savers Series includes seven books, as well as several companion novellas and short stories. Over 1.2 million Soul Savers books have been downloaded. She has also written The Book of Phoenix trilogy, a New Adult paranormal romance series. Her books have been featured in *USA Today's* HEA section, on Good Morning America, and in the Emmy's Gifting Suite.

Kristie also created, writes in, and publishes the award-winning Havenwood Falls shared world, a collaborative project with multiple series, dozens of authors, and countless stories.

Besides writing, Kristie enjoys reading, cooking, traveling, getting her hippie on, and feeding her addictions to coffee, chocolate, cheese, and her latest TV obsession. She has lived in eleven states, but currently calls Florida home.

CONNECT WITH ME ONLINE

I love to hear from and connect with readers. Please don't be shy.

Facebook Reader Group: https://www.facebook.com/
groups/KristieCook.AKAngels.KnightRiders/

Email: kristie@kristiecook.com

Author's Website & Blog: http://www.KristieCook.com

Facebook: http://www.facebook.com/AuthorKristieCook

Twitter: http://twitter.com/kristiecookauth

Goodreads: https://www.goodreads.com/KristieCook

Instagram: http://instagram.com/kristiecookauth

BookBub: https://www.bookbub.com/authors/kristie-cook

Word of mouth is very important for any author. If you enjoyed the book, please consider leaving a review, even if it's only a sentence or two. This is one of the most important and appreciated things you can do for an author.

ACKNOWLEDGMENTS

First and foremost, my thanks go to the Creator for the many blessings the Spirit has showered on me.

Shawn, Zakary, Austin, and Nathan, thank you for sharing your lives with me, for your continued support and love, for understanding when Mom can't make dinner every night, and for being you. I love you.

Brenda, thank you for being a true friend who not only takes a beating from me but dishes it right back (yes, "it"!). Without your nit-picky, old school marm self, this book would be a mess. And without your encouragement, your understanding like only another writer can provide, and your shoulder to cry on, I would be a complete disaster.

Thank you to Lily Rowserein for my gorgeous new covers. I can't get over how perfect they are.

Jessica, I'm so grateful you emailed me over a little book no one had ever heard of to review on a little blog that was only a baby at the time. Look what we've grown, girl. Thank you for all of your help. Mindy and Jennifer, thank you for coming through at the last minute and helping out a crazed author. Chrissi and Lisa, thank you (again) for all you did.

Thank you also to Heather and the Indie Elite, and to the

many bloggers who have helped spread the word about the Soul Savers, especially to Jessica, Lisa, Mindy, Michele, Stacey, Inga, Jennifer, Brittany, Damaris, Stella, Tanya, Angela, Savannah, Katelyn, Jessica, Colleen, Lisa, Cynthia and Christina. Thank you to the Warriors for your love and enthusiasm. And as always, my deepest love and gratitude to the readers for taking a little time out of your life to spend with me. You have no idea what your posts, comments, reviews and recommendations to friends mean to an author. You're the best fans in the world. I dare anyone to deny it.

AN EXCERPT

SOUL SAVERS BOOK 5

Sacred
WRATH

KRISTIE COOK

The world is on the brink of war, the enemy have increased their attacks on humans, and my team and I have been assigned the mission of building the Angels' army on Earth. However, the unthinkable happens, and my biggest fear comes true. *Nothing* will stop me from recovering what is mine.

Except everything and everyone tries.

Suspicious humans have set traps to ensnare the supernatural. The world powers have closed their borders as they prepare for war. The Demons' army grows exponentially by taking innocent souls—souls that we're supposed to protect. And a power-hungry sorceress schemes to rule us all, with revenge on my grandmother topping her priority list. I'm forced to choose between those I love dearly and the souls of all of humanity, but when there's no right answer, I'm destined to lose. The question is—who will it be?

SACRED WRATH

AN EXCERPT

*H*e was gone. Really gone.

My little boy, my baby, the light of my life. Gone.

No matter how hard I tried, how far I pushed the boundaries of my mind to feel across the sea of mind signatures, I couldn't find his. Of course I couldn't. But I knew where I could.

My fingers curled into Sasha's white and gray striped fur, trying to soothe her, though I had no soothing vibes within me. I sat on my knees in the bedroom part of the safe house suite where I had left Dorian, where I thought he'd be safe when I couldn't be there to protect him myself. Barely bigger than my hand, the lykora lay on her side in her natural form, her silver blood staining the blue-and-cream Oriental rug under her. More coagulated on her back where one of her wings had been severed. Who could be so cruel? Stupid question. I knew that answer, too. He'd left my dagger under her to ensure I knew.

Heavy arms hung over my shoulders, arms that usually gave me comfort but now trembled with sobs.

"Can you heal her?" I asked, my voice sounding rough and

distant. When I received no answer, I asked again, each word discrete and deliberate. "Tristan. Can you heal her?"

He lifted his head from my shoulder, but Blossom answered first.

"She's an Angelic being," she said from behind me. "She'll heal on her own."

"Good," I said. I picked up my dagger, wiped her blood off of it and onto my leather pants, put it back where it belonged on my hip, and flashed.

Tampa. Gainesville. Tallahassee. Rural Alabama and Mississippi. From here, I followed the path Vanessa and I had taken only two days before, barely seeing the landscape of each place before flashing to the next one. Tristan finally caught up to me outside of Kansas City, where the March air was significantly cooler than at home.

He wrapped his arms around me and held me tight against his chest, preventing me from flashing again.

"Where are you going?" he asked, his lovely voice distorted with the two primary emotions roiling within me—anger and grief. Mostly anger. The kind that didn't dissipate but built with each passing moment.

"To Hades," I answered flatly.

"Alone?"

"Unless you're coming with me, yes."

"Alexis, we can't just waltz into Hades—"

"Not waltz. Storm." Like the raging storm building inside me.

"Still. We can't—"

"I guess that's your answer then." I pushed a spark of electricity into him and used the moment of surprise to flip my way out of his hold. Then I flashed.

Again and again.

But my power was waning. After flashing halfway across the world once already in the last two days, fighting my way out of Hades, and escaping Lucas, the sperm donor, I hadn't been able to truly regenerate. I had to pause longer between each flash, but each time I did, I envisioned what I would do when I arrived in Hades. The throats I would slash. The Demons I would fry to a crisp. Lucas's life I would take, but only after slicing the smirk off his face, and carving his eyeballs out with my silver dagger and stuffing them into his lipless mouth.

The thoughts should have terrified me, but they only pushed me on.

Until Tristan stopped me once again in Wyoming.

"Alexis, you can't—"

I ignored him and flashed.

"Take them on by yourself," he finished in Idaho.

"Watch me." I flashed again.

"But we can't—" he started again in Washington.

"Damn it, Tristan. I don't want to hear 'can't'!" I yelled, and I flashed again.

And slammed into a wall.

At least, that's what it felt like. An invisible wall that blocked my flash, causing me to materialize in an empty field somewhere near the Canadian border. I tried again and appeared by a stream, the lights of Seattle not far off. I screamed with frustration.

"The border's been shielded," Tristan said from behind me. "And not a normal shield, either, but more like an invisible fence we can't flash through. No one can pass through at all, not even norms, except at guarded border crossings."

I didn't reply before I flashed again, farther inland. No mage could have possibly shielded the entire border between the United States and Canada. I would find a way through. Focusing on the nearest state highway, I flashed to about two hundred yards outside a border crossing.

Several armed soldiers guarded a barbed-wire-topped steel gate that stretched across the two-lane highway, blocking anyone from simply crossing. Lines of cars waited from both directions. More guards surrounded the first car, pulling the driver and passengers out and training their flashlights on their eyes and hands. Others were searching the car and its contents. I absorbed all of this in a few seconds and knew that gate provided my way into Canada, and then I could resume flashing to Siberia. A steel gate and a few soldiers weren't about to stop me.

I sprinted for the crossing, planning to blur past them all, hurdle it, and be on my way without anyone noticing. But someone did. Perhaps those soldiers weren't all Norman. Gunfire tore through the night. Bullets flew at me. *You've got to be kidding me.* I flicked my fingers, and the bullets fell to the ground. As I ran, I lifted my left hand, a purplish-silver current already sparking. More gunfire erupted. I shot electricity, not aiming for any particular guard, but simply shooting bolts wildly as a warning. People screamed. More soldiers shot at me, but I was almost there. Almost to the gate.

And nobody—not even a dozen men with automatic assault rifles—could stop me from getting to my son.

Just as I was about to make the leap, though, something hard slammed into my side. The breath whooshed out of my lungs. My vision went dark.

Buy Sacred Wrath where books are sold.

BOOKS BY KRISTIE COOK

SOUL SAVERS

Recommended Reading Order:

A Demon's Promise

An Angel's Purpose

Genesis: A Soul Savers Novella

Dangerous Devotion

Dark Power

Sacred Wrath

Unholy Torment

Fractured Faith

Age of Angels Part I: Awakened

Age of Angels Part II: Lost

Age of Angels Part III: Marked

Prophecy of the Wolves: (A Soul Savers Tie-In Novella)

Wonder: A Soul Savers Collection of Holiday Short Stories & Recipes

HAVENWOOD FALLS

Recommended Reading Order:

Forget You Not

Lose You Not

Break Me Not

The Collector: Awakening

Savage Salvation (Sin & Silk)

Sun & Moon Academy Book One: Fall Semester

Sun & Moon Academy Book Two: Fall Semester

The Winged & the Wicked (with T.V. Hahn)

Havenwood Falls Short Story Anthology 2018

Havenwood Falls Short Story Anthology 2019

Havenwood Falls Short Story Anthology 2020

BOOK OF PHOENIX

The Space Between

The Space Beyond

The Space Within